DAVID EDDINGS was born in Spokane, Washington, in 1931, and was raised in the Puget Sound area north of Seattle. He received a Bachelor of Arts degree from Reed College in Portland, Oregon, in 1954 and a Master of Arts degree from the University of Washington in 1961. He has served in the United Sates Army, worked as a buyer for the Boeing Company, has been a grocery clerk and has taught college English. He has lived in many parts of the United States. His first novel, *High Hunt*, was a contemporary adventure story. The field of fantasy has always been of interest to him, however, and he turned to *The Belgariad* in an effort to develop certain technical and philosophical ideas concerning that genre. Eddings currently resides with his wife, Leigh, in northwest America.

By David Eddings

THE BELGARIAD

Book One: PAWN OF PROPHECY
Book Two: QUEEN OF SORCERY
Book Three: MAGICIAN'S GAMBIT
Book Four: CASTLE OF WIZARDRY
Book Five: ENCHANTERS' END GAME

THE MALLOREON

Book One: GUARDIANS OF THE WEST
Book Two: KING OF THE MURGOS
Book Three: DEMON LORD OF KARANDA
Book Four: SORCERESS OF DARSHIVA
Book Five: SEERESS OF KELL

and published by Corgi Books

David Eddings

Book Four of The Belgariad

Castle of Wizardry

CORGI BOOKS

Book Four of The Belgariad:
CASTLE OF WIZARDRY
A CORGI BOOK : 0 552 14810 5

First publication in Great Britain
This edition published by arrangement with Ballantine Books,
a division of Random House, Inc.

PRINTING HISTORY
Corgi edition published 1984

19 20 18

Set in 10pt Linotron Times by
Falcon Oast Graphic Art.

Corgi Books are published by Transworld Publishers,
61–63 Uxbridge Road, London W5 5SA,
a division of The Random House Group Ltd,
in Australia by Random House Australia (Pty) Ltd,
20 Alfred Street, Milsons Point, Sydney, NSW 2061, Australia,
in New Zealand by Random House New Zealand Ltd,
18 Poland Road, Glenfield, Auckland 10, New Zealand
and in South Africa by Random House (Pty) Ltd,
Endulini, 5a Jubilee Road, Parktown 2193, South Africa.

Printed and bound in Great Britain by
Cox & Wyman Ltd, Reading, Berkshire.

For Bibbidie,
    and for Chopper Jack
    and for Jimmy and Eddie
    – close and special friends who have
    given support from the start.

Prologue

Being an account of how Riva Iron-grip became Guardian of the Orb of Aldur and of the evil wrought by Nyissa.
—Based upon *The Book of Alorn* and later accounts.

Now a time came when Cherek and his three sons went with Belgarath the Sorcerer into Mallorea. Together they sought to reclaim the Orb of Aldur, which had been stolen by the maimed God Torak. And when they came to the place in the iron tower of Torak where the Orb was hidden, only Riva Iron-grip, youngest of the sons, dared seize the great jewel and bear it forth. For Riva alone was free of evil intent within his soul.

And when they were come again to the West, Belgarath gave unto Riva and his descendants eternal guardianship of the Orb, saying: 'So long as the Orb rests with you and your line, so long shall the West be safe.'

Then Riva took the Orb and sailed with his people to the Isle of the Winds. There, upon the one place where ships might land, Riva caused to be built a Citadel and a walled city around it, which men named *Riva*. It was a fortress city, built for war.

Within the Citadel was built a great hall, with a throne carved of black rock set against the wall. And men called this throne room the Hall of the Rivan King.

Then a deep sleep fell upon Riva, and Belar, Bear-God of the Alorns, appeared to him in a dream, saying:

'Behold, Guardian of the Orb, I will cause two stars to fall from the sky. And thou shalt take up the two stars and place them in a fire and forge them. One shalt thou forge into a blade, the other into a hilt, and together they shall be a sword to guard the Orb of my brother Aldur.'

When Riva awoke, he saw two stars fall and he sought and found them in the high mountains. And he did with them as Belar had instructed. But when it was done, the blade and hilt could not be joined. Then Riva cried out, 'Behold, I have marred the work, for the sword will not become one.'

A fox, which had sat nearby to watch him, said to Riva, 'The work is not marred, Riva. Take the hilt and place the Orb upon it as a pommel stone.' And when Riva did as the fox instructed, the Orb became one with the hilt. But blade and hilt were still unjoined. Again the fox counseled him. 'Take the blade in your left hand and the hilt in the right and join them.'

'They will not join. It is not possible,' Riva said.

'Wise are you, indeed,' the fox said, 'to know what is not possible before you have made the attempt.'

Then Riva was ashamed. He set blade and hilt together, and the blade passed into the hilt as a stick slides into water. The sword was joined forever.

The fox laughed and said, 'Take the sword and smite the rock which stands before you.'

Riva feared for the blade, lest the blow shatter it, but he smote the rock. The rock broke in two, and water gushed forth in a river and flowed down to the city below. And far to the east in the darkness of Mallorea, maimed Torak started up from his bed as a chill coursed through his heart.

Again the fox laughed. Then it ran away, but stopped to look back. Riva saw that it was a fox no longer, but the great silver wolf form of Belgarath.

Riva had the sword placed upon the face of the black rock wall that stood at the back of his throne with its blade downward so that the Orb at its pommel stood at the highest point. And the sword cleaved itself to the rock. None but Riva could take it down.

As the years passed, men saw that the Orb burned with a cold fire when Riva sat upon the throne; and when he took down the sword and raised it, it became a great tongue of blue flame.

In the early spring of the year after the sword was forged, a small boat came across the dark waters of the Sea of the Winds, moving without oars or sails. Alone within the boat was the fairest maid in all the world. Her name was Beldaran, beloved daughter of Belgarath, and she had come to be a wife to Riva. And Riva's heart melted with love for her, as had been ordained from the beginning of time.

In the year that followed the wedding of Beldaran to Riva, a son was born to them upon Erastide. And upon the right hand of this son of Riva was the mark of the Orb. Straightaway, Riva carried his infant manchild to the Hall of the Rivan King and placed the tiny hand upon the Orb. The Orb knew the child and glowed with love for him. Ever afterward, the hand of each descendant of Riva bore the mark of the Orb that it might know him and not destroy him when he touched it, for only one of Riva's line could touch the Orb in safety. With each touch of infant hand upon the Orb the bond between Riva's line and the Orb grew stronger. And with each joining, the brilliance of the Orb increased.

Thus it was in the city of Riva for a thousand years. Sometimes strangers sailed into the Sea of Winds, seeking trade, but the ships of Cherek, bound to defend the Isle of the Winds, fell upon the strangers and destroyed them. But in time, the Alorn Kings met and determined in council that these strangers were not the servants of Torak, but bowed instead to the God Nedra. Then they agreed to let the ships sail the Sea of the Winds unmolested. 'For,' the Rivan King told his fellow monarchs, 'a time may come when the sons of Nedra will join with us in our struggle against the Angaraks of Torak One-Eye. Let us not offend Nedra by sinking the ships of his children.' The ruler of Riva spoke wisely, and the Alorn Kings agreed, knowing that the world was changing.

Then treaties were signed with the sons of Nedra, who took a childish delight in signing scraps of parchment. But when they sailed into the harbor at Riva, with their ships bearing full loads of gaudy trinkets upon which they placed high value, the Rivan King laughed at their folly and closed the gates of the city to them.

The sons of Nedra importuned their king, whom they called Emperor, to force the city gates so that they might hawk their wares in the streets, and the Emperor sent his army to the Isle. Now to permit these strangers from the kingdom they called Tolnedra passage upon the Sea was one thing, but to let them land an army at the gates of Riva without challenge was quite another. The Rivan King ordered that the strand before the city be cleared and the harbor be swept clean of the ships of Tolnedra. And it was done.

Great was the wrath of the Emperor of Tolnedra. He assembled his armies to cross the Sea of the Winds and do war. Then the peaceloving Alorns held council to try reason upon this rash Emperor. And they sent out a message to advise him that, should he persist, they would rise up and destroy Emperor and kingdom and sweep the wreckage thereof into the sea. And the Emperor gave heed to this quiet remonstrance and abandoned his desperate adventure.

As years passed and the Rivan King realized that these merchants from Tolnedra were harmless, he allowed them to build a village upon the strand before his city and there to display their useless goods. Their desperation to sell or trade came to amuse him, and he asked his people to buy some few items from them – though no purpose could be found for the goods thus purchased.

Then, four thousand and two years from the day when Accursed Torak raised the stolen Orb and cracked open the world, other strange people came to the village which the sons of Nedra had built outside the walls of Riva. And it was learned of these strangers that they were the sons of the God Issa. They called themselves Ny-Issans, and they claimed that their ruler was a woman, which seemed unnatural to all who heard. The name of this queen was Salmissra.

They came in dissembling guise, saying that they brought rich gifts from their queen for the Rivan King and his family. Hearing this, Gorek the Wise, aged king in the line of Riva, grew curious to know more of these children of Issa and their queen. With his wife, his two sons and their wives, and all his royal grandchildren, he went from out the fortress and the city to visit the pavilion of the Ny-Issans, to greet them courteously, and to receive from them the valueless gifts sent by the harlot of Sthiss Tor. With smiles of greeting, the Rivan King and his family were welcomed into the pavilion of the strangers.

Then the foul and accursed sons of Issa struck at all who were the fruit and the seed of the line of Riva. And venom was anointed upon their weapons, so that the merest scratch was death.

Mighty even in age, Gorek struggled with the assassins – not to save himself, for he felt death in his veins from the frst blow – but to save at least one of his grandsons that his line might continue. Alas, all were doomed, save only one child who fled and cast himself into the sea. When Gorek saw this, he covered his head with his cloak, groaned, and fell dying beneath the knives of Nyissa.

When word of this reached Brand, Warder of the Citadel, his wrath was dreadful. The traitorous assassins were overcome, and Brand questioned each in turn in ways that made brave men tremble. And the truth was wrung from them. Gorek and his family had been foully murdered at the instructions of Salmissra, Snake Queen of the Nyissans.

Of the child who had cast himself into the sea there was no trace. One assassin claimed that he had seen a snowy owl swoop down and bear the child away, but he was not believed, though even the severest urging would not make him change his story.

Then all Aloria made dreadful war upon the sons of Issa and tore down their cities and put all they could find to the sword. And in her final hour, Salmissra confessed that the evil deed had been done at the urging of Torak One-Eye and his servant Zedar.

Thus there was no longer a Rivan King and Guardian of the Orb, though Brand and those of the same name who followed reluctantly took up rule of Riva. Rumor, ever vagrant, persisted in the years that followed, saying that the seed of Riva still lay hidden in some remote land. But gray-cloaked Rivans scoured the world in search of him and never found him.

The sword remained as Riva had placed it, and the Orb was still affixed to its pommel, though now the jewel was ever dull and seeming without life. And men began to feel that so long as the Orb was there, the West was safe, even though there was no Rivan King. Nor did there seem aught of danger that the Orb could ever be removed, since any man who touched it would be instantly and utterly consumed, were he not truly of the line of Riva.

But now that his minions had removed the Rivan King and Guardian of the Orb, Torak One-Eye again dared begin plans for the conquest of the West. And after many years, he led forth an enormous army of Angaraks to destroy all who opposed him. His hordes raved through Algaria and down through Arendia, to the city of Vo Mimbre.

Now Belgarath and his daughter Polgara the Sorceress came to the one who was Brand and Warder of Riva to advise and counsel with him. With them, Brand led his army to Vo Mimbre. And in the bloody battle before that city, Brand drew upon the power of the Orb to overcome Torak. Zedar spirited the body of his master away and hid it, but not all the disciple's skill could again awaken his God. And again men of the West felt safe, protected by the Orb and Aldur.

Now there came rumors of a prophecy that a Rivan King, true seed of the line of Riva, should again appear and sit upon the throne in the Hall of the Rivan King. And in later years, some claimed that each daughter of an Emperor of Tolnedra appeared on her sixteenth birthday to be the bride of the new king, should he appear. But few regarded such tales. Time passed into centuries, and still the West was safe. The Orb remained, quiet and dark upon the pommel of the sword. And somewhere fearful Torak was said to sleep until the return of the Rivan King – which came to mean never.

And thus the account should be ended. But no true account can ever end. And nothing can ever be safe or sure so long as cunning men plot to steal or destroy.

Again, long centuries passed. And then new rumors came, this time to disturb those in the highest places of power. And it was whispered that somehow the Orb had been stolen. Then Belgarath and Polgara were seen to be moving through the lands of the West again. This time they took with them a young man named Garion who named Belgarath his grandfather and called Polgara his aunt. And as they moved through the kingdoms, they gathered upon them a strange company.

To the Alorn Kings who gathered in council, Belgarath revealed that it was the Apostate Zedar who had somehow contrived to steal the Orb from the sword and who was even then fleeing with it to the East, presumably to use it to awaken sleeping Torak. And it was there Belgarath must go with his company to rescue it.

Then Belgarath discovered that Zedar had found a boy of total innocence who could safely touch the Orb. But now the way led to the grim and dangerous headquarters of the Grolim priests of Torak, where the magician Ctuchik had seized the Orb and the boy from Zedar.

In time this quest of Belgarath and his company to regain the Orb would come to be known as the *Belgariad*. But the end thereof lay entangled within the Prophecy. And even to the Prophecy was the ultimate conclusion unknown.

Part One

ALGARIA

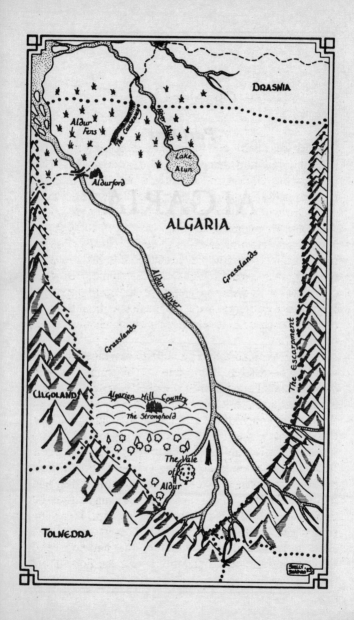

Chapter One

Ctuchik was dead – and more than dead – and the earth itself heaved and groaned in the aftershock of his destruction. Garion and the others fled down through the dim galleries that honeycombed the swaying basalt pinnacle, with the rocks grinding and cracking about them and fragments shattering away from the ceilings and raining down on them in the darkness. Even as he ran, Garion's mind jerked and veered, his thoughts tumbling over each other chaotically, stunned out of all coherence by the enormity of what had just happened. Flight was a desperate need, and he fled without thought or even awareness, his running steps as mechanical as his heartbeat.

His ears seemed full of a swelling, exultant song that rang and soared in the vaults of his mind, erasing thought and filling him with stupefied wonder. Through all his confusion, however, he was sharply conscious of the trusting touch of the small hand he held in his. The little boy they had found in Ctuchik's grim turret ran beside him with the Orb of Aldur clasped tightly to his little chest. Garion knew that it was the Orb that filled his mind with song. It had whispered to him as they had mounted the steps of the turret, and its song had soared as he had entered the room where it had lain. It was the song of the Orb that obliterated all thought – more than shock or the thunderous detonation that had destroyed Ctuchik and tumbled Belgarath across the floor like a rag doll or the deep sullen boom of the earthquake that had followed.

Garion struggled with it as he ran, trying desperately to pull his wits into some kind of order, but the song intruded on his every effort, scattering his mind so that chance impression and random memory fluttered and scurried this way and that and left him to flee without design or direction.

The dank reek of the slave pens lying just beneath the disintegrating city of Rak Cthol came sharply through the shadowy galleries. As if suddenly awakened by that single stimulus, a flood of memories of other smells crashed in on Garion's consciousness – the warm smell of fresh-baked bread in Aunt Pol's kitchen back at Faldor's farm, the salt smell of the sea when they had reached Darine on the north coast of Sendaria on the first leg of their quest for the Orb, the stink of the swamps and jungles of Nyissa, the stomach-turning smell of the burning bodies of the sacrificed slaves in the Temple of Torak which even now shattered and fell in upon itself among the collapsing walls of Rak Cthol. But, oddly, the smell that came sharpest to his confused memory was the sun-warmed scent of Princess Ce'Nedra's hair.

'Garion!' Aunt Pol's voice came sharply to him in the near dark through which they ran. 'Watch where you're going!' And he struggled to pull his mind back from its wandering even as he stumbled over a pile of broken rock where a large stretch of ceiling had fallen to the floor.

The terrified wails of the imprisoned slaves locked in clammy cells rose all around them now, joining in a weird counterharmony with the rumble and boom of earthquake. Other sounds came from the darkness as well – confused shouts in harshly accented Murgo voices, the lurching stagger of running feet, the clanging of an unlatched iron cell door swinging wildly as the huge rock pinnacle swayed and shuddered and heaved in the surging roll. Dust billowed through the dark caves, a thick, choking rock dust that stung their eyes and made them all cough almost continually as they clambered over the broken rubble.

Garion carefully lifted the trusting little boy over the pile of shattered rock, and the child looked into his face, calm and smiling despite the chaos of noise and stink all around them in the oppressive dimness. He started to set the child down again, but changed his mind. It would be easier and safer to carry the boy. He turned to go on along the passageway, but he recoiled sharply as his foot came down on something soft. He peered at the floor, then felt his stomach suddenly heave with revulsion as he saw that he had stepped on a lifeless human hand protruding from the rockfall.

They ran on through the heaving darkness with the black Murgo robes which had disguised them flapping around their legs and the dust still thick in the air about them.

'Stop!' Relg, the Ulgo zealot, raised his hand and stood with his head cocked to one side, listening intently.

'Not here!' Barak told him, still lumbering forward with the dazed Belgarath in his arms. 'Move, Relg!'

'Be still!' Relg ordered. 'I'm trying to listen.' Then he shook his head. 'Go back!' he barked, turning quickly and pushing at them. 'Run!'

'There are Murgos back there!' Barak objected.

'Run!' Relg repeated. 'The side of the mountain's breaking away!'

Even as they turned, a new and dreadful creaking roar surrounded them. Screeching in protest, the rock ripped apart with a long, hideous tearing. A sudden flood of light filled the gallery along which they fled as a great crack opened in the side of the basalt peak, widening ponderously as a vast chunk of the mountainside toppled slowly outward to fall to the floor of the wasteland thousands of feet below. The red glow of the new-risen sun was blinding as the dark world of the caves was violently opened, and the great wound in the side of the peak revealed a dozen or more dark openings both above and beneath, where caves suddenly ran out into nothingness.

'There!' a shout came from overhead. Garion jerked his head around. Perhaps fifty feet above and out along the sharp angle of the face, a half dozen black-robed Murgos, swords drawn, stood in a cave mouth with the dust billowing about them. One was pointing excitedly at the fleeing fugitives. And then the peak heaved again, and another great slab of rock sheared away, carrying the shrieking Murgos into the abyss beneath.

'Run!' Relg shouted again, and they all pounded along at his heels, back into the darkness of the shuddering passageway.

'Stop a minute,' Barak gasped, plowing to a sudden halt after they had retreated several hundred yards. 'Let me get my breath.' He lowered Belgarath to the floor, his huge chest heaving.

'Can I help thee, my Lord?' Mandorallen offered quickly.

'No,' Barak panted. 'I can manage all right, I'm just a little winded.' The big man peered around. 'What happened back there? What set all this off?'

'Belgarath and Ctuchik had a bit of a disagreement,' Silk told him with sardonic understatement. 'It got a little out of hand toward the end.'

'What happened to Ctuchik?' Barak asked, still

gasping for breath. 'I didn't see anybody else when Mandorallen and I broke into that room.'

'He destroyed himself,' Polgara replied, kneeling to examine Belgarath's face.

'We saw no body, my Lady,' Mandorallen noted, peering into the darkness with his great broadsword in his hand.

'There wasn't that much left of him,' Silk said.

'Are we safe here?' Polgara asked Relg.

The Ulgo set the side of his head against the wall of the passageway, listening intently. Then he nodded. 'For the moment,' he replied.

'Let's stop here for a while then. I want to have a look at my father. Make me some light.'

Relg fumbled in the pouches at his belt and mixed the two substances that gave off that faint Ulgo light.

Silk looked curiously at Polgara. 'What really happened?' he asked her. 'Did Belgarath do that to Ctuchik?'

She shook her head, her hands lightly touching her father's chest. 'Ctuchik tried to unmake the Orb for some reason,' she said. 'Something happened to frighten him so much that he forgot the first rule.'

A momentary flicker of memory came to Garion as he set the little boy down on his feet – that brief glimpse of Ctuchik's mind just before the Grolim had spoken the fatal 'Be Not' that had exploded him into nothingness. Once again he caught that single image that had risen in the High Priest's mind – the image of himself holding the Orb in his hand – and he felt the blind, unreasoning panic the image had caused Ctuchik. Why? Why would that have frightened the Grolim into that deadly mistake? 'What happened to him, Aunt Pol?' he asked. For some reason he had to know.

'He no longer exists,' she replied. 'Even the substance that formed him is gone.'

'That's not what I meant,' Garion started to object, but Barak was already speaking.

'Did he destroy the Orb?' the big man asked with a kind of weak sickness in his voice.

'Nothing can destroy the Orb,' she told him calmly.

'Where is it then?'

The little boy pulled his hand free from Garion's and went confidently to the big Cherek. 'Errand?' he asked, holding out the round, grey stone in his hand.

Barak recoiled from the offered stone. 'Belar!' he swore, quickly putting his hands behind his back. 'Make him stop waving it around like that, Polgara. Doesn't he knew how dangerous it is?'

'I doubt it.'

'How's Belgarath?' Silk asked.

'His heart's still strong,' Polgara replied. 'He's exhausted, though. The fight nearly killed him.'

With a long, echoing shudder the quaking subsided, and the silence seemed very loud. 'Is it over?' Durnik asked, looking around nervously.

'Probably not,' Relg replied, his voice hushed in the sudden quiet. 'An earthquake usually goes on for quite some time.'

Barak was peering curiously at the little boy. 'Where did he come from?' he asked, his rumbling voice also subdued.

'He was in the turret with Ctuchik,' Polgara told him. 'He's the child Zedar raised to steal the Orb.'

'He doesn't look all that much like a thief.'

'He isn't precisely.' She looked gravely at the blond-headed waif. 'Somebody's going to have to keep an eye on him,' she observed. 'There's something very peculiar about him. After we get down, I'll look into it, but I've got too much on my mind for that at the moment.'

'Could it be the Orb?' Silk asked curiously. 'I've heard that it has strange effects on people.'

'Perhaps that's it.' But she didn't sound very convinced. 'Keep him with you, Garion, and don't let him lose the Orb.'

'Why me?' He said it without thinking.

She gave him a level gaze.

'All right, Aunt Pol.' He knew there was no point in arguing with her.

'What was that?' Barak asked, holding up his hand for silence.

Somewhere off in the darkness there was the murmur of voices – harsh, guttural voices.

'Murgos!' Silk whispered sharply, his hand going to his dagger.

'How many?' Barak asked Aunt Pol.

'Five,' she replied. 'No – six. One's lagging behind.'

'Are any of them Grolims?'

She shook her head.

'Let's go, Mandorallen,' the big Cherek muttered, grimly drawing his sword.

The knight nodded, shifting his own broadsword in his hands.

'Wait here,' Barak whispered to the rest of them. 'We shouldn't be long.' And then he and Mandorallen moved off into the darkness, their black Murgo robes blending into the shadows.

The others waited, their ears straining to catch any sound. Once again that strange song began to intrude itself upon Garion's awareness, and once again his thoughts scattered before its compulsion. Somewhere a long, hissing slither of dislodged pebbles rattled down a slope, and that sound raised a confused welter of memory in him. He seemed to hear the ring of Durnik's hammer on the anvil at Faldor's farm, and then the plodding step of the horses and the creak of the wagons in which they had carried turnips to Darine back when this had all begun. As clearly as if he were there, he heard again the squealing rush of the boar he had killed in the snowy woods outside Val Alorn, and then the aching song of the Arendish serf-boy's flute that had soared to the sky from the stump-dotted field where Asharak the Murgo had watched with hate and fear on his scarred face.

Garion shook his head, trying to clear his thoughts, but the song drew him back into that bemused reverie. Sharply, he heard the awful, hissing crackle of Asharak burning beneath the vast, ancient trees in the Wood of the Dryads and heard the Grolim's desperate plea, 'Master, have mercy.' Then there were the screams in Salmissra's palace as Barak, transformed into that dreadful bear shape, clawed and ripped his way toward the throne room with Aunt Pol in her icy fury striding at his side.

And then the voice that had always been in his mind was there again. '*Stop fighting with it.*'

'*What is it?*' Garion demanded, trying to focus his thoughts.

'*It's the Orb.*'

'*What's it doing?*'

'*It wants to know you. This is its way of finding things out.*'

'*Can't it wait? We don't really have time just now.*'

'*You can try to explain that, if you'd like.*' The voice sounded amused. '*It might listen, but I doubt it. It's been waiting for you for a very long time.*'

'*Why me?*'

'*Don't you ever get tired of saying that?*'

'*Is it doing the same thing to the others?*'

'*To a lesser degree. You might as well relax. One way or another, it's going to get what it wants.*'

There was a sudden ring of steel against steel

somewhere off in the dark passageways and a startled cry. Then Garion heard the crunch of blows, and someone groaned. After that, there was silence.

A few moments later they heard the scuff of footsteps, and Barak and Mandorallen returned. 'We couldn't find that one who was coming along behind the rest of them,' Barak reported. 'Is Belgarath showing any signs of coming around yet?'

Polgara shook her head. 'He's still completely dazed,' she replied.

'I'll carry him then. We'd better go. It's a long way back down, and these caves are going to be full of Murgos before long.'

'In a moment,' she said. 'Relg, do you know where we are?'

'Roughly.'

'Take us back to the place where we left the slave woman,' she instructed in a tone that tolerated no objection.

Relg's face went hard, but he said nothing.

Barak bent and picked up the unconscious Belgarath. Garion held out his arms, and the little boy obediently came to him, the Orb still held protectively against his chest. The child seemed peculiarly light, and Garion carried him with almost no effort. Relg lifted his faintly glowing wooden bowl to illuminate their path, and they started out again, twisting, turning, following a zigzag course that went deeper and deeper into the gloomy caves. The darkness of the peak above them seemed to bear down on Garion's shoulders with a greater and greater weight the farther they went. The song in his mind swelled again, and the faint light Relg carried sent his thoughts roving once more. Now that he understood what was happening, it seemed to go more easily. The song opened his mind, and the Orb leeched out every

27

thought and memory, passing through his life with a light, flickering touch. It had a peculiar kind of curiosity lingering often on things Garion did not think were all that important and barely touching matters that had seemed so dreadfully urgent when they had occurred. It traced out in detail each step they had taken in their long journey to Rak Cthol. It passed with them to the crystal chamber in the mountains above Maragor where Garion had touched the stillborn colt and given life in that oddly necessary act of atonement that had somehow made up for the burning of Asharak. It went down with them into the Vale where Garion had turned over the large white rock in his first conscious attempt to use the Will and the Word objectively. It scarcely noticed the dreadful fight with Grul the Eldrak nor the visit to the caves of Ulgo, but seemed to have a great curiosity about the shield of imagining which Garion and Aunt Pol had erected to conceal their movements from the searching minds of the Grolims as they had approached Rak Cthol. It ignored the death of Brill and the sickening ceremonies in the Temple of Torak, but lingered instead on the conversation between Belgarath and Ctuchik in the Grolim High Priest's hanging turret. And then, most peculiarly, it went back to sift through every one of Garion's memories of Princess Ce'Nedra – of the way the sun caught her coppery hair, of the lithe grace of her movements, of her scent, of each unconscious gesture, of the flicker and play of emotion across her tiny exquisite face. It lingered on her in a way that Garion eventually found unsettling. At the same time he found himself a bit surprised that so much of what the princess had said and done had stuck so firmly in his memory.

'Garion,' Aunt Pol said, 'what *is* the matter with you? I told you to hold onto the child. Pay attention. This isn't the time for daydreaming.'

28

'I wasn't. I was—' How could he explain it?

'You were what?'

'Nothing.'

They moved on, and there were periodic tremors as the earth settled uneasily. The huge basalt pinnacle swayed and groaned each time the earth shuddered and convulsed under its base; and at each new quiver, they stopped, almost fearing to breathe.

'How far down have we come?' Silk asked, looking around nervously.

'A thousand feet perhaps,' Relg replied.

'That's all? We'll be penned up in here for a week at this rate.'

Relg shrugged his heavy shoulders. 'It will take as long as it takes,' he said in his harsh voice as they moved on.

There were Murgos in the next gallery, and another nasty little fight in the darkness. Mandorallen was limping when he came back.

'Why didn't you wait for me as I told you to?' Barak demanded crossly.

Mandorallen shrugged. 'They were but three, my Lord.'

'There's just no point in trying to talk to you, do you know that?' Barak sounded disgusted.

'Are you all right?' Polgara asked the knight.

'A mere scratch, my lady,' Mandorallen replied indifferently. 'It is of no moment.'

The rock floor of the gallery shuddered and heaved again, and the booming noise echoed up through the caves. They all stood frozen, but the uneasy movement of the earth subsided after a few moments.

They moved steadily downward through the passageways and caves. The aftershocks of the earthquake that had shattered Rak Cthol and sent Ctuchik's turret crashing to the floor of the wasteland of Murgos continued at intervals. At one point, hours later it seemed, a party of Murgos, perhaps a dozen strong, passed through a gallery not far ahead, their torches casting flickering shadows on the walls and their harsh voices echoing. After a brief, whispered conference, Barak and Mandorallen let them go by unmolested and unaware of the terrible violence lurking in the shadows not twenty yards away. After they were out of earshot, Relg uncovered his light again and selected yet another passageway. They moved on, descending, twisting, zigzagging their way down through the caves toward the foot of the pinnacle and the dubious safety of the wasteland which lay outside.

While the song of the Orb did not diminish in any way, Garion was at least able to think as he followed Silk along the twisting passageways with the little boy in his arms. He thought that perhaps it was because he had grown at least partially accustomed to it – or maybe its attention was concentrated on one of the others.

They had done it; that was the amazing thing. Despite all the odds against them, they had retrieved the Orb. The search that had so abruptly interrupted his quiet life at Faldor's farm was over, but it had changed him in so many ways that the boy who had crept out through the gate at Faldor's farm in the middle of a windswept autumn night no longer even existed. Garion could feel the power he had discovered within himself even now and he knew that power was there for a reason. There had been hints along the way – vague, half-spoken, sometimes only implied – that the return of the Orb to its proper place was only a beginning of something much larger and much more serious. Garion was absolutely certain that this was not the end of it.

'*It's about time,*' the dry voice in his mind said.

'*What's that supposed to mean?*'

'Why do I have to explain this every single time?'

'Explain what?'

'That I know what you're thinking. It's not as if we were completely separate, you know.'

'All right, then. Where do we go from here?'

'To Riva.'

'And after that?'

'We'll see.'

'You aren't going to tell me?'

'No. Not yet. You haven't come nearly as far as you think you have. There's still a very long way to go.'

'If you aren't going to tell me anything, why don't you just leave me alone?'

'I just wanted to advise you not to make any long-term plans. The recovery of the Orb was only a step – an important one – but only a beginning.'

And then, as if mention of it somehow reminded the Orb of Garion's presence, its song returned in full force, and Garion's concentration dissolved.

Not much later, Relg stopped, lifting the faint light aloft.

'What's the trouble?' Barak demanded, lowering Belgarath to the floor again.

'The ceiling fell in,' Relg replied, pointing at the rubble choking the passageway ahead. 'We can't get through.' He looked at Aunt Pol. 'I'm sorry,' he said, and Garion felt that he really meant it. 'That woman we left down here is on the other side of the cave-in.'

'Find another way,' she told him shortly.

'There isn't any. This was the only passageway leading to the pool where we found her.'

'We'll have to clear it then.'

Relg shook his head gravely. 'We'd just bring more of it down on top of us. It probably fell in on her as well – at least we can hope so.'

'Isn't that just a bit contemptible, Relg?' Silk asked pointedly.

The Ulgo turned to regard the little man. 'She has water there and sufficient air to breathe. If the cave-in didn't kill her, she could live for weeks before she starves to death.' There was a peculiar, quiet regret in Relg's voice.

Silk stared at him for a moment. 'Sorry, Relg,' he said finally. 'I misunderstood.'

'People who live in caves have no desire to see anyone trapped like that.'

Polgara, however, was considering the rubble-blocked passageway. 'We have to get her out of there,' she declared.

'Relg could be right, you know,' Barak pointed out. 'For all we know, she's buried under half the mountain.'

She shook her head. 'No,' she disagreed. 'Taiba's still alive, and we can't leave without her. She's as important to all of this as any one of us.' She turned back to Relg. 'You'll have to go get her,' she told him firmly.

Relg's large, dark eyes widened. 'You can't ask that,' he protested.

'There's no alternative.'

'You can do it, Relg,' Durnik encouraged the zealot. 'You can go through the rock and bring her out the same way you carried Silk out of that pit where Taur Urgas had him.'

Relg had begun to tremble violently. 'I can't!' his voice was choked. 'I'd have to touch her – put my hands on her. It's sin.'

'This is most uncharitable of thee, Relg,' Mandorallen told him. 'There is no sin in giving aid to the weak and helpless. Consideration for the unfortunate is a paramount responsibility of all decent men, and no force in all the world can corrupt the pure spirit. If compassion

32

doth not move thee to fly to her aid, then mayest thou not perhaps regard her rescue a test of thy purity?'

'You don't understand,' Relg told him in an anguished voice. He turned back to Polgara. 'Don't make me do this, I beg you.'

'You must,' she replied quietly. 'I'm sorry, Relg, but there's no other way.'

A dozen emotions played across the fanatic's face as he shrank under Aunt Pol's unrelenting gaze. Then with a strangled cry, he turned and put his hand to the solid rockface at the side of the passageway. With a dreadful concentration, he pushed his fingers into the rock, demonstrating once more his uncanny ability to slip his very substance through seemingly unyielding stone.

Silk quickly turned his back. 'I can't stand to watch that,' the little man choked. And then Relg was gone, submerged in the rock.

'Why does he make so much fuss about touching people?' Barak demanded.

But Garion knew why. His enforced companionship with the ranting zealot during the ride across Algaria had given him a sharp insight into the workings of Relg's mind. The harsh-voiced denunciations of the sins of others served primarily to conceal Relg's own weakness. Garion had listened for hours at a time to hysterical and sometimes incoherent confessions about the lustful thoughts that raged through the fanatic's mind almost continually. Taiba, the lush-bodied Marag slave woman, would represent for Relg the ultimate temptation, and he would fear her more than death itself.

In silence they waited. Somewhere a slow drip of water measured the passing seconds. The earth shuddered from time to time as the last uneasy shocks of earthquake trembled beneath their feet. The minutes dragged on in the dim cavern.

33

And then there was a flicker of movement, and Relg emerged from the rock wall carrying the half-naked Taiba. Her arms were desperately clasped about his neck, and her face was buried in his shoulder. She was whimpering in terror and trembling uncontrollably.

Relg's face was twisted into an agony. Tears of anguish streamed openly from his eyes, and his teeth were clenched as if he were in the grip of intolerable pain. His arms, however, cradled the terrified slave woman protectively, almost gently, and even when they were free of the rock, he held her closely against him as if he intended to hold her thus forever.

Chapter Two

It was noon by the time they reached the foot of the basalt tower and the large cave where they had left the horses. Silk went to the cave mouth to stand watch as Barak carefully lowered Belgarath to the floor. 'He's heavier than he looks,' the big man grunted, wiping the sweat from his face. 'Shouldn't he be starting to come around?'

'It may be days before he's fully conscious,' Polgara replied. 'Just cover him and let him sleep.'

'How's he going to ride?'

'I'll take care of that.'

'Nobody's going to be riding anywhere for a while,' Silk announced from the narrow mouth of the cave. 'The Murgos are swarming around out there like hornets.'

'We'll wait until dark,' Polgara decided. 'We all need some rest anyway.' She pushed back the hood of her Murgo robe and went to one of the packs they had piled against the cave wall when they had entered the night before. 'I'll see about something to eat, then you'd all better sleep.'

Taiba, the slave woman, wrapped once again in Garion's cloak, had been watching Relg almost continually. Her large, violet eyes glowed with gratitude mingled with a faint puzzlement. 'You saved my life,' she said to him in a rich, throaty voice. She leaned slightly toward him as she spoke. It was an unconscious gesture, Garion was certain, but it was distinctly

35

noticeable. 'Thank you,' she added, her hand moving to rest lightly on the zealot's arm.

Relg cringed back from her. 'Don't touch me,' he gasped.

She stared at him in amazement, her hand still half-extended.

'You must *never* put your hands on me,' he told her. 'Never.'

Taiba's look was incredulous. Her life had been spent almost entirely in darkness, and she had never learned to keep her emotions from showing on her face. Amazement gave way to humiliation, and her expression settled then into a kind of stiff, sullen pout as she turned quickly away from the man who had just so harshly rejected her. The cloak slipped from her shoulders as she turned, and the few rags she had for clothing scarcely concealed her nakedness. Despite her tangled hair and the dirty smudges on her limbs, there was a lush, inviting ripeness about her. Relg stared at her and he began to tremble. Then he quickly turned, moved as far away from her as possible, and dropped to his knees, praying desperately and pressing his face against the rocky floor of the cave.

'Is he all right?' Taiba asked quickly.

'He's got some problems,' Barak replied. 'You'll get used to it.'

'Taiba,' Polgara said. 'Come over here.' She looked critically at the woman's scanty clothing. 'We're going to have to get something together for you to wear. It's very cold outside. There are other reasons too, it appears.'

'I'll see what I can find in the packs,' Durnik offered. 'We'll need something for the boy too, I think. That smock of his doesn't look any too warm.' He looked over at the child, who was curiously examining the horses.

'You won't need to bother about me,' Taiba told

them. 'There's nothing out there for me. As soon as you leave, I'm going back to Rak Cthol.'

'What are you talking about?' Polgara asked her sharply.

'I still have something to settle with Ctuchik,' Taiba replied, fingering her rusty knife.

Silk laughed from the cave mouth. 'We took care of that for you. Rak Cthol's falling to pieces up there, and there isn't enough left of Ctuchik to make a smudge on the floor.'

'Dead?' she gasped. 'How?'

'You wouldn't believe it,' Silk told her.

'Did he suffer?' She said it with a terrible eagerness.

'More than you could ever imagine,' Polgara replied.

Taiba drew in a long, shuddering breath, and then she began to cry. Aunt Pol opened her arms and took the sobbing woman into them, comforting her even as she had comforted Garion so often when he was small.

Garion sank wearily to the floor, resting his back against the rocky wall of the cave. Waves of exhaustion washed over him, and a great lassitude drained him of all consciously directed thought. Once again the Orb sang to him, but lulling now. Its curiosity about him apparently was satisfied, and its song seemed to be there only to maintain the contact between them. Garion was too tired even to be curious about why the stone took such pleasure in his company.

The little boy turned from his curious examination of the horses and went to where Taiba sat with one of Aunt Pol's arms about her shoulders. He looked puzzled, and reached out with one hand to touch his fingers to her tear-streaked face.

'What does he want?' Taiba asked.

'He's probably never seen tears before,' Aunt Pol replied.

Taiba stared at the child's serious little face, then suddenly laughed through her tears and gave him a quick embrace.

The little boy smiled then. 'Errand?' he asked, offering her the Orb.

'Don't take it, Taiba,' Polgara told her very quietly. 'Don't even touch it.'

Taiba looked at the smiling child and shook her head.

The little boy sighed, then came across the cave, sat down beside Garion, and nestled against him.

Barak had gone a short distance back up the passageway they had followed; now he returned, his face grim. 'I can hear Murgos moving around up there,' the big man reported. 'You can't tell how far away they are with all the echoes in these caves, but it sounds as if they're exploring every cave and passageway.'

'Let us find some defensible spot then, my Lord, and give them reason to look for us elsewhere,' Mandorallen suggested gaily.

'Interesting notion,' Barak replied, 'but I'm afraid it wouldn't work. Sooner or later they're going to find us.'

'I'll take care of it,' Relg said quietly, breaking off his praying and getting to his feet. The ritual formulas had not helped him, and his eyes were haunted.

'I'll go with you,' Barak offered.

Relg shook his head. 'You'd just be in my way,' he said shortly, already moving toward the passage leading back into the mountain.

'What's come over him?' Barak asked, puzzled.

'I think our friend's having a religious crisis,' Silk observed from the mouth of the cave where he kept watch.

'Another one?'

'It gives him something to occupy his spare moments,' Silk replied lightly.

'Come and eat,' Aunt Pol told them, laying slices of

38

bread and cheese on top of one of the packs. 'Then I want to have a look at the cut on your leg, Mandorallen.'

After they had eaten and Polgara had bandaged Mandorallen's knee, she dressed Taiba in a peculiar assortment of clothes Durnik had taken from the packs. Then she turned her attention to the little boy. He returned her grave look with one just as serious, then reached out and touched the white lock at her brow with curious fingers. With a start of remembrance, Garion recalled how many times he had touched that lock with the selfsame gesture, and the memory of it raised a momentary irrational surge of jealousy, which he quickly suppressed.

The little boy smiled with sudden delight. 'Errand,' he said firmly, offering the Orb to Aunt Pol.

She shook her head. 'No, child,' she told him. 'I'm afraid I'm not the one.' She dressed him in clothing that had to be rolled up and taken in with bits of twine in various places, then sat down with her back against the wall of the cave and held out her arms to him. Obediently he climbed into her lap, put one arm about her neck and kissed her. Then he nestled his face down against her, sighed and immediately fell asleep. She looked down at him with a strange expression on her face – a peculiar mixture of wonder and tenderness – and Garion fought down another wave of jealousy.

There was a grinding rumble in the caves above them.

'What's that?' Durnik asked, looking around with apprehension.

'Relg, I'd imagine,' Silk told him. 'He seems to be taking steps to head off the Murgos.'

'I hope he doesn't get carried away,' Durnik said nervously, glancing at the rock ceiling.

'How long's it going to take to get to the Vale?' Barak asked.

'A couple of weeks, probably,' Silk replied. 'A lot's going to depend on the terrain and how quickly the Grolims can organize a search for us. If we can get enough of a headstart to put down a good false trail, we can send them all running off to the west toward the Tolnedran border, and we can move toward the Vale without needing to waste all that time dodging and hiding.' The little man grinned. 'The notion of deceiving the whole Murgo nation appeals to me,' he added.

'You don't have to get *too* creative,' Barak told him. 'Hettar's going to be waiting for us in the Vale – along with King Cho-Hag and half the clans of Algaria. They'll be awfully disappointed if we don't bring them at least a *few* Murgos.'

'Life's full of little disappointments,' Silk told him sardonically. 'As I remember it, the eastern edge of the Vale is very steep and rough. It will take a couple of days at least to make it down, and I don't think we'll want to try it with all of Murgodom snapping at our heels.'

It was midafternoon when Relg returned. His exertions seemed to have quieted some of the turmoil in his mind, but there was still a haunted look in his eyes, and he deliberately avoided Taiba's violet-eyed gaze. 'I pulled down the ceilings of all the galleries leading to this cave,' he reported shortly. 'We're safe now.'

Polgara, who had seemed asleep, opened her eyes. 'Get some rest,' she told him.

He nodded and went immediately to his blankets.

They rested in the cave through the remainder of the day, taking turns on watch at the narrow opening. The wasteland of black sand and wind-scoured rock lying out beyond the tumbled scree at the base of the pinnacle was alive with Murgo horsemen scurrying this way and that in a frenzied, disorganized search.

'They don't seem to know what they're doing,' Garion

observed quietly to Silk as the two of them watched. The sun was just sinking into a bank of cloud on the western horizon, staining the sky fiery red, and the stiff wind brought a dusty chill with it as it seeped into the cave opening.

'I imagine that things are a bit scrambled up in Rak Cthol,' Silk replied. 'No one's in charge any more, and that confuses Murgos. They tend to go all to pieces when there's nobody around to give them orders.'

'Isn't that going to make it hard for us to get out of here?' Garion asked. 'What I mean is that they're not going anyplace. They're just milling around. How are we going to get through them?'

Silk shrugged. 'We'll just pull up our hoods and mill around with the rest of them.' He pulled the coarse cloth of the Murgo robe he wore closer about him to ward off the chill and turned to look back into the cave. 'The sun's going down,' he reported.

'Let's wait until it's completely dark,' Polgara replied. She was carefully bundling the little boy up in one of Garion's old tunics.

'Once we get out a ways, I'll drop a few odds and ends,' Silk said. 'Murgos can be a little dense sometimes, and we wouldn't want them to miss our trail.' He turned to look back out at the sunset. 'It's going to be a cold night,' he remarked to no one in particular.

'Garion,' Aunt Pol said, rising to her feet, 'you and Durnik stay close to Taiba. She's never ridden before, and she might need some help at first.'

'What about the little boy?' Durnik asked.

'He'll ride with me.'

'And Belgarath?' Mandorallen inquired, glancing over at the still-sleeping old sorcerer.

'When the time comes, we'll just put him on his horse,' Polgara replied. 'I can keep him in his saddle – as long as we don't make any sudden changes in direction. Is it getting any darker?'

'We'd better wait for a little longer,' Silk answered. 'There's still quite a bit of light out there.'

They waited. The evening sky began to turn purple, and the first stars came out, glittering cold and very far away. Torches began to appear among the searching Murgos. 'Shall we go?' Silk suggested, rising to his feet.

They led their horses quietly out of the cave and down across the scree to the sand. There they stopped for several moments while a group of Murgos carrying torches galloped by several hundred yards out. 'Don't get separated,' Silk told them as they mounted.

'How far is it to the edge of the wasteland?' Barak asked the little man, grunting as he climbed up onto his horse.

'Two days' hard riding,' Silk replied. 'Or nights in this case. We'll probably want to take cover when the sun's out. We don't look all *that* much like Murgos.'

'Let's get started,' Polgara told him.

They moved out at a walk, going slowly until Taiba became more sure of herself and Belgarath showed that he could stay in his saddle even though he could not yet communicate with anyone. Then they nudged their horses into a canter that covered a great deal of ground without exhausting the horses.

As they crossed the first ridge, they rode directly into a large group of Murgos carrying torches.

'Who's there?' Silk demanded sharply, his voice harsh with the characteristic accents of Murgo speech. 'Identify yourselves.'

'We're from Rak Cthol,' one of the Murgos answered respectfully.

'I know that, blockhead,' Silk barked. 'I asked your identity.'

'Third Phalanx,' the Murgo said stiffly.

'That's better. Put out those torches. How do you expect to see anything beyond ten feet with them flaring in your eyes?'

The torches were immediately extinguished.

'Move your search to the north,' Silk commanded. 'The Ninth Phalanx is covering this sector.'

'But—'

'Are you going to argue with me?'

'No, but—'

'Move! Now!'

The Murgos wheeled their horses about and galloped off into the darkness.

'Clever,' Barak said admiringly.

Silk shrugged. 'Pretty elementary,' he replied. 'People are grateful for a bit of direction when they're confused. Let's move along, shall we?'

There were other encounters during the long, cold, moonless night as they rode west. They were inescapable, in view of the hordes of Murgos scouring the wasteland in search of them, but Silk handled each such meeting smoothly, and the night passed without significant incident.

Toward morning the little man began artfully dropping various articles to mark their trail. 'A bit overdone, perhaps,' he said critically, looking at an old shoe he had just tossed into the hoof-churned sand behind them.

'What are you talking about?' Barak asked him.

'Our trail,' Silk replied. 'We want them to follow us, remember? They're supposed to think we're headed toward Tolnedra.'

'So?'

'I was just suggesting that this is a bit crude.'

'You worry too much about things like that.'

'It's a question of style, my dear Barak,' Silk replied loftily. 'Sloppy work tends to be habit-forming.'

As the first steel-gray light of dawn began to creep across the wintry sky, they took shelter among the boulders of one of the ridges that laced the floor of the wasteland. Durnik, Barak and Mandorallen stretched the canvas of their tents tautly over a narrow ravine on the west side of the ridge and sprinkled sand on top of it to disguise their makeshift shelter.

'It's probably best not to build a fire,' Durnik said to Polgara as they led their horses in under the canvas, 'what with the smoke and all.'

She nodded her agreement. 'We could all use a hot meal,' she said, 'but I suppose we'll have to wait.'

They ate a cold breakfast of bread and cheese and began to settle in, hoping to sleep out the day so that they could ride on the next night.

'I could definitely use a bath,' Silk said, brushing sand out of his hair.

The little boy looked at him, frowning slightly. Then he walked over and offered him the Orb. 'Errand?' he asked.

Silk carefully put his hands behind his back and shook his head. 'Is that the only word he knows?' he asked Polgara.

'It seems to be,' she replied.

'I don't quite get the connection,' Silk said. 'What does he mean by it?'

'He's probably been told that he has an errand to run,' she explained, 'to steal the Orb. I imagine that Zedar's been telling him that over and over since he was a baby, and the word stuck in his mind.'

'It's a bit disconcerting.' Silk was still holding his hands behind his back. 'It seems oddly appropriate sometimes.'

'He doesn't appear to think the way we do,' she told him. 'The only purpose he has in life is to give the Orb to someone – anyone, it would seem.' She frowned thoughtfully. 'Durnik, why don't you see if you can make him some kind of pouch to carry it in, and we'll fasten it to his waist. Maybe if he doesn't have it right there in his hand all the time, he won't think about it so much.'

'Of course, Mistress Pol,' Durnik agreed. 'I should have thought of that myself.' He went to one of the packs and took out an old, burn-scarred leather apron and fashioned a pouch out of a wide piece of leather he cut from it. 'Boy,' he said when he had finished, 'come here.'

The little boy was curiously examining a small, very dry bush at the upper end of the ravine and gave no indication that he knew the smith was calling him.

'You – Errand!' Durnik said.

The little boy looked around quickly and smiled as he went to Durnik.

'Why did you call him that?' Silk asked curiously.

Durnik shrugged. 'He seems to be fond of the word and he answers to it. It will do for a name until we can find something more suitable, I suppose.'

'Errand?' the child asked, offering the Orb to Durnik.

Durnik smiled at him, bent over and held the mouth of the pouch open. 'Put it in here, Errand,' he instructed, 'and we'll tie it up all nice and safe so you won't lose it.'

The little boy delightedly deposited the Orb in the leather pouch. 'Errand,' he declared firmly.

'I suppose so,' Durnik agreed. He pulled the draw-string tight and then tied the pouch to the bit of rope the boy wore as a belt. 'There we are, Errand. All safe and secure now.'

Errand examined the pouch carefully, tugging at it a

few times as if to be sure it was tightly tied. Then he gave a happy little laugh, put his arms about Durnik's neck and kissed his cheek.

'He's a good lad,' Durnik said, looking a trifle embarrassed.

'He's totally innocent,' Aunt Pol told him from where she was examining the sleeping Belgarath. 'He has no idea of the difference between good and evil, so everything in the world seems good to him.'

'I wonder what it's like to see the world that way,' Taiba mused, gently touching the child's smiling face. 'No sorrow; no fear; no pain – just to love everything you see because you believe that everything is good.'

Relg, however, had looked up sharply. The troubled expression that had hovered on his face since he had rescued the trapped slave woman fell away to be replaced by that look of fanatic zeal that it had always worn before. 'Monstrous!' he gasped.

Taiba turned on him, her eyes hardening. 'What's so monstrous about happiness?' she demanded, putting her arm about the boy.

'We aren't here to be happy,' he replied, carefully avoiding her eyes.

'Why are we here then?' she challenged.

'To serve our God and to avoid sin.' He still refused to look at her, and his tone seemed a trifle less certain.

'Well, I don't have a God,' she retorted, 'and the child probably doesn't either, so if it's all the same to you, he and I will just concentrate on trying to be happy – and if a bit of sin gets involved in it, so what?'

'Have you no shame?' His voice was choked.

'I am what I am,' she replied, 'and I won't apologize, since I didn't have very much to say about it.'

'Boy,' Relg snapped at the child, 'come away from her at once.'

46

Taiba straightened, her face hardening even more, and she faced him defiantly. 'What do you think you're going to do?' she demanded.

'I will fight sin wherever I find it,' he declared.

'Sin, sin, sin!' she flared. 'Is that all you ever think about?'

'It's my constant care. I guard against it every moment.'

She laughed. 'How tedious. Can't you think of anything better to do? Oh, I forgot,' she added mockingly. 'There's all that praying too, isn't there? All that bawling at your God about how vile you are. I think you must bore this UL of yours tremendously sometimes, do you know that?'

Enraged, Relg raised his fist. 'Don't *ever* speak UL's name again!'

'Will you hit me if I do? It doesn't matter that much. People have been hitting me all my life. Go ahead, Relg. Why don't you hit me?' She lifted her smudged face to him.

Relg's hand fell.

Sensing her advantage, Taiba put her hands to the throat of the rough grey dress Polgara had given her. 'I can stop you, Relg,' she told him. She began unfastening the dress. 'Watch me. You look at me all the time anyway – I've seen you with your hot eyes on me. You call me names and say that I'm wicked, but still you watch. Look then. Don't try to hide it.' She continued to unfasten the front of the dress. 'If you're free of sin, my body shouldn't bother you at all.'

Relg's eyes were bulging now.

'My body doesn't bother me, but it bothers you very much, doesn't it? But is the wickedness in my mind or yours? I can sink you in sin any time I want to. All I have to do is this.' And she pulled open the front of her dress.

47

Relg spun about, making strangled noises.

'Don't you want to look, Relg?' she mocked him as he fled.

'You have a formidable weapon there, Taiba,' Silk congratulated her.

'It was the only weapon I had in the slave pens,' she told him. 'I learned to use it when I had to.' She carefully rebuttoned her dress and turned back to Errand as if nothing had happened.

'What's all the shouting?' Belgarath mumbled, rousing slightly, and they all turned quickly to him.

'Relg and Taiba were having a little theological discussion,' Silk replied lightly. 'The finer points were very interesting. How are you?'

But the old man had already drifted back into sleep.

'At least he's starting to come around,' Durnik noted.

'It will be several days before he's fully recovered,' Polgara told him, putting her hand to Belgarath's forehead. 'He's still terribly weak.'

Garion slept for most of the day, wrapped in his blankets and lying on the stony ground. When the chill and a particularly uncomfortable rock under his hip finally woke him, it was late afternoon. Silk sat guard near the mouth of the ravine, staring out at the black sand and the greyish salt flats, but the rest were all asleep. As he walked quietly down to where the little man sat, Garion noticed that Aunt Pol slept with Errand in her arms, and he pushed away a momentary surge of jealousy. Taiba murmured something as he passed, but a quick glance told him that she was not awake. She was lying not far from Relg; in her sleep, her hand seemed to be reaching out toward the slumbering Ulgo.

Silk's sharp little face was alert and he showed no signs of weariness. 'Good morning,' he murmured, 'or whatever.'

'Don't you ever get tired?' Garion asked him, speaking quietly so that his voice would not disturb the others.

'I slept a bit,' Silk told him.

Durnik came out from under the canvas roof to join them, yawning and rubbing at his eyes. 'I'll relieve you now,' he said to Silk. 'Did you see anything?' He squinted out toward the lowering sun.

Silk shrugged. 'Some Murgos. They were a couple of miles off to the south. I don't think anyone's found our trail yet. We might have to make it a little more obvious for them.'

Garion felt a peculiar, oppressive sort of weight on the back of his neck. He glanced around uncomfortably. Then, with no warning, there was a sudden sharp stab that seemed to go straight into his mind. He gasped and tensed his will, pushing the attack away.

'What's wrong?' Silk asked sharply.

'A Grolim,' Garion snarled, clenching his will as he prepared to fight.

'Garion!' It was Aunt Pol, and her voice sounded urgent. He turned and darted back in under the canvas with Silk and Durnik on his heels.

She had risen to her feet and was standing with her arms protectively about Errand.

'That was a Grolim, wasn't it?' Garion demanded, his voice sounding a bit shrill.

'It was more than one,' she replied tensely. 'The Hierarchs control the Grolims now that Ctuchik's dead. They've joined their wills to try to kill Errand.'

The others, awakened by her sharp cry, were stumbling to their feet and reaching for weapons.

'Why are they after the boy?' Silk asked.

'They know that he's the only one who can touch the Orb. They think that if he dies, we won't be able to get it out of Cthol Murgos.'

'What do we do?' Garion asked her, looking around helplessly.

'I'm going to have to concentrate on protecting the child,' she told him. 'Step back, Garion.'

'What?'

'Get back away from me.' She bent and drew a circle in the sand, enclosing herself and the little boy in it. 'Listen to me, all of you,' she said. 'Until we're out of this, none of you come any closer to me than this. I don't want any of you getting hurt.' She drew herself up, and the white lock in her hair seemed to blaze.

'Wait,' Garion exclaimed.

'I don't dare. They could attack again at any moment. It's going to be up to you to protect your grandfather and the others.'

'Me?'

'You're the only one who can do it. You have the power. Use it.' She raised her hand.

'How many of them are there that I have to fight off?' Garion demanded, but he already felt the sudden surge and the peculiar roaring sound in his mind as Aunt Pol's will thrust out. The air about her seemed to shimmer, distorting like heatwaves on a summer afternoon. Garion could actually feel the barrier encircling her. 'Aunt Pol?' he said to her. Then he raised his voice and shouted, 'Aunt Pol!'

She shook her head and pointed at her ear. She seemed to say something, but no sound penetrated the shimmering shield she had erected.

'How many?' Garion mouthed the words exaggeratedly.

She held up both hands with one thumb folded in.

'Nine?' he mouthed again.

She nodded and then drew her cloak in around the little boy.

'Well, Garion?' Silk asked then, his eyes penetrating, 'what do we do now?'

'Why are you asking me?'

'You heard her. Belgarath's still in a daze, and she's busy. You're in charge now.'

'*Me?*'

'What do we do?' Silk pressed. 'You've got to learn to make decisions.'

'I don't know.' Garion floundered helplessly.

'Never admit that,' Silk told him. 'Act as if you know – even if you don't.'

'We – uh – we'll wait until it gets dark, I guess – then we'll keep going the same way we have been.'

'There.' Silk grinned. 'See how easy it is?'

Chapter Three

There was the faintest sliver of a moon low over the horizon as they started out across the black sand of the wasteland in the biting chill. Garion felt distinctly uncomfortable in the role Silk had thrust upon him. He knew that there had been no need for it, since they all knew where they were going and what they had to do. If any kind of leadership had actually been required, Silk himself was the logical one to provide it; but instead, the little man had placed the burden squarely on Garion's shoulders and now seemed to be watching intently to see how he would handle it.

There was no time for leadership or even discussion when shortly after midnight, they ran into a party of Murgos. There were six of them, and they came galloping over a low ridge to the south and blundered directly into the middle of Garion's party. Barak and Mandorallen reacted with that instant violence of trained warriors, their swords whistling out of their sheaths to crunch with steely ringing sounds into the mail-shirted bodies of the startled Murgos. Even as Garion struggled to draw his own sword, he saw one of the black-robed intruders tumble limply out of his saddle, while another, howling with pain and surprise, toppled slowly backward, clutching at his chest. There was a confusion of shouts and shrill screams from terrified horses as the men fought in the darkness. One frightened Murgo wheeled his mount to flee, but

Garion, without even thinking, pulled his horse in front of him, sword raised to strike. The desperate Murgo made a frantic swing with his own weapon, but Garion easily parried the badly aimed swipe and flicked his blade lightly, whiplike, across the Murgo's shoulder. There was a satisfying crunch as the sharp edge bit into the Murgo's mail shirt. Garion deftly parried another clumsy swing and whipped his blade again, slashing the Murgo across the face. All the instruction he had received from his friends seemed to click together into a single, unified style that was part Cherek, part Arendish, part Algar, and was distinctly Garion's own. This style baffled the frightened Murgo, and his efforts became more desperate. But each time he swung, Garion easily parried and instantly countered with those light, flicking slashes that inevitably drew blood. Garion felt a wild, surging exultation boiling in his veins as he fought, and there was a fiery taste in his mouth.

Then Relg darted in out of the shadows, jerked the Murgo off balance, and drove his hook-pointed knife up under the man's ribs. The Murgo doubled over sharply, shuddered, then fell dead from his saddle.

'What did you do that for?' Garion demanded without thinking. 'That was *my* Murgo.'

Barak, surveying the carnage, laughed, his sudden mirth startling in the darkness. 'He's turning savage on us, isn't he?'

'His skill is noteworthy, however,' Mandorallen replied approvingly.

Garion's spirits soared. He looked around eagerly for someone else to fight, but the Murgos were all dead. 'Were they alone?' he demanded, somewhat out of breath. 'I mean, were there any others coming along behind them? Maybe we should go look.'

'We *do* want them to find our trail, after all,' Silk

reminded him. 'It's up to you of course, Garion, but if we exterminate all the Murgos in the area, there won't be anyone left to report our direction back to Rak Cthol, will there?'

'Oh,' Garion said, feeling a little sheepish, 'I forgot about that.'

'You have to keep the grand plan in view, Garion, and not lose sight of it during these little side adventures.'

'Maybe I got carried away.'

'A good leader can't afford to do that.'

'All right.' Garion began to feel embarrassed.

'I just wanted to be sure you understood, that's all.'

Garion didn't answer, but he began to see what it was about Silk that irritated Belgarath so much. Leadership was enough of a burden without these continual sly comments from the weasel-faced little man to complicate things.

'Are you all right?' Taiba was saying to Relg with a strange note of concern in her voice. The Ulgo was still on his knees beside the body of the Murgo he had killed.

'Leave me alone,' he told her harshly.

'Don't be stupid. Are you hurt? Let me see.'

'Don't touch me!' He cringed away from her out-stretched hand. 'Belgarion, make her get away from me.'

Garion groaned inwardly. 'What's the trouble now?' he asked.

'I killed this man,' Relg replied. 'There are certain things I have to do – certain prayers – purification. She's interfering.'

Garion resisted an impulse to swear. 'Please, Taiba,' he said as calmly as he could, 'just leave him alone.'

'I just wanted to see if he was all right,' Taiba answered a bit petulantly. 'I wasn't hurting him.' She had an odd look on her face that Garion could not begin to understand. As she stared at the kneeling Ulgo, a curious little smile flickered across her lips. Without warning, she reached her hand out toward him again.

Relg shrank back. 'No!' he gasped. Taiba chuckled, a throaty, wicked little sound, and walked away, humming softly to herself.

After Relg had performed his ritual of purification over the dead Murgo's body, they remounted and rode on. The sliver of moon stood high overhead in the chill sky, casting a pale light down on the black sands, and Garion looked about constantly as he rode, trying to pick out any possible dangers lurking ahead. He glanced frequently at Aunt Pol, wishing that she were not so completely cut off from him, but she seemed to be totally absorbed in maintaining her shield of will. She rode with Errand pulled closely against her, and her eyes were distant, unfathomable. Garion looked hopefully at Belgarath, but the old man, though he looked up from his doze at times, seemed largely unaware of his surroundings. Garion sighed, and his eyes resumed their nervous scrutiny of the trail ahead. They rode on through the tag-end of night in the biting chill with the faint moonlight about them and the stars glittering like points of ice in the sky above.

Suddenly Garion heard a roaring in his mind – a sound that had a peculiar echo to it – and the shield of force surrounding Aunt Pol shimmered with an ugly orange glow. He jerked his will in sharply and gestured with a single word. He had no idea what word he used, but it seemed to work. Like a horse blundering into a covey of feeding birds, his will scattered the concerted attack on Aunt Pol and Errand. There had been more than one mind involved in the attack – he sensed that – but it seemed to make no difference. He caught a momentary flicker of chagrin and even fear as the joined wills of Aunt Pol's attackers broke and fled from him.

'Not bad,' the voice in his mind observed. *'A little clumsy, perhaps, but not bad at all.'*

'It's the first time I ever did it,' Garion replied. *'I'll get better with more practice.'*

'Don't get overconfident,' the voice advised dryly, and then it was gone.

He was growing stronger, there was no doubt about that. The ease with which he had dispersed the combined wills of that group of Grolims Aunt Pol had called the Hierarchs amazed him. He faintly began to understand what Aunt Pol and Belgarath meant in their use of the word 'talent.' There seemed to be some kind of capacity, a limit beyond which most sorcerers could not go. Garion realized with a certain surprise that he was already stronger than men who had been practicing this art for centuries, and that he was only beginning to touch the edges of his talent. The thought of what he might eventually be able to do was more than a little frightening.

It did, however, make him feel somewhat more secure. He straightened in his saddle and rode a bit more confidently. Perhaps leadership wasn't so bad after all. It took some getting used to, but once you knew what you were doing, it didn't seem all that hard.

The next attack came as the eastern horizon had begun to grow pale behind them. Aunt Pol, her horse, and the little boy all seemed to vanish as absolute blackness engulfed them. Garion struck back instantly and he added a contemptuous little twist to it – a stinging slap at the joined minds that had mounted the attack. He felt a glow of self-satisfaction at the surprise and pain in the minds as they flinched back from his quick counter-blow. There was a glimpse – just a momentary one – of nine very old men in black robes seated around a table in a room somewhere. One of the walls of the room had a large crack in it, and part of the ceiling had collapsed as a result of the earthquake that had convulsed Rak Cthol. Eight of the evil old men looked surprised and frightened; the ninth one had fainted. The darkness surrounding Aunt Pol disappeared.

'What are they doing?' Silk asked him.

'They're trying to break through Aunt Pol's shield,' Garion replied. 'I gave them something to think about.' He felt a little smug about it.

Silk looked at him, his eyes narrowed shrewdly. 'Don't overdo things, Garion,' he advised.

'Somebody had to do something,' Garion protested.

'That's usually the way it works out. All I'm saying is that you shouldn't lose your perspective.'

The broken wall of peaks that marked the western edge of the wasteland was clearly visible as the light began to creep up the eastern sky. 'How far would you say it is?' Garion asked Durnik.

The smith squinted at the mountains ahead. 'Two or three leagues at least,' he judged. 'Distances are deceiving in this kind of light.'

'Well?' Barak asked. 'Do we take cover for the day here or do we make a run for it?'

Garion thought about that. 'Are we going to change direction as soon as we get to the mountains?' he asked Mandorallen.

' 'Twould seem better mayhap to continue our present course for some little distance first,' the knight replied thoughtfully. 'A natural boundary such as that which lies ahead might attract more than passing scrutiny.'

'That's a good point,' Silk agreed.

Garion scratched at his cheek, noticing that his whiskers had begun to sprout again. 'Maybe we should stop here then,' he suggested. 'We could start out again when the sun goes down, get up into the mountains a way and then rest. When the sun comes up tomorrow morning, we can change our route. That way, we'll have light enough to see any tracks we leave and cover them up.'

'Seems like a good plan,' Barak approved.

'Let's do it that way then,' Garion decided.

They sought out another ridge and another ravine, and once again concealed it with their tent canvas. Although he was tired, Garion was reluctant to lose himself in sleep. Not only did the cares of leadership press heavily on him, but he also felt apprehensive about the possibility of an attack by the Hierarchs coming while he was asleep. As the others began to unroll their blankets, he walked about rather aimlessly, stopping to look at Aunt Pol, who sat with her back against a large rock, holding the sleeping Errand and looking as distant as the moon behind her shimmering shield. Garion sighed and went on down to the mouth of the ravine where Durnik was attending to the horses. It had occurred to him that all their lives depended on the well-being of their mounts, and that gave him something else to worry about.

'How are they?' he asked Durnik as he approached.

'They're bearing up fairly well,' Durnik replied. 'They've come a long way, though, and it's beginning to show on some of them.'

'Is there anything we can do for them?'

'A week's rest in a good pasture, perhaps,' Durnik answered with a wry smile.

Garion laughed. 'I think we could all use a week's rest in a good pasture.'

'You've really grown, Garion,' Durnik observed as he lifted another horse's hind hoof to examine it for cuts or bruises.

58

Garion glanced at his arm and saw that his wrist stuck an inch or two out of his sleeve. 'Most of my clothes still fit – pretty much,' he replied.

'That's not the way I meant.' Durnik hesitated. 'What's it like, Garion? Being able to do things the way you do?'

'It scares me, Durnik,' Garion admitted quietly. 'I didn't really want any of this, but it didn't give me any choice.'

'You mustn't let it frighten you, you know,' Durnik said, carefully lowering the horse's hoof. 'If it's part of you, it's part of you – just like being tall or having blond hair.'

'It's not really like that, Durnik. Being tall or having blond hair doesn't hurt anybody. This can.'

Durnik looked out at the long shadows of the ridge stretching away from the newly risen sun. 'You just have to learn to be careful with it, that's all. When I was about your age, I found out that I was much stronger than the other young men in our village – probably because I worked in the smithy. I didn't want to hurt anybody, so I wouldn't wrestle with my friends. One of them thought I was a coward because of that and he pushed me around for about six months until I finally lost my temper.'

'Did you fight him?'

Durnik nodded. 'It wasn't really much of a contest. After it was over, he realized that I wasn't a coward after all. We even got to be good friends again – after his bones all healed up and he got used to the missing teeth.'

Garion grinned at him, and Durnik smiled back a bit ruefully. 'I was ashamed of myself afterward, of course.'

Garion felt very close to this plain, solid man. Durnik was his oldest friend – somebody he could always count on.

'What I'm trying to say, Garion,' Durnik continued seriously, 'is that you can't go through life being afraid of what you are. If you do that, sooner or later somebody will come along who'll misunderstand, and you'll have to do something to show him that it's not *him* that you're afraid of. When it goes that far, it's usually much worse for you – and for him, too.'

'As it was with Asharak?'

Durnik nodded. 'It's always best in the long run to be what you are. It isn't proper to behave as if you were more, but it isn't good to behave as if you were less, either. Do you understand what I'm trying to say?'

'The whole problem seems to be finding out just exactly *what* you really are,' Garion observed.

Durnik smiled again. 'That's the part that gets most of us in trouble at times,' he agreed. Suddenly the smile fell away from his face and he gasped. Then he fell writhing to the ground, clutching at his stomach.

'Durnik!' Garion cried, 'What's wrong?'

But Durnik could not answer. His face was ashen and contorted with agony as he twisted in the dirt.

Garion felt a strange, alien pressure and he understood instantly. Thwarted in their attempts to kill Errand, the Hierarchs were directing their attacks at the others in the hope of forcing Aunt Pol to drop her shield. A terrible rage boiled up in him. His blood seemed to burn, and a fierce cry came to his lips.

'*Calmly.*' It was the voice within his mind again.

'*What do I do?*'

'*Get out into the sunlight.*'

Garion did not understand that, but he ran out past the horses into the pale morning light.

'*Put yourself into your shadow.*'

He looked down at the shadow stretching out on the ground in front of him and obeyed the voice. He wasn't sure exactly how he did it, but he poured his will and his awareness into the shadow.

60

'Now, follow the trail of their thought back to them. Quickly.'

Garion felt himself suddenly flying. Enclosed in his shadow, he touched the still-writhing Durnik once like a sniffing hound, picked up the direction of the concerted thought that had felled his friend, and then flashed through the air back over the miles of wasteland toward the wreckage of Rak Cthol. He had, it seemed, no weight, and there was an odd purplish cast to everything he saw.

He felt his immensity as he entered the room with the cracked wall where the nine black-robed old men sat, trying with the concerted power of their minds to kill Durnik. Their eyes were all focused on a huge ruby, nearly the size of a man's head, which lay flickering in the center of the table around which they sat. The slanting rays of the morning sun had distorted and enlarged Garion's shadow, and he filled one corner of the room, bending slightly so that he could fit under the ceiling. 'Stop!' he roared at the evil old men. 'Leave Durnik alone!'

They flinched back from his sudden apparition, and he could feel the thought they were directing at Durnik through the stone on the table falter and begin to fall apart. He took a threatening step and saw them cringe away from him in the purple light that half-clouded his vision.

Then one of the old men – very thin and with a long dirty beard and completely hairless scalp – seemed to recover from his momentary fright. 'Stand firm!' he snapped at the others. 'Keep the thought on the Sendar!'

'Leave him alone!' Garion shouted at them.

'Who says so?' the thin old man drawled insultingly.

'I do.'

'And just who are you?'

'I am Belgarion. Leave my friends alone.'

The old man laughed, and his laugh was as chilling as Ctuchik's had been. 'Actually, you're only Belgarion's shadow,' he corrected. 'We know the trick of the shadow. You can talk and bluster and threaten, but that's all you can do. You're just a powerless shade, Belgarion.'

'Leave us alone!'

'And what will you do if we don't?' The old man's face was filled with contemptuous amusement.

'Is he right?' Garion demanded of the voice within his mind.

'Perhaps – perhaps not,' the voice replied. *'A few men have been able to go beyond the limitation. You won't know unless you try.'*

Despite his dreadful anger, Garion did not want to kill any of them. 'Ice!' he said, focusing on the idea of cold and lashing out with his will. It felt odd – almost tenuous, as if it had no substance behind it, and the roaring was hollow and puny-sounding.

The bald old man sneered and waggled his beard insultingly.

Garion ground his insubstantial teeth and drew himself in with dreadful concentration. 'Burn!' he said then, driving his will. There was a flicker and then a sudden flash. The force of Garion's will burst forth, directed not at the bald man himself, but rather at his whiskers.

The Hierarch jumped up and stumbled back with a hoarse exclamation, trying desperately to beat the flames out of his beard.

The concerted thought of the Hierarchs shattered as the rest of them scrambled to their feet in terrified astonishment. Grimly, Garion gathered his swelling will and began to lay about him with his immensely long arms. He tumbled the Hierarchs across the rough stone floor and slammed them into walls. Squealing with fright, they scurried this way and that, trying to escape, but he methodically reached out and grasped them one by one to administer his chastisement. With a peculiar kind of detachment, he even stuffed one of them headfirst into the crack in the wall, pushing quite firmly until only a pair of wriggling feet were sticking out.

Then, when it was done, he turned back to the bald Hierarch, who had managed finally to beat the last of the fire out of his beard. 'It's impossible – impossible,' the Hierarch protested, his face stunned. 'How did you do it?'

'I told you – I am Belgarion. I can do things you can't even imagine.'

'*The jewel,*' the voice told him. '*They're using the jewel to focus their attacks. Destroy it.*'

'How?'

'*It can only hold so much. Look.*'

Garion suddenly found that he could actually see into the interior of the still-flickering ruby on the table. He saw the minute stress lines within its crystalline structure, and then he understood. He turned his will on it and poured all his anger into it. The stone blazed with light and began to pulsate as the force within it swelled. Then, with a sharp detonation, the stone exploded into fragments.

'No!' the bald Hierarch wailed. 'You idiot! That stone was irreplaceable.'

'Listen to me, old man,' Garion said in an awful voice, 'you *will* leave us alone. You will *not* pursue us, or try to injure any of us any more.' He reached out with his shadowy hand and slid it directly into the bald man's chest. He could feel the heart flutter like a terrified bird and the lungs falter as the Hierarch's breath stopped and he gaped with horror at the arm sticking out of his chest.

Garion slowly opened his fingers very wide. 'Do you understand me?' he demanded.

The Hierarch gurgled and tried to take hold of the arm, but his fingers found nothing to grasp.

'Do you understand me?' Garion repeated and suddenly clenched his fist.

The Hierarch screamed.

'Are you going to leave us alone?'

'Please, Belgarion! No more! I'm dying!'

'Are you going to leave us alone?' Garion demanded again.

'Yes, yes – anything, but please stop! I beg you! I'll do anything. Please!'

Garion unclenched his fist and drew his hand out of the Hierarch's heaving chest. He held it up, clawlike, directly in front of the old man's face. 'Look at this and remember it,' he said in a dreadfully quiet voice. 'Next time I'll reach into your chest and pull your heart out.'

The Hierarch shrank back, his eyes filled with horror as he stared at the awful hand. 'I promise you,' he stammered. 'I promise.'

'Your life depends on it,' Garion told him, then turned and flashed back across the empty miles toward his friends. Quite suddenly he was standing at the mouth of the ravine staring down at his shadow slowly reforming on the ground before him. The purple haze was gone; strangely enough, he didn't even feel tired.

Durnik drew in a shuddering breath and struggled to rise.

Garion turned quickly and ran back to his friend. 'Are you all right?' he asked, taking hold of the smith's arm.

'It was like a knife twisting inside me,' Durnik replied in a shaking voice. 'What was it?'

'The Grolim Hierarchs were trying to kill you,' Garion told him. Durnik looked around, his eyes frightened.

'Don't worry, Durnik. They won't do it again.' Garion helped him to his feet and together they went back into the ravine.

Aunt Pol was looking directly at him as he approached her. Her eyes were penetrating. 'You're growing up very fast,' she said to him.

'I had to do something,' he replied. 'What happened to your shield?'

'It doesn't seem to be necessary any more.'

'Not bad,' Belgarath said. The old man was sitting up. He looked weak and drawn, but his eyes were alert. 'Some of it was a bit exotic; but on the whole, it wasn't bad at all. The business with the hand was just a little overdone, though.'

'I wanted to be sure he understood that I meant what I was saying.' Garion felt a tremendous wave of relief at his grandfather's return to consciousness.

'I think you convinced him,' Belgarath said dryly. 'Is there anything to eat somewhere nearby?' he asked Aunt Pol.

'Are you all right now, Grandfather?' Garion asked him.

'Aside from being as weak as a fresh-hatched baby chick and as hungry as a she-wolf with nine puppies, I'm just fine,' Belgarath replied. 'I could *really* use something to eat, Polgara.'

'I'll see what I can find, father,' she told him, turning to the packs.

'I don't know that you need to bother cooking it,' he added.

The little boy had been looking curiously at Garion, his wide, blue eyes serious and slightly puzzled. Quite suddenly he laughed; smiling, he looked into Garion's face. 'Belgarion,' he said.

65

Chapter Four

'No regrets?' Silk asked Garion that evening as they rode toward the sharply rising peaks outlined against the gliaering stars ahead.

'Regrets about what?'

'Giving up command.' Silk had been watching him curiously ever since the setting sun had signalled the resumption of their journey.

'No,' Garion replied, not quite sure what the little man meant. 'Why should there be?'

'It's a very important thing for a man to learn about himself, Garion,' Silk told him seriously. 'Power can be very sweet for some men, and you never know how a man's going to handle it until you give him the chance to try.'

'I don't know why you went to all the trouble. It's not too likely that I'm going to be put in charge of things very often.'

'You never know, Garion. You never know.'

They rode on across the barren black sands of the wasteland toward the mountains looming ahead. The quarter moon rose behind them, and its light was cold and white. Near the edge of the wasteland there were a few scrubby thornbushes huddling low to the sand and silvered with frost. It was an hour or so before midnight when they finally reached rocky ground, and the hooves of their horses clattered sharply as they climbed up out of the sandy waste. When they topped the first ridge, they stopped to look back. The dark expanse of the wasteland behind them was dotted with the watch fires of the Murgos, and far back along their trail they saw moving torches.

'I was starting to worry about that,' Silk said to Belgarath, 'but it looks as if they found our trail after all.'

'Let's hope they don't lose it again,' the old man replied.

'Not too likely, really. I made it pretty obvious.'

'Murgos can be a bit undependable sometimes.' Belgarath seemed to have recovered almost completely, but Garion noted a weary slump to his shoulders and was glad that they did not plan to ride all night.

The mountains into which they rode were as arid and rocky as the ones lying to the north had been. There were looming cliffs and patches of alkali on the ground and a bitingly cold wind that seemed to wail endlessly through the rocks and to tug at the coarse-woven Murgo robes that disguised them. They pushed on until they were well into the mountains; then, several hours before dawn, they stopped to rest and to wait for the sun to rise.

When the first faint light appeared on the eastern horizon, Silk rode out and located a rocky gap passing to the northwest between two ocherous cliff faces. As soon as he returned, they saddled their horses again and moved out at a trot.

'We can get rid of these now, I think,' Belgarath said, pulling off his Murgo robe.

'I'll take them,' Silk suggested as he reined in. 'The gap's just ahead there.' He pointed. 'I'll catch up in a couple of hours.'

'Where are you going?' Barak asked him.

'I'll leave a few miles more of false trail,' Silk replied.

'Then I'll double back and make sure that you haven't left any tracks. It won't take long.'

'You want some company?' the big man offered.

Silk shook his head. 'I can move faster alone.'

'Be careful.'

Silk grinned. 'I'm always careful.' He took the Murgo garments from them and rode off to the west.

The gap into which they rode appeared to be the bed of a stream that had dried up thousands of years before. The water had cut down through the rock, revealing layer upon layer of red, brown, and yellow stone lying in bands, one atop the other. The sound of their horses' hooves was very loud as they clattered along between the cliffs, and the wind whistled as it poured through the cut.

Taiba drew her horse in beside Garion's. She was shivering and she had the cloak he had given her pulled tightly about her shoulders. 'Is it always this cold?' she asked, her large, violet eyes very wide.

'In the wintertime,' he replied. 'I imagine it's pretty hot here in the summer.'

'The slave pens were always the same,' she told him. 'We never knew what season it was.'

The twisting streambed made a sharp bend to the right, and they rode into the light of the newly risen sun. Taiba gasped.

'What's wrong?' Garion asked her quickly.

'The light,' she cried, covering her face with her hands. 'It's like fire in my eyes.'

Relg, who rode directly in front of them, was also shielding his eyes. He looked back over his shoulder at the Marag woman. 'Here,' he said. He took one of the veils he usually bound across his eyes when they were in direct sunlight and handed it back to her. 'Cover your face with this until we're back into the shadows again.' His voice was peculiarly neutral.

'Thank you,' Taiba said, binding the cloth across her eyes. 'I didn't know that the sun could be so bright.'

'You'll get used to it,' Relg told her. 'It just takes some time. Try to protect your eyes for the first few days.' He seemed about to turn and ride on, then he looked at her curiously. 'Haven't you ever seen the sun before?' he asked her.

'No,' she replied. 'Other slaves told me about it, though. The Murgos don't use women on their work gangs, so I was never taken out of the pens. It was always dark down there.'

'It must have been terrible.' Garion shuddered.

She shrugged. 'The dark wasn't so bad. It was the light we were afraid of. Light meant that the Murgos were coming with torches to take someone to the Temple to be sacrificed.'

The trail they followed turned again, and they rode out of the bright glare of sunlight. 'Thank you,' Taiba said to Relg, removing the veil from her eyes and holding it out to him.

'Keep it,' he told her. 'You'll probably need it again.' His voice seemed oddly subdued, and his eyes had a strange gentleness in them. As he looked at her, the haunted expression crept back over his face.

Since they had left Rak Cthol, Garion had covertly watched these two. He knew that Relg, despite all his efforts, could not take his eyes off the Marag woman he had been forced to rescue from her living entombment in the caves. Although Relg still ranted about sin continually, his words no longer carried the weight of absolute conviction; indeed quite often, they seemed to be little more than a mechanical repetition of a set of formulas. Occasionally, Garion had noted, even those formulas had faltered when Taiba's deep violet eyes had turned to regard the Ulgo's face. For her part, Taiba was quite obviously puzzled. Relg's rejection of her simple gratitude had humiliated her, and her resentment had been hot and immediate. His constant scrutiny, however, spoke to her with a meaning altogether different from the words coming from his lips. His eyes told her one thing, but his mouth said something else. She was baffled by him, not knowing whether to respond to his look or his words.

'You've lived your whole life in the dark, then?' Relg asked her curiously.

'Most of it,' she replied. 'I saw my mother's face once – the day the Murgos came and took her to the Temple. I was alone after that. Being alone is the worst of it. You can bear the dark if you aren't alone.'

'How old were you when they took your mother away?'

'I don't really know. I must have been almost a woman, though, because not long after that the Murgos gave me to a slave who had pleased them. There were a lot of slaves in the pens who did anything the Murgos wanted, and they were rewarded with extra food – or with women. I cried at first; but in time I learned to accept it. At least I wasn't alone any more.'

Relg's face hardened, and Taiba saw the expression. 'What should I have done?' she asked him. 'When you're a slave, your body doesn't belong to you. They can sell you or give you to anybody they want to, and there's nothing you can do about it.'

'There must have been *something*.'

'Such as what? I didn't have any kind of weapon to fight with – or to kill myself with – and you can't strangle yourself.' She looked at Garion. 'Did you know that? Some of the slaves tried it, but all you do is fall into unconsciousness, and then you start to breathe again. Isn't that curious?'

'Did you try to fight?' It seemed terribly important to Relg for some reason.

'What would have been the point? The slave they gave me to was stronger than I. He'd have just hit me until I did what he wanted.'

'You should have fought,' Relg declared adamantly. 'A little pain is better than sin, and giving up like that is sin.'

'Is it? If somebody forces you to do something and there's no possible way to avoid it, is it really sin?'

Relg started to answer, but her eyes, looking directly into his face, seemed to stop up his tongue. He faltered, unable to face that gaze. Abruptly he turned his mount and rode back toward the pack animals.

'Why does he fight with himself so much?' Taiba asked.

'He's completely devoted to his God,' Garion explained. 'He's afraid of anything that might take away some of what he feels he owes to UL.'

'Is this UL of his really that jealous?'

'No, I don't think so, but Relg does.'

Taiba pursed her lips into a sensual pout and looked back over her shoulder at the retreating zealot. 'You know,' she said, 'I think he's actually afraid of me.' She laughed then, that same low, wicked little laugh, and lifted her arms to run her fingers through the glory of her midnight hair. 'No one's ever been afraid of me before – not ever. I think I rather like it. Will you excuse me?' She turned her horse without waiting for a reply and quite deliberately rode back after the fleeing Relg.

Garion thought about it as he rode on through the narrow, twisting canyon. He realized that there was a strength in Taiba that none of them had suspected, and he finally concluded that Relg was in for a very bad time.

He trotted on ahead to speak to Aunt Pol about it as she rode with her arms about Errand.

71

'It's really none of your business, Garion,' she told him. 'Relg and Taiba can work out their problems without any help from you.'

'I was just curious, that's all. Relg's tearing himself apart, and Taiba's all confused about him. What's *really* going on between them, Aunt Pol?'

'Something very necessary,' she replied.

'You could say that about nearly everything that happens, Aunt Pol.' It was almost an accusation. 'You could even say that the way Ce'Nedra and I quarrel all the time is necessary too, couldn't you?'

She looked slightly amused. 'It's not exactly the same thing, Garion,' she answered, 'but there's a certain necessity about that too.'

'That's ridiculous,' he scoffed.

'Is it really? Then why do you suppose the two of you go out of your way so much to aggravate each other?'

He had no answer for that, but the entire notion worried him. At the same time the very mention of Ce'Nedra's name suddenly brought her sharply into his mind, and he realized that he actually missed her. He rode along in silence beside Aunt Pol for a while, feeling melancholy. Finally he sighed.

'And why so great a sigh?'

'It's all over, isn't it?'

'What's that?'

'This whole thing. I mean – we've recovered the Orb. That's what this was all about, wasn't it?'

'There's more to it than that, Garion – much more – and we're not out of Cthol Murgos yet, are we?'

'You're not really worried about that, are you?' But then, as if her question had suddenly uncovered some lingering doubts in his own mind, he stared at her in sudden apprehension. 'What would happen if we didn't?' he blurted. 'If we didn't make it out, I mean.

What would happen to the West if we didn't get the Orb back to Riva?'

'Things would become unpleasant.'

'There'd be a war, wouldn't there? And the Angaraks would win, and there'd be Grolims everywhere with their knives and their altars.' The thought of Grolims marching up to the gates of Faldor's farm outraged him.

'Don't go borrowing trouble, Garion. Let's worry about one thing at a time, shall we?'

'But what if—'

'Garion,' she said with a pained look, 'don't belabor the "what ifs," please. If you start that, you'll just worry everybody to death.'

'*You* say "what if" to grandfather all the time,' he accused.

'That's different,' she replied.

They rode hard for the next several days through a series of passes with the dry, bitter chill pressing at them like some great weight. Silk rode back often to look for any signs of pursuit, but their ruse seemed to have fooled the Murgos. Finally, about noon on a cold, sunless day when the wind was kicking up dust clouds along the horizon, they reached the broad, arid valley through which the south caravan route wound. They took cover behind a low hill while Silk rode on ahead to take a quick look.

'Thinkest thou that Taur Urgas hath joined in the search for us?' Mandorallen, dressed again in his armor, asked Belgarath.

'It's hard to say for sure,' the old sorcerer replied. 'He's a very unpredictable man.'

'There's a Murgo patrol headed east on the caravan route,' Silk reported when he returned. 'It will be another half hour or so until they're out of sight.'

Belgarath nodded.

'Do you think we'll be safe once we cross over into Mishrak ac Thull?' Durnik asked.

'We can't count on it,' Belgarath replied. 'Gethel, the king of the Thulls, is afraid of Taur Urgas, so he wouldn't make any kind of fuss about a border violation if Taur Urgas decided to follow us.'

They waited until the Murgos had crossed a low ridge to the east and then moved out again.

For the next two days they rode steadily to the northwest. The terrain grew less rocky after they crossed into the land of the Thulls, and they saw the telltale dust clouds far behind them that spoke of mounted Murgo search parties. It was late in the afternoon of a murky day when they finally reached the top of the eastern escarpment.

Barak glanced back over his shoulder at the dust clouds behind them, then pulled his horse in beside Belgarath's. 'Just how rough is the ground leading down into the Vale?' he asked.

'It's not the easiest trail in the world.'

'Those Murgos are less than a day behind us, Belgarath. If we have to pick our way down, they'll be on top of us before we make it.'

Belgarath pursed his lips, squinting at the dust clouds on the southern horizon. 'Perhaps you're right,' he said. 'Maybe we'd better think this through.' He raised his hand to call a halt. 'It's time to make a couple of decisions,' he told the rest of them. 'The Murgos are a little closer than we really want them to be. It takes two to three days to make the descent into the Vale, and there are places where one definitely doesn't want to be rushed.'

'We could always go on to that ravine we followed coming up,' Silk suggested. 'It only takes a half-day to go down that way.'

'But Lord Hettar and the Algar clans of King Cho-Hag await us in the Vale,' Mandorallen objected. 'Were we to go on, would we not lead the Murgos down into undefended country?'

'Have we got any choice?' Silk asked him.

'We could light fires along the way,' Barak suggested. 'Hettar will know what they mean.'

'So would the Murgos,' Silk said. 'They'd ride all night and be right behind us every step of the way down.'

Belgarath scratched sourly at his short white beard. 'I think we're going to have to abandon the original plan,' he decided. 'We have to take the shortest way down, and that means the ravine, I'm afraid. We'll be on our own once we get down, but that can't be helped.'

'Surely King Cho-Hag will have scouts posted along the foot of the escarpment,' Durnik said, his plain face worried.

'We can *hope* so,' Barak replied.

'All right,' Belgarath said firmly, 'we'll use the ravine. I don't altogether like the idea, but our options seem to have been narrowed a bit. Let's ride.'

It was late afternoon when they reached the shallow gully at the top of the steep notch leading down to the plain below. Belgarath glanced once down the precipitous cut and shook his head. 'Not in the dark,' he decided. 'Can you see any signs of the Algars?' he asked Barak, who was staring out at the plain below.

'I'm afraid not,' the red-bearded man answered. 'Do you want to light a fire to signal them?'

'No,' the old man replied. 'Let's not announce our intentions.'

'I *will* need a small fire, though,' Aunt Pol told him. 'We all need a hot meal.'

'I don't know if that's wise, Polgara,' Belgarath objected.

'We'll have a hard day tomorrow, father,' she said firmly. 'Durnik knows how to build a small fire and keep it hidden.'

'Have it your own way, Pol,' the old man said in a resigned tone of voice.

'Naturally, father.'

It was cold that night, and they kept their fire small and well sheltered. As the first light of dawn began to stain the cloudy sky to the east, they rose and prepared to descend the rocky cut toward the plain below.

'I'll strike the tents,' Durnik said.

'Just knock them down,' Belgarath told him. He turned and nudged one of the packs thoughtfully with his foot. 'We'll take only what we absolutely have to have,' he decided. 'We're not going to have the time to waste on these.'

'You're not going to leave them?' Durnik sounded shocked.

'They'll just be in the way, and the horses will be able to move faster without them.'

'But – all of our belongings!' Durnik protested.

Silk also looked a bit chagrined. He quickly spread out a blanket and began rummaging through the packs, his quick hands bringing out innumerable small, valuable items and piling them in a heap on the blanket.

'Where did you get all those?' Barak asked him.

'Here and there,' Silk replied evasively.

'You stole them, didn't you?'

'Some of them,' Silk admitted. 'We've been on the road for a long time, Barak.'

'Do you really plan to carry all of that down the ravine?' Barak asked, curiously eyeing Silk's treasures.

Silk looked at the heap, mentally weighing it. Then he sighed with profound regret. 'No,' he said, 'I guess not.' He stood up and scattered the heap with his foot. 'It's all very pretty though, isn't it? Now I guess I'll have to start all over again.' He grinned then. 'It's the stealing that's fun, anyway. Let's go down.' And he started toward the top of the steeply descending streambed that angled sharply down toward the base of the escarpment.

The unburdened horses were able to move much more rapidly, and they all passed quite easily over spots Garion remembered painfully from the upward climb weeks before. By noon they were more than halfway down.

Then Polgara stopped and raised her face. 'Father,' she said calmly, 'they've found the top of the ravine.'

'How many of them?'

'It's an advance patrol – no more than twenty.'

Far above them they heard a sharp clash of rock against rock, and then, after a moment, another. 'I was afraid of that,' Belgarath said sourly.

'What?' Garion asked.

'They're rolling rocks down on us.' The old man grimly hitched up his belt. 'All right, the rest of you go on ahead. Get down as fast as you can.'

'Are you strong enough, father?' Aunt Pol asked, sounding concerned. 'You still haven't really recovered, you know.'

'We're about to find out,' the old man replied, his face set. 'Move – all of you.' He said it in a tone that cut off any possible argument.

As they all began scrambling down over the steep rocks, Garion lagged farther and farther behind. Finally, as Durnik led the last packhorse over a jumble of broken stone and around a bend, Garion stopped entirely and stood listening. He could hear the clatter and slide of hooves on the rocks below and, from above, the clash and bounce of a large stone tumbling over the ravine, coming closer and closer. Then there was a familiar surge and roaring sound. A rock, somewhat larger than a man's head, went whistling over him, angling sharply up out of the cut to fall harmlessly far out on the tumbled debris at the floor of the escarpment. Carefully Garion began climbing back up the ravine, pausing often to listen.

Belgarath was sweating as Garion came into sight around a bend in the ravine a goodly way above and ducked back out of the old man's sight. Another rock, somewhat larger than the first, came bounding and crashing down the narrow ravine, bouncing off the walls and leaping into the air each time it struck the rocky streambed. About twenty yards above Belgarath, it struck solidly and spun into the air. The old man gestured irritably, grunting with the effort, and the rock sailed out in a long arc, clearing the walls of the ravine and falling out of sight.

Garion quickly crossed the streambed and went down several yards more, staying close against the rocky wall and peering back to be sure he was concealed from his grandfather.

When the next rock came bouncing and clashing down toward them, Garion gathered his will. He'd have to time it perfectly, he knew, and he peered around a corner, watching the old man intently. When Belgarath raised his hand, Garion pushed his own will in to join his grandfather's, hoping to slip a bit of unnoticed help to him.

Belgarath watched the rock go whirling far out over the plain below, then he turned and looked sternly down the ravine. 'All right, Garion,' he said crisply, 'step out where I can see you.'

Somewhat sheepishly Garion went out into the center of the streambed and stood looking up at his grandfather.

'Why is it that you can never do what you're told to do?' the old man demanded.

'I just thought I could help, that's all.'

'Did I ask for help? Do I look like an invalid?'

'There's another rock coming.'

'Don't change the subject. I think you're getting above yourself, young man.'

'Grandfather!' Garion said urgently, staring at the large rock bounding down the ravine directly for the old man's back. He threw his will under the rock and hurled it out of the ravine.

Belgarath looked up at the stone soaring over his head. 'Tacky, Garion,' he said disapprovingly, 'very tacky. You don't have to throw them all the way to Prolgu, you know. Stop trying to show off.'

'I got excited,' Garion apologized. 'I pushed a little too hard.'

The old man grunted. 'All right,' he said a bit ungraciously, 'as long as you're here anyway – but stick to your own rocks. I can manage mine, and you throw me off-balance when you come blundering in like that.'

'I just need a little practice, that's all.'

'You need some instruction in etiquette, too,' Belgarath told him, coming on down to where Garion stood. 'You don't just jump in with help until you're asked. That's very bad form, Garion.'

'Another rock coming,' Garion informed him politely. 'Do you want to get it or shall I?'

'Don't get snippy, young man,' Belgarath told him, then turned and flipped the approaching rock out of the ravine.

They moved on down together, taking turns on the rocks the Murgos were rolling down the ravine. Garion discovered that it grew easier each time he did it, but Belgarath was drenched with sweat by the time they neared the bottom. Garion considered trying once again to slip his grandfather a bit of assistance, but the old sorcerer glared at him so fiercely as he started to gather in his will that he quickly abandoned the idea.

'I wondered where you'd gone,' Aunt Pol said to Garion as the two clambered out over the rocks at the mouth of the ravine to rejoin the rest of the party. She looked closely at Belgarath. 'Are you all right?' she asked.

'I'm just fine,' he snapped. 'I had all this assistance – unsolicited, of course.' He glared at Garion again.

'When we get a bit of time, we're going to have to give him some lessons in controlling the noise,' she observed. 'He sounds like a thunderclap.'

'That's not all he has to learn to control.' For some reason the old man was behaving as if he'd just been dreadfully insulted.

'What now?' Barak asked. 'Do you want to light signal fires and wait here for Hettar and Cho-Hag?'

'This isn't a good place, Barak,' Silk pointed out. 'Half of Murgodom's going to come pouring down that ravine very shortly.'

'The passage is not wide, Prince Kheldar,' Mandorallen observed. 'My Lord Barak and I can hold it for a week or more if need be.'

'You're backsliding again, Mandorallen,' Barak told him.

'Besides, they'd just roll rocks down on you,' Silk said. 'And they're going to be dropping boulders off the edge up there before long. We're probably going to have to get out on the plain a ways to avoid that sort of thing.'

Durnik was staring thoughtfully at the mouth of the ravine. 'We need to send something up there to slow them down, though,' he mused. 'I don't think we want them right behind us.'

'It's a little hard to make rocks roll uphill,' Barak said.

'I wasn't thinking of rocks,' Durnik replied. 'We'll need something much lighter.'

'Like what?' Silk asked the smith.

'Smoke would be good,' Durnik answered. 'The ravine should draw just like a chimney. If we build a fire and fill the whole thing with smoke, nobody's going to come down until the fire goes out.'

Silk grinned broadly. 'Durnik,' he said, 'you're a treasure.'

Chapter Five

There were bushes, scrub and bramble for the most part, growing here and there along the base of the cliff, and they quickly fanned out with their swords to gather enough to build a large, smoky fire. 'You'd better hurry,' Belgarath called to them as they worked. 'There are a dozen Murgos or more already halfway down the ravine.'

Durnik, who had been gathering dry sticks and splintered bits of log, ran back to the mouth of the ravine, knelt and began striking sparks from his flint into the tinder he always carried. In a few moments he had a small fire going, the orange flames licking up around the weathered grey sticks. Carefully he added larger pieces until his fire was a respectable blaze. Then he began piling thornbushes and brambles atop it, critically watching the direction of the smoke. The bushes hissed and smoldered fitfully at first, and a great cloud of smoke wafted this way and that for a moment, then began to pour steadily up the ravine. Durnik nodded with satisfaction. 'Just like a chimney,' he observed. From far up the cut came shouts of alarm and a great deal of coughing and choking.

'How long can a man breathe smoke before he chokes to death?' Silk asked.

'Not very long,' Durnik replied.

'I didn't think so.' The little man looked happily at the smoking blaze. 'Good fire,' he said, holding his hands out to the warmth.

'The smoke's going to delay them, but I think it's time to move on out,' Belgarath said, squinting at the cloud-obscured ball of the sun hanging low over the horizon to the west. 'We'll move on up the face of the escarpment and then make a run for it. We'll want to surprise them a bit, to give us time to get out of range before they start throwing rocks down on us.'

'Is there any sign of Hettar out there?' Barak asked, peering out at the grassland.

'We haven't seen any yet,' Durnik replied.

'You do know that we're going to lead half of Cthol Murgos out onto the plain?' Barak pointed out to Belgarath.

'That can't be helped. For right now, we've got to get out of here. If Taur Urgas is up there, he's going to send people after us, even if he has to throw them off the cliff personally. Let's go.'

They followed the face of the cliff for a mile or more until they found a spot where the rockfall did not extend so far out onto the plain. 'This will do,' Belgarath decided. 'As soon as we get to level ground, we ride hard straight out. An arrow shot off the top of that cliff will carry a long way. Is everybody ready?' He looked around at them. 'Let's move, then.'

They led their horses down the short, steep slope of rock to the grassy plain below, mounted quickly and set off at a dead run.

'Arrow!' Silk said sharply, looking up and back over his shoulder.

Garion, without thinking, slashed with his will at the tiny speck arching down toward them. In the same instant he felt a peculiar double surge coming from either side of him. The arrow broke into several pieces in midair.

'If you two don't mind!' Belgarath said irritably to Garion and Aunt Pol, half-reining in his horse.

'I just didn't want you to tire yourself, father,' Aunt Pol replied coolly. 'I'm sure Garion feels the same way.'

'Couldn't we discuss it later?' Silk suggested, looking apprehensively back at the towering escarpment.

They plunged on, the long, brown grass whipping at the legs of their horses. Other arrows began to fall, dropping farther and farther behind them as they rode. By the time they were a half mile out from the sheer face, the arrows were sheeting down from the top of the cliff in a whistling black rain.

'Persistent, aren't they?' Silk observed.

'It's a racial trait,' Barak replied. 'Murgos are stubborn to the point of idiocy.'

'Keep going,' Belgarath told them. 'It's just a question of time until they bring up a catapult.'

'They're throwing ropes down the face of the cliff,' Durnik reported, peering back at the escarpment. 'As soon as a few of them get to the bottom, they'll pull the fire clear of the ravine and start bringing horses down.'

'At least it slowed them down a bit,' Belgarath said.

Twilight, hardly more than a gradual darkening of the cloudy murk that had obscured the sky for several days, began to creep across the Algarian plain. They rode on.

Garion glanced back several times as he rode and noticed moving pinpoints of light along the base of the cliff. 'Some of them have reached the bottom, grandfather,' he called to the old man, who was pounding along in the lead. 'I can see their torches.'

'It was bound to happen,' the sorcerer replied.

It was nearly midnight by the time they reached the Aldur River, lying black and oily-looking between its frosty banks.

'Does anybody have any idea how we're going to find that ford in the dark?' Durnik asked.

'I'll find it,' Relg told him. 'It isn't all that dark for me. Wait here.'

'That could give us a certain advantage,' Silk noted. 'We'll be able to ford the river, but the Murgos will flounder around on this side in the dark for half the night. We'll be leagues ahead of them before they get across.'

'That was one of the things I was sort of counting on,' Belgarath replied smugly.

It was a half an hour before Relg returned. 'It isn't far,' he told them.

They remounted and rode through the chill darkness, following the curve of the river bank until they heard the unmistakable gurgle and wash of water running over stones. 'That's it just ahead,' Relg said.

'It's still going to be dangerous fording in the dark,' Barak pointed out.

'It isn't that dark,' Relg said. 'Just follow me.' He rode confidently a hundred yards farther upriver, then turned and nudged his horse into the shallow rippling water.

Garion felt his horse flinch from the icy chill as he rode out into the river, following closely behind Belgarath. Behind him he heard Durnik coaxing the now-unburdened pack animals into the water.

The river was not deep, but it was very wide – almost a half mile – and in the process of fording, they were all soaked to the knees.

'The rest of the night promises to be moderately unpleasant,' Silk observed, shaking one sodden foot.

'At least you've got the river between you and Taur Urgas,' Barak reminded him.

'That does brighten things up a bit,' Silk admitted.

They had not gone a half mile, however, before Mandorallen's charger went down with a squeal of agony. The knight, with a great clatter, tumbled in the grass as he was pitched out of the saddle. His great horse floundered with threshing legs, trying futilely to rise.

'What's the matter with him?' Barak demanded sharply.

Behind them, with another squeal, one of the pack-horses collapsed.

'What is it?' Garion asked Durnik, his voice shrill.

'It's the cold,' Durnik answered, swinging down from his saddle. 'We've ridden them to exhaustion, and then we made them wade across the river. The chill's settled into their muscles.'

'What do we do?'

'We have to rub them down – all of them – with wool.'

'We don't have time for that,' Silk objected.

'It's that or walk,' Durnik declared, pulling off his stout wool cloak and beginning to rub vigorously at his horse's legs with it.

'Maybe we should build a fire,' Garion suggested, also dismounting and beginning to rub down his horse's shivering legs.

'There isn't anything around here to burn,' Durnik told him. 'This is all open grassland.'

'And a fire would set up a beacon for every Murgo within ten miles,' Barak added, massaging the legs of his grey horse.

They all worked as rapidly as possible, but the sky to the east had begun to pale with the first hints of dawn before Mandorallen's horse was on his feet again and the rest of their mounts were able to move.

'They won't be able to run,' Durnik declared somberly. 'We shouldn't even ride them.'

'Durnik,' Silk protested, 'Taur Urgas is right behind us.'

'They won't last a league if we try to make them run,' the smith said stubbornly. 'There's nothing left in them.'

They rode away from the river at a walk. Even at that pace, Garion could feel the trembling of his horse under him. They all looked back frequently, watching the dark-shrouded plain beyond the river as the sky grew gradually lighter. When they reached the top of the first low hills, the deep shadow which had obscured the grasslands behind them faded and they were able to see movement. Then, as the light grew stronger, they saw an army of Murgos swarming toward the river. In the midst of them were the flapping black banners of Taur Urgas himself.

The Murgos came on in waves until they reached the far bank of the river. Then their mounted scouts ranged out until they located the ford. The bulk of the army Taur Urgas had brought down to the plain was still on foot, but clusters of horses were being driven up from the rear as rapidly as they could be brought down the narrow cut leading from the top of the escarpment.

As the first units began splashing across the ford, Silk turned to Belgarath. 'Now what?' the little man asked in a worried voice.

'We'd better get off the top of this hill,' the old man replied. 'I don't think they've seen us yet, but it's just a question of time, I'm afraid.'

They rode down into a little swale just beyond the hill. The overcast which had obscured the sky for the past week or more had begun to blow off, and broad patches of pale, icy blue had begun to appear, though the sun had not yet come up.

'My guess is that he's going to hold the bulk of his army on the far side,' Belgarath told them after they had all dismounted. 'He'll bring them on across as their horses catch up. As soon as they get to this side, they're going to spread out to look for us.'

'That's the way I'd do it,' Barak agreed.

'Somebody ought to keep an eye on them,' Durnik

87

suggested. He started back up the hill on foot. 'I'll let you know if they start doing anything unusual.'

Belgarath seemed lost in thought. He paced up and down, his hands clasped together behind his back and an angry look on his face. 'This isn't working out the way I'd expected,' he said finally. 'I hadn't counted on the horses playing out on us.'

'Is there any place we can hide?' Barak asked.

Belgarath shook his head. 'This is all grassland,' he replied. 'There aren't any rocks or caves or trees, and it's going to be impossible to cover our tracks.' He kicked at the tall grass. 'This isn't turning out too well,' he admitted glumly. 'We're all alone out here on exhausted horses.' He chewed thoughtfully at his lower lip. 'The nearest help is in the Vale. I think we'd better turn south and make for it. We're fairly close.'

'*How* close?' Silk asked.

'Ten leagues or so.'

'That's going to take all day, Belgarath. I don't think we've got that long.'

'We might have to tamper with the weather a bit,' Belgarath conceded. 'I don't like doing that, but I might not have any choice.'

There was a distant low rumble somewhere off to the north. The little boy looked up and smiled at Aunt Pol. 'Errand?' he asked.

'Yes, dear,' she replied absently.

'Can you pick up any traces of Algars in the vicinity, Pol?' Belgarath asked her.

She shook her head. 'I think I'm too close to the Orb, father. I keep getting an echo that blots things out more than a mile or so away.'

'It always has been noisy,' he grunted sourly.

'Talk to it, father,' she suggested. 'Maybe it will listen to you.'

He gave her a long, hard look – a look she returned quite calmly. 'I can do without that, miss,' he told her finally in a crisp voice.

There was another low rumble, from the south this time.

'Thunder?' Silk said, looking a bit puzzled. 'Isn't this an odd time of year for it?'

'This plain breeds peculiar weather,' Belgarath said. 'There isn't anything between here and Drasnia but eight hundred leagues of grass.'

'Do we try for the Vale then?' Barak asked.

'It looks as if we'll have to,' the old man replied.

Durnik came back down the hill. 'They're coming across the river,' he reported, 'but they aren't spreading out yet. It looks as if they want to get more men across before they start looking for us.'

'How hard can we push the horses without hurting them?' Silk asked him.

'Not very,' Durnik replied. 'It would be better to save them until we absolutely have to use up whatever they've got left. If we walk and lead them for an hour or so, we might be able to get a canter out of them – for short periods of time.'

'Let's go along the back side of the crest,' Belgarath said, picking up the reins of his horse. 'We'll stay pretty much out of sight that way, but I want to keep an eye on Taur Urgas.' He led them at an angle back up out of the swale.

The clouds had broken even more now, and the tatters raced in the endless winds that swept the vast grassland. To the east, the sky was turning a pale pink. Although the Algarian plain did not have that bitter, arid chill that had cut at them in the uplands of Cthol Murgos and Mishrak ac Thull, it was still very cold. Garion shivered, drew his cloak in tight about him, and kept walking, trailing his weary horse behind him.

There was another brief rumble, and the little boy, perched in the saddle of Aunt Pol's horse laughed. 'Errand,' he announced.

'I wish he'd stop that,' Silk said irritably.

They glanced from time to time over the crest of the long hill as they walked. Below, in the broad valley of the Aldur River, the Murgos of Taur Urgas were fording in larger and larger groups. It appeared that fully half his army had reached the west bank by now, and the red and black standard of the king of the Murgos stood planted defiantly on Algarian soil.

'If he brings too many more men down the escarpment, it's going to take something pretty significant to dislodge him,' Barak rumbled, scowling down at the Murgos.

'I know,' Belgarath replied, 'and that's the one thing I've wanted to avoid. We aren't ready for a war just yet.'

The sun, huge and red, ponderously moved up from behind the eastern escarpment, turning the sky around it rosy. In the still-shadowed valley below them, the Murgos continued to splash across the river in the steely morning light.

'Methinks he will await the sun before he begins the search for us,' Mandorallen observed.

'And that's not very far off,' Barak agreed, glancing at the slowly moving band of sunlight just touching the hill along which they moved. 'We've probably got half an hour at the most. I think it's getting to the point where we're going to have to gamble on the horses. Maybe if we switch mounts every mile or so, we can get some more distance out of them.'

The rumble that came then could not possibly have been thunder. The ground shook with it, and it rolled on and on endlessly from both the north and south.

And then, pouring over the crests of the hills

surrounding the valley of the Aldur like some vast tide suddenly released by the bursting of a mighty dam, came the clans of the Algars. Down they plunged upon the startled Murgos thickly clustered along the banks of the river, and their great war cry shook the very heavens as they fell like wolves upon the divided army of Taur Urgas.

A lone horseman veered out of the great charge of the clans and came pounding up the hillside toward Garion and his friends. As the warrior drew closer, Garion could see his long scalp lock flowing behind him and his drawn sabre catching the first rays of the morning sun. It was Hettar. A vast surge of relief swept over Garion. They were safe.

'Where have you been?' Barak demanded in a great voice as the hawk-faced Algar rode closer.

'Watching,' Hettar replied calmly as he reined in. 'We wanted to let the Murgos get out a ways from the escarpment so we could cut them off. My father sent me to see how you all are.'

'How considerate,' Silk observed sardonically. 'Did it ever occur to you to let us know you were out there?'

Hettar shrugged. 'We could see that you were all right.' He looked critically at their exhausted mounts. 'You didn't take very good care of them,' he said accusingly.

'We were a bit pressed,' Durnik apologized.

'Did you get the Orb?' the tall man asked Belgarath, glancing hungrily down toward the river where a vast battle had been joined.

'It took a bit, but we got it,' the old sorcerer replied.

'Good.' Hettar turned his horse, and his lean face had a fierce look on it. 'I'll tell Cho-Hag. Will you excuse me?' Then he stopped as if remembering something. 'Oh,' he said to Barak, 'congratulations, by the way.'

'For what?' the big man asked, looking puzzled.

'The birth of your son.'

'What?' Barak sounded stunned. 'How?'

'In the usual way, I'd imagine,' Hettar replied.

'I mean how did you find out?'

'Anheg sent word to us.'

'When was he born?'

'A couple months ago.' Hettar looked nervously down at the battle which was raging on both sides of the river and in the middle of the ford as well. 'I really have to go,' he said. 'If I don't hurry, there won't be any Murgos left.' And he drove his heels into his horse's flanks and plunged down the hill.

'He hasn't changed a bit,' Silk noted.

Barak was standing with a somewhat foolish grin on his big, red-bearded face.

'Congratulations, my Lord,' Mandorallen said to him, clasping his hand.

Barak's grin grew broader.

It quickly became obvious that the situation of the encircled Murgos below was hopeless. With his army cut in two by the river, Taur Urgas was unable to mount even an orderly retreat. The forces he had brought across the river were quickly swarmed under by King Cho-Hag's superior numbers, and the few survivors of that short, ugly mêlée plunged back into the river, protectively drawn up around the red and black banner of the Murgo king. Even in the ford, however, the Algar warriors pressed him. Some distance upriver Garion could see horsemen plunging into the icy water to be carried down by the current to the shallows of the ford in an effort to cut off escape. Much of the fight in the river was obscured by the sheets of spray kicked up by struggling horses, but the bodies floating downstream testified to the savagery of the clash.

Briefly, for no more than a moment, the red and black banner of Taur Urgas was confronted by the burgundy-and-white horse-banner of King Cho-Hag, and then the two were swept apart.

'That could have been an interesting meeting,' Silk noted. 'Cho-Hag and Taur Urgas have hated each other for years.'

Once the king of the Murgos regained the east bank, he rallied what forces he could, turned, and fled back across the open grassland toward the escarpment with Algar clansmen hotly pursuing him. For the bulk of his army, however, there was no escape. Since their horses had not yet descended the narrow ravine from the top of the escarpment, they were forced to fight on foot. The Algars swept down upon them in waves, sabres flashing in the morning sun. Faintly, Garion could hear the screams. Sickened finally, he turned away, unable to watch the slaughter any longer.

The little boy, who was standing close beside Aunt Pol with his hand in hers, looked at Garion gravely. 'Errand,' he said with a sad conviction.

By midmorning the battle was over. The last of the Murgos on the far bank of the river had been destroyed, and Taur Urgas had fled with the tattered remnants of his army back up the ravine. 'Good fight,' Barak observed professionally, looking down at the bodies littering both banks of the river and bobbing limply in the shallows downstream from the ford.

'The tactics of thy Algar cousins were masterly,' Mandorallen agreed. 'Taur Urgas will take some time to recover from this morning's chastisement.'

'I'd give a great deal to see the look on his face just now.' Silk laughed. 'He's probably frothing at the mouth.'

King Cho-Hag, dressed in steel-plated black leather

and with his horse-banner streaming triumphantly in the bright morning sun, came galloping up the hill toward them, closely surrounded by the members of his personal guard. 'Interesting morning,' he said with typical Algar understatement as he reined in. 'Thanks for bringing us so many Murgos.'

'He's as bad as Hettar,' Silk observed to Barak.

The king of the Algars grinned openly as he slowly dismounted. His weak legs seemed almost to buckle as he carefully put his weight on them, and he held onto his saddle for support. 'How did things go in Rak Cthol?' he asked.

'It wound up being rather noisy,' Belgarath replied.

'Did you find Ctuchik in good health?'

'Moderately. We corrected that, however. The whole affair set off an earthquake. Most of Rak Cthol slid off its mountaintop, I'm afraid.'

Cho-Hag grinned again. 'What a shame.'

'Where's Hettar?' Barak asked.

'Chasing Murgos, I imagine,' Cho-Hag replied. 'Their rear guard got cut off, and they're out there trying to find someplace to hide.'

'There aren't very many hiding places on this plain, are there?' Barak asked.

'Almost none at all,' the Algar king agreed pleasantly.

A dozen or so Algar wagons crested a nearby hill, rolling toward them through the tall, brown grass. They were squareboxed conveyances, looking not unlike houses on wheels. They had roofs, narrow windows, and steps at the rear leading up to the doorway on the back of each wagon. It looked, Garion thought, almost like a moving city as they approached.

'I imagine Hettar's going to be a while,' Cho-Hag noted. 'Why don't we have a bit of lunch? I'd like to get word to Anheg and Rhodar about what's happened here as soon as possible, but I'm sure you'll want to pass a few things along as well. We can talk while we eat.'

Several of the wagons were drawn up close together and their sides were let down and joined to form a spacious, low-ceilinged dining hall. Braziers provided warmth, and candles illuminated the interior of the quickly assembled hall, supplementing the bright winter sunlight streaming in through the windows.

They dined on roasted meat and mellow ale. Garion soon found that he was wearing far too many clothes. It seemed that he had not been warm in months, and the glowing braziers shimmered out a welcome heat. Although he was tired and very dirty, he felt warm and safe, and he soon found himself nodding over his plate, almost drowsing as Belgarath recounted the story of their escape to the Algar king.

Gradually, however, as the old man spoke, something alerted Garion. There was, it seemed, a trace too much vivacity in his grandfather's voice, and Belgarath's words sometimes seemed almost to tumble over each other. His blue eyes were very bright, but seemed occasionally a bit unfocused.

'So Zedar got away,' Cho-Hag was saying. 'That's the only thing that mars the whole affair.'

'Zedar's no problem,' Belgarath replied, smiling in a slightly dazed way.

His voice seemed strange, uncertain, and King Cho-Hag looked at the old man curiously. 'You've had a busy year, Belgarath,' he said.

'A good one, though.' The sorcerer smiled again and lifted his ale cup. His hand was trembling violently, and he stared at it in astonishment.

'Aunt Pol!' Garion called urgently.

'Are you all right, father?'

'Fine, Pol, perfectly fine.' He smiled vaguely at her,

his unfocused eyes blinking owlishly. He rose suddenly to his feet and began to move toward her, but his steps were lurching, almost staggering. And then his eyes rolled back in his head and he fell to the floor like a pole-axed cow.

'Father!' Aunt Pol exclaimed, leaping to his side.

Garion, moving almost as fast as his Aunt, knelt on the other side of the unconscious old man. 'What's wrong with him?' he demanded.

But Aunt Pol did not answer. Her hands were at Belgarath's wrist and brow, feeling for his pulse. She peeled back one of his eyelids and stared intently into his blank, unseeing eyes. 'Durnik!' she snapped. 'Get my herb-bag – quickly!'

The smith bolted for the door.

King Cho-Hag had half-risen, his face deathly pale. 'He isn't—'

'No,' she answered tensely. 'He's alive, but only barely.'

'Is something attacking him?' Silk was on his feet, looking around wildly, his hand unconsciously on his dagger.

'No. It's nothing like that.' Aunt Pol's hands had moved to the old man's chest. 'I should have known,' she berated herself. 'The stubborn, proud old fool! I should have been watching him.'

'Please, Aunt Pol,' Garion begged desperately, 'what's wrong with him?'

'He never really recovered from his fight with Ctuchik,' she replied. 'He's been forcing himself, drawing on his will. Then those rocks in the ravine – but he wouldn't quit. Now he's burned up all his vital energy and will. He barely has enough strength left to keep breathing.'

Garion had lifted his grandfather's head and cradled it on his lap.

'Help me, Garion!'

He knew instinctively what she wanted. He gathered his will and held out his hand to her. She grasped it quickly, and he felt the force surge out of him.

Her eyes were very wide as she intently watched the old man's face. 'Again!' And once more she pulled the quickly gathered will out of him.

'What are we doing?' Garion's voice was shrill.

'Trying to replace some of what he has lost. Maybe—' She glanced toward the door. 'Hurry, Durnik!' she shouted.

Durnik rushed back into the wagon.

'Open the bag,' she instructed, 'and give me that black jar – the one that's sealed with lead – and a pair of iron tongs.'

'Should I open the jar, Mistress Pol?' the smith asked.

'No. Just break the seal – carefully. And give me a glove – leather, if you can find one.'

Wordlessly, Silk pulled a leather gauntlet from under his belt and handed it to her. She pulled it on, opened the black jar, and reached inside with the tongs. With great care, she removed a single dark, oily-looking green leaf. She held it very carefully in the tongs. 'Pry his mouth open, Garion,' she ordered.

Garion wedged his fingers between Belgarath's clenched teeth and carefully pried the old man's jaws apart. Aunt Pol pulled down her father's lower lip, reached inside his mouth with the shiny leaf, and lightly brushed his tongue with it, once and once only.

Belgarath jumped violently, and his feet suddenly scraped on the floor. His muscles heaved, and his arms began to flail about.

'Hold him down,' Aunt Pol commanded. She pulled back sharply and held the leaf out of the way while Mandorallen and Barak jumped in to hold down

Belgarath's convulsing body. 'Give me a bowl,' she ordered. 'A wooden one.'

Durnik handed her one, and she deposited the leaf and the tongs in it. Then, with great care, she took off the gauntlet and laid it atop the leaf. 'Take this,' she told the smith. 'Don't touch any part of the glove.'

'What do you want me to do with it, Mistress Pol?'

'Take it out and burn it – bowl and all – and don't let anyone get into the smoke from it.'

'Is it *that* dangerous?' Silk asked.

'It's even worse, but those are the only precautions we can take out here.'

Durnik swallowed very hard and left the wagon, holding the bowl as if it were a live snake.

Polgara took a small mortar and pestle and began grinding certain herbs from her bag into a fine powder as she watched Belgarath intently. 'How far is it to the Stronghold, Cho-Hag?' she asked the Algar king.

'A man on a good horse could make it in half a day,' he replied.

'How long by wagon – a wagon driven carefully to avoid bouncing?'

'Two days.'

She frowned, still mixing the herbs in the mortar. 'All right, there's no help for it, I guess. Please send Hettar to Queen Silar. Have him tell her that I'm going to need a warm, well-lighted chamber with a good bed and no drafts. Durnik, I want you to drive the wagon. Don't hit any bumps – even if it means losing an hour.'

The smith nodded.

'He's going to be all right, isn't he?' Barak asked, his voice strained and his face shocked by Belgarath's sudden collapse.

'It's really too early to say,' she replied. 'He's been on the point of collapse for days maybe. But he wouldn't let himself go. I think he's past this crisis, but there may be others.' She laid one hand on her father's chest. 'Put him in bed – carefully. Then I want a screen of some kind around the bed – blankets will do. We have to keep him very quiet and out of drafts. No loud noises.'

They all stared at her as the significance of her extreme precautions struck them.

'Move, gentlemen,' she told them firmly. 'His life may depend on a certain speed.'

Chapter Six

The wagon seemed barely to crawl. The high, thin cloud had swept in again to hide the sun, and a kind of leaden chill descended on the featureless plain of southern Algaria. Garion rode inside the wagon, thick-headed and numb with exhaustion, watching with dreadful concern as Aunt Pol hovered over the unconscious Belgarath. Sleep was out of the question. Another crisis could arise at any time and he had to be ready to leap to her aid, joining his will and the power of his amulet with hers. Errand, his small face grave, sat quietly in a chair at the far side of the wagon, his hands firmly clasped around the pouch Durnik had made for him. The sound of the Orb still hung in Garion's ears, muted but continual. He had grown almost accustomed to the song in the weeks since they had left Rak Cthol; but at quiet moments or when he was tired, it always seemed to return with renewed strength. It was somehow a comforting sound.

Aunt Pol leaned forward to touch Belgarath's chest.

'What's wrong?' Garion asked in a sharp whisper.

'Nothing's wrong, Garion,' she replied calmly. 'Please don't keep saying that every time I so much as move. If something's wrong, I'll tell you.'

'I'm sorry – I'm just worried, that's all.'

She turned to give him a steady look. 'Why don't you take Errand and go up and ride on top of the wagon with Silk and Durnik?'

'What if you need me?'

'I'll call you, dear.'

'I'd really rather stay, Aunt Pol.'

'I'd really rather you didn't. I'll call if I need you.'

'But—'

'Now, Garion.'

Garion knew better than to argue. He took Errand out the back door of the wagon and up the steps to the top.

'How is he?' Silk asked.

'How should I know? All I know is that she chased me out.' Garion's reply was a bit surly.

'That might be a good sign, you know.'

'Maybe.' Garion looked around. Off to the west there was a range of low hills. Rearing above them stood a vast pile of rock.

'The Algar Stronghold,' Durnik told Garion, pointing.

'Are we that close?'

'That's still a good day's ride.'

'How high is it?' Garion asked.

'Four or five hundred feet at least,' Silk told him. 'The Algars have been building at it for several thousand years. It gives them something to do after the calving season.'

Barak rode up. 'How's Belgarath?' he asked as he approached.

'I think he might be improving just a little,' Garion answered. 'I don't know for sure, though.'

'That's something, anyway.' The big man pointed toward a gully just ahead. 'You'd better go around that,' he told Durnik. 'King Cho-Hag says that the ground gets a bit rough through there.'

Durnik nodded and changed the wagon's direction.

Throughout the day, the Stronghold of the Algars

loomed higher and higher against the western horizon. It was a vast, towering fortress rearing out of the dun-colored hills.

'A monument to an idea that got out of hand,' Silk observed as he lounged idly atop the wagon.

'I don't quite follow that,' Durnik said.

'Algars are nomads,' the little man explained. 'They live in wagons like this one and follow their herds. The Stronghold gives Murgo raiders something to attack. That's its only real purpose. Very practical, really. It's much easier than looking for them all over these plains. The Murgos always come here, and it's a convenient place to wipe them out.'

'Don't the Murgos realize that?' Durnik looked a bit skeptical.

'Quite possibly, but they come here anyway because they can't resist the place. They simply can't accept the fact that nobody really lives here.' Silk grinned his ferretlike little grin. 'You know how stubborn Murgos are. Anyway, over the years the Algar clans have developed a sort of competition. Every year they try to outdo one another in hauling rock, and the Stronghold keeps growing higher and higher.'

'Did Kal Torak *really* lay siege to it for eight years?' Garion asked him.

Silk nodded. 'They say that his army was like a sea of Angaraks dashing itself to pieces against the walls of the Stronghold. They might still be here, but they ran out of food. That's always been the problem with large armies. Any fool can raise an army, but you start running into trouble around suppertime.'

As they approached the man-made mountain, the gates opened and a party emerged to greet them. In the lead on a white palfrey rode Queen Silar with Hettar close behind. At a certain point they stopped and sat waiting.

Garion lifted a small trapdoor in the roof of the wagon. 'We're here, Aunt Pol,' he reported in a hushed voice.

'Good,' she replied.

'How's grandfather?'

'He's sleeping. His breathing seems a bit stronger. Go ask Cho-Hag to take us inside immediately. I want to get father into a warm bed as soon as possible.'

'Yes, Aunt Pol.' Garion lowered the trapdoor and then went down the steps at the rear of the slowly moving wagon. He untied his horse, mounted and rode to the front of the column where the Algar queen was quietly greeting her husband.

'Excuse me,' he said respectfully, swinging down from his horse, 'but Aunt Pol wants to get Belgarath inside at once.'

'How is he?' Hettar asked.

'Aunt Pol says that his breathing's getting stronger, but she's still worried.'

From the rear of the group that had emerged from the Stronghold, there was a flurry of small hooves. The colt that had been born in the hills above Maragor burst into view and came charging directly at them. Garion immediately found himself swarmed under by the colt's exuberant greetings. The small horse nuzzled him and butted at him with its head, then pranced away only to gallop back again. When Garion put his hand on the animal's neck to calm him, the colt quivered with joy at his touch.

'He's been waiting for you,' Hettar said to Garion. 'He seems to have known you were coming.'

The wagon drew up and stopped. The door opened, and Aunt Pol looked out.

'Everything's ready, Polgara,' Queen Silar told her.

'Thank you, Silar.'

'Is he recovering at all?'

'He seems better, but it's very hard to say for sure at this point.'

Errand, who had been watching from the top of the wagon, suddenly clambered down the steps at the rear, hopped to the ground, and ran out among the legs of the horses.

'Catch him, Garion,' Aunt Pol said. 'I think he'd better ride in here with me until we get inside the Stronghold.'

As Garion started after the little boy, the colt scampered away, and Errand, laughing with delight, ran after him. 'Errand!' Garion called sharply. The colt, however, had turned in midgallop and suddenly bore down on the child, his hooves flailing wildly. Errand, showing no signs of alarm, stood smiling directly in its path. Startled, the little horse stiffened his legs and skidded to a stop. Errand laughed and held out his hand. The colt's eyes were wide as he sniffed curiously at the hand, and then the boy touched the small animal's face.

Again within the vaults of his mind Garion seemed to hear that strange, bell-like note, and the dry voice murmured, *'Done,'* with a peculiar sort of satisfaction.

'What's that supposed to mean?' Garion asked silently, but there was no answer. He shrugged and picked Errand up to avoid any chance collision between horse and child. The colt stood staring at the two of them, its eyes wide as if in amazement; when Garion turned to carry Errand back to the wagon, it trotted alongside, sniffing and even nuzzling at the child. Garion wordlessly handed Errand up to Aunt Pol and looked her full in the face. She said nothing as she took the child, but her expression told him plainly that something very important had just happened.

As he turned to remount his horse, he felt that

someone was watching him, and he turned quickly toward the group of riders that had accompanied Queen Silar from the Stronghold. Just behind the queen was a tall girl mounted on a roan horse. She had long, dark brown hair, and the eyes she had fixed on Garion were gray, calm, and very serious. Her horse pranced nervously, and she calmed him with a quiet word and a gentle touch, then turned to gaze openly at Garion again. He had the peculiar feeling that he ought to know her.

The wagon creaked as Durnik shook the reins to start the team, and they all followed King Cho-Hag and Queen Silar through a narrow gate into the Stronghold. Garion saw immediately that there were no buildings inside the towering fortress. Instead there was a maze of stone walls perhaps twenty feet high twisting this way and that without any apparent plan.

'But where is thy city, your Majesty?' Mandorallen asked in perplexity.

'Inside the walls themselves,' King Cho-Hag replied. 'They're thick enough and high enough to give us all the room we could possibly need.'

'What purpose hath all this, then?'

'It's just a trap.' The king shrugged. 'We permit attackers to break through the gates, and then we deal with them in here. We want to go this way.' He led them along a narrow alleyway.

They dismounted in a courtyard beside the vast wall. Barak and Hettar unhooked the latches and swung the side of the wagon down. Barak tugged thoughtfully at his beard as he looked at the sleeping Belgarath. 'It would probably disturb him less if we just took him inside bed and all,' he suggested.

'Right,' Hettar agreed, and the two of them climbed up into the wagon to lift out the sorcerer's bed.

'Just don't bounce him around,' Polgara cautioned. 'And don't drop him.'

'We've got him, Polgara,' Barak assured her. 'I know you might not believe it, but we're almost as concerned about him as you are.'

With the two big men carrying the bed, they passed through an arched doorway into a wide, torch-lighted corridor and up a flight of stairs, then along another hallway to another flight. 'Is it much farther?' Barak asked. Sweat was running down his face into his beard. 'This bed isn't getting any lighter, you know.'

'Just up here,' the Algar Queen told him.

'I hope he appreciates all this when he wakes up,' Barak grumbled.

The room to which they carried Belgarath was large and airy. A glowing brazier stood in each corner and a broad window overlooked the maze inside the walls of the Stronghold. A canopied bed stood against one wall and a large wooden tub against the other.

'This will be just fine,' Polgara said approvingly. 'Thank you, Silar.'

'We love him too, Polgara,' Queen Silar replied quietly.

Polgara drew the drapes, darkening the room. Then she turned back the covers, and Belgarath was transferred to the canopied bed so smoothly that he did not even stir.

'He *looks* a little better,' Silk said.

'He needs sleep, rest and quiet more than anything right now,' Polgara told him, her eyes intent on the old man's sleeping face.

'We'll leave you with him, Polgara,' Queen Silar said. She turned to the rest of them. 'Why don't we all go down to the main hall? Supper's nearly ready, but in the meantime I'll have some ale brought in.'

106

Barak's eyes brightened noticeably, and he started toward the door.

'Barak,' Polgara called to him, 'aren't you and Hettar forgetting something?' She looked pointedly at the bed they had used for a stretcher.

Barak sighed. He and Hettar picked up the bed again.

'I'll send some supper up for you, Polgara,' the queen said.

'Thank you, Silar.' Aunt Pol turned to Garion, her eyes grave. 'Stay for a few moments, dear,' she asked, and he remained as the others all quietly left.

'Close the door, Garion,' she said, pulling a chair up beside the sleeping old man's bed.

He shut the door and crossed the room back to her. 'Is he really getting better, Aunt Pol?'

She nodded. 'I think we're past the immediate danger. He seems stronger physically. But it's not his physical body I'm worried about – it's his mind. That's why I wanted to talk to you alone.'

Garion felt a sudden cold grip of fear. 'His mind?'

'Keep your voice down, dear,' she told him quietly. 'This has to be kept strictly between us.' Her eyes were still on Belgarath's face. 'An episode like this can have very serious effects, and there's no way to know how it will be with him when he recovers. He could be very seriously weakened.'

'Weakened? How?'

'His will could be greatly reduced – to that of any other old man. He drained it to the utter limit, and he might have gone so far that he could never regain his powers.'

'You mean he wouldn't be a sorcerer any more?'

'Don't repeat the obvious, Garion,' she said wearily. 'If that happens, it's going to be up to you and me to conceal it from everybody. Your grandfather's power is the one thing that has held the Angaraks in check for all these years. If something has happened to that power, then you and I will have to make it *look* as if he's the same as he always was. We'll have to conceal the truth even from him, if that is possible.'

'What can we do without him?'

'We'd go on, Garion,' she replied quietly, looking directly into his eyes. 'Our task is too important for us to falter because a man falls by the wayside – even if that man happens to be your grandfather. We're racing against time in all this, Garion. We absolutely must fulfill the Prophecy and get the Orb back to Riva by Erastide, and there are people who must be gathered up to go with us.'

'Who?'

'Princess Ce'Nedra, for one.'

'Ce'Nedra?' Garion had never really forgotten the little princess, but he failed to see why Aunt Pol was making such an issue of her going with them to Riva.

'In time you'll understand, dear. All of this is part of a series of events that must occur in proper sequence and at the proper time. In most situations, the present is determined by the past. This series of events is different, however. In this case, what's happening in the present is determined by the future. If we don't get it exactly the way it's supposed to be, the ending will be different, and I don't think any of us would like that at all.'

'What do you want me to do?' he asked, placing himself unquestioningly in her hands.

She smiled gratefully at him. 'Thank you, Garion,' she said simply. 'When you rejoin the others, they're going to ask you how father's coming along, and I want you to put on your best face and tell them that he's doing fine.'

'You want me to lie to them.' It was not even a question.

'No place in the world is safe from spies, Garion. You

know that as well as I, and no matter what happens, we can't let any hint that father might not recover fully get back to the Angaraks. If necessary, you'll lie until your tongue turns black. The whole fate of the West could depend on how well you do it.'

He stared at her.

'It's possible that all this is totally unnecessary,' she reassured him. 'He may be exactly the same as always after he's had a week or two of rest, but we've got to be ready to move smoothly, just in case he's not.'

'Can't we do something?'

'We're doing all we can. Go back to the others now, Garion – and smile. Smile until your jaws ache if you have to.'

There was a faint sound in the corner of the room, and they both turned sharply. Errand, his blue eyes very serious, stood watching them.

'Take him with you,' Aunt Pol said. 'See that he eats and keep an eye on him.'

Garion nodded and beckoned to the child. Errand smiled his trusting smile and crossed the room. He reached out and patted the unconscious Belgarath's hand, then turned to follow Garion from the room.

The tall, brown-haired girl who had accompanied Queen Silar out through the gates of the Stronghold was waiting for him in the corridor outside. Her skin, Garion noticed, was very pale, almost translucent, and her grey eyes were direct. 'Is the Eternal Man really any better?' she asked.

'Much better,' Garion replied with all the confidence he could muster. 'He'll be out of bed in no time at all.'

'He seems so weak,' she said. 'So old and frail.'

'Frail? Belgarath?' Garion forced a laugh. 'He's made out of old iron and horseshoe nails.'

'He *is* seven thousand years old, after all.'

'That doesn't mean anything to him. He stopped paying attention to the years a long time ago.'

'You're Garion, aren't you?' she asked. 'Queen Silar told us about you when she returned from Val Alorn last year. For some reason I thought you were younger.'

'I was then,' Garion replied. 'I've aged a bit this last year.'

'My name is Adara,' the tall girl introduced herself. 'Queen Silar asked me to show you the way to the main hall. Supper should be ready soon.'

Garion inclined his head politely. In spite of the worry gnawing at him, he could not shake off the peculiar feeling that he ought to know this quiet, beautiful girl. Errand reached out and took the girl's hand, and the three of them passed hand in hand down the torch-lighted corridor.

King Cho-Hag's main hall was on a lower floor. It was a long, narrow room where chairs and padded benches sat in little clusters around braziers filled with glowing coals. Barak, holding a large ale tankard in one huge fist, was describing with some embellishment their descent from the top of the escarpment.

'We didn't really have any choice, you see,' the big man was saying. 'Taur Urgas had been frothing on our heels for several days, and we had to take the shortest way down.'

Hettar nodded. 'Plans sometimes have a way of changing when the unexpected crops up,' he agreed. 'That's why we put men to watching every known pass down from the top of the escarpment.'

'I still think you might have let us know you were there.' Barak sounded a little injured.

Hettar grinned wolfishly. 'We couldn't really take the chance, Barak,' he explained. 'The Murgos might have seen us, and we didn't want to frighten them off. It would have been a shame if they'd gotten away, wouldn't it?'

'Is that all you ever think about?'

Hettar considered the question for a moment. 'Pretty much, yes,' he admitted.

Supper was announced then, and they all moved to the long table at the far end of the hall. The general conversation at the table made it unnecessary for Garion to lie directly to anyone about the frightening possibility Aunt Pol had raised, and after supper he sat beside Adara and lapsed into a kind of sleepy haze, only half-listening to the talk.

There was a stir at the door, and a guard entered. 'The priest of Belar!' he announced in a loud voice, and a tall man in a white robe strode into the room, followed by four men dressed in shaggy furs. The four walked with a peculiar shuffling gait, and Garion instantly recognized them as Bear-cultists, indistinguishable from the Cherek members of the same group he had seen in Val Alorn.

'Your Majesty,' the man in the white robe boomed.

'Hail, Cho-Hag,' the cultists intoned in unison, 'Chief of the Clan-Chiefs of the Algars and guardian of the southern reaches of Aloria.'

King Cho-Hag inclined his head briefly. 'What is it, Elvar?' he asked the priest.

'I have come to congratulate your Majesty upon the occasion of your great victory over the forces of the Dark God,' the priest replied.

'You are most kind, Elvar,' Cho-Hag answered politely.

'Moreover,' Elvar continued, 'it has come to my attention that a holy object has come into the Stronghold of the Algars. I presume that your Majesty will wish to place it in the hands of the priesthood for safekeeping.'

Garion, alarmed at the priest's suggestion, half rose

from his seat, but stopped, not knowing how to voice his objection. Errand, however, with a confident smile, was already walking toward Elvar. The knots Durnik had so carefully tied were undone, and the child took the Orb out of the pouch at his waist and offered it to the startled priest. 'Errand?' he said.

Elvar's eyes bulged and he recoiled from the Orb, lifting his hands above his head to avoid touching it.

'Go ahead, Elvar,' Polgara's voice came mockingly from the doorway. 'Let him who is without ill intent in the silence of his soul stretch forth his hand and take the Orb.'

'Lady Polgara,' the priest stammered. 'We thought – that is – I—'

'He seems to have some reservations,' Silk suggested dryly. 'Perhaps he has some lingering and deep-seated doubts about his own purity. That's a serious failing in a priest, I'd say.'

Elvar looked at the little man helplessly, his hands still held aloft.

'You should never ask for something you're not prepared to accept, Elvar,' Polgara suggested.

'Lady Polgara,' Elvar blurted, 'we thought that you'd be so busy caring for your father that—' He faltered.

'—That you could take possession of the Orb before I knew about it? Think again, Elvar. I won't allow the Orb to fall into the hands of the Bear-cult.' She smiled rather sweetly at him. 'Unless *you* happen to be the one destined to wield it, of course. My father and I would both be overjoyed to hand the burden over to someone else. Why don't we find out? All you have to do is reach out your hand and take the Orb.'

Elvar's face blanched, and he backed away from Errand fearfully.

'I believe that will be all, Elvar,' King Cho-Hag said firmly.

The priest looked about helplessly, then turned and quickly left the hall with his cultists close behind him.

'Make him put it away, Durnik,' Polgara told the smith. 'And see if you can do something about the knots.'

'I could seal them up with lead,' Durnik mused. 'Maybe that would keep him from getting it open.'

'It might be worth a try.' Then she looked around. 'I thought you might all like to know that my father's awake,' she told him. 'The old fool appears to be stronger than we thought.'

Garion, immediately alert, looked at her sharply, trying to detect some hint that she might not be telling them everything, but her calm face was totally unreadable.

Barak, laughing loudly with relief, slapped Hettar on the back. 'I *told* you he'd be all right,' he exclaimed delightedly. The others in the room were already crowding around Polgara, asking for details.

'He's awake,' she told them. 'That's about all I can say at the moment – except that he's his usual charming self. He's already complaining about lumps in the bed and demanding strong ale.'

'I'll send some at once,' Queen Silar said.

'No, Silar,' Polgara replied firmly. 'He gets broth, not ale.'

'He won't like that much,' Silk suggested.

'Isn't that a shame?' She smiled. She half-turned, as if about to go back to the sickroom, then stopped and looked rather quizzically at Garion who sat, relieved, but still apprehensive about Belgarath's true condition, beside Adara. 'I see that you've met your cousin,' she observed.

'*Who?*'

'Don't sit there with your mouth open, Garion,' she

advised him. 'It makes you look like an idiot. Adara's the youngest daughter of your mother's sister. Haven't I ever told you about her?'

It all came crashing in on him. 'Aunt Pol!' he protested. 'How could you forget something that important?'

But Adara, obviously as startled by the announce-ment as he had been, gave a low cry, put her arms about his neck and kissed him warmly. 'Dear cousin!' she exclaimed.

Garion flushed, then went pale, then flushed again. He stared first at Aunt Pol, then at his cousin, unable to speak or even to think coherently.

Chapter Seven

In the days that followed while the others rested and Aunt
Pol nursed Belgarath back to health, Garion and his cousin
spent every waking moment together. From the time he
had been a very small child he had believed that Aunt Pol
was his only family. Later, he had discovered that Mister
Wolf – Belgarath – was also a relative, though infinitely far
removed. But Adara was different. She was nearly his own
age, for one thing, and she seemed immediately to fill that
void that had always been there. She became at once all
those sisters and cousins and younger aunts that others
seemed to have but that he did not.

She showed him the Algar Stronghold from top to
bottom. As they wandered together down long, empty
corridors, they frequently held each others' hands. Most
of the time, however, they talked. They sat together in
out-of-the-way places with their heads close together,
talking, laughing, exchanging confidences and opening
their hearts to each other. Garion discovered a hunger
for talk in himself that he had not suspected. The
circumstances of the past year had made him reticent,
and now all that flood of words broke loose. Because he
loved his tall, beautiful cousin, he told her things he
would not have told any other living soul.

Adara responded to his affection with a love of her
own that seemed as deep, and she listened to his
outpourings with an attention that made him reveal
himself even more.

'Can you really do that?' she asked when, one bright winter afternoon, they sat together in an embrasure high up in the fortress wall with a window behind them overlooking the vast sea of winter-brown grass stretching to the horizon. 'Are you really a sorcerer?'

'I'm afraid so,' he replied.

'Afraid?'

'There are some pretty awful things involved in it, Adara. At first I didn't want to believe it, but things kept happening because I wanted them to happen. It finally reached the point where I couldn't doubt it any more.'

'Show me,' she urged him.

He looked around a bit nervously. 'I don't really think I should,' he apologized. 'It makes a certain kind of noise, you see, and Aunt Pol can hear it. For some reason I don't think she'd approve if I just did it to show off.'

'You're not afraid of her, are you?'

'It's not exactly that. I just don't want her to be disappointed in me.' He considered that. 'Let me see if I can explain. We had an awful argument once – in Nyissa. I said some things I didn't really mean, and she told me exactly what she'd gone through for me.' He looked somberly out of the window, remembering Aunt Pol's words on the steamy deck of Greldik's ship. 'She's devoted a thousand years to me, Adara – to my family actually, but finally all because of me. She's given up every single thing that's ever been important to her for me. Can you imagine the kind of obligation that puts on me? I'll do anything she wants me to, and I'd cut off my arm before I'd ever hurt her again.'

'You love her very much, don't you, Garion?'

'It goes beyond that. I don't think there's even been a word invented yet to describe what exists between us.'

Wordlessly Adara took his hand, her eyes warm with a wondering affection.

Later that afternoon, Garion went alone to the room where Aunt Pol was caring for her recalcitrant patient. After the first few days of bed rest, Belgarath had steadily grown more testy about his enforced confinement. Traces of that irritability lingered on his face even as he dozed, propped up by many pillows in his canopied bed. Aunt Pol, wearing her familiar grey dress, sat nearby, her needle busy as she altered one of Garion's old tunics for Errand. The little boy, sitting not far away, watched her with that serious expression that always seemed to make him look older than he really was.

'How is he?' Garion asked softly, looking at his sleeping grandfather.

'Improving,' Aunt Pol replied, setting aside the tunic. 'His temper's getting worse, and that's always a good sign.'

'Are there any hints that he might be getting back his—? Well, you know.' Garion gestured vaguely.

'No,' she replied. 'Nothing yet. It's probably too early.'

'Will you two stop that whispering?' Belgarath demanded without opening his eyes. 'How can I possibly sleep with all that going on?'

'You were the one who said he didn't want to sleep,' Polgara reminded him.

'That was before,' he snapped, his eyes popping open. He looked at Garion. 'Where have you been?' he demanded.

'Garion's been getting acquainted with his cousin Adara,' Aunt Pol explained.

'He *could* stop by to visit me once in a while,' the old man complained.

'There's not much entertainment in listening to you snore, father.'

'I do *not* snore, Polgara.'

'Whatever you say, father,' she agreed placidly.

'Don't patronize me, Pol!'

'Of course not, father. Now, how would you like a nice hot cup of broth?'

'I would *not* like a nice hot cup of broth. I want meat – rare, red meat – and a cup of strong ale.'

'But you won't get meat and ale, father. You'll get what I decide to give you – and right now it's broth and milk.'

'Milk?'

'Would you prefer gruel?'

The old man glared indignantly at her, and Garion quietly left the room.

After that, Belgarath's recovery was steady. A few days later he was out of bed, though Polgara raised some apparently strenuous objections. Garion knew them both well enough to see directly to the core of his Aunt's behavior. Prolonged bed rest had never been her favorite form of therapy. She had always wanted her patients ambulatory as soon as possible. By *seeming* to want to coddle her irrascible father, she had quite literally forced him out of bed. Even beyond that, the precisely calibrated restrictions she imposed on his movements were deliberately designed to anger him, to goad his mind to activity – never anything more than he could handle at any given time, but always just enough to force his mental recovery to keep pace with his physical recuperation. Her careful manipulation of the old man's convalescence stopped beyond the mere practice of medicine into the realm of art.

When Belgarath first appeared in King Cho-Hag's hall, he looked shockingly weak. He seemed actually to totter as he leaned heavily on Aunt Pol's arm, but a bit later when the conversation began to interest him, there were hints that this apparent fragility was not wholly genuine. The old man was not above a bit of self-dramatization once in a while, and he soon demonstrated that no matter how skillfully Aunt Pol played, he could play too. It was marvellous to watch the two of them subtly maneuvering around each other in their elaborate little game.

The final question, however, still remained unanswered. Belgarath's physical and mental recovery now seemed certain, but his ability to bring his will to bear had not yet been tested. That test, Garion knew, would have to wait.

Quite early one morning, perhaps a week after they had arrived at the Stronghold, Adara tapped on the door of Garion's room; even as he came awake, he knew it was she. 'Yes?' he said through the door, quickly pulling on his shirt and hose.

'Would you like to ride today, Garion?' she asked. 'The sun's out, and it's a little warmer.'

'Of course,' he agreed immediately, sitting to pull on the Algar boots Hettar had given him. 'Let me get dressed. I'll just be a minute.'

'There's no great hurry,' she told him. 'I'll have a horse saddled for you and get some food from the kitchen. You should probably tell Lady Polgara where you're going, though. I'll meet you in the west stables.'

'I won't be long,' he promised.

Aunt Pol was seated in the great hall with Belgarath and King Cho-Hag, while Queen Silar sat nearby, her fingers flickering through warp and woof on a large loom upon which she was weaving. The click of her shuttle was a peculiarly drowsy sort of sound.

'Travel's going to be difficult in midwinter,' King Cho-Hag was saying. 'It will be savage in the mountains of Ulgo.'

'I think there's a way we can avoid all that,' Belgarath

replied lazily. He was lounging deeply in a large chair. 'We'll go back to Prolgu the way we came, but I need to talk to Relg. Do you suppose you could send for him?'

Cho-Hag nodded and gestured to a serving man. He spoke briefly to him as Belgarath negligently hung one leg over the arm of his chair and settled in even deeper. The old man was wearing a soft, grey woolen tunic; although it was early, he held a tankard of ale.

'Don't you think you're overdoing that a bit?' Aunt Pol asked him, looking pointedly at the tankard.

'I have to regain my strength, Pol,' he explained innocently, 'and strong ale restores the blood. You seem to forget that I'm still practically an invalid.'

'I wonder how much of your invalidism's coming out of Cho-Hag's ale-barrel,' she commented. 'You looked terrible when you came down this morning.'

'I'm feeling much better now, though.' He smiled, taking another drink.

'I'm sure you are. Yes, Garion?'

'Adara wants me to go riding with her,' Garion said. 'I – that is, she – thought I should tell you where I was going.'

Queen Silar smiled gently at him. 'You've stolen away my favorite lady in waiting, Garion,' she told him.

'I'm sorry,' Garion quickly replied. 'If you need her, we won't go.'

'I was only teasing you.' The queen laughed. 'Go ahead and enjoy your ride.'

Relg came into the hall just then, and not far behind him, Taiba. The Marag woman, once she had bathed and been given decent clothes to wear, had surprised them all. She was no longer the hopeless, dirty slave woman they had found in the caves beneath Rak Cthol. Her figure was full and her skin very pale. She moved with a kind of unconscious grace, and King Cho-Hag's clansmen looked after her as she passed, their lips pursed speculatively. She seemed to know she was being watched, and, far from being offended by the fact, it seemed rather to please her and to increase her self-confidence. Her violet eyes glowed, and she smiled often now. She was, however, never very far from Relg. At first Garion had believed that she was deliberately placing herself where the Ulgo would have to look at her out of a perverse enjoyment of the discomfort it caused him, but now he was not so sure. She no longer even seemed to think about it, but followed Relg wherever he went, seldom speaking, but always there.

'You sent for me, Belgarath?' Relg asked. Some of the harshness had gone out of his voice, but his eyes still looked peculiarly haunted.

'Ah, Relg,' Belgarath said expansively. 'There's a good fellow. Come, sit down. Take a cup of ale.'

'Water, thank you,' Relg replied firmly.

'As you wish.' Belgarath shrugged. 'I was wondering, do you by any chance know a route through the caves of Ulgo that reaches from Prolgu to the southern edge of the land of the Sendars?'

'That's a very long way,' Relg told him.

'Not nearly as long as it would be if we rode over the mountains,' Belgarath pointed out. 'There's no snow in the caves, and no monsters. *Is* there such a way?'

'There is,' Relg admitted.

'And would you be willing to guide us?' the old man pressed.

'If I must,' Relg agreed with some reluctance.

'I think you must, Relg,' Belgarath told him.

Relg sighed. 'I'd hoped that I could return home now that our journey's almost over,' he said regretfully.

Belgarath laughed. 'Actually, our journey's only just started, Relg. We have a long way to go yet.'

Taiba smiled a slow, pleased little smile at that.

Garion felt a small hand slip into his, and he smiled down at Errand, who had just come into the hall. 'Is it all right, Aunt Pol?' he asked. 'If I go riding, I mean?'

'Of course, dear,' she replied. 'Just be careful. Don't try to show off for Adara. I don't want you falling off a horse and breaking anything.'

Errand let go of Garion's hand and walked over to where Relg stood. The knots on the pouch that Durnik had so carefully sealed with lead were undone again, and the little boy took the Orb out and offered it to Relg. 'Errand?' he said.

'Why don't you take it, Relg?' Taiba asked the startled man. 'No one in the world questions *your* purity.'

Relg stepped back and shook his head. 'The Orb is the holy object of another religion,' he declared. 'It is from Aldur, not UL, so it wouldn't be proper for me to touch it.'

Taiba smiled knowingly, her violet eyes intent on the zealot's face.

'Errand,' Aunt Pol said, 'come here.'

Obediently he went to her. She took hold of the pouch at his belt and held it open. 'Put it away,' she told him.

Errand sighed and deposited the Orb in the pouch.

'How *does* he manage to keep getting this open?' she said half to herself as she examined the strings of the pouch.

Garion and Adara rode out from the Stronghold into the rolling hills to the west. The sky was a deep blue, and the sunlight was very bright. Although the morning was crisp, it was not nearly as cold as it had been for the past week or so. The grass beneath their horses' hooves was brown and lifeless, lying dormant under the winter sky. They rode together without speaking for an hour or so, and finally they stopped and dismounted on the sunny south side of a hill where there was shelter from the stiff breeze. They sat together looking out at the featureless miles of the Algarian plain.

'How much can actually be done with sorcery, Garion?' she asked after a long silence.

He shrugged. 'It depends on who's doing it. Some people are very powerful; others can hardly do anything at all.'

'Could you—' She hesitated. 'Could you make this bush bloom?' She went on quickly, and he knew that was not the question she had originally intended to ask. 'Right now, I mean, in the middle of wintertime,' she added.

Garion looked at the dry, scrubby bit of gorse, putting the sequence of what he'd have to do together. 'I suppose I could,' he replied, 'but if I did that in the wrong season, the bush wouldn't have any defense against the cold, and it would die.'

'It's only a bush, Garion.'

'Why kill it?'

She avoided his eyes. 'Could you make something happen for me, Garion?' she asked. 'Some small thing. I need something to believe in very much just now.'

'I can try, I guess.' He did not understand her suddenly somber mood. 'How about something like this?' He picked up a twig and turned it over in his hands, looking carefully at it. Then he wrapped several strands of dry grass around it and studied it again until he had what he wanted to do firmly in his mind. When he released his will on it, he did not do it all at once, so the change was gradual. Adara's eyes widened as the sorry-looking clump of twig and dry grass was transmuted before her.

It really wasn't much of a flower. It was a kind of pale

lavender color, and it was distinctly lopsided. It was quite small, and its petals were not very firmly attached. Its fragrance, however, was sweet with all the promise of summer. Garion felt very strange as he wordlessly handed the flower to his cousin. The sound of it had not been that rushing noise he'd always associated with sorcery, but rather was very much like the bell-tone he'd heard in the glowing cave when he'd given life to the colt. And when he had begun to focus his will, he had not drawn anything from his surroundings. It had all come from within him, and there had been a deep and peculiar joy in it.

'It's lovely,' Adara said, holding the little flower gently in her cupped hands and inhaling its fragrance. Her dark hair fell across her cheek, hiding her face from him. Then she lifted her chin, and Garion saw that her eyes were filled with tears. 'It seems to help,' she said, 'for a little while, anyway.'

'What's wrong, Adara?'

She did not answer, but looked out across the dun-brown plain. 'Who's Ce'Nedra?' she asked suddenly. 'I've heard the others mention her.'

'Ce'Nedra? She's an Imperial Princess – the daughter of Ran Borune of Tolnedra.'

'What's she like?'

'Very small – she's part Dryad – and she has red hair and green eyes and a bad temper. She's a spoiled little brat, and she doesn't like me very much.'

'But you could change that, couldn't you?' Adara laughed and wiped at the tears.

'I'm not sure I follow you.'

'All you'd have to do is—' She made a vague kind of gesture.

'Oh.' He caught her meaning. 'No, we can't do very much with other people's thoughts and feelings. What I

124

Chapter Eight

The Ulgo girls had pale skin, white-blond hair and huge, dark eyes. Princess Ce'Nedra sat in the midst of them like a single red rose in a garden of lilies. They watched her every move with a sort of gentle astonishment as if overwhelmed by this vibrant little stranger who had quite suddenly become the center of their lives. It was not merely her coloring, though that was astonishing enough. Ulgos by nature were a serious, reserved people, seldom given to laughter or outward displays of emotion. Ce'Nedra, however, lived as always on the extreme outside of her skin. They watched, enthralled, the flicker and play of mood and emotion across her exquisite little face. They blushed and giggled nervously at her outrageous and often wicked little jokes. She drew them into confidences, and each of the dozen or so who had become her constant companions had at one time or another opened her heart to the little princess.

There were bad days, of course, days when Ce'Nedra was out of sorts, impatient, willful, and when she drove the gentle-eyed Ulgo girls from her with savage vituperation, sending them fleeing in tears from her unexplained tantrums. Later, though they all resolved after such stormy outbursts never to go near her again, they would hesitantly return to find her smiling and laughing as if nothing at all had happened.

It was a difficult time for the princess. She had not fully realized the implications of her unhesitating acquiescence to the command of UL when he had told her to remain behind in the caves while the others journeyed to Rak Cthol. For her entire life, Ce'Nedra had been at the center of events, but here she was, shunted into the background, forced to endure the tedious passage of hours spent doing nothing but waiting. She was not emotionally constructed for waiting, and the outbursts that scattered her companions like startled doves were at least in part generated by her enforced inactivity.

The wild swings of her moods were particularly trying for the Gorim. The frail, ancient holy man had lived for centuries a life of quiet contemplation, and Ce'Nedra had exploded into the middle of that quiet like a comet. Though sometimes tried to the very limits of his patience, he endured the fits of bad temper, the storms of weeping, the unexplained outbursts – and just as patiently her sudden exuberant displays of affection when she would throw her arms about his neck and cover his startled face with kisses.

On those days when Ce'Nedra's mood was congenial, she gathered her companions among the columns on the shore of the Gorim's island to talk, laugh, and play the little games she had invented, and the dim silent cavern was filled with the babble and laughter of adolescent girls. When her mood was pensive, she and the Gorim sometimes took short walks to view the strange splendors of this subterranean world of cave and gallery and cavern beneath the abandoned city of Prolgu. To the unpracticed eye, it might have appeared that the princess was so involved in her own emotional pyrotechnics that she was oblivious to anything around her, but such was not the case. Her complex little mind was quite capable of observing, analyzing, and questioning, even in the very midst of an outburst. To the Gorim's surprise, he found her mind quick and retentive. When he told her the stories of his people, she questioned him closely, moving always to the meaning that lay behind the stories.

The princess made many discoveries during those talks. She discovered that the core of Ulgo life was religion, and that the moral and theme of all their stories was the duty of absolute submission to the will of UL. A Tolnedran might quibble or even try to strike bargains with his God. Nedra expected it, and seemed to enjoy the play of offer and counteroffer as much as did his people. The Ulgo mind, however, was incapable of such casual familiarity. 'We were nothing,' the Gorim explained. 'Less than nothing. We had no place and no God, but wandered outcast in the world until UL consented to become our God. Some of the zealots have even gone so far as to suggest that if one single Ulgo displeases our God, he will withdraw himself from us. I don't pretend to know the mind of UL entirely, but I don't think he's quite that unreasonable. Still, he didn't really want to be our God in the first place, so it's best probably not to offend him.'

'He loves *you*,' Ce'Nedra pointed out quickly. 'Anyone could see that in his face when he came to us that time.'

The Gorim looked doubtful. 'I *hope* I haven't disappointed him too much.'

'Don't be silly,' the princess said airily. 'Of course he loves you. Everyone in the whole world loves you.' Impulsively, as if to prove her point, she kissed his pale cheek fondly.

The Gorim smiled at her. 'Dear child,' he observed, 'your own heart is so open that you automatically assume that everyone loves those whom you love. It's not always that way, I'm afraid. There are a good number of people in our caves who aren't all that fond of me.'

'Nonsense,' she said. 'Just because you argue with someone doesn't mean that you don't love him. I love my father very much, but we fight all the time. We enjoy fighting with each other.' Ce'Nedra knew that she was safe using such terms as 'silly' and 'nonsense' with the Gorim. She had by now so utterly charmed him that she was quite sure she could get away with almost anything.

Although it might have been difficult to persuade anyone around her that such was the case, there had been a few distinct but subtle changes in Ce'Nedra's behavior. Impulsive though she might seem to these serious, reserved people, she now gave at least a moment's thought – however brief – before acting or speaking. She had on occasion embarrassed herself here in the caves, and embarrassment was the one thing Ce'Nedra absolutely could not bear. Gradually, imperceptibly, she learned the value of marginal self-control, and sometimes she almost appeared ladylike.

She had also had time to consider the problem of Garion. His absence during the long weeks had been particularly and inexplicably painful for her. It was as if she had misplaced something – something very valuable – and its loss left an aching kind of vacancy. Her emotions had always been such a jumble that she had never fully come to grips with them. Usually they changed so rapidly that she never had time to examine one before another took its place. This yearning sense of something missing, however, had persisted for so long that she finally had to face it.

It could not be love. That was impossible. Love for a peasant scullion – no matter how nice he was – was quite out of the question! She was, after all, an Imperial Princess, and her duty was crystal clear. If there had been even the faintest suspicion in her mind that her feelings had moved beyond casual friendship, she would have an absolute obligation to break off any further contact. Ce'Nedra did not *want* to send Garion away and never see him again. The very thought of doing so made her lip tremble. So, quite obviously, what she felt was not – could not – be love. She felt much better once she had worked that out. The possibility had been worrying her, but now that logic had proved beyond all doubt that she was safe, she was able to relax. It was a great comfort to have logic on her side.

That left only the waiting, the seemingly endless, unendurable waiting for her friends. Where *were* they? When were they coming back? What were they doing out there that could take so long? The longer she waited, the more frequently her newfound self-control deserted her, and her pale-skinned companions learned to watch apprehensively for those minute danger signs that announced imminent eruption.

Then finally the Gorim told her that word had reached him that her friends were returning, and the little princess went absolutely wild with anticipation. Her preparations were lengthy and elaborate. She would greet them properly of course. No little girl enthusiasm this time. Instead, she would be demure, reserved, imperial and altogether grown up. Naturally, she would have to look the part.

She fretted for hours before selecting the perfect gown, a floor-length Ulgo dress of glistening white. Ulgo gowns, however, were perhaps a trifle too modest for Ce'Nedra's taste. While she wished to appear reserved, she did not want to be that reserved. Thoughtfully, she removed the sleeves from the gown and made a few modifications to the neckline. Some elaborate cross-tying at bodice and waist with a slender gold sash accentuated things a bit. Critically she examined the results of her efforts and found them to her liking.

Then there was the problem of her hair. The loose, tumbled style she had always worn would never do. It needed to be up, piled in a soft mass of curls atop her head and then cascading elegantly down over one shoulder to add that splash of color across the pristine whiteness of her bodice that would set things off just right. She worked on it until her arms ached from being raised over her head for so long. When she was finished, she studied the entire effect of gown and hair and demurely regal expression. It wasn't bad, she congratulated herself. Garion's eyes would fall out when he saw her. The little princess exulted.

When the day finally arrived, Ce'Nedra, who had scarcely slept, sat nervously with the Gorim in his now-familiar study. He was reading from a long scroll, rolling the top with one hand while he unrolled the bottom with another. As he read, the princess fidgeted, nibbling absently on a lock.

'You seem restless today, child,' he observed.

'It's just that I haven't seen him – them – for so long,' she explained quickly. 'Are you sure I look all right?' She had only asked the question six or eight times that morning already.

'You're lovely, child,' he assured her once again.

She beamed at him.

A servingman came into the Gorim's study. 'Your guests have arrived, Holy One,' he said with a respectful bow.

Ce'Nedra's heart began to pound.

'Shall we go greet them, child?' the Gorim suggested, laying aside his scroll and rising to his feet.

Ce'Nedra resisted her impulse to spring from her chair and run out of the room. With an iron grip she controlled herself. Instead, she walked at the Gorim's side, silently repeating to herself, 'Dignity. Reserve. Imperially demure.'

Her friends were travel-stained and weary-looking as they entered the Gorim's cavern, and there were strangers with them whom Ce'Nedra did not recognize. Her eyes however, sought out only one face.

He looked older than she remembered him. His face, which had always been so serious, had a gravity to it now that had not been there before. Things had obviously happened to him while he had been gone – important things – and the princess felt a little pang at having been excluded from such momentous events in his life.

And then her heart froze. Who was that great gangling girl at his side? And why was he being so deferential to the big cow? Ce'Nedra's jaws clenched as she glared across the calm waters of the lake at the perfidious young man. She had *known* it would happen. The minute she had let him out of her sight, he had run headlong into the arms of the first girl who happened by. How *dared* he? *How dared he!*

As the group on the far side of the lake began to come across the causeway, Ce'Nedra's heart sank. The tall girl was lovely. Her dark hair was lustrous, and her features were perfect. Desperately, Ce'Nedra looked for some flaw, some blemish. And the way the girl moved! She actually seemed to flow with a grace that nearly brought tears of despair to Ce'Nedra's eyes.

The greetings and introductions seemed hardly more than some incoherent babble to the suffering princess. Absently she curtsied to the king of the Algars and his lovely queen. Politely she greeted the lushly beautiful woman – Taiba, her name was – whom Lady Polgara introduced to her. The moment she was dreading was approaching, and there was no way she could forestall it.

'And this is Adara,' Lady Polgara said, indicating the lovely creature at Garion's side. Ce'Nedra wanted to cry. It wasn't fair! Even the girl's name was beautiful. Why couldn't it have been something ugly?

'Adara,' Lady Polgara continued, her eyes intently on Ce'Nedra's face, 'this is her Imperial Highness, the Princess Ce'Nedra.'

Adara curtsied with a grace that was like a knife in Ce'Nedra's heart. 'I've so wanted to meet your Highness,' the tall girl said. Her voice was vibrant, musical.

'Charmed, I'm sure,' Ce'Nedra replied with a lofty superiority. Though every nerve within her screamed with the need to lash out at this detested rival, she held herself rigid and silent. Any outburst, even the faintest trace of dismay showing in her expression or her voice would make this Adara's victory complete. Ce'Nedra was too much a princess – too much a *woman* – to permit that ultimate defeat. Though her pain was as real as if she were in the hands of a torturer, she stood erect, enclosed in all the imperial majesty she could muster. Silently she began to repeat all of her titles over and over to herself, steeling herself with them, reminding herself grimly just who she was. An Imperial Princess did not cry. The daughter of Ran Borune did not snivel. The flower of Tolnedra would *never* grieve because some clumsy scullery boy had chosen to love somebody else.

'Forgive me, Lady Polgara,' she said, pressing a trembling hand to her forehead, 'but I suddenly seem to have the most dreadful headache. Would you excuse me, please?' Without waiting for an answer, she turned to walk slowly toward the Gorim's house. She paused only once, just as she passed Garion. 'I hope you'll be very happy,' she lied to him.

He looked baffled.

It had gone too far. It had been absolutely necessary

to conceal her emotions from Adara, but this was Garion, and she had to let him know exactly how she felt. 'I *despise* you, Garion,' she whispered at him with a terrible intensity, 'and I don't ever want to lay eyes on you again.'

He blinked.

'I don't think you can even begin to imagine how much I *loathe* the very sight of you,' she added. And with that she continued on into the Gorim's house, her back straight and her head unbowed.

Once she was inside, she fled to her room, threw herself on the bed, and wept in broken-hearted anguish.

She heard a light step near the doorway, and then the Lady Polgara was there. 'All right, Ce'Nedra,' she said, 'what's this all about?' She sat down on the edge of the bed and put one hand on the shoulder of the sobbing little princess.

'Oh, Lady Polgara,' Ce'Nedra wailed, suddenly throwing herself into Polgara's arms. 'I-I've l-lost him. He-he's in love with h-h-her.'

'Who's that, dear?' Polgara asked her calmly.

'Garion. He's in love with that Adara, and he doesn't even know I'm alive any m-m-more.'

'You silly little goose,' Polgara chided her gently.

'He *does* love her, doesn't he?' Ce'Nedra demanded.

'Of course he does, dear.'

'I knew it,' Ce'Nedra wailed, collapsing into a fresh storm of weeping.

'It's only natural for him to love her,' Polgara continued. 'She's his cousin, after all.'

'His cousin?' Ce'Nedra's tear-streaked face came up suddenly.

'The daughter of his mother's sister,' Polgara explained. 'You did know that Garion's mother was an Algar, didn't you?'

Ce'Nedra shook her head mutely.

'Is that what all this is about?'

Ce'Nedra nodded. Her weeping had suddenly stopped.

Lady Polgara took a handkerchief from her sleeve and offered it to the tiny girl. 'Blow your nose, dear,' she instructed. 'Don't sniff like that. It's very unbecoming.'

Ce'Nedra blew her nose.

'And so you've finally admitted it to yourself,' Polgara observed. 'I was wondering how long it was going to take you.'

'Admitted what?'

Polgara gave her a long, steady look, and Ce'Nedra flushed slowly, lowering her eyes. 'That's better,' Polgara said. 'You mustn't try to hide things from me, Ce'Nedra. It doesn't do any good, you know, and it only makes things more difficult for you.'

Ce'Nedra's eyes had widened as the full impact of her tacit admission struck her. 'It's not possible,' she gasped in absolute horror. 'It can't happen.'

'As my father's so fond of saying, just about anything is possible,' Polgara told her.

'What am I going to do?'

'First you ought to go wash your face,' Polgara told her. 'Some girls can cry without making themselves ugly, but you don't have the right coloring for it. You're an absolute fright. I'd advise you never to cry in public if you can help it.'

'That's not what I meant,' Ce'Nedra said. 'What am I going to do about Garion?'

'I don't know that you really need to do anything, dear. Things will straighten themselves out eventually.'

'But I'm a princess, and he's – well, he's just Garion. This sort of thing isn't permitted.'

'Everything will probably turn out all right,' Lady

Polgara assured her. 'Trust me, Ce'Nedra. I've been handling matters like this for a very long time. Now go wash your face.'

'I made a terrible fool of myself out there, didn't I?' Ce'Nedra said.

'It's nothing that can't be fixed,' Polgara said calmly. 'We can pass it off as something brought on by the excitement of seeing your friends again after so long. You *are* glad to see us, aren't you?'

'Oh, Lady Polgara,' Ce'Nedra said, embracing her and laughing and crying at the same time.

After the ravages of Ce'Nedra's crying fit had been repaired, they rejoined the others in the Gorim's familiar study.

'Are you recovered, my child?' the Gorim asked her gently, concern written all over his dear old face.

'Just a touch of nerves, Holy One,' Lady Polgara reassured him. 'Our princess, as you've probably noticed, is somewhat high-strung.'

'I'm so sorry that I ran off like that,' Ce'Nedra apologized to Adara. 'It was silly of me.'

'Your Highness could never be silly,' Adara told her.

Ce'Nedra lifted her chin. 'Oh yes I can,' she declared. 'I've got as much right to make a fool of myself in public as anyone else.'

Adara laughed, and the entire incident was smoothed over.

There was still, however, a problem. Ce'Nedra had, she realized, gone perhaps a bit too far in her impulsive declaration of undying hatred for Garion. His expression was confused, even a trifle hurt. Ce'Nedra decided somewhat loftily to ignore the injury she had inflicted upon him. *She* had suffered through that dreadful scene on the shore of the Gorim's island, and it seemed only fair that *he* should suffer a little as well – not

136

too much, of course, but a little anyway. He did, after all, have it coming. She allowed him a suitable period of anguish – at least she hoped it was anguish – then spoke to him warmly, even fondly, as if those spiteful words had never passed her lips. His expression became even more baffled, and then she turned the full force of her most winsome smile on him, noting with great satisfaction its devastating effect. After that she ignored him.

While Belgarath and Lady Polgara were recounting the events of their harrowing journey to Rak Cthol, the princess sat demurely beside Adara on a bench, half-listening, but for the most part turning the amazing discovery of the past hour over and over in her mind. Suddenly, she felt eyes on her, and she looked up quickly. The little blond boy Lady Polgara called Errand was watching her, his small face very serious. There was something about his eyes. With a sudden and absolute certainty, she knew that the child was looking directly into her heart. He smiled at her then; without knowing why, she felt a sudden overwhelming surge of joy at his smile. He walked toward her, still smiling, and his little hand dipped into the pouch at his waist. He took out a round, grey stone and offered it to her. 'Errand?' he said. For an instant Ce'Nedra seemed to see a faint blue flicker deep within the stone.

'Don't touch it, Ce'Nedra,' Lady Polgara told her in a tone that made Ce'Nedra's hand freeze in the very act of reaching for the stone.

'Durnik!' Lady Polgara said to the smith with an odd note of complaint in her voice.

'Mistress Pol,' he said helplessly, 'I don't know what else to do. No matter how I seal it up, he always manages to get it open.'

'Make him put it away,' she told him with just a hint of exasperation.

Durnik went to the little boy, knelt and took hold of the pouch. Without a word he held it open, and the child dropped the stone into it. Durnik tied the pouch shut, pulling the knots as tight as he could. When he had finished, the little boy put his arms affectionately around the smith's neck. Durnik looked a bit embarrassed and was about to lead the child away, but Errand pulled his hand free and climbed instead into Ce'Nedra's lap. Quite seriously he kissed her, then nestled down in her arms and promptly fell asleep.

Feelings moved in Ce'Nedra that she had never felt before. Without knowing why, she was happier than she had ever been in her life. She held the child close against her, her arms protectively about him and her cheek laid snugly against his pale blond curls. She felt an impulse to rock him and perhaps to croon a very soft lullaby to him.

'We'll have to hurry,' Belgarath was saying to the Gorim. 'Even with Relg's help, it will take a week or more to reach the Sendarian border. Then we'll have to cross the whole country, and the snow in Sendaria can pile up in a hurry this time of year. To make things even worse, this is the season for storms in the Sea of the Winds, and it's a long way over open water from Sendar to Riva.'

The word 'Riva' jerked Ce'Nedra out of her reverie. From the very moment that she and Jeebers had crept from the Imperial Palace at Tol Honeth, one single thought had dominated her thinking. She was *not* going to Riva. Though she might have seemed on occasion to have surrendered on that point, her acquiescence had always been a subterfuge. Now, however, she would have to take a stand. The reasons for her adamant refusal to obey the provisions of the Accords of Vo Mimbre were no longer entirely clear to her. So much had happened that she was not even the same person, but one thing was absolutely certain no matter who she was. She was *not* going to Riva. It was a matter of principle.

'I'm sure that once we reach Sendaria, I'll be able to make my way to an Imperial garrison,' she said as casually as if the matter had already been decided.

'And why would you want to do that, dear?' Lady Polgara asked her.

'As I said earlier, I'm not going to Riva,' Ce'Nedra replied. 'The legionnaires will be able to make arrangements to return me to Tol Honeth.'

'Perhaps you *should* visit your father,' Polgara said quite calmly.

'You mean you're just going to let me go?'

'I didn't say that. I'm sure we'll be able to find a ship bound for Tol Honeth sometime in the late spring or early summer. Rivan commerce with the Empire is extensive.'

'I don't think you fully understand me, Lady Polgara. I said that I'm *not* going to go to Riva – under any circumstances.'

'I heard you, Ce'Nedra. You're wrong, however. You *are* going to Riva. You have an appointment there, remember?'

'I *won't* go!' Ce'Nedra's voice went up an octave or two.

'Yes, you will.' Polgara's voice was deceptively calm, but there was a hint of steel in it.

'I absolutely refuse,' the princess declared. She was about to say more, but a small finger gently brushed her lips. The sleepy child in her arms raised his hand to touch her mouth. She moved her head irritably. 'I've told you all before that I will not submit to—' The child touched her lips again. His eyes were drowsy as he looked up at her, but his gaze was calm and reassuring. Ce'Nedra forgot what she had been saying. 'I am not going to the Isle of the Winds,' she concluded rather lamely, 'and that's final.' The trouble was that it didn't sound all that final.

'It seems that we've had this discussion once or twice before,' Polgara observed.

'You have no right to—' Ce'Nedra's words trailed off again as her thoughts went astray once more. The child's eyes were so blue – so very blue. She found herself unable to look away from them and seemed to be sinking into that incredible color. She shook her head. It was so completely unlike her to keep losing track of an argument this way. She tried to concentrate. 'I refuse to be publicly humiliated,' she declared. 'I will *not* stand in the Hall of the Rivan King like a beggar while all the Alorns snicker up their sleeves at me.' That was better. Her momentary distraction seemed to be fading. Inadvertently she glanced down at the child and it all went out the window again. 'I don't even have the right kind of dress,' she added plaintively. Now what had made her say that?

Polgara said nothing, but her eyes seemed very wise as she watched the princess flounder. Ce'Nedra stumbled along, her objections growing less and less relevant. Even as she argued, she realized that there was no real reason for her not going to Riva. Her refusal seemed frivolous – even childish. Why on earth had she made such a fuss about it? The little boy in her arms smiled encouragingly at her, and, unable to help herself, she smiled back at him, her defences crumbling. She made one last try. 'It's only some silly old formality anyway, Lady Polgara,' she said. 'There won't be anyone waiting for me in the Hall of the Rivan King – there never has been. The Rivan line is extinct.' She tore her eyes away from the child's face. 'Do I really *have* to go?'

mean is – well, there's nothing to get hold of. I wouldn't even know where to start.'

Adara looked at him for a moment, then she buried her face in her hands and began to cry.

'What's the matter?' he asked, alarmed.

'Nothing,' she said. 'It's not important.'

'It *is* important. Why are you crying?'

'I'd hoped – when I first heard that you were a sorcerer – and then when you made this flower, I thought you could do anything. I thought that maybe you might be able to do something for me.'

'I'll do anything you ask, Adara. You know that.'

'But you can't, Garion. You just said so yourself.'

'What was it that you wanted me to do?'

'I thought that perhaps you might be able to make somebody fall in love with me. Isn't that a foolish idea?'

'Who?'

She looked at him with a quiet dignity, her eyes still full of tears. 'It doesn't really matter, does it? You can't do anything about it, and neither can I. It was just a foolish notion, and I know better now. Why don't we just forget that I ever said anything?' She rose to her feet. 'Let's go back now. It's not nearly as nice a day as I'd thought, and I'm starting to get cold.'

They remounted and rode in silence back toward the looming walls of the Stronghold. They did not speak any more. Adara did not wish to talk, and Garion did not know what to say.

Behind them, forgotten, lay the flower he had created. Protected by the slope and faintly warmed by the winter sun, the flower that had never existed before swelled with silent, vegetative ecstasy and bore its fruit. A tiny seed pod at its heart opened, scattering infinitesimal seeds that sifted down to the frozen earth through the stalks of winter grass, and there they lay, awaiting spring.

Lady Polgara nodded gravely.

Ce'Nedra heaved a great sigh. All this bickering seemed so unnecessary. What was the point of making such an issue of a simple trip? It was not as if there was any danger involved. If it would make people happy, why be stubborn about it? 'Oh, all right,' she surrendered. 'If it's so important to everyone, I suppose I can go to Riva.' For some reason, saying it made her feel much better. The child in her arms smiled again, gently patted her cheek and went back to sleep. Lost in a sudden inexplicable happiness, the princess nestled her cheek against his curls again and began to rock back and forth gently, crooning very softly.

Part Two

RIVA

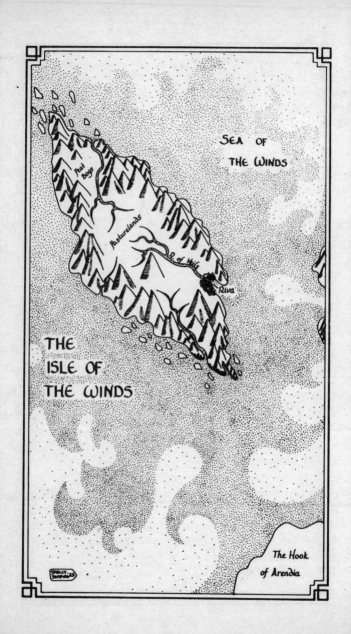

SEA OF
THE WINDS

Peat Bogs

Pasturelands

Q of Vile

Riva

THE
ISLE OF
THE WINDS

The Hook
of Arendia

Chapter Nine

Once more Relg led them through the dark, silent world of the caves, and once more Garion hated every moment of it. It seemed an eternity ago that they had left Prolgu, where Ce'Nedra's farewells to the frail old Gorim had been long and tearful. The princess rather baffled Garion, and he gave himself over to some speculation about her as he stumbled along in the musty-smelling darkness. Something had happened at Prolgu. In some very subtle ways, Ce'Nedra was different – and the differences made Garion jumpy for some reason.

When at last, after uncountable days in the dark, twisting galleries, they emerged once again into the world of light and air, it was through an irregular, brush-choked opening in the wall of a steep ravine. It was snowing heavily outside with large flakes settling softly down through the windless air.

'Are you sure this is Sendaria?' Barak asked Relg as he bulled his way through the obstructing brush at the cave mouth.

Relg shrugged, once more binding a veil across his face to protect his eyes from the light. 'We're no longer in Ulgo.'

'There are a lot of places that aren't in Ulgo, Relg,' Barak reminded him sourly.

'It sort of looks like Sendaria,' King Cho-Hag observed, leaning over in his saddle to stare out of the cave at the softly falling snow. 'Can anybody make a guess at the time of day?'

'It's really very hard to say when it's snowing this hard, father,' Hettar told him. 'The horses think it's about noon, but their idea of time is a bit imprecise.'

'Wonderful,' Silk noted sardonically. 'We don't know where we are or what time it is. Things are getting off to a splendid start.'

'It's not really that important, Silk,' Belgarath said wearily. 'All we have to do is go north. We're bound to run into the Great North Road eventually.'

'Fine,' Silk replied. 'But which way is north?'

Garion looked closely at his grandfather as the old man squeezed out into the snowy ravine. The old man's face was etched with lines of weariness, and the hollows under his eyes were dark again. Despite the two weeks or more of convalescence at the Stronghold and Aunt Pol's considered opinion that he was fit to travel, Belgarath had obviously not yet fully recovered from his collapse.

As they emerged from the cave, they pulled on their heavy cloaks and tightened the cinches on their saddles in preparation to move out.

'Uninviting sort of place, isn't it?' Ce'Nedra observed to Adara, looking around critically.

'This is mountain country,' Garion told her, quickly coming to the defense of his homeland. 'It's no worse than the mountains of eastern Tolnedra.'

'I didn't say it was, Garion,' she replied in an infuriating way.

They rode for several hours until they heard the sound of axes somewhere off in the forest. 'Woodcutters,' Durnik surmised. 'I'll go talk with them and get directions.' He rode off in the directions of the sound. When he returned, he had a slightly disgusted look on his face. 'We've been going south,' he told them.

'Naturally,' Silk said sardonically. 'Did you find out what time it is?'

'Late afternoon,' Durnik told him. 'The woodcutters say that if we turn west, we'll strike a road that runs northwesterly. It will bring us to the Great North Road about twenty leagues on this side of Muros.'

'Let's see if we can find this road before dark, then,' Belgarath said.

It took them several days to ride down out of the mountains and several more before they had passed through the sparsely inhabited stretches of eastern Sendaria to the more thickly populated plains around Lake Sulturn. It snowed intermittently the entire time, and the heavily travelled roads of south-central Sendaria were slushy and lay like ugly brown scars across the snowy hills. Their party was large, and they usually had to split up among several inns in the neat, snow-covered villages at which they stopped. Princess Ce'Nedra quite frequently used the word 'quaint' to describe both the villages and the accommodations, and Garion found her fondness for the word just a trifle offensive.

The kingdom through which they travelled was not the same Sendaria he had left more than a year before. Garion saw quiet evidence of mobilization in almost every village along the way. Groups of country militia drilled in the brown slush in village squares; old swords and bent pikes, long forgotten in dusty attics or damp cellars, had been located and scraped free of rust in preparation for the war everyone knew was coming. The efforts of these peaceful farmers and villagers to look warlike were often ludicrous. Their homemade uniforms were in every possible shade of red or blue or green, and their bright-colored banners obviously showed that treasured petticoats had been sacrificed to the cause. The faces of these simple folk, however, were

147

serious. Though young men strutted in their uniforms for the benefit of village girls, and older men tried to look like veterans, the atmosphere in each village was grave. Sendaria stood quietly on the brink of war.

At Sulturn, Aunt Pol, who had been looking thoughtfully at each village through which they passed, apparently reached a decision. 'Father,' she said to Belgarath as they rode into town, 'you and Cho-Hag and the rest go straight on to Sendar. Durnik, Garion, and I need to make a little side trip.'

'Where are you going?'

'To Faldor's farm.'

'Faldor's? What for?'

'We all left things behind, father. You hustled us out of there so fast that we barely had time to pack.' Her tone and expression were so matter-of-fact that Garion immediately suspected subterfuge, and Belgarath's briefly raised eyebrow indicated that he also was fairly certain that she was not telling him everything.

'We're starting to trim this a bit close, Pol,' the old man pointed out.

'There's still plenty of time, father,' she replied. 'It's not really all that far out of our way. We'll only be a few days behind you.'

'Is it really that important, Pol?'

'Yes, father. I think it is. Keep an eye on Errand for me, won't you? I don't think he really needs to go with us.'

'All right, Pol.'

A silvery peal of laughter burst from the lips of the Princess Ce'Nedra, who was watching the stumbling efforts of a group of militiamen to execute a right turn without tripping over their own weapons. Aunt Pol's expression did not change as she turned her gaze on the giggling jewel of the Empire. 'I think we'll take that one with us, however,' she added.

Ce'Nedra protested bitterly when she was advised that she would not be travelling directly to the comforts of King Fulrach's palace at Sendar, but her objections had no impact on Aunt Pol.

'Doesn't she *ever* listen to *anybody*?' the little princess grumbled to Garion as they rode along behind Aunt Pol and Durnik on the road to Medalia.

'She always listens,' Garion replied.

'But she never changes her mind, does she?'

'Not very often – but she *does* listen.'

Aunt Pol glanced over her shoulder at them. 'Pull up your hood, Ce'Nedra,' she instructed. 'It's starting to snow again, and I don't want you riding with a wet head.'

The princess drew in a quick breath as if preparing to retort.

'I wouldn't,' Garion advised her softly.

'But—'

'She's not in the mood for discussion just now.'

Ce'Nedra glared at him, but pulled up her hood in silence.

It was still snowing lightly when they reached Medalia that evening. Ce'Nedra's reaction to the lodgings offered at the inn was predictable. There was, Garion had noted, a certain natural rhythm to her outbursts. She never began at the top of her voice, but rather worked her way up to it with an impressively swelling crescendo. She had just reached the point of launching herself into full voice when she was suddenly brought up short.

'What an absolutely charming display of good breeding,' Aunt Pol observed calmly to Durnik. 'All of Garion's old friends will be terribly impressed by this sort of thing, don't you think?'

Durnik looked away, hiding a smile. 'I'm sure of it, Mistress Pol.'

Ce'Nedra's mouth was still open, but her tirade had been cut off instantly. Garion was amazed at her sudden silence. 'I *was* being a bit silly, wasn't I?' she said after a moment. Her tone was reasonable – almost sweet-natured.

'Yes, dear – just a bit,' Aunt Pol agreed.

'Please forgive me – all of you.' Ce'Nedra's voice dripped honey.

'Don't overdo it, Ce'Nedra,' Aunt Pol told her.

It was perhaps noon of the following day when they turned off the main road leading to Erat into the country lane that led to Faldor's farm. Since that morning, Garion's excitement had risen to almost intolerable heights. Every milepost, every bush and tree was familiar to him now. And over there – wasn't that old Cralto riding an unsaddled horse on some errand for Faldor? Finally, at the sight of a tall, familiar figure clearing brush and twigs from a drainage ditch, he was no longer able to restrain himself. He drove his heels into his horse's flanks, smoothly jumped a fence and galloped across the snowy field toward the solitary worker.

'Rundorig!' he shouted, hauling his horse to a stop and flinging himself from his saddle.

'Your Honor?' Rundorig replied, blinking with astonishment.

'Rundorig, it's me – Garion. Don't you recognize me?'

'Garion?' Rundorig blinked several more times, peering intently into Garion's face. The light dawned slowly in his eyes like a sunrise on a murky day. 'Why, I believe you're right,' he marvelled. 'You *are* Garion, aren't you?'

'Of course I am, Rundorig,' Garion exclaimed, reaching out to take his friend's hand.

But Rundorig shoved both hands behind him and stepped back. 'Your clothing, Garion! Have a care. I'm all over mud.'

'I don't care about my clothes, Rundorig. You're my friend.'

The tall lad shook his head stubbornly. 'You mustn't get mud on them. They're too splendid. Plenty of time to shake hands after I clean up.' He stared curiously at Garion. 'Where did you get such fine things? And a sword? You'd better not let Faldor see you wearing a sword. You know he doesn't approve of that sort of thing.'

Somehow things were not going the way they were supposed to be going. 'How's Doroon?' Garion asked, 'and Zubrette?'

'Doroon moved away last summer,' Rundorig replied after a moment's struggle to remember. 'I think his mother remarried – anyway, they're on a farm down on the other side of Winold. And Zubrette – well, Zubrette and I started walking out together not too long after you left.' The tall young man suddenly blushed and looked down in embarrassed confusion. 'There's a sort of an understanding between us, Garion,' he blurted.

'How splendid, Rundorig!' Garion exclaimed quickly to cover the little dagger cut of disappointment.

Rundorig, however, had already taken the next step. 'I know that you and she were always fond of each other,' he said, his long face miserably unhappy. 'I'll have a talk with her.' He looked up, tears standing in his eyes. 'It wouldn't have gone so far, Garion, except that none of us thought that you were ever coming back.'

'I haven't really, Rundorig,' Garion quickly assured his friend. 'We only came by to visit and to pick up some things we left behind. Then we'll be off again.'

'Have you come for Zubrette, too?' Rundorig asked

in a numb, stricken sort of voice that tore at Garion's heart.

'Rundorig,' he said it very calmly, 'I don't even have a home any more. One night I sleep in a palace; the next night in the mud beside the road. Would either one of us want that kind of life for Zubrette?'

'I think she'd go with you if you asked her to, though,' Rundorig said. 'I think she'd endure anything to be with you.'

'But we won't let her, will we? So far as we're concerned, the understanding between the two of you is official."

'I could never lie to her, Garion,' the tall boy objected.

'*I* could,' Garion said bluntly. 'Particularly if it will keep her from living out her life as a homeless vagabond. All you have to do is keep your mouth shut and let me do the talking.' He grinned suddenly. 'Just as in the old days.'

A slow smile crept shyly across Rundorig's face.

The gate of the farm stood open, and good, honest Faldor, beaming and rubbing his hands with delight, was bustling around Aunt Pol, Durnik, and Ce'Nedra. The tall, thin farmer seemed as lean as always, and his long jaw appeared to have grown even longer in the year and more since they had left. There was a bit more grey at his temples, but his heart had not changed.

Princess Ce'Nedra stood demurely to one side of the little group, and Garion carefully scanned her face for danger signs. If anyone could disrupt the plan he had in mind, it would most likely be Ce'Nedra; but, try though he might, he could not read her face.

Then Zubrette descended the stairs from the gallery that encircled the interior of the courtyard. Her dress was a country dress, but her hair was still golden, and she was even more beautiful than before. A thousand memories flooded over Garion all at once, together with an actual pain at what he had to do. They had grown up together, and the ties between them were so deep that no outsider could ever fully understand what passed between them in a single glance. And it was with a glance that Garion lied to her. Zubrette's eyes were filled with love, and her soft lips were slightly parted as if almost ready to answer the question she was sure he would ask, even before he gave it voice. Garion's look, however, feigned friendship, affection even, but no love. Incredulity flickered across her face and then a slow flush. The pain Garion felt as he watched the hope die in her blue eyes was as sharp as a knife. Even worse, he was forced to retain his pose of indifference while she wistfully absorbed every feature of his face as if storing up those memories which would have to last her a lifetime. Then she turned and, pleading some errand, she walked away from them. Garion knew that she would avoid him thereafter and that he had seen her for the last time in his life.

It had been the right thing to do, but it had very nearly broken Garion's heart. He exchanged a quick glance with Rundorig that said all that needed saying, then he sadly watched the departure of the girl he had always thought that one day he might marry. When she turned a corner and disappeared, he sighed rather bitterly, turned back and found Ce'Nedra's eyes on him. Her look plainly told him that she understood precisely what he had just done and how much it had cost him. There was sympathy in that look – and a peculiar questioning.

Despite Faldor's urgings, Polgara immediately rejected the role of honored guest. It was as if her fingers itched to touch all the familiar things in the kitchen once more. No sooner had she entered than her cloak went on a peg, an apron went about her waist, and her hands fell to work. Her polite suggestions remained so for almost a full minute and a half before they became commands, and then everything was back to normal again. Faldor and Durnik, their hands clasped behind their back, strolled about the courtyard, looking into storage sheds, talking about the weather and other matters, and Garion stood in the kitchen doorway with Princess Ce'Nedra.

'Will you show me the farm, Garion?' she asked very quietly.

'If you wish.'

'Does Lady Polgara really like to cook that much?' She looked across the warm kitchen to where Aunt Pol, humming happily to herself, was rolling out a pie crust.

'I believe she does,' Garion answered. 'Her kitchen is an orderly kind of place, and she likes order. Food goes in one end and supper comes out the other.' He looked around at the low-beamed room with all the polished pots and pans hanging on the wall. His life seemed to have come full-circle. 'I grew up in this room,' he said quietly. 'There are worse places to grow up, I suppose.'

Ce'Nedra's tiny hand crept into his. There was a kind of tentativeness in her touch – almost as if she were not entirely certain how the gesture would be received. There was something peculiar and rather comforting about holding her hand. It was a very small hand; sometimes Garion found himself forgetting just how diminutive Ce'Nedra really was. At the moment she seemed very tiny and very vulnerable, and Garion felt protective for some reason. He wondered if it would be appropriate to put his arm about her shoulder.

Together they wandered about the farmstead, looking into barns and stables and hen roosts. Finally they reached the hayloft that had always been Garion's favorite hiding place. 'I used to come here when I knew that Aunt Pol had work for me to do,' he confessed with a rueful little laugh.

'Didn't you want to work?' Ce'Nedra asked him. 'Everybody here seems to be busy every single moment.'

'I don't mind working,' Garion told her. 'It's just that some of the things she wanted me to do were pretty distasteful.'

'Like scrubbing pots?' she asked, her eyes twinkling.

'That's not one of my favorites – no.'

They sat together on the soft, fragrant hay in the loft. Ce'Nedra, her fingers now locked firmly in Garion's, absently traced designs on the back of his hand with her other forefinger. 'You were very brave this afternoon, Garion,' she told him seriously.

'Brave?'

'You gave up something that's always been very special and very important to you.'

'Oh,' he said. 'You mean Zubrette. I think it was for the best, really. Rundorig loves her, and he can take care of her in ways that I probably won't be able to.'

'I'm not sure I understand.'

'Zubrette needs a lot of special attention. She's clever and pretty, but she's not really very brave. She used to run away from trouble a lot. She needs someone to watch over her and keep her warm and safe – somebody who can devote his entire life to her. I don't think I'll be able to do that.'

'If you'd stayed here at the farm, though, you'd have married her, wouldn't you?'

'Probably,' he admitted, 'but I didn't stay at the farm.'

'Didn't it hurt – giving her up like that?'

Garion sighed. 'Yes,' he said, 'it did, sort of, but it was best for all of us, I think. I get a feeling that I'm going to spend a lot of my life travelling about, and Zubrette's really not the sort of person you can ask to sleep on the ground.'

'You people never hesitated to ask *me* to sleep on the ground,' Ce'Nedra pointed out a trifle indignantly.

Garion looked at her. 'We didn't, did we? I guess I never thought about that before. Maybe it's because you're braver.'

The following morning after extended farewells and many promises to return, the four of them set out for Sendar.

'Well, Garion?' Aunt Pol said as they rode across the hill that put Faldor's farm irrevocably behind them.

'Well what?'

She gave him a long, silent look.

He sighed. There was really not much point in trying to hide things from her. 'I won't be able to go back there, will I?'

'No, dear.'

'I guess I always thought that when this was all finished, maybe we could go back to the farm – but we won't, will we?'

'No, Garion, we won't. You had to see it again to realize it, though. It was the only way to get rid of the little bits and pieces of it you've been trailing behind you all these months. I'm not saying that Faldor's is a bad place, you understand. It's just that it's not right for certain people.'

'We made the trip all the way up there just so I could find that out?'

'It is fairly important, Garion – of course I enjoyed visiting with Faldor, too – and there were a few special things I left in the kitchen – things I've had for a very long time and that I'd rather not lose.'

A sudden thought had occurred to Garion, however. 'What about Ce'Nedra? Why did you insist that she come along?'

Aunt Pol glanced back once at the little princess, who was riding some yards behind them with her eyes lost in thought. 'It didn't hurt her, and she saw some things there that were important for her to see.'

'I'm fairly sure that I'll never understand that.'

'No, dear,' she agreed, 'probably not.'

It snowed fitfully for the next day and a half as they rode along the road that crossed the white central plain toward the capital at Sendar. Though it was not particularly cold, the sky remained overcast and periodic flurries swept in on them as they rode west. Near the coastline, the wind picked up noticeably, and the occasional glimpses of the sea were disquieting. Great waves ran before the wind, their tops ripped to frothy tatters.

At King Fulrach's palace, they found Belgarath in a foul humor. It was little more than a week until Erastide, and the old man stood glaring out a window at the stormy sea as if it were all some kind of vast, personal insult. 'So nice you could join us,' he said sarcastically to Aunt Pol when she and Garion entered the room where he brooded.

'Be civil, father,' she replied calmly, removing her blue cloak and laying it across a chair.

'Do you see what it's doing out there, Pol?' He jabbed an angry finger toward the window.

'Yes, father,' she said, not even looking. Instead, she peered intently at his face. 'You aren't getting enough rest,' she accused him.

'How can I rest with all that going on?' He waved at the window again.

'You're just going to agitate yourself, father, and that's bad for you. Try to keep your composure.'

'We have to be in Riva by Erastide, Pol.'

'Yes, father, I know. Have you been taking your tonic?'

'There's just no talking with her.' The old man appealed directly to Garion. 'You can see that, can't you?'

'You don't really expect me to answer a question like that, do you, Grandfather? Not right here in front of her?'

Belgarath scowled at him. 'Turncoat,' he muttered spitefully.

The old man's concern, however, was unfounded. Four days before Erastide, Captain Greldik's familiar ship sailed into the harbor out of a seething sleet storm. Her masts and bulwarks were coated with ice, and her mainsail was ripped down the center.

When the bearded sailor arrived at the palace, he was escorted to the room where Belgarath waited with Captain – now Colonel – Brendig, the sober baronet who had arrested them all in Camaar so many months before. Brendig's rise had been very rapid, and he was now, along with the Earl of Seline, among King Fulrach's most trusted advisors.

'Anheg sent me,' Greldik reported laconically to Belgarath. 'He's waiting at Riva with Rhodar and Brand. They were wondering what was keeping you.'

'I can't find any ship captain willing to venture out of the harbor during this storm,' Belgarath replied angrily.

'Well, I'm here now,' Greldik told him. 'I've got to patch my sail, but that won't take too long. We can leave in the morning. Is there anything to drink around here?'

'How's the weather out there?' Belgarath asked.

'A little choppy,' Greldik admitted with an indifferent shrug. He glanced through a window at the twelve-foot waves crashing green and foamy against the icy stone wharves in the harbor below. 'Once you get out past the breakwater it isn't too bad.'

'We'll leave in the morning then,' Belgarath decided.

'You'll have twenty or so passengers. Have you got room?'

'We'll make room,' Greldik said. 'I hope you're not planning to take horses this time. It took me a week to get my bilges clean after the last trip.'

'Just one,' Belgarath replied. 'A colt that seems to have become attached to Garion. He won't make that much mess. Do you need anything?'

'I could still use that drink,' Greldik replied hopefully.

The following morning the queen of Sendaria went into hysterics. When she learned that *she* was going to accompany the party to Riva, Queen Layla went all to pieces. King Fulrach's plump little wife had an absolute horror of sea travel – even in the calmest weather. She could not so much as look at a ship without trembling. When Polgara informed her that she *had* to go with them to Riva, Queen Layla promptly collapsed.

'Everything will be all right, Layla,' Polgara kept repeating over and over again, trying to calm the agitated little queen. 'I won't let anything happen to you.'

'We'll all drown like rats,' Queen Layla wailed in stark terror. 'Like rats! Oh, my poor orphaned children.'

'Now stop that at once!' Polgara told her.

'The sea monsters will eat us all up,' the queen added morbidly, 'crunching all our bones with their horrid teeth.'

'There aren't any monsters in the Sea of the Winds, Layla,' Polgara said patiently. 'We *have* to go. We *must* be in Riva on Erastide.'

'Couldn't you tell them that I'm sick – that I'm dying?' Queen Layla pleaded. 'If it would help, I *will* die. Honestly, Polgara, I'll die right here and now on this very spot. Only, please, don't make me get on that awful ship. *Please*.'

'You're being silly, Layla,' Polgara chided her firmly. 'You have no choice in the matter – none of us do. You and Fulrach and Seline and Brendig all have to go to Riva with the rest of us. That decision was made long before any of you were born. Now stop all this foolishness and start packing.'

'I *can't*!' the queen sobbed, flinging herself into a chair.

Polgara looked at the panic-stricken queen with a kind of understanding sympathy, but when she spoke there was no trace of it in her voice. 'Get up, Layla,' she commanded briskly. 'Get on your feet and pack your clothes. You *are* going to Riva. You'll go even if I have to drag you down to the ship and tie you to the mast until we get there.'

'You *wouldn't*!' Queen Layla gasped, shocked out of her hysteria as instantly as if she had just been doused with a pail full of cold water. 'You wouldn't do that to me, Polgara.'

'Wouldn't I?' Polgara replied. 'I think you'd better start packing, Layla.'

The queen weakly struggled to her feet. 'I'll be seasick every inch of the way,' she promised.

'You can if it makes you happy, dear,' Polgara said sweetly, patting the plump little queen gently on the cheek.

Chapter Ten

They were two days at sea from Sendar to Riva, running before a quartering wind with their patched sail booming and the driving spray that froze to everything it touched. The cabin belowdecks was crowded, and Garion spent most of his time topside, trying to stay out of the wind and out from under the sailors' feet at the same time. Inevitably, he moved finally to the sheltered spot in the prow, sat with his back against the bulwark and his blue hooded cloak tight about him, and gave himself over to some serious thinking. The ship rocked and pitched in the heavy swells and frequently slammed head-on into monstrous black waves, shooting spray in all directions. The sea around them was flecked with whitecaps, and the sky was a threatening, dirty gray.

Garion's thoughts were almost as gloomy as the weather. His life for the past fifteen months had been so caught up in the pursuit of the Orb that he had not had time to look toward the future. Now the quest was almost over, and he began to wonder what would happen once the Orb had been restored to the Hall of the Rivan King. There would no longer be any reason for his companions to remain together. Barak would return to Val Alorn; Silk would certainly find some other part of the world more interesting; Hettar and Mandorallen and Relg would return home; and even Ce'Nedra, once she had gone through the ceremony of presenting herself in the throne room, would be called back to Tol

Honeth. The adventure was almost over, and they would all pick up their lives again. They would promise to get together someday and probably be quite sincere about it; but Garion knew that once they parted, he would never see them all together again.

He wondered also about his own life. The visit to Faldor's farm had forever closed that door to him, even if it had ever really been open. The bits and pieces of information he had been gathering for the past year and more told him quite plainly that he was not going to be in a position to make his own decisions for quite some time.

'I don't suppose you'd consider telling me what I'm supposed to do next?' He didn't really expect any kind of satisfactory answer from that other awareness.

'It's a bit premature,' the dry voice in his mind replied.

'We'll be in Riva tomorrow,' Garion pointed out. *'As soon as we put the Orb back where it belongs, this part of the adventure will be all finished. Don't you think that a hint or two might be in order along about now?'*

'I wouldn't want to spoil anything for you.'

'You know, sometimes I think you keep secrets just because you know that it irritates people.'

'What an interesting idea.'

The conversation got absolutely nowhere after that.

It was about noon on the day before Erastide when Greldik's ice-coated ship tacked heavily into the sheltered harbor of the city of Riva on the east coast of the Isle of the Winds. A jutting promontory of wind-lashed rock protected the harbor basin and the city itself. Riva, Garion saw immediately, was a fortress. The wharves were backed by a high, thick city wall, and the narrow, snow-choked gravel strand stretching out to either side of the wharves was also cut off from access to the city. A cluster of makeshift buildings and low, varicolored tents stood on the strand, huddled against the city wall and half-buried in snow. Garion thought he recognized Tolnedrans and a few Drasnian merchants moving quickly through the little enclave in the raw wind.

The city itself rose sharply up the steep slope upon which it was built, each succeeding row of grey stone houses towering over the ones below. The windows facing out toward the harbor were all very narrow and very high up in the buildings, and Garion could see the tactical advantage of such construction. The terraced city was a series of successive barriers. Breaching the gates would accomplish virtually nothing. Each terrace would be as impregnable as the main wall. Surmounting the entire city and brooding down at it rose the final fortress, its towers and battlements as gray as everything else in the bleak city of the Rivans. The blue and white sword-banners of Riva stood out stiffly in the wind above the fortress, outlined sharply against the dark gray clouds scudding across the winter sky.

King Anheg of Cherek, clad in fur, and Brand, the Rivan Warder, wearing his gray cloak, stood on the wharf before the city gates waiting for them as Greldik's sailors rowed the ship smartly up to the wharf. Beside them, his reddish-gold hair spread smoothly out over his green-cloaked shoulders, stood Lelldorin of Wildantor. The young Asturian was grinning broadly. Garion took one incredulous look at his friend; then, with a shout of joy, he jumped to the top of the rail and leaped across to the stone wharf. He and Lelldorin caught each other in a rough bear hug, laughing and pounding each other on the shoulders with their fists.

'Are you all right?' Garion demanded. 'I mean, did you completely recover and everything?'

'I'm as sound as ever,' Lelldorin assured him with a laugh.

Garion looked at his friend's face dubiously. 'You'd say that even if you were bleeding to death, Lelldorin.'

'No, I'm really fine,' the Asturian protested. 'The young sister of Baron Oltorain leeched the Algroth poison from my veins with poultices and vile-tasting potions and restored me to health with her art. She's a marvellous girl.' His eyes glowed as he spoke of her.

'What are you doing here in Riva?' Garion demanded.

'Lady Polgara's message reached me last week,' Lelldorin explained. 'I was still at Baron Oltorain's castle.' He coughed a bit uncomfortably. 'For one reason or another, I had kept putting off my departure. Anyway, when her instruction to travel to Riva with all possible haste reached me, I left at once. Surely you knew about the message.'

'This is the first I'd heard of it,' Garion replied, looking over to where Aunt Pol, followed by Queen Silar and Queen Layla, was stepping down from the ship to the wharf.

'Where's Rhodar?' Cho-Hag was asking King Anheg.

'He stayed up at the Citadel.' Anheg shrugged. 'There isn't really that much point to his hauling that paunch of his up and down the steps to the harbor any more than he has to.'

'How is he?' King Fulrach asked.

'I think he's lost some weight,' Anheg replied. 'The approach of fatherhood seems to have had some impact on his appetite.'

'When's the child due?' Queen Layla asked curiously.

'I really couldn't say, Layla,' the king of Cherek told her. 'I have trouble keeping track of things like that. Porenn had to stay at Boktor, though. I guess she's too far along to travel. Islena's here though.'

'I need to talk with you, Garion,' Lelldorin said nervously.

'Of course.' Garion led his friend several yards down the snowy pier away from the turmoil of disembarking.

'I'm afraid that the Lady Polgara's going to be cross with me, Garion,' Lelldorin said quietly.

'Why cross?' Garion said it suspiciously.

'Well—' Lelldorin hesitated. 'A few things went wrong along the way – sort of.'

'What exactly are we talking about when we say "went wrong – sort of?" '

'I was at Baron Oltorain's castle,' Lelldorin began.

'I got that part.'

'Ariana – the Lady Ariana, that is, Baron Oltorain's sister—'

'The blond Mimbrate girl who nursed you back to health?'

'You remember her,' Lelldorin sounded very pleased about that. 'Do you remember how lovely she is? How—'

'I think we're getting away from the point, Lelldorin,' Garion said firmly. 'We were talking about why Aunt Pol's going to be cross with you.'

'I'm getting to it, Garion. Well – to put it briefly – Ariana and I had become – well – friends.'

'I see.'

'Nothing improper, you understand,' Lelldorin said quickly. 'But our friendship was such that – well – we didn't want to be separated.' The young Asturian's face appealed to his friend for understanding. 'Actually,' he went on, 'it was a bit more than "didn't want to." Ariana told me that she'd die if I left her behind.'

'Possibly she was exaggerating,' Garion suggested.

'How could I risk it, though?' Lelldorin protested. 'Women are much more delicate than we are – besides, Ariana's a physician. She'd know if she'd die, wouldn't she?'

'I'm sure she would.' Garion sighed. 'Why don't you just plunge on with the story, Lelldorin? I think I'm ready for the worst now.'

'It's not that I really meant any harm,' Lelldorin said plaintively.

'Of course not.'

'Anyway, Ariana and I left the castle very late one evening. I knew the knight on guard at the drawbridge, so I hit him over the head because I didn't want to hurt him.'

Garion blinked.

'I knew that he'd be honor-bound to try to stop us,' Lelldorin explained. 'I didn't want to have to kill him, so I hit him over the head.'

'I suppose that makes sense,' Garion said dubiously.

'Ariana's almost positive that he won't die.'

'*Die?*'

'I hit him just a little too hard, I think.'

The others had all disembarked and were preparing to follow Brand and King Anheg up the steep, snow-covered stairs toward the upper levels of the city.

'So that's why you think Aunt Pol might be cross with you,' Garion said as he and Lelldorin fell in at the rear of the group.

'Well, that's not exactly the whole story, Garion,' Lelldorin admitted. 'A few other things happened, too.'

'Such as what?'

'Well – they chased us – a little – and I had to kill a few of their horses.'

'I see.'

'I specifically aimed my arrows at the horses and not at the men. It wasn't my fault that Baron Oltorain couldn't get his foot clear of the stirrup, was it?'

'How badly was he hurt?' Garion was almost resigned by now.

'Nothing serious at all – at least I don't think so. A broken leg perhaps – the one he broke before when Sir Mandorallen unhorsed him.'

'Go on,' Garion told him.

'The priest *did* have it coming, though,' Lelldorin declared hotly.

'What priest?'

'The priest of Chaldan at that little chapel who wouldn't marry us because Ariana couldn't give him a document proving that she had her family's consent. He was very insulting.'

'Did you break anything?'

'A few of his teeth is about all – and I stopped hitting him as soon as he agreed to perform the ceremony.'

'And so you're married? Congratulations. I'm sure you'll both be very happy – just as soon as they let you out of prison.'

Lelldorin drew himself up. 'It's a marriage in name only, Garion. I would never take advantage of it – you know me better than that. We reasoned that Ariana's reputation might suffer if it became known that we were travelling alone like that. The marriage was just for the sake of appearances.'

As Lelldorin described his disastrous journey through Arendia, Garion glanced curiously at the city of Riva. There was a kind of unrelieved bleakness about its snow-covered streets. The buildings were all very tall and were of a uniform grey color. The few evergreen boughs, wreaths, and brightly-hued buntings hung in celebration of the Erastide season seemed somehow to accentuate the stiff grimness of the city. There were, however, some very interesting smells coming from kitchens where Erastide feasts simmered and roasted under the watchful eyes of the women of Riva.

'That was all of it, then?' Garion asked his friend.

'You stole Baron Oltorain's sister, married her without his consent, broke his leg and assaulted several of his people – and a priest. That was everything that happened?'

'Well – not exactly.' Lelldorin's face was a bit pained.

'There's *more*?'

'I didn't really *mean* to hurt Torasin.'

'Your cousin?'

Lelldorin nodded moodily. 'Ariana and I took refuge at my Uncle Reldegin's house, and Torasin made some remarks about Ariana – she *is* a Mimbrate after all, and Torasin's very prejudiced. My remonstrances were quite temperate, I thought – all things considered – but after I knocked him down the stairs, nothing would satisfy him but a duel.'

'You killed him?' Garion asked in a shocked voice.

'Of course I didn't kill him. All I did was run him through the leg – just a little bit.'

'How can you run somebody through just a little bit, Lelldorin?' Garion demanded of his friend in exasperation.

'You're disappointed in me, aren't you, Garion?' The young Asturian seemed almost on the verge of tears.

Garion rolled his eyes skyward and gave up. 'No, Lelldorin, I'm not disappointed – a little startled perhaps – but not really disappointed. Was there anything else you can remember? – anything you might have left out?'

'Well, I hear that I've sort of been declared an outlaw in Arendia.'

'Sort of?'

'The crown's put a price on my head,' Lelldorin admitted, 'or so I understand.'

Garion began to laugh helplessly.

'A true friend wouldn't laugh at my misfortunes,' the young man complained, looking injured.

'You managed to get into that much trouble in just a week?'

'None of it was really my fault, Garion. Things just got out of hand, that's all. Do you think Lady Polgara's going to be angry?'

'I'll talk to her,' Garion assured his impulsive young friend. 'Maybe if she and Mandorallen appeal to King Korodullin, they can get him to take the price off your head.'

'Is it true that you and Sir Mandorallen destroyed the Murgo Nachak and all his henchmen in the throne room at Vo Mimbre?' Lelldorin asked suddenly.

'I think the story might have gotten a bit garbled,' Garion replied. 'I denounced Nachak, and Mandorallen offered to fight him to prove that what I said was true. Nachak's men attacked Mandorallen then, and Barak and Hettar joined in. Hettar's the one who actually killed Nachak. We *did* manage to keep your name – and Torasin's – out of it.'

'You're a true friend, Garion.'

'Here?' Barak was saying. 'What's she doing here?'

'She came with Islena and me,' King Anheg replied.

'Did she—?'

Anheg nodded. 'Your son's with her – and your daughters. His birth seems to have mellowed her a bit.'

'What does he look like?' Barak asked eagerly.

'He's a great, red-haired brute of a boy.' Anheg laughed. 'And when he gets hungry, you can hear him yell for a mile.'

Barak grinned rather foolishly.

When they reached the top of the stairs and came out in the shallow square before the great hall, two rosy-cheeked little girls in green cloaks were waiting impatiently for them. They both had long, reddish-blond braids and seemed to be only slightly older than

Errand. 'Poppa,' the youngest of the two squealed, running to Barak. The huge man caught her up in his arms and kissed her soundly. The second girl, a year or so older than her sister, joined them with a show of dignity but was also swept up in her father's embrace.

'My daughters,' Barak introduced the girls to the rest of the party. 'This is Gundred.' He poked his great red beard into the face of the eldest girl, and she giggled as his whiskers tickled her face. 'And this is little Terzie.' He smiled fondly at the youngest.

'We have a little brother, Poppa,' the elder girl informed him gravely.

'What an amazing thing,' Barak replied, feigning a great show of astonishment.

'You knew about it already!' Gundred accused him. 'We wanted to be the ones to tell you.' She pouted.

'His name's Unrak, and he's got red hair – just the same as you have,' Terzie announced, 'but he doesn't have a beard yet.'

'I expect that will come in time,' Barak assured her.

'He yells a lot,' Gundred reported, 'and he hasn't got any teeth.'

Then the broad gateway to the Rivan Citadel swung open and Queen Islena, wearing a dark red cloak, emerged from within, accompanied by a lovely blond Arendish girl and by Merel, Barak's wife. Merel was dressed all in green and she was carrying a blanket-wrapped bundle in her arms. Her expression was one of pride.

'Hail Barak, Earl of Trellheim and husband,' she said with great formality. 'Thus have I fulfilled my ultimate duty.' She extended the bundle. 'Behold your son Unrak, Trellheim's heir.'

With a strange expression, Barak gently set his daughters down, approached his wife, and took the bundle from her. Very gently, his great fingers trembling, he turned back the blanket to gaze for the first time at his son's face. Garion could see only that the baby had bright red hair, much the same color as Barak's.

'Hail, Unrak, heir to Trellheim and my son,' Barak greeted the infant in his rumbling voice. Then he kissed the child in his hands. The baby boy giggled and cooed as his father's great beard tickled his face. His two tiny hands reached up and clutched at the beard, and he burrowed his face into it like a puppy.

'He's got a good strong grip,' Barak commented to his wife, wincing as the infant tugged at his beard.

Merel's eyes seemed almost startled, and her expression was unreadable.

'This is my son Unrak,' Barak announced to the rest of them, holding the baby up so that they could see him. 'It may be a bit early to tell, but he shows some promise.'

Barak's wife had drawn herself up with pride. 'I have done well then, my Lord?'

'Beyond all my expectations, Merel,' he told her. Then, holding the baby in one arm, he caught her in the other and kissed her exuberantly. She seemed even more startled than before.

'Let's go inside,' the brutish-looking King Anheg suggested. 'It's very cold out here, and I'm a sentimental man. I'd rather not have tears freezing in my beard.'

The Arendish girl joined Lelldorin and Garion as they entered the fortress.

'And this is my Ariana,' Lelldorin told Garion with an expression of total adoration on his face.

For a moment – for just a moment – Garion had some hope for his impossible friend. Lady Ariana was a slim, practical-looking Mimbrate girl, whose medical studies had given her face a certain seriousness. The look she directed at Lelldorin, however, immediately dispelled any hope. Garion shuddered inwardly at the total lack of anything resembling reason in the gaze these two exchanged. Ariana would not restrain Lelldorin as he crashed headlong into disaster after disaster; she would encourage him; she would cheer him on.

'My Lord hath awaited thy coming most eagerly,' she said to Garion as they followed the others along a broad stone corridor. The very slight stress she put on 'My Lord' indicated that while Lelldorin might think that their marriage was one in name only, *she* did not.

'We're very good friends,' Garion told her. He looked around, a bit embarrassed by the way these two kept staring into each others' eyes. 'Is this the Hall of the Rivan King, then?' he asked.

' 'Tis generally called so,' Ariana replied. 'The Rivans themselves speak with more precision, however. Lord Olban, youngest son of the Rivan Warder, hath most graciously shown us throughout the fortress, and he doth speak of this as the Citadel. The Hall of the Rivan King is the throne room itself.'

'Ah,' Garion said, 'I see.' He looked away quickly, not wanting to see the way all thought vanished from her eyes when they returned to their contemplation of Lelldorin's face.

King Rhodar of Drasnia, wearing his customary red robe, was sitting in the large, low-beamed dining room where a fire crackled in a cavelike fireplace and a multitude of candles gave off a warm, golden light. Rhodar vastly filled a chair at the head of a long table with the ruins of his lunch spread before him. His crown was hung negligently on the back of his chair, and his round, red face was gleaming with perspiration. 'Finally!' he said with a grunt. He waddled ponderously to greet them. He fondly embraced Polgara, kissed Queen Silar and Queen Layla, and took the hands of

King Cho-Hag and King Fulrach in his own. 'It's been a long time,' he said to them. Then he turned to Belgarath. 'What took you so long?' he asked.

'We had a long way to go, Rhodar,' the old sorcerer replied, pulling off his cloak and backing up to the broad-arched fireplace. 'You don't go from here to Rak Cthol in a week, you know.'

'I hear that you and Ctuchik finally had it out,' the king said.

Silk laughed sardonically. 'It was a splendid little get-together, uncle.'

'I'm sorry I missed it.' King Rhodar looked inquiringly at Ce'Nedra and Adara, his expression openly admiring. 'Ladies,' he said to them bowing politely, 'if someone will introduce us, I'll be more than happy to bestow a few royal kisses.'

'If Porenn catches you kissing pretty girls, she'll carve out your tripes, Rhodar.' King Anheg laughed crudely.

As Aunt Pol made the introductions, Garion drew back a few paces to consider the havoc Lelldorin had caused in one short week. It was going to take months to unravel it, and there was no guarantee that it would not happen again – indeed, that it would not happen every time the young man got loose.

'What's the matter with your friend?' It was the Princess Ce'Nedra, and she was tugging on Garion's sleeve.

'What do you mean, what's the matter with him?'

'You mean he's always like that?'

'Lelldorin—' Garion hesitated. 'Well, Lelldorin's very enthusiastic about things, and sometimes he speaks or acts without stopping to think.' Loyalty made him want to put the best face on it.

'Garion.' Ce'Nedra's gaze was very direct. 'I know Arends, and he's the most Arendish Arend I've ever met. He's so Arendish that he's almost incapacitated.'

Garion quickly came to the defense of his friend. 'He's not *that* bad.'

'Really? And Lady Ariana. She's a lovely girl, a skilled physician – and utterly devoid of anything remotely resembling thought.'

'They're in love,' Garion said, as if that explained everything.

'What's that got to do with it?'

'Love does things to people,' Garion told her. 'It seems to knock holes in their judgment or something.'

'What a fascinating observation,' Ce'Nedra replied. 'Do go on.'

Garion was too preoccupied with the problem to catch the dangerous lilt in her voice. 'As soon as somebody falls in love all the wits seem to dribble out of the bottom of his head,' he continued moodily.

'What a *colorful* way to put it,' Ce'Nedra said.

Garion even missed *that* warning. 'It's almost as if it were some kind of disease,' he added.

'Do you know something, Garion?' the princess said in a conversational, almost casual tone of voice. 'Sometimes you make me positively sick.' And she turned and walked away, leaving him staring after her in openmouthed astonishment.

'What did I say?' he called after her, but she ignored him.

After they had all dined, King Rhodar turned to Belgarath. 'Do you suppose we might have a look at the Orb?' he asked.

'Tomorrow,' the old man answered. 'We'll reveal it when it's returned to its proper place in the Hall of the Rivan King at midday.'

'We've all seen it before, Belgarath,' King Anheg asserted. 'What's the harm in our having a look now?'

Belgarath shook his head stubbornly. 'There are

174

reasons, Anheg,' he said. 'I think it may surprise you tomorrow, and I wouldn't want to spoil it for anyone.'

'Stop him, Durnik,' Polgara said as Errand slipped from his seat and walked around the table toward King Rhodar, his hand fumbling with the strings of the pouch at his waist.

'Oh no, little fellow,' Durnik said, catching the boy from behind and lifting him up into his arms.

'What a beautiful child,' Queen Islena observed. 'Who is he?'

'That's our thief,' Belgarath replied. 'Zedar found him someplace and raised him as a total innocent. At the moment, he seems to be the only one in the world who can touch the Orb.'

'Is that it in the pouch?' Anheg asked.

Belgarath nodded. 'He's caused us all some anxiety along the way. He keeps trying to give it to people. If he decides to offer you something, I don't really advise taking it.'

'I wouldn't dream of it,' Anheg agreed.

As was usually the case, once Errand's attention had been diverted, he immediately seemed to forget about the Orb. His gaze focused on the infant Barak was holding; as soon as Durnik set him down, he went over to look at the baby. Unrak returned the look and some kind of peculiar recognition seemed to pass between them. Then Errand gently kissed the child in Barak's arms, and Unrak, smiling, took hold of the strange little boy's finger. Gundred and Terzie gathered close, and Barak's great face rose from the garden of children clustered about him. Garion could clearly see the tears glistening in his friend's eyes as he looked at his wife Merel. The look she returned him was strangely tender; for the first time Garion could remember, she smiled at her husband.

Chapter Eleven

That night a sudden, savage storm howled down from the northwest to claw at the unyielding rock of the Isle of the Winds. Great waves crashed and thundered against the cliffs, and a shrieking gale howled among the ancient battlements of Iron-grip's Citadel. The firm-set rock of the fortress seemed almost to shudder as the seething storm lashed again and again at the walls.

Garion slept fitfully. There was not only the shriek and bellow of wind and the rattle of sleet against close-shuttered windows to contend with, nor the gusting drafts that blew suddenly down every corridor to set unlatched doors banging, but there were also those peculiar moments of oppressive silence that were almost as bad as the noise. Strange dreams stalked his sleep that night. Some great, momentous, and unexplained event was about to take place, and there were all manner of peculiar things that he had to do in preparation for it. He did not know why he had to do them, and no one would tell him if he were doing them right or not. There seemed to be some kind of dreadful hurry, and people kept rushing him from one thing to the next without ever giving him time to make sure that anything was really finished.

Even the storm seemed to be mixed up in it – like some howling enemy trying with noise and wind and crashing waves to break the absolute concentration necessary to complete each task.

'Are you ready?' It was Aunt Pol, and she was placing a long-handled kitchen kettle on his head like a helmet and handing him a pot-lid shield and a wooden stick sword.

'What am I supposed to do?' he demanded of her.

'You know,' she replied. 'Hurry. It's getting late.'

'No, Aunt Pol, I don't – really.'

'Of course you do. Now stop wasting time.'

He looked around, feeling very confused and apprehensive. Not far away, Rundorig stood with that same rather foolish look on his face that had always been there. Rundorig also had a kettle on his head, a pot-lid shield, and a wooden sword. Apparently he and Rundorig were supposed to do this together. Garion smiled at his friend, and Rundorig grinned back.

'That's right,' Aunt Pol said encouragingly. 'Now kill him. Hurry, Garion. You have to be finished by suppertime.'

He spun around to stare at her. Kill Rundorig? But when he looked back, it was not Rundorig. Instead the face that looked at him from beneath the kettle was maimed and hideous.

'No, no,' Barak said impatiently. 'Don't hold it like that. Grip it in both hands and keep it pointed at his chest. Keep the point low so that, when he charges, he doesn't knock the spear aside with his tusks. Now do it again. Try to get it right this time. Hurry, Garion. We don't have all day, you know.' The big man nudged the dead boar with his foot, and the boar got up and began to paw at the snow. Barak gave Garion a quick look. 'Are you ready?' he demanded.

Then he was standing on a strange, colorless plain, and there seemed to be statues all around him. No. Not statues – figures. King Anheg was there – or a figure that looked like him – and King Korodullin, and Queen

Islena, and there was the Earl of Jarvik, and over there was Nachak, the Murgo ambassador at Vo Mimbre.

'Which piece do you want to move?' It was the dry voice in his mind.

'I don't know the rules,' Garion objected.

'That doesn't matter. You have to move. It's your turn.'

When Garion turned back, one of the figures was rushing at him. It wore a cowled robe, and its eyes bulged with madness. Without thinking, Garion raised his hand to ward off the figure's attack.

'Is that the move you want to make?' the voice asked him.

'I don't know.'

'It's too late to change it now. You've already touched him. From now on, you have to make your own moves.'

'Is that one of the rules?'

'That's the way it is. Are you ready?'

There was the smell of loam and of ancient oak trees. 'You really must learn to control your tongue, Polgara,' Asharak the Murgo said with a bland smile, slapping Aunt Pol sharply across the face.

'It's your move again,' the dry voice said. 'There's only one that you can make.'

'Do I have to do it? Isn't there anything else I can do?'

'It's the only move there is. You'd better hurry.'

With a deep sigh of regret, Garion reached out and set fire to Asharak with the palm of his hand.

A sudden, gusting draft banged open the door of the room Garion shared with Lelldorin, and the two of them sat bolt upright in their beds.

'I'll latch it again,' Lelldorin said, throwing back the covers and stumbling across the chilly stones of the floor.

'How long's it going to keep blowing like this?' Garion

178

asked peevishly. 'How's anyone supposed to sleep with all this noise?'

Lelldorin closed the door again, and Garion heard him fumbling around in the darkness. There was a scraping click and a sudden bright spark. The spark went out, and Lelldorin tried again. This time it caught in the tinder. The young Asturian blew on it, and it grew brighter, then flared into a small finger of flame.

'Have you got any idea what time it is?' Garion asked as his friend lighted the candle.

'Some hours before dawn, I imagine,' Lelldorin replied.

Garion groaned. 'It feels like this night's already been about ten years long.'

'We can talk for a while,' Lelldorin suggested. 'Maybe the storm will die down toward dawn.'

'Talking's better than lying here in the dark, jumping at every sound,' Garion agreed, sitting up and pulling his blanket around his shoulders.

'Things have happened to you since we saw each other last haven't they, Garion?' Lelldorin asked, climbing back into his own bed.

'A lot of things,' Garion told him, 'not all of them good, either.'

'You've changed a great deal,' Lelldorin noted.

'I've *been* changed. There's a difference. Most of it wasn't my idea. You've changed, too, you know.'

'Me?' Lelldorin laughed ruefully. 'I'm afraid not, my friend. The mess I've made of things in the past week is proof that I haven't changed at all.'

'That *will* take a bit of straightening out, won't it?' Garion agreed. 'The funny part about it all is that there *is* a perverse sort of logic about the whole thing. There wasn't one single thing you did that was actually insane. It's just when you put them all together that it starts to look like a catastrophe.'

Lelldorin sighed. 'And now my poor Ariana and I are doomed to perpetual exile.'

'I think we'll be able to fix it,' Garion assured him. 'Your uncle will forgive you, and Torasin probably will, too. He likes you too much to stay angry for long. Baron Oltorain is probably very put out with you, but he's a Mimbrate Arend. He'll forgive anything if it's done for love. We might have to wait until his leg heals up again, though. That was the part that was a real blunder, Lelldorin. You shouldn't have broken his leg.'

'Next time I'll try to avoid that,' Lelldorin promised quickly.

'Next time?'

They both laughed then and talked on as their candle flickered in the vagrant drafts stirred by the raging storm. After an hour or so, the worst of the gale seemed to pass, and the two of them found their eyes growing heavy once more.

'Why don't we try to sleep again?' Garion suggested.

'I'll blow out the candle,' Lelldorin agreed. He got up out of bed and stepped to the table. 'Are you ready?' he asked Garion.

Garion slept again almost immediately, and almost immediately heard a sibilant whisper in his ear and felt a dry, cold touch. 'Are you ready?' the whispering voice hissed, and he turned to look with uncomprehending eyes at the face of Queen Salmissra, a face that shifted back and forth from woman to snake to something midway between.

Then he stood beneath the shimmering dome of the cave of the Gods and moved without thought to touch the unblemished, walnut-colored shoulder of the still-born colt, thrusting his hand into the absolute silence of death itself.

'Are you ready?' Belgarath asked quite calmly.

'I think so.'

'All right. Put your will against it and push.'

'It's awfully heavy, Grandfather.'

'You don't have to pick it up, Garion. Just push it. It will roll over if you do it right. Hurry up. We have a great deal more to do.'

Garion began to gather his will.

And then he sat on a hillside with his cousin Adara. In his hand he held a dead twig and a few wisps of dry grass.

'Are you ready?' the voice in his mind asked him.

'Is this going to mean anything?' Garion asked. 'I mean, will it make any difference?'

'That depends on you and how well you do it.'

'That's not a very good answer.'

'It wasn't a very good question. If you're ready, turn the twig into a flower.'

Garion did that and looked critically at the result. 'It's not a very good flower, is it?' he apologized.

'It will have to do,' the voice told him.

'Let me try it again.'

'What are you going to do with this one?'

'I'll just—' Garion raised his hand to obliterate the defective bloom he had just created.

'That's forbidden, you know,' the voice reminded him.

'I made it, didn't I?'

'That has nothing to do with it. You can't unmake it. It will be fine. Come along now. We have to hurry.'

'I'm not ready yet.'

'That's too bad. We can't wait any longer.'

And then Garion woke up. He felt oddly light-headed, as if his troubled sleep had done him more harm than good. Lelldorin was still deep in slumber, and Garion found his clothes in the dark, pulled them on and quietly left the room. The strange dream nagged at his mind as he wandered in the dimly lighted corridors of Iron-grip's Citadel. He still felt that pressing urgency and the peculiar sense that everyone was waiting impatiently for him to do something.

He found a windswept courtyard where snow had piled up in the corners and the stones were black and shiny with ice. Dawn was just breaking, and the battlements surrounding the courtyard were etched sharply against a sky filled with scudding cloud.

Beyond the courtyard lay the stables – warm, smelling of fragrant hay and of horses. Durnik had already found his way there. As was so frequently the case, the smith was uncomfortable in the presence of nobility, and he sought the company of animals instead. 'Couldn't you sleep either?' he asked as Garion entered the stable.

Garion shrugged. 'For some reason sleep just made things worse. I feel as if my head's stuffed full of straw.'

'Joyous Erastide, Garion,' Durnik said then.

'That's right. It is, isn't it?' In all the rush, the holiday seemed to have crept up on him. 'Joyous Erastide, Durnik.'

The colt, who had been sleeping in a back stall, nickered softly as he caught Garion's scent, and Garion and Durnik went back to where the small animal stood.

'Joyous Erastide, horse,' Garion greeted him a bit whimsically. The colt nuzzled at him. 'Do you think that the storm has blown over completely?' Garion asked Durnik as he rubbed the colt's ears. 'Or is there more on the way?'

'It has the smell of being over,' Durnik answered. 'Weather could smell differently here on this island, though.'

Garion nodded his agreement, patted the colt's neck

and turned toward the door. 'I suppose I'd better go find Aunt Pol,' he said. 'She was saying something last night about wanting to check my clothes. If I make her look for me, she'll probably make me wish I hadn't.'

'Age is bringing you wisdom, I see.' Durnik grinned at him. 'If anyone wants me, I'll be here.'

Garion put his hand briefly on Durnik's shoulder and then left the stable to go looking for Aunt Pol.

He found her in the company of women in the apartment that appeared to have been set aside for her personal use centuries before. Adara was there and Taiba, Queen Layla and Ariana, the Mimbrate girl; in the center of the room stood Princess Ce'Nedra.

'You're up early,' Aunt Pol observed, her needle flickering as she made some minute modification to Ce'Nedra's creamy gown.

'I had trouble sleeping,' he told her, looking at the princess with a certain puzzlement. She looked different somehow.

'Don't stare at me, Garion,' she told him rather primly.

'What have you done to your hair?' he asked her.

Ce'Nedra's flaming hair had been elaborately arranged, caught at brow and temples by a gold coronet in the form of a band of twined oak leaves. There was some rather intricate braiding involved at the back and then the coppery mass flowed smoothly down over one of her tiny shoulders. 'Do you like it?' she asked him.

'That's not the way you usually wear it,' he noted.

'We're all aware of that, Garion,' she replied loftily. Then she turned and looked rather critically at her reflection in the mirror. 'I'm still not convinced about the braiding, Lady Polgara,' she fretted. 'Tolnedran ladies don't braid their hair. This makes me look like an Alorn.'

'Not entirely, Ce'Nedra,' Adara murmured.

'You know what I mean, Adara – all those buxom blondes with their braids and their milk-maid complexions.'

'Isn't it a little early to be getting ready?' Garion asked. 'Grandfather said that we weren't going to take the Orb to the throne room until noon.'

'That's not really that far off, Garion,' Aunt Pol told him, biting a thread and stepping back to look critically at Ce'Nedra's dress. 'What do you think, Layla?'

'She looks just like a princess, Pol,' Queen Layla gushed.

'She *is* a princess, Layla,' Aunt Pol reminded the plump little queen. Then she turned to Garion. 'Get some breakfast and have someone show you the way to the baths,' she instructed. 'They're in the cellars under the west wing. After you've bathed, you'll need a shave. Try not to cut yourself. I don't want you bleeding all over your good clothes.'

'Do I have to wear all that?'

She gave him a look that immediately answered that question – as well as several others he might have asked.

'I'll go find Silk,' he agreed quickly. 'He'll know where the baths are.'

'Do that,' she told him quite firmly. 'And don't get lost. When the time comes, I want you to be ready.'

Garion nodded and left. Her words had somehow strangely echoed the words of his dream, and he wondered about that as he went looking for Silk.

The little man was lounging in the company of the others in a large, torch-lighted room in the west wing. The kings were there, with Brand, Belgarath and Garion's other friends. They were breakfasting on cakes and hot spiced wine.

'Where did you go this morning?' Lelldorin asked him. 'You were gone when I woke up.'

'I couldn't sleep any more,' Garion replied.

'Why didn't you wake me?'

'Why should you lose sleep just because I'm having a restless night?' Garion could see that they were deep in a discussion, and he sat down quietly to wait for the opportunity to speak to Silk.

'I think we've managed to aggravate Taur Urgas pretty thoroughly in the past couple of months,' Barak was saying. The big man was sprawled deep in a high-backed chair with his face sunk in the shadows from the flaring torch behind him. 'First Relg steals Silk right out from under his nose, then Belgarath destroys Ctuchik and knocks down Rak Cthol in the process of taking back the Orb, and finally Cho-Hag and Hettar exterminate a sizable piece of his army when he tries to follow us. The king of the Murgos has had a bad year.' The big man's chuckle rumbled out of the shadows. For a moment – a fleeting instant – Garion seemed to see a different shape sprawled there. Some trick of the flickering light and dancing shadows made it appear momentarily that a great, shaggy bear sat in Barak's place. Then it was gone. Garion rubbed at his eyes and tried to shake off the half-bemused reverie that had dogged him all morning.

'I still don't quite follow what you mean about Relg going into the rock to rescue Prince Kheldar.' King Fulrach frowned. 'Do you mean that he can burrow through?'

'I don't think you'd understand unless you saw it, Fulrach,' Belgarath told him. 'Show him, Relg.'

The Ulgo zealot looked at the old man, then walked over to the stone wall beside the large window. Silk instantly turned his back, shuddering. 'I still can't stand to watch that,' he declared to Garion.

'Aunt Pol said I was supposed to ask you the way to

the baths,' Garion said quietly. 'She wants me to get cleaned up and shaved, and then I guess I'm supposed to put on my best clothes.'

'I'll go with you,' Silk offered. 'I'm sure that all these gentlemen are going to be fascinated by Relg's demonstration, and they'll want him to repeat it. What's he doing?'

'He stuck his arm through the wall and he's wiggling his fingers at them from outside the window,' Garion reported.

Silk glanced once over his shoulder, then shuddered again and quickly averted his eyes. 'That makes my blood cold,' he said with revulsion. 'Let's go bathe.'

'I'll go along,' Lelldorin said, and the three of them quietly left the room.

The baths were in a cavernous cellar beneath the west wing of the Citadel. There were hot springs deep in the rock, and they bubbled up to fill the tiled chambers with steam and a faintly sulfurous smell. There were but few torches and only one attendant who wordlessly handed them towels and then went off into the steam to manage the valves that adjusted the water temperature.

'The big pool there gets hotter the closer you go toward the far end,' Silk told Garion and Lelldorin as they all disrobed. 'Some people say you should go in until it's as hot as you can stand it, but I prefer just to pick a comfortable temperature and soak.' He splashed down into the water.

'Are you sure we'll be alone here?' Garion asked nervously. 'I don't think I'd care to have a group of ladies come trooping in while I'm trying to bathe.'

'The women's baths are separate,' Silk assured him. 'The Rivans are very proper about that sort of thing. They aren't nearly as advanced as the Tolnedrans yet.'

'Are you *really* sure that bathing in the wintertime is

healthy?' Lelldorin asked, eyeing the steaming water suspiciously.

Garion plunged into the pool and moved quickly out of the tepid water at the near end toward the hotter area. The steam rose more thickly as he waded out into the pool, and the pair of torches set in rings on the back wall receded into a kind of ruddy glow. The tiled walls echoed back the sounds of their voices and splashing with a peculiar, cavernlike hollowness. The steam eddied up out of the water, and he found himself suddenly shut off by it, separated from his friends in the hazy dimness. The hot water relaxed him, and he seemed almost to want to float, half-aware, and let it soak out all memory – all the past and all the future. Dreamily he lay back, and then, not knowing why, he allowed himself to sink beneath the dark, steaming water. How long he floated, his eyes closed and all sense suspended, he could not have said, but finally his face rose to the surface and he stood up, the water streaming out of his hair and down across his shoulders. He felt strangely purified by his immersion. And then the sun broke through the tattered cloud outside for a moment, and a single shaft of sunlight streamed down through a small grilled window to fall fully upon Garion. The sudden light was diffused by the steam and seemed to flicker with an opalescent fire.

'Hail, Belgarion,' the voice in his mind said to him. 'I greet thee on this Erastide.' There was no hint of the usual amusement in the voice, and the formality seemed strange, significant.

'Thank you,' Garion replied gravely, and they did not speak again.

The steam rose and eddied about him as he waded back toward the cooler reaches of the pool where Silk and Lelldorin, both sunk to their necks in warm water, were talking quietly together.

187

About half an hour before noon, Garion, in response to a summons from Aunt Pol, walked down a long stone corridor toward a room a few steps from the huge, carved doors that gave entrance into the Hall of the Rivan King. He was wearing his best doublet and hose, and his soft leather half-boots had been brushed until they glowed. Aunt Pol wore a deep blue robe, cowled and belted at the waist. For once Belgarath, also blue-robed, did not look rumpled or spotted. The old man's face was very serious; as he and Aunt Pol spoke together, there was no hint of the banter that usually marked their conversation. Seated quietly in the corner of the little room, Errand, dressed all in white linen, gravely watched.

'You look very nice, Garion,' Aunt Pol said, reaching out to smooth his sandy hair back from his forehead.

'Shouldn't we go inside?' Garion asked. He had seen others, gray-clad Rivans and the more brightly garbed visitors entering the hall.

'We will, Garion,' she replied. 'All in good time.' She turned to Belgarath. 'How long?' she asked.

'Another quarter-hour or so,' he replied.

'Is everything ready?'

'Ask Garion,' the old man told her. 'I've taken care of everything I can. The rest is up to him.'

Aunto Pol turned to Garion then, her eyes very serious and the white lock at her brow gleaming silver in the darkness of her hair. 'Well, Garion,' she asked, 'are you ready?'

He looked at her, baffled. 'I had the oddest dream last night,' he said. 'Everyone kept asking me that same question. What does it mean, Aunt Pol? Am I ready for what?'

'That will become clearer in a bit,' Belgarath told him. 'Take out your amulet. You'll wear it on the outside of your clothes today.'

'I thought it was supposed to be out of sight.'

'Today's different,' the old man replied. 'As a matter of fact, today's unlike any day I've ever seen – and I've seen a lot of them.'

'Because it's Erastide?'

'That's part of it.' Belgarath reached inside his robe and drew out his own silver medallion. He glanced at it briefly. 'It's getting a little worn,' he noted. Then he smiled. '—but then, so am I, I suppose.'

Aunt Pol drew out her own amulet. She and Belgarath each reached out to take Garion's hands and then to join their own.

'It's been a long time coming, Polgara,' Belgarath said.

'Yes it has, father,' Aunt Pol agreed.

'Any regrets?'

'I can live with them, Old Wolf.'

'Let's go in then.'

Garion started toward the door.

'Not you, Garion,' Aunt Pol told him. 'You'll wait here with Errand. You two will come in late.'

'You'll send somebody for us?' he asked her. 'What I mean is, how will we know when we're supposed to come in?'

'You'll know,' Belgarath told him. And then they left him alone with Errand.

'They didn't give us very complete instructions, did they?' Garion said to the child. 'I hope we don't make any mistakes.'

Errand smiled confidently, reached out and put his small hand in Garion's. At his touch, the song of the Orb filled Garion's mind again, sponging away his worries and doubts. He could not have said how long he stood holding the child's hand and immersed in that song.

'*It's come at last, Belgarion.*' The voice seemed to

189

come from outside somehow, no longer confined within Garion's mind, and the look on Errand's face made it quite clear that he also could hear the words.

'*Is this what I'm supposed to do?*' Garion asked.

'*It's part of it.*'

'*What are they doing in there?*' Garion looked rather curiously toward the door.

'*They're getting the people in the Hall ready for what's going to happen.*'

'*Will they be ready?*'

'*Will you?*' There was a pause. '*Are you ready, Belgarion?*'

'*Yes,*' Garion replied. '*Whatever it is, I think I'm ready for it.*'

'*Let's go then.*'

'*You'll tell me what to do?*'

'*If it's necessary.*'

With his hand still holding Errand's, Garion walked toward the door. He raised his other hand to push it open, but it swung inexplicably open ahead of him before he touched it.

There were two guards at the huge, carved door a few steps down the hall, but they seemed frozen into immobility as Garion and Errand approached. Once again Garion raised his hand, and the immense doors to the Hall of the Rivan King swung silently open in response to his hand alone.

The Hall of the Rivan King was a huge, vaulted throne room with massive and ornately carved wooden buttresses supporting the ceiling beams. The walls were festooned with banners and green boughs, and hundreds of candles burned in iron sconces. Three great stone firepits were set at intervals in the floor; instead of logs, blocks of peat glowed in the pits, radiating an even, fragrant warmth. The Hall was crowded, but there was a broad avenue of blue carpet leading from the doors to the throne. Garion's eyes, however, scarcely noted the crowd. His thoughts seemed suspended by the song of the Orb, which now filled his mind completely. Bemused, freed of all thought or fear or hint of self-consciousness, he walked with Errand close beside him toward the front of the Hall where Aunt Pol and Belgarath stood, one on each side of the throne.

The throne of the Rivan King had been chiseled from a single basalt block. Its back and arms were all one height, and there was a massiveness about it that made it seem more permanent than the mountains themselves. It sat solidly against the wall and, hanging point downward above it, was a great sword.

Somewhere in the Citadel, a bell had begun to peal, and the sound of it mingled with the song of the Orb as Garion and Errand moved down the long, carpeted pathway toward the front of the hall. As they passed each sconce, the candles inexplicably dropped to the merest pinpoint. There was no draft, no flickering, as, one by one, the candles dimmed and the Hall filled with deepening shadow.

When they reached the front of the Hall, Belgarath, his face a mystery, looked gravely at them for a moment, then looked out at the throng assembled in the Hall of the Rivan King. 'Behold the Orb of Aldur,' he announced in a solemn voice.

Errand released Garion's hand, tugged open the pouch, and reached inside. As he turned to face the darkened Hall, Errand drew the round gray stone out of the pouch and lifted it with both hands, displaying it for all to see.

The song of the Orb was overpowering; joining with it, there was a kind of vast, shimmering sound. The sound seemed to soar, rising, ringing higher and higher as Garion stood beside the child, looking at the faces of the assemblage. Within the stone Errand held aloft there seemed to be a pinpoint of intense blue light. The light grew brighter as the shimmering sound rose higher. The faces before him were all familiar, Garion could see. Barak was there and Lelldorin, Hettar, Durnik, Silk, and Mandorallen. Seated in a royal box beside the Tolnedran ambassador, with Adara and Ariana directly behind her, was Ce'Nedra, looking every inch an Imperial Princess. But, mingled somehow with the familiar faces were others – strange, stark faces, each so caught up in a single overriding identity that they seemed almost masklike. Mingled with Barak was the Dreadful Bear, and Hettar bore with him the sense of thousands upon thousands of horses. With Silk stood the figure of the Guide and with Relg that of the Blind Man. Lelldorin was the Archer and Mandorallen the Knight Protector. Seeming to hover in the air above Taiba was the sorrowing form of the Mother of the Race That Died, and her sorrow was like the sorrow of Mara. And Ce'Nedra was no longer a princess but now a queen – the one Ctuchik had called the Queen of the World. Strangest of all, Durnik, good solid Durnik, stood with his two lives plainly evident on his face. In the searing blue light of the Orb and with the strange sound shimmering in his ears, Garion looked in wonder at his friends, realizing with amazement that he was seeing for the first time what Belgarath and Aunt Pol had seen all along.

From behind him he heard Aunt Pol speak, her voice calm and very gentle. 'Your task is completed, Errand. You may now give up the Orb.'

The little boy crowed with delight, turned, and presented the glowing Orb to Garion. Uncomprehending, Garion stared at the fiery stone. He could not take it. It was death to touch the Orb.

'*Reach forth thy hand, Belgarion, and receive thy birthright from the child who hath borne it unto thee.*' It was the familiar voice, and yet at the same time it was not. When *this* voice spoke, there was no possibility of refusal. Garion's hand stretched out without his even being aware that it was moving.

'Errand!' the child declared, firmly depositing the Orb in Garion's outstretched hand. Garion felt the peculiar, seething touch of it against the mark on his palm. It was alive! He could feel the life in it, even as he stared in blank incomprehension at the living fire he held in his naked hand.

'*Return the Orb to the pommel of the sword of the Rivan King,*' the voice instructed, and Garion turned with instant, unthinking obedience. He stepped up onto the seat of the basalt throne and then onto the wide ledge formed by its back and arms. He stretched up, taking hold of the huge sword hilt to steady himself, and placed the Orb on the great sword's pommel. There was a faint but clearly audible click as the Orb and the sword became one, and Garion could feel the living force of the Orb surging down through the hilt he gripped in one hand. The great blade began to glow, and the shimmering sound rose yet another octave. Then the huge weapon quite suddenly came free from the wall to which it had been attached for so many centuries. The throng in the hall gasped. As the sword began to drop free, Garion caught hold of the hilt with both hands, half-turning as he did so, striving to keep the great blade from falling to the floor.

What pulled him off balance was the fact that it had no apparent weight. The sword was so huge that he should not have been able to hold it, much less lift it; but as he braced himself with his feet widespread and his shoulders pressed back against the wall, the point of the sword rose easily until the great blade stood upright before him. He stared at it in amazement, feeling a strange throbbing between the hands he had clasped about the hilt. The Orb flared and began to pulsate. Then, as the shimmering sound soared into a mighty crescendo of jubilation, the sword of the Rivan King burst into a great tongue of searing blue flame. Without knowing why, Garion lifted the flaming sword over his head with both hands, staring up at it in wonder.

'Let Aloria rejoice!' Belgarath called out in a voice like thunder, 'for the Rivan King has returned! All hail Belgarion, King of Riva and Overlord of the West!'

And yet in the midst of the turmoil that followed and even with the shimmering chorus of what seemed a million million voices raised in an exultation echoing from one end of the universe to the other, there was a sullen clang of iron as if the rust-scoured door of some dark tomb had suddenly burst open, and the sound of that clanging chilled Garion's heart. A voice echoed hollowly from the tomb, and it did not join the universal rejoicing. Ripped from its centuries of slumber, the voice in the tomb awoke raging and crying out for blood.

Stunned past all thought, Garion stood with his flaming sword aloft as, with a steely rustle, the assembled Alorns unsheathed their swords to raise them in salute.

'Hail Belgarion, my King,' Brand, the Rivan Warder, boomed, sinking to one knee and lifting his sword. His four sons knelt behind him, their swords also lifted. 'Hail Belgarion, King of Riva!' they cried.

'Hail Belgarion!' The great shout shook the Hall of the Rivan King, and a forest of upraised swords glittered in the fiery blue light of the flaming blade in Garion's hands. Somewhere within the Citadel, a bell began to peal. As the news raced through the breathless city below, other bells caught the sound, and their iron rejoicing echoed back from the rocky crags to announce to the icy waters of the sea the return of the Rivan King.

One in the Hall, however, did not rejoice. In the instant that the kindling of the sword had irrevocably announced Garion's identity, Princess Ce'Nedra had started to her feet, her face deathly pale and her eyes wide with absolute consternation. She had instantly grasped something that eluded him – something so unsettling that it drained the color from her face and brought her to her feet to stare at him with an expression of total dismay. Then there suddenly burst from the lips of the Imperial Princess Ce'Nedra a wail of outrage and protest.

With a voice that rang in the rafters she cried out, '*OH NO!*'

Chapter Twelve

The worst part of it all was that people kept bowing to him. Garion had not the slightest idea of how he should respond. Should he bow back? Should he nod slightly in acknowledgment? Or perhaps might it not be better just to ignore the whole business and act as if he hadn't seen it, or something? But what was he supposed to do when someone called him, 'Your Majesty'?

The events of the previous day were still a confused blur in his mind. He seemed to remember being presented to the people of the city – standing on the battlements of Iron-grip's Citadel with a great, cheering throng below and the huge sword that somehow seemed weightless still blazing in his hands. Stupendous as they were, however, the overt events of the day were unimportant when compared to things which were taking place on a different level of reality. Enormous forces had focused on the moment of the revelation of the Rivan King, and Garion was still numb as a result of things he had seen and perceived in that blinding instant when he had at last discovered who he was.

There had been endless congratulations and a great many preparations for his coronation, but all of that blurred in his mind. Had his life depended upon it, he could not have given a rational, coherent account of the day's events.

Today promised to be even worse, if that were possible. He had not slept well. For one thing, the great bed in the royal apartments to which he had been escorted the previous evening was definitely uncomfortable. It had great round posts rising from each corner and it was canopied and curtained in purple velvet. It seemed much too large for him and it was noticeably on the soft side. For the past year and more he had done most of his sleeping on the ground, and the down-filled mattress on the royal bed was too yielding to be comfortable. There was, moreover, the sure and certain knowledge that as soon as he arose, he was going to be the absolute center of attention.

On the whole, he decided, it might just be simpler to stay in bed. The more he thought about that, the better it sounded. The door to the royal bedchamber, however, was not locked. Sometime not long after sunrise it swung open, and Garion could hear someone moving around. Curious he peeked through the purple drapery enclosing his bed. A sober-looking servant was busily opening the drapes at the window and stirring up the fire. Garion's attention, however, moved immediately to the large, covered silver tray sitting on the table by the fireplace. His nose recognized sausage and warm, fresh-baked bread – and butter – there was definitely butter involved somewhere on that tray. His stomach began to speak to him in a loud voice.

The servant glanced around the room to make sure everything was in order, then came to the bed with a no-nonsense expression. Garion burrowed quickly back under the covers.

'Breakfast, your Majesty,' the servant announced firmly, drawing the curtains open and tying them back.

Garion sighed. Quite obviously, decisions about staying in bed were not his to make. 'Thank you,' he replied.

'Does your Majesty require anything else?' the

servant asked solicitously, holding open a robe for Garion to put on.

'Uh – no – not right now, thank you,' Garion answered, climbing out of the royal bed and down the three carpeted steps leading up to it. The servant helped him into the robe, then bowed and quietly left the room. Garion went to the table, seated himself, lifted the cover from the tray, and assaulted breakfast vigorously.

When he had finished eating, he sat for a time in a large, blue-upholstered armchair looking out the window at the snowy crags looming above the city. The storm that had raked the coast for days had blown off – at least for the moment; the winter sun was bright, and the morning sky very blue. The young Rivan King stared for a time out his window, lost in thought.

Something nagged at the back of his memory – something he had heard once but had since forgotten. It seemed that there was something he ought to remember that involved Princess Ce'Nedra. The tiny girl had fled from the Hall of the Rivan King almost immediately after the sword had so flamboyantly announced his identity the previous day. He was fairly sure that it was all mixed together. Whatever it was that he was trying to recall had been directly involved in her flight. With some people it might be better to let things quiet down before clearing the air, but Garion knew that this was not the proper way to deal with Ce'Nedra. Things should never be allowed to fester in her mind. That only made matters worse. He sighed and began to dress.

As he walked purposefully through the corridors, he met with startled looks and hasty bows. He soon realized that the events of the preceding day had forever robbed him of his anonymity. Someone – Garion could never catch a glimpse of his face – even went so far as to follow him, probably in the hope of performing some service.

Whoever it was kept a discreet distance behind, but Garion caught occasional glimpses of him far back along the corridor – a gray-cloaked man who moved on strangely noiseless feet. Garion did not like being followed, whatever the reason, but he resisted the urge to turn around and tell the man to go away.

The Princess Ce'Nedra had been given several rooms just down the hall from Aunt Pol's apartments, and Garion steeled himself as he raised his hand to rap on the door.

'Your Majesty,' Ce'Nedra's maid greeted him with a startled curtsy.

'Would you please ask her Highness if I might have a word with her?' Garion asked.

'Certainly, your Majesty,' the girl replied and darted into the next chamber.

There was a brief murmur of voices and then Ce'Nedra swept into the room. She wore a plain gown, and her face was as pale as it had been the previous day. 'Your Majesty,' she greeted him in an icy voice, and then she curtsied, a stiff little curtsy that spoke whole volumes.

'Something's bothering you,' Garion said bluntly. 'Would you like to get it out in the open?'

'Whatever your Majesty wishes,' she replied.

'Do we have to do this?'

'I can't imagine what your Majesty is talking about.'

'Don't you think we know each other well enough to be honest?'

'Of course. I suppose I'd better accustom myself to obeying your Majesty immediately.'

'What's that supposed to mean?'

'Don't pretend that you don't know,' she flared.

'Ce'Nedra, I haven't the faintest idea what you're talking about.'

She looked at him suspiciously, then her eyes softened just a bit. 'Perhaps you don't at that,' she murmured. 'Have you ever read the Accords of Vo Mimbre?'

'You taught me how to read yourself,' he reminded her, 'about six or eight months ago. You know every book I've read. You gave me most of them yourself.'

'That's true, isn't it?' she said. 'Wait just a moment. I'll be right back.' She went briefly into the adjoining room and returned with a rolled parchment. 'I'll read it to you,' she told him. 'Some of the words are a little diffficult."

'I'm not *that* stupid,' he objected.

But she had already begun to read. ' "—And when it shall come to pass that the Rivan King returns, he shall have Lordship and Dominion, and swear we all fealty to him as Overlord of the Kingdoms of the West. And he shall have an Imperial Princess of Tolnedra to wife, and—" '

'Wait a minute,' Garion interrupted her with a strangled note in his voice.

'Was there something you didn't understand? It all seems quite clear to me.'

'What was that last part again?'

'—"he shall have an Imperial Princess of Tolnedra to wife, and—" '

'Are there any other princesses in Tolnedra?'

'Not that I know of.'

'Then that means—' He gaped at her.

'Precisely.' She said it like a steel trap suddenly snapping shut.

'Is that why you ran out of the Hall yesterday?'

'I did *not* run.'

'You don't want to marry me.' It was almost an accusation.

'I didn't say that.'

'Then you *do* want to marry me?'

'I didn't say that either – but it doesn't really matter, does it? We don't have any choice at all – neither one of us.'

'Is that what's bothering you?'

Her look was lofty. 'Of course not. I've always known that my husband would be selected for me.'

'What's the problem, then?'

'I'm an Imperial Princess, Garion.'

'I know that.'

'I'm not accustomed to being anyone's inferior.'

'Inferior? To who – whom?'

'The Accords state that you are the Overlord of the West.'

'What does that mean?'

'It means, your Majesty, that you outrank me.'

'Is that all that's got you so upset?'

Her look was like a drawn dagger. 'With your Majesty's permission, I believe I'd like to withdraw.' And without waiting for an answer, she swept from the room.

Garion stared after her. This was going too far. He considered going immediately to Aunt Pol to protest, but the more he thought about it, the more convinced he became that she would be totally unsympathetic. Too many little things began to click together all at once. Aunt Pol was not merely a party to this absurd notion; she had actively done everything in her power to make absolutely sure that there was no escape for him. He needed someone to talk to – someone devious enough and unscrupulous enough to think a way out of this. He left Ce'Nedra's sitting room and went looking for Silk.

The little man was not in his room, and the servant who was making up the bed kept bowing as he stammered out his apologies at not having the slightest notion of where Silk might be. Garion left quickly.

Since the apartment Barak shared with his wife and children was only a few steps down the corridor, Garion went there, trying not to look back at the gray-cloaked attendant he knew was still following him. 'Barak,' he said, knocking on the big Cherek's door, 'it's me, Garion. May I come in?'

The Lady Merel opened the door immediately and curtsied respectfully.

'Please, don't do that,' Garion begged her.

'What's the trouble, Garion?' Barak asked from the green-covered chair where he sat, bouncing his infant son on his knee.

'I'm looking for Silk,' Garion replied, entering the large, comfortable room that was littered with clothes and children's toys.

'You're a little wild around the eyes,' the big man noted. 'Is something wrong?'

'I've just had some very unsettling news,' Garion told him, shuddering. 'I need to talk to Silk. Maybe he can come up with an answer for me.'

'Would you like some breakfast?' Lady Merel suggested.

'I've already eaten, thank you,' Garion replied. He looked at her a bit more closely. She had undone the rather severe braids she customarily wore, and her blond hair framed her face softly. She wore her usual green gown, but her carriage seemed not to have the rigidity it had always had. Barak, Garion noted, had also lost a bit of the grim defensiveness that had always been there previously when he was in the presence of his wife.

Barak's two daughters entered the room then, one on each side of Errand. They all sat down in the corner

202

and began playing an elaborate little game that seemed to involve a great deal of giggling.

'I think my daughters have decided to steal him.' Barak grinned. 'Quite suddenly I'm up to my ears in wife and children, and the funny part about it is that I don't seem to mind it at all.'

Merel threw him a quick, almost shy smile. Then she looked over at the laughing children. 'The girls absolutely adore him,' she said, and then turned back to Garion. 'Have you ever noticed that you can't look directly into his eyes for more than a moment or so? He seems to be looking right into your heart.'

Garion nodded. 'I think it might have something to do with the way he trusts everybody,' he suggested. He turned back to Barak. 'Do you have any idea where I might find Silk?'

Barak laughed. 'Walk up and down the halls and listen for the rattle of dice. The little thief's been gambling ever since we got here. Durnik might know. He's been hiding out in the stables. Royalty makes him nervous.'

'It does the same thing to me,' Garion said.

'But you *are* royalty, Garion,' Merel reminded him.

'That makes me even more nervous,' he replied.

There was a series of back hallways that led to the stables, and Garion decided to follow that route rather than pass through the more stately corridors where he might encounter members of the nobility. These narrower passageways were used for the most part by servants going to and from the kitchen, and Garion reasoned that most of the minor household staff would probably not recognize him yet. As he walked quickly along one of the passageways with his head down to avoid any chance recognition, he caught another glimpse behind him of the man who had dogged his steps ever since he had left the royal apartment. Irritated finally to the point where he no longer cared about concealing his identity, Garion turned to confront his pursuer. 'I know you're there,' he declared. 'Come out where I can see you.' He waited, tapping his foot impatiently.

The hallway behind him remained empty and silent.

'Come out here at once,' Garion repeated, his voice taking on an unaccustomed note of command. But there was no movement, no sound. Garion thought for a moment of retracing his steps to catch this persistent attendant in the act of creeping along behind him, but just then a servant carrying a tray of dirty dishes came along from the direction Garion had just come.

'Did you see anybody back there?' Garion asked him.

'Back where?' the servant said, obviously not recognizing his king.

'Back along the hall.'

The servant shook his head. 'I haven't seen anyone since I left the apartments of the King of Drasnia,' he replied. 'Would you believe that this is his third breakfast? I've never seen anybody eat so much.' He looked curiously at Garion. 'You shouldn't be back here, you know,' he warned. 'If the head cook catches you, he'll thrash you. He doesn't like anybody in this hall who doesn't have business here.'

'I'm just on my way to the stables,' Garion told him.

'I'd move right along, then. The head cook's got a vicious temper.'

'I'll keep that in mind,' Garion assured him.

Lelldorin was coming out of the stable, and he gave Garion a startled look as the two of them approached each other in the snowy courtyard. 'How did you manage to escape from all the officials?' he asked. Then, as if remembering, he bowed.

'Please don't do that, Lelldorin,' Garion told him.

'The situation *is* a bit awkward, isn't it?' Lelldorin agreed.

'We'll behave toward each other the same as we always have behaved,' Garion said firmly. 'At least until they tell us we can't. Have you any idea where Silk might be?'

'I saw him earlier this morning,' Lelldorin replied. 'He said he was going to visit the baths. He looked a bit unwell. I think he celebrated last night.'

'Let's go find him,' Garion suggested. 'I've got to talk to him.'

They found Silk sitting in a tiled stone room thick with steam. The little man had a towel about his waist and he was sweating profusely.

'Are you sure this is good for you?' Garion asked, waving his hand in front of his face to clear an eddying cloud of steam.

'Nothing would really be good for me this morning, Garion,' Silk replied sadly. He put his elbows on his knees and sank his face miserably into his hands.

'Are you sick?'

'Horribly.'

'If you knew it was going to make you feel this way, why did you drink so much last night?'

'It seemed like a good idea at the time – at least I think it did. I seem to have lost track of several hours.' An attendant brought the suffering man a foaming tankard, and Silk drank deeply.

'Is that really wise?' Lelldorin asked him.

'Probably not,' Silk admitted with a shudder, 'but it's the best I could come up with on short notice.' He shuddered again. 'I feel absolutely wretched,' he declared. 'Was there anything in particular you wanted?'

'I've got a problem,' Garion blurted. He looked

quickly at Lelldorin. 'I'd rather this didn't go beyond the three of us,' he said.

'You have my oath on it,' Lelldorin responded instantly.

'Thank you, Lelldorin.' It was easier to accept the oath than to try to explain why it wasn't really necessary. 'I've just read the Accords of Vo Mimbre,' he told them. 'Actually, I had them read to me. Did you know that I'm supposed to marry Ce'Nedra?'

'I hadn't actually put that part together yet,' Silk admitted, 'but the Accords do mention something about it, don't they?'

'Congratulations, Garion!' Lelldorin exclaimed, suddenly clapping his friend on the shoulder. 'She's a beautiful girl.'

Garion ignored that. 'Can you think of some way I can get out of it?' he demanded of Silk.

'Garion, right now I can't really think of anything except how awful I feel. My first hunch though, is that there isn't any way out for you. Every kingdom in the west is signatory to the Accords – and then I think the Prophecy's involved too.'

'I'd forgotten about that,' Garion admitted glumly.

'I'm sure they'll give you time to get used to the idea,' Lelldorin said.

'But how much time will they give Ce'Nedra? I talked to her this morning, and she's not happy about the idea at all.'

'She doesn't actually dislike you,' Silk told him.

'That's not what the problem is. She seems to think that I outrank her, and that's what's got her upset.'

Silk began to laugh weakly.

'A real friend wouldn't laugh,' Garion accused him.

'Is rank really that important to your princess?' Lelldorin asked.

'Probably not much more important than her right arm,' Garion replied sourly. 'I think she reminds herself that she's an Imperial Princess six or eight times every hour. She makes a pretty big issue about it. Now I come along from out of nowhere, and suddenly I outrank her. It's the sort of thing that's going to set her teeth on edge – permanently, I expect.' He stopped and looked rather closely at Silk. 'Do you think there's any chance of your getting well today?'

'What have you got in mind?'

'Do you know your way around Riva at all?'

'Naturally.'

'I was sort of thinking that I ought to go down into the city – not with trumpets blowing and all that – but just dressed like somebody ordinary. I don't know anything at all about the Rivans, and now—' He faltered with it.

'And now you're their king,' Lelldorin finished for him.

'It's probably not a bad idea,' Silk agreed. 'Though I can't really say for sure. My brain isn't working too well just now. It will have to be today, of course. Your coronation's scheduled for tomorrow, and your movements are likely to be restricted after they've put the crown on your head.'

Garion didn't want to think about that.

'I hope the two of you don't mind if I take a little while to pull myself together first, though,' Silk added, drinking from the tankard again. 'Actually it doesn't really matter if you mind or not. It's a question of necessity.'

It took the rat-faced little man only about an hour to recuperate. His remedies were brutally direct. He soaked up hot steam and cold ale in approximately equal amounts, then emerged from the steamroom to plunge directly into a pool of icy water. He was blue and shaking when he came out, but the worst of his indisposition seemed to be gone. He carefully selected nondescript clothes for the three of them, then led the way out of the Citadel by way of a side gate. As they left, Garion glanced back several times, but he seemed to have shaken off the persistent attendant who had been following him all morning.

As they wandered down into the city, Garion was struck again by the bleak severity of the place. The outsides of the houses were uniformly gray and totally lacking any form of exterior decoration. They were solid, square, and absolutely colorless. The gray cloak which was the oustanding feature of the Rivan national costume gave the people in the narrow streets an appearance of that same grimness. Garion quailed a bit at the thought of spending the rest of his life in so uninviting a place.

They walked down a long street in pale winter sunshine with the salt smell of the harbor strong in their nostrils and passed a house from which came the sound of children singing. Their voices were very clear and merged together in subtle harmonies. Garion was astonished at the complexity of the children's song.

'A national pastime,' Silk said. 'Rivans are very much involved in music. I suppose it helps relieve the boredom. I'd hate to offend your Majesty, but your kingdom's a tedious sort of place.' He looked around. 'I have an old friend who lives not far from here. Why don't we pay him a visit?'

He led them down a long stairway to the street below. Not far up that street a large building stood solidly on the downhill side. Silk strode up to the door and knocked. After a moment, a Rivan in a burn-spotted leather smock answered. 'Radek, old friend,' he said with a certain surprise. 'I haven't seen you in years.'

'Torgan.' Silk grinned at him. 'I thought I'd stop by and see how you were doing.'

'Come in, come in,' Torgan said, opening the door wider.

'You've expanded things a bit, I see,' Silk noticed, looking around.

'The market's been good to me,' Torgan replied modestly. 'The perfume makers in Tol Borune are buying just about any kind of bottle they can get.' The Rivan was a solid-looking man with iron-gray hair and strangely rounded and rosy cheeks. He glanced curiously at Garion and frowned slightly as if trying to remember something. Garion turned to examine a row of delicate little glass bottles standing neatly on a nearby table, trying to keep his face turned away.

'You're concentrating on bottle making then?' Silk asked.

'Oh, we still try to turn out a few good pieces,' Torgan replied a bit ruefully. 'I've got an apprentice who's an absolute genius. I have to let him spend a certain amount of time on his own work. I'm afraid that if I kept him blowing bottles all day, he'd leave me.' The glassmaker opened a cabinet and carefully took out a small velvet-wrapped bundle. 'This is a piece of his work,' he said, folding back the cloth.

It was a crystal wren, wings half-spread, and it was perched on a leafy twig with buds at its tip. The entire piece was so detailed that even the individual feathers were clearly visible. 'Amazing,' Silk gasped, examining the glass bird. 'This is exquisite, Torgan. How did he get the colors so perfect?'

'I have no idea,' Torgan admitted. 'He doesn't even measure when he mixes, and the colors always come out exactly right. As I said, he's a genius.' He carefully rewrapped the crystal bird and placed it back in the cabinet.

There were living quarters behind the workshop, and the rooms were filled with warmth and affection and vibrant colors. Brightly colored cushions were everywhere, and paintings hung on the walls in every room. Torgan's apprentices seemed to be not so much workers as members of his family, and his eldest daughter played for them as they concentrated on the molten glass, her fingers touching the strings of her harp in cascading waterfalls of music.

'It's so unlike the outside,' Lelldorin observed, his face puzzled.

'What's that?' Silk asked him.

'The outside is so grim – so stiff and gray – but once you come inside the building, it's all warmth and color.'

Torgan smiled. 'It's something outsiders don't expect,' he agreed. 'Our houses are very much like ourselves. Out of necessity, the outside is bleak. The city of Riva was built to defend the Orb, and every house is part of the overall fortifications. We can't change the outside, but inside we have art and poetry and music. We ourselves wear the gray cloak. It's a useful garment – woven from the wool of goats – light, warm, nearly waterproof – but it won't accept dye, so it's always gray. But even though we're gray on the outside, that doesn't mean that we have no love of beauty.'

The more Garion thought about that, the more he began to understand these bleak-appearing islanders. The stiff reserve of the gray-cloaked Rivans was a face they presented to the world. Behind that face, however, was an altogether different kind of people.

The apprentices for the most part were blowing the delicate little bottles that were the major item in the trade with the perfume makers of Tol Borune. One apprentice, however, worked alone, fashioning a glass ship cresting a crystal wave. He was a sandy-haired young man with an intent expression. When he looked up from his work and saw Garion, his eyes widened, but he lowered his head quickly to his work again.

Back at the front of the shop as they were preparing to leave, Garion asked to look once more at the delicate glass bird perched on its gleaming twig. The piece was so beautiful that it made his heart ache.

'Does it please your Majesty?' It was the young apprentice, who had quietly entered from the work-room. He spoke softly. 'I was in the square yesterday when Brand introduced you to the people,' he explained. 'I recognized you as soon as I saw you.'

'What's your name?' Garion asked curiously.

'Joran, your Majesty,' the apprentice replied.

'Do you suppose we could skip the "Majesties"?' Garion said rather plaintively. 'I'm not really comfortable with that sort of thing yet. The whole business came as a complete surprise to me.'

Joran grinned at him. 'There are all kinds of rumors in the city. They say you were raised by Belgarath the Sorcerer in his tower in the Vale of Aldur.'

'Actually I was raised in Sendaria by my Aunt Pol, Belgarath's daughter.'

'Polgara the Sorceress?' Joran looked impressed. 'Is she as beautiful as men say she is?'

'I've always thought so.'

'Can she really turn herself into a dragon?'

'I suppose she could if she wanted to,' Garion admitted, 'but she prefers the shape of an owl. She loves birds for some reason – and birds go wild at the sight of her. They talk to her all the time.'

'What an amazing thing,' Joran marvelled. 'I'd give anything to be able to meet her.' He pursed his lips thoughtfully, hesitating a moment. 'Do you think she'd like this little thing?' he blurted finally, touching the crystal wren.

'Like it?' Garion said. 'She'd love it.'

'Would you give it to her for me?'

'Joran!' Garion was startled at the idea. 'I couldn't take it. It's too valuable, and I don't have any money to pay you for it.'

Joran smiled shyly. 'It's only glass,' he pointed out, 'and glass is only melted sand – and sand's the cheapest thing in the world. If you think she'd like it, I'd really like for her to have it. Would you take it to her for me – please? Tell her it's a gift from Joran the glassmaker.'

'I will, Joran,' Garion promised, impulsively clasping the young man's hand. 'I'll be proud to carry it to her for you.'

'I'll wrap it,' Joran said then. 'It's not good for glass to go out in the cold from a warm room.' He reached for the piece of velvet, then stopped. 'I'm not being entirely honest with you,' he admitted, looking a bit guilty. 'The wren's a very good piece, and if the nobles up at the Citadel see it, they might want me to make other things for them. I need a few commissions if I'm ever going to open my own shop, and—' He glanced once at Torgan's daughter, his heart in his eyes.

'—And you can't get married until you've established your own business?' Garion suggested.

'Your Majesty will be a very wise king,' Joran said gravely.

'If I can get past all the blunders I'll make during the first few weeks,' Garion added ruefully.

Later that afternoon he delivered the crystal bird to Aunt Pol in her private apartment.

'What's this?' she asked, taking the cloth-wrapped object.

'It's a present for you from a young glassmaker I met down in the city,' Garion replied. 'He insisted that I give it to you. His name's Joran. Be careful. I think it's kind of fragile.'

Aunt Pol gently unwrapped the crystal piece. Her eyes slowly widened as she stared at the exquisitely wrought bird. 'Oh Garion,' she murmured, 'it's the most beautiful thing I've ever seen.'

'He's awfully good,' Garion told her. 'He works for a glassmaker called Torgan, and Torgan says he's a genius. He wants to meet you.'

'And I want to meet him,' she breathed, her eyes lost in the glowing detail of the glass figure. Then she carefully set the crystal wren down on a table. Her hands were trembling and her glorious eyes were full of tears.

'What's wrong, Aunt Pol?' Garion asked her, slightly alarmed.

'Nothing, Garion,' she replied. 'Nothing at all.'

'Why are you crying then?'

'You'd never understand, dear,' she told him. Then she put her arms around him and pulled him to her in an almost fierce embrace.

The coronation took place at noon the following day. The Hall of the Rivan King was full to overflowing with nobles and royalty, and the city below was alive with the sound of bells.

Garion could never actually remember very much of his coronation. He did remember that the ermine-bordered cape was hot and that the plain gold crown the Rivan Deacon placed on his head was very heavy. What stood out most in his mind was the way the Orb of Aldur filled the entire Hall with an intense blue light that grew brighter and brighter as he approached the throne and overwhelmed his ears with that strange, exultant song he always seemed to hear whenever he came near it. The song of the Orb was so loud that he scarcely heard the great cheer that greeted him as he turned, robed and crowned, to face the throng in the Hall of the Rivan King.

He did, however, hear one voice very clearly.

'Hail, Belgarion,' the voice in his mind said quietly to him.

Chapter Thirteen

King Belgarion sat somewhat disconsolately on his throne in the Hall of the Rivan King, listening to the endless, droning voice of Valgon, the Tolnedran ambassador. It had not been an easy time for Garion. There were so many things he did not know how to do. For one thing, he was totally incapable of giving orders; for another, he discovered that he had absolutely no time to himself and that he had not the faintest idea of how to dismiss the servants who continually hovered near him. He was followed wherever he went, and he had even given up trying to catch the overzealous bodyguard or valet or messenger who was always in the passageways behind him.

His friends seemed uncomfortable in his presence and they persisted in calling him 'your Majesty' no matter how many times he asked them not to. He didn't feel any different, and his mirror told him that he didn't look any different, but everyone behaved as if he had changed somehow. The look of relief that passed over their faces each time he left injured him, and he retreated into a kind of protective shell, nursing his loneliness in silence.

Aunt Pol stood continually at his side now, but there was a difference there as well. Before, he had always been an adjunct to her, but now it was the other way around, and that seemed profoundly unnatural.

'The proposal, if your Majesty will forgive my saying so, is most generous,' Valgon observed, concluding his reading of the latest treaty offered by Ran Borune. The Tolnedran ambassador was a sardonic man with an aquiline nose and an aristocratic bearing. He was a Honethite, a member of that family which had founded the Empire and from which three Imperial dynasties had sprung, and he had a scarcely concealed contempt for all Alorns. Valgon was a continual thorn in Garion's side. Hardly a day passed that some new treaty or trade agreement did not arrive from the Emperor. Garion had quickly perceived that the Tolnedrans were desperately nervous about the fact that they did not have his signature on a single piece of parchment, and they were proceeding on the theory that if they kept shoving documents in front of a man, eventually he would sign something just to get them to leave him alone.

Garion's counterstrategy was very simple; he refused to sign anything.

'It's exactly the same as the one they offered last week,' Aunt Pol's voice observed in the silence of his mind. *'All they did was switch the clauses around and change a few words. Tell him no.'*

Garion looked at the smug ambassador with something very close to active dislike. 'Totally out of the question,' he replied shortly.

Valgon began to protest, but Garion cut him short. 'It's identical to last week's proposal, Valgon, and we both know it. The answer was no then, and it's still no. I will *not* give Tolnedra preferred status in trade with Riva; I will *not* agree to ask Ran Borune's permission before I sign any agreement with any other nation; and I most certainly will *not* agree to any modification of the terms of the Accords of Vo Mimbre. Please ask Ran Borune not to pester me any more until he's ready to talk sense.'

'Your Majesty!' Valgon sounded shocked. 'One does not speak so to the Emperor of Tolnedra.'

'I'll speak any way I please,' Garion told him. 'You have my – *our* permission to leave.'

'Your Majesty—'

'You're dismissed, Valgon,' Garion cut him off.

The ambassador drew himself up, bowed coldly, and stalked from the Hall.

'Not bad,' King Anheg drawled from the partially concealed embrasure where he and the other kings generally gathered. The presence of these royal on-lookers made Garion perpetually uneasy. He knew they were watching his every move, judging, evaluating his decisions, his manner, his words. He knew he was bound to make mistakes during these first few months, and he'd have greatly preferred to make them without an audience, but how could he tell a group of sovereign kings that he would prefer not to be the absolute center of their attention?

'A trifle blunt, though, wouldn't you say?' King Fulrach suggested.

'He'll learn to be more diplomatic in time,' King Rhodar predicted. 'I expect that Ran Borune will find this directness refreshing – just as soon as he recovers from the fit of apoplexy our Belgarion's reply is going to give him.'

The assembled kings and nobles all laughed at King Rhodar's sally, and Garion tried without success to keep from blushing. 'Do they have to do that?' he whispered furiously to Aunt Pol. 'Every time I so much as hiccup, I get all this commentary.'

'Don't be surly, dear,' she replied calmly. 'It *was* a trifle impolite, though. Are you really sure you want to take that tone with your future father-in-law?'

That was something of which Garion most definitely did not wish to be reminded. The Princess Ce'Nedra had still not forgiven him for his sudden elevation, and

Garion was having grave doubts about the whole notion of marrying her. Much as he liked her – and he *did* like her – he regretfully concluded that Ce'Nedra would not make him a good wife. She was clever and spoiled, and she had a streak of stubbornness in her nature as wide as an oxcart. Garion was fairly certain that she would take a perverse delight in making his life as miserable as she possibly could. As he sat on his throne listening to the jocular comments of the Alorn Kings, he began to wish that he had never heard of the Orb.

As always, the thought of the jewel made him glance up to where it glowed on the pommel of the massive sword hanging above the throne. There was something so irritatingly smug about the way it glowed each time he sat on the throne. It always seemed to be congratulating itself – as if he, Belgarion of Riva, were somehow its own private creation. Garion did not understand the Orb. There was an awareness about it; he knew that. His mind had tentatively touched that awareness and then had carefully retreated. Garion had been touched on occasion by the minds of Gods, but the consciousness of the Orb was altogether different. There was a power in it he could not even begin to comprehend. More than that, its attachment for him seemed quite irrational. Garion knew himself, and he was painfully aware that he was not that lovable. But each time he came near it, it would begin to glow insufferably, and his mind would fill with that strange, soaring song he had first heard in Ctuchik's turret. The song of the Orb was a kind of compelling invitation. Garion knew that if he should take it up, its will would join with his, and there would be nothing that between them they could not do. Torak had raised the Orb and had cracked the world with it. Garion knew that if he chose, *he* could raise the Orb and mend that crack. More alarming was the fact that as soon as the notion occurred to him, the Orb began to provide him with precise instructions on how to go about it.

'Pay attention, Garion,' Aunt Pol's voice said to him.

The business of the morning, however, was very nearly completed. There were a few other petitions and a peculiar note of congratulation that had arrived that morning from Nyissa. The tone of the note was tentatively conciliatory, and it appeared over the signature of Sadi the eunuch. Garion decided that he wanted to think things through rather carefully before he drafted a reply. The memory of what had happened in Salmissra's throne room still bothered him, and he was not entirely sure he wanted to normalize relations with the snake-people just yet.

Then, since there was no further court business, he excused himself and left the Hall. His ermine-trimmed robe was very hot, and the crown was beginning to give him a headache. He most definitely wanted to return to his apartment and change clothes.

The guards at the side door to the Hall bowed respectfully as he passed them and drew up into formation to accompany him. 'I'm not really going anyplace,' Garion told the sergeant in charge. 'Just back to my rooms, and I know the way. Why don't you and your men go have some lunch?'

'Your Majesty is very kind,' the sergeant replied. 'Will you need us later?'

'I'm not sure. I'll send somebody to let you know.'

The sergeant bowed again, and Garion went on along the dimly lighted corridor. He had found this passageway about two days after his coronation. It was relatively unused and it was the most direct route from the royal apartment to the throne room. Garion liked it because he could follow it to and from the great Hall with a minimum of pomp and ceremony. There were only a few doors, and the candles on the walls were spaced far enough apart to keep the light subdued. The dimness seemed comforting for some reason, almost as if it restored in some measure his anonymity.

He walked along, lost in thought. There were so many things to worry about. The impending war between the West and the Angarak kingdoms was uppermost in his mind. He, as Overlord of the West, would be expected to lead the West; and Kal Torak, awakened from his slumber, would come against him with the multitudes of Angarak. How could he possibly face so terrible an adversary? The very name of Torak chilled him, and what did he know about armies and battles? Inevitably, he would blunder, and Torak would smash all the forces of the West with one mailed fist.

Not even sorcery could help him. His own power was still too untried to risk a confrontation with Torak. Aunt Pol would do her best to aid him, of course, but without Belgarath they had little hope of success; and Belgarath had still not given any indication that his collapse had not permanently impaired his abilities.

Garion did not want to think about that any more, but his other problems were nearly as bad. Very soon he was going to have to come to grips with Ce'Nedra's adamant refusal to make peace. If she would only be reasonable, Garion was sure that the marginal difference in their rank would not make all that much difference. He liked Ce'Nedra. He was even prepared to admit that his feelings for her went quite a bit deeper than that. She could – usually when she wanted something – be absolutely adorable. If they could just get past this one minor problem, things might turn out rather well. That possibility brightened his thoughts considerably. Musing about it, he continued on down the corridor.

He had gone only a few more yards when he heard

that furtive step behind him again. He sighed, wishing that his everpresent attendant would find some other amusement. Then he shrugged and, deep in thought about the Nyissan question, he continued on along the corridor.

The warning was quite sharp and came at the last instant. '*Look out!*' the voice in his mind barked at him. Not knowing exactly why, not even actually thinking about it, Garion reacted instantly, diving headlong to the floor. His crown went rolling as, with a great shower of sparks, a thrown dagger clashed into the stone wall and went bouncing and skittering along the flagstones. Garion swore, rolled quickly and came to his feet with his own dagger in his hand. Outraged and infuriated by this sudden attack, he ran back along the corridor, his ermine-trimmed robe flapping and tangling cumbersomely around his legs.

He caught only one or two momentary glimpses of his gray-cloaked attacker as he ran after the knife thrower. The assassin dodged into a recessed doorway some yards down the corridor, and Garion heard a heavy door slam behind the fleeing man. When he reached the door and wrenched it open, his dagger still in his fist, he found only another long, dim passageway. There was no one in sight.

His hands were shaking, but it was more from anger than from fright. He briefly considered calling the guards, but almost immediately dismissed that idea. To continue following the assailant was, the more he thought about it, even more unwise. He had no weapon but his dagger, and the possibility of meeting someone armed with a sword occurred to him. There might even be more than one involved in this business, and these dimly lighted and deserted corridors were most certainly not a good place for confrontations.

As he started to close the door, something caught his eye. A small scrap of gray wool lay on the floor just at the edge of the door frame. Garion bent, picked it up and carried it over to one of the candles hanging along the wall. The bit of wool was no more than two fingers wide and seemed to have been torn from the corner of a gray Rivan cloak. In his haste to escape, the assassin had, Garion surmised, inadvertently slammed the door on his own cape, and then had ripped off this fragment in his flight. Garion's eyes narrowed and he turned and hurried back up the corridor, stooping once to retrieve his crown and again to pick up his assailant's dagger. He looked around once. The hallway was empty and somehow threatening. If the unknown knife thrower were to return with three or four companions, things could turn unpleasant. All things considered, it might be best to get back to his own apartments as quickly as possible – and to lock his door. Since there was no one around to witness any lack of dignity, Garion lifted the skirts of his royal robe and bolted like a rabbit for safety.

He reached his own door, jerked it open and jumped inside, closing and locking it behind him. He stood with his ear against the door, listening for any sounds of pursuit.

'Is something wrong, your Majesty?'

Garion almost jumped out of his skin. He whirled to confront his valet, whose eyes widened as he saw the daggers in the king's hands. 'Uh – nothing' he replied quickly, trying to cover his confusion. 'Help me out of this thing.' He struggled with the fastenings of his robe. His hands seemed to be full of daggers and crowns. With a negligent flip he tossed his crown into a nearby chair, sheathed his own dagger and then carefully laid the other knife and the scrap of wool cloth on the polished table.

The valet helped him to remove the robe and then carefully folded it over his arm. 'Would your Majesty like to have me get rid of these for you?' he asked, looking a bit distastefully at the dagger and the bit of wool on the table.

'No,' Garion told him firmly. Then a thought occurred to him. 'Do you know where my sword is?' he asked.

'Your Majesty's sword hangs in the throne room,' the valet replied.

'Not that one,' Garion said. 'The other one. The one I was wearing when I first came here.'

'I suppose I could find it,' the valet answered a bit dubiously.

'Do that,' Garion said. 'I think I'd like to have it where I can get my hands on it. And please see if you can find Lelldorin of Wildantor for me. I need to talk to him.'

'At once, your Majesty.' The valet bowed and quietly left the room.

Garion took up the dagger and the scrap of cloth and examined both rather closely. The dagger was just a commonplace knife, heavy, sturdily made and with a wirebound hilt. It bore no ornaments or identifying marks of any kind. Its tip was slightly bent, the result of its contact with the stone wall. Whoever had thrown it had thrown very hard. Garion developed a definitely uncomfortable sensation between his shoulder blades. The dagger would probably not be very useful. There were undoubtedly a hundred like it in the Citadel. The wool scrap, on the other hand, might prove to be very valuable. Somewhere in this fortress, there was a man with the corner of his cloak torn off. The torn cloak and this little piece of cloth would very likely match rather closely.

About a half an hour later Lelldorin arrived. 'You sent for me, Garion?' he asked.

'Sit down, Lelldorin,' Garion told his friend, then pointedly waited until the valet left the room. 'I think I've got a little bit of a problem,' he said then, sprawling deeper in the chair by the table. 'I wondered if I might ask your help.'

'You know you don't have to ask, Garion,' the earnest young Asturian told him.

'This has to be just between the two of us,' Garion cautioned. 'I don't want anyone else to know.'

'My word of honor on it,' Lelldorin replied instantly.

Garion slid the dagger across the table to his friend. 'A little while ago when I was on my way back here, somebody threw this at me.'

Lelldorin gasped and his eyes went wide. 'Treason?' he gasped.

'Either that or something personal,' Garion replied. 'I don't know what it's all about.'

'You must alert your guards,' Lelldorin declared, jumping to his feet.

'No,' Garion answered firmly. 'If I do that, they'll lock me up entirely. I don't have very much freedom left at all, and I don't want to lose it.'

'Did you see him at all?' Lelldorin asked, sitting down again and examining the dagger.

'Just his back. He was wearing one of those gray cloaks.'

'All Rivans wear gray cloaks, Garion.'

'We do have something to work with, though.' Garion took the scrap of wool out from under his tunic. 'After he threw the knife, he ran through a door and slammed it shut behind him. He caught his cloak in the door and this got ripped off.'

Lelldorin examined the bit of cloth. 'It looks like a corner,' he noted.

'That's what I think, too,' Garion agreed. 'If we both

keep our eyes open, we might just happen to see somebody with the corner of his cloak missing. Then, if we can get our hands on his cloak, we might be able to see if this piece matches.'

Lelldorin nodded his agreement, his face hardening. 'When we find him, though, *I* want to deal with him. A king isn't supposed to become personally involved in that sort of thing.'

'I might decide to suspend the rules,' Garion said grimly. 'I don't like having knives thrown at me. But let's find out who it is first.'

'I'll start at once,' Lelldorin said, rising quickly. 'I'll examine every corner of every cloak in Riva if I have to. We'll find this traitor, Garion. I promise you.'

Garion felt better after that, but it was still a wary young king who, in the company of a detachment of guards, went late that afternoon to the private apartments of the Rivan Warder. He looked about constantly as he walked, and his hand was never far from the hilt of the sword at his waist.

He found Brand seated before a large harp. The Warder's big hands seemed to caress the strings of the instrument, bringing forth a plaintively rippling melody. The big, grim man's face was soft and reflective as he played, and Garion found that the music was even more beautiful because it was so unexpected.

'You play very well, my Lord,' he said respectfully as the last notes of the song lingered in the strings.

'I play often, your Majesty,' Brand replied. 'Sometimes as I play I can even forget that my wife is no longer with me.' He rose from the chair in front of the harp and squared his shoulders, all softness going out of his face. 'How may I serve you, King Belgarion?'

Garion cleared his throat a trifle nervously. 'I'm probably not going to say this very well,' he admitted, 'but please take it the way I mean it and not the way it might come out.'

'Certainly, your Majesty.'

'I didn't ask for all this, you know,' Garion began with a vague gesture that took in the entire Citadel. 'The crown, I mean, and being king – all of it. I was really pretty happy the way I was.'

'Yes, your Majesty?'

'What I'm trying to get at is – well – you were the ruler here in Riva until I came along.'

Brand nodded soberly.

'I didn't really want to be king,' Garion rushed on, 'and I certainly didn't want to push you out of your position.'

Brand looked at him, and then he slowly smiled. 'I'd wondered why you seemed so uneasy whenever I came into the room, your Majesty. Is that what's been making you uncomfortable?'

Mutely, Garion nodded.

'You don't really know us yet, Belgarion,' Brand told him. 'You've only been here for a little more than a month. We're a peculiar sort of people. For over three thousand years we've been protecting the Orb – ever since Iron-grip came to this island. That's why we exist, and I think that one of the things we've lost along the way is that sense of self other men seem to feel is so important. Do you know why I'm called Brand?'

'I never really thought about it,' Garion admitted.

'I do have another name, of course,' Brand said, 'but I'm not supposed ever to mention it. Each Warder has been called Brand so that there could never be any sense of personal glory in the office. We serve the Orb; that's our only purpose. To be quite honest with you, I'm really rather glad you came when you did. It was getting close to the time when I was supposed to choose my

226

successor – with the help of the Orb, of course. But I didn't have the faintest idea whom to choose. Your arrival has relieved me of that task.'

'We can be friends, then?'

'I think we already are, Belgarion,' Brand replied gravely. 'We both serve the same master, and that always brings men close together.'

Garion hesitated. 'Am I doing all right?' he blurted.

Brand considered that. 'Some of the things you've done weren't exactly the way I might have done them, but that's to be expected. Rhodar and Anheg don't always do things the same way either. Each of us has his own particular manner.'

'They make fun of me, don't they – Anheg, Rhodar, and the others. I hear all the clever remarks every time I make a decision.'

'I wouldn't worry too much about that, Belgarion. They're Alorns, and Alorns don't take kings very seriously. They make fun of each other too, you know. You could almost say that as long as they're joking, everything is all right. If they suddenly become very serious and formal, then you'll know that you're in trouble.'

'I suppose I hadn't thought of it that way,' Garion admitted.

'You'll get used to it in time,' Brand assured him.

Garion felt much better after his conversation with Brand. In the company of his guards he started back toward the royal apartments; but part way there, he changed his mind and went looking for Aunt Pol instead. When he entered her rooms, his cousin Adara was sitting quietly with her, watching as Aunt Pol carefully mended one of Garion's old tunics. The girl rose and curtsied formally.

'Please Adara,' he said in a pained voice, 'don't do

227

that when we're alone. I see enough of it out there.' He gestured in the direction of the more public parts of the building.

'Whatever your Majesty wishes,' she replied.

'And don't call me that. I'm still just Garion.'

She looked gravely at him with her calm, beautiful eyes. 'No, cousin,' she disagreed, 'you'll never be "just Garion" any more.'

He sighed as the truth of that struck his heart.

'If you'll excuse me,' she said then, 'I must go attend Queen Silar. She's a bit unwell, and she says it comforts her to have me near.'

'It comforts all of us when you're near,' Garion told her without even thinking about it.

She smiled at him fondly.

'There might be some hope for him after all,' Aunt Pol observed, her needle busy.

Adara looked at Garion. 'He has never really been that bad, Lady Polgara,' she said. She inclined her head toward them both and quietly left the room.

Garion wandered around for a few moments and then flung himself into a chair. A great deal had happened that day, and he felt suddenly at odds with the whole world.

Aunt Pol continued to sew.

'Why are you doing that?' Garion demanded finally. 'I'll never wear that old thing again.'

'It needs fixing, dear,' she told him placidly.

'There are a hundred people around who could do it for you.'

'I prefer to do it myself.'

'Put it down and talk to me.'

She set the tunic aside and looked at him inquiringly. 'And what did your Majesty wish to discuss?' she inquired.

'Aunt Pol!' Garion's voice was stricken. 'Not you too.'

'Don't give orders then, dear,' she recommended, picking up the tunic again.

Garion watched her at her sewing for a few moments, not really knowing what to say. A strange thought occurred to him. 'Why *are* you doing that, Aunt Pol?' he asked, really curious this time. 'Probably nobody'll ever use it again, so you're just wasting time on it.'

'It's my time, dear,' she reminded him. She looked up from her sewing, her eyes unreadable. Then, without explanation she held up the tunic with one hand and ran the forefinger of her other hand carefully up the rip. Garion felt a very light surge, and the sound was only a whisper. The rip mended itself before his eyes, rewoven as if it had never existed. 'Now you can see how completely useless mending it really is,' she told him.

'Why do you do it then?'

'Because I like to sew, dear,' she replied. With a sharp little jerk she ripped the tunic again. Then she picked up her needle and patiently began repairing the rip. 'Sewing keeps the hands and eyes busy, but leaves the mind free for other things. It's very relaxing.'

'Sometimes you're awfully complicated, Aunt Pol.'

'Yes, dear. I know.'

Garion paced about for a bit, then suddenly knelt beside her chair and, pushing her sewing aside, he put his head into her lap. 'Oh, Aunt Pol,' he said, very close to tears.

'What's the matter, dear?' she asked, carefully smoothing his hair.

'I'm so *lonely*.'

'Is *that* all?'

He lifted his head and stared at her incredulously. He had not expected that.

'Everyone is lonely, dear,' she explained, drawing

him close to her. 'We touch other people only briefly, then we're alone again. You'll get used to it in time.'

'Nobody will talk to me now – not the way they did before. They're always bowing and saying "Your Majesty" to me.'

'You are the king, after all,' she replied.

'But I don't want to be.'

'That's too bad. It's the destiny of your family, so there's not a thing you can do about it. Did anyone ever tell you about Prince Gared?'

'I don't think so. Who was he?'

'He was the only survivor when the Nyissan assassins killed King Gorek and his family. He escaped by throwing himself into the sea.'

'How old was he?'

'Six. He was a very brave child. Everyone thought that he had drowned and that his body had been washed out to sea. Your grandfather and I encouraged that belief. For thirteen hundred years we've hidden Prince Gared's descendants. For generations they've lived out their lives in quiet obscurity for the single purpose of bringing *you* to the throne – and now you say that you don't want to be king?'

'I don't know any of those people,' he said sullenly. He knew he was behaving badly, but he couldn't seem to help himself.

'Would it help if you did know them – some of them anyway?'

The question baffled him.

'Perhaps it might,' she decided. She laid her sewing aside and stood up, drawing him to his feet. 'Come with me,' she told him and led him to the tall window that looked out over the city below. There was a small balcony outside; in one corner where a rain-gutter had cracked, there had built up during the fall and winter a sheet of shiny black ice, curving down over the railing and spreading out on the balcony floor.

Aunt Pol unlatched the window and it swung open, admitting a blast of icy air that made the candles dance. 'Look directly into the ice, Garion,' she told him, pointing at the glittering blackness. 'Look deep into it.'

He did as she told him and felt the force of her mind at work.

Something was in the ice – shapeless at first but emerging slowly and becoming more and more visible. It was, he saw finally, the figure of a pale blonde woman, quite lovely and with a warm smile on her lips. She seemed young, and her eyes were directly on Garion's face. 'My baby,' a voice seemed to whisper to him. 'My little Garion.'

Garion began to tremble violently. 'Mother?' he gasped.

'So tall now,' the whisper continued. 'Almost a man.'

'And already a king, Ildera,' Aunt Pol told the phantom in a gentle voice.

'Then he *was* the chosen one,' the ghost of Garion's mother exulted. 'I knew it. I could feel it when I carried him under my heart.'

A second shape had begun to appear beside the first. It was a tall young man with dark hair but a strangely familiar face. Garion clearly saw its resemblance to his own. 'Hail Belgarion, my son,' the second shape said to him.

'Father,' Garion replied, not knowing what else to say.

'Our blessings, Garion,' the second ghost said as the two figures started to fade.

'I avenged you, father,' Garion called after them. It seemed important that they know that. He was never sure, however, if they had heard him.

Aunt Pol was leaning against the window frame with a look of exhaustion on her face.

'Are you all right?' Garion asked her, concerned.

'It's a very difficult thing to do, dear,' she told him, passing a weary hand over her face.

But there was yet another flicker within the depths of the ice, and the familiar shape of the blue wolf appeared – the one who had joined Belgarath in the fight with Grul the Eldrak in the mountains of Ulgo. The wolf sat looking at them for a moment, then flickered briefly into the shape of a snowy owl and finally became a tawny-haired woman with golden eyes. Her face was so like Aunt Pol's that Garion could not help glancing quickly back and forth to compare them.

'You left it open, Polgara,' the golden-eyed woman said gently. Her voice was as warm and soft as a summer evening.

'Yes, mother,' Aunt Pol replied. 'I'll close it in a moment.'

'It's all right, Polgara,' the wolf-woman told her daughter. 'It gave me the chance to meet him.' She looked directly into Garion's face. 'A touch or two is still there,' she observed. 'A bit about the eyes and in the shape of the jaw. Does he know?'

'Not everything, mother,' Aunt Pol answered.

'Perhaps it's as well,' Poledra noted.

Once again another figure emerged out of the dark depths of the ice. The second woman had hair like sunlight, and her face was even more like Aunt Pol's than Poledra's. 'Polgara, my dear sister,' she said.

'Beldaran,' Aunt Pol responded in a voice over-whelmed with love.

'And Belgarion,' Garion's ultimate grandmother said, 'the final flower of my love and Riva's.'

'Our blessings also, Belgarion,' Poledra declared.

'Farewell for now, but know that we love thee.' And then the two were gone.

'Does that help?' Aunt Pol asked him, her voice deep with emotion and her eyes filled with tears.

Garion was too stunned by what he had just seen and heard to answer. Dumbly he nodded.

'I'm glad the effort wasn't wasted then,' she said. 'Please close the window, dear. It's letting the winter in.'

Chapter Fourteen

It was the first day of spring, and King Belgarion of Riva was terribly nervous. He had watched the approach of Princess Ce'Nedra's sixteenth birthday with a steadily mounting anxiety and, now that the day had finally arrived, he hovered on the very edge of panic. The deep blue brocade doublet over which a half dozen tailors had labored for weeks still did not seem to feel just right. Somehow it was a bit tight across the shoulders, and the stiff collar scratched his neck. Moreover, his gold crown seemed unusually heavy on this particular day, and, as he fidgeted, his throne seemed even more uncomfortable than usual.

The Hall of the Rivan King had been decorated extensively for the occasion, but even the banners and garlands of pale spring flowers could not mask the ominous starkness of the great throne room. The assembled notables, however, chatted and laughed among themselves as if nothing significant were taking place. Garion felt rather bitter about their heartless lack of concern in the face of what was about to happen to him.

Aunt Pol stood at the left side of his throne, garbed in a new silver gown and with a silver circlet about her hair. Belgarath lounged indolently on the right, wearing a new green doublet which had already become rumpled.

'Don't squirm so much, dear,' Aunt Pol told Garion calmly.

'That was easy enough for *you* to say,' Garion retorted in an accusing tone.

'Try not to think about it,' Belgarath advised. 'It will all be over in a little while.'

Then Brand, his face seeming even more bleak than usual, entered the Hall from the side door and came to the dais. 'There's a Nyissan at the gate of the Citadel, your Majesty,' he said quietly. 'He says that he's an emissary of Queen Salmissra and that he's here to witness the ceremony.'

'Isn't that impossible?' Garion asked Aunt Pol, startled by the Warder's surprising announcement.

'Not entirely,' she replied. 'More likely, though, it's a diplomatic fiction. I'd imagine that the Nyissans would prefer to keep Salmissra's condition a secret.'

'What do I do?' Garion asked.

Belgarath shrugged. 'Let him in.'

'In here?' Brand's voice was shocked. 'A Nyissan in the throne room? Belgarath, you're not serious.'

'Garion is Overlord of the West, Brand,' the old man replied, 'and that includes Nyissa. I don't imagine that the snakepeople will be much use to us at any time, but let's be polite, at least.'

Brand's face went stiff with disapproval. 'What is your Majesty's decision?' he asked Garion directly.

'Well—' Garion hesitated. 'Let him come in, I guess.'

'Don't vacillate, Garion,' Aunt Pol told him firmly.

'I'm sorry,' Garion said quickly.

'And don't apologize,' she added. 'Kings do not apologize.'

He looked at her helplessly. Then he turned back to Brand. 'Tell the emissary from Nyissa to join us,' he said, though his tone was placating.

'By the way, Brand,' Belgarath suggested, 'I wouldn't let anyone get too excited about this. The Nyissan has

235

ambassadorial status, and it would be a serious breach of protocol if he were to die unexpectedly.'

Brand bowed rather stiffly, turned, and left the Hall.

'Was that really necessary, father?' Aunt Pol asked.

'Old grudges die hard, Pol,' Belgarath replied. 'Sometimes it's best to get everything right out in front so that there aren't any misunderstandings later.'

When the emissary of the Snake Queen entered the Hall, Garion started with surprise. It was Sadi, the chief eunuch in Salmissra's palace. The thin man with the dead-looking eyes and shaved head wore the customary iridescent blue-green Nyissan robe, and he bowed sinuously as he approached the throne. 'Greetings to his Majesty, Belgarion of Riva, from Eternal Salmissra, Queen of the Snake-People,' he intoned in his peculiarly contralto voice.

'Welcome, Sadi,' Garion replied formally.

'My queen sends her regards on this happy day,' Sadi continued.

'She didn't really, did she?' Garion asked a bit pointedly.

'Not precisely, your Majesty,' Sadi admitted without the least trace of embarrassment. 'I'm sure she would have, however, if we'd been able to make her understand what was happening.'

'How is she?' Garion remembered the dreadful transformation Salmissra had undergone.

'Difficult,' Sadi answered blandly. 'Of course that's nothing new. Fortunately she sleeps for a week or two after she's been fed. She moulted last month, and it made her dreadfully short-tempered.' He rolled his eyes ceilingward. 'It was ghastly,' he murmured. 'She bit three servants before it was over. They all died immediately, of course.'

'She's venomous?' Garion was a bit startled at that.

'She's always been venomous, your Majesty.'

'That's not the way I mean.'

'Forgive my little joke,' Sadi apologized. 'Judging from the reactions of people she's bitten, I'd guess that she's at least ten times more deadly than a common cobra.'

'Is she terribly unhappy?' Garion felt a strange pity for the hideously altered queen.

'That's really rather hard to say, your Majesty,' Sadi replied clinically. 'It's difficult to tell what a snake's really feeling, you understand. By the time she'd learned to communicate her wishes to us, she seemed to have become reconciled to her new form. We feed her and keep her clean. As long as she has her mirror and someone to bite when she's feeling peevish, she seems quite content.'

'She still looks at herself in the mirror? I wouldn't think she'd want to now.'

'Our race has a somewhat different view of the serpent, your Majesty,' Sadi explained. 'We find it a rather attractive creature, and our queen is a splendid-looking snake, after all. Her new skin is quite lovely, and she seems very proud of it.' He turned and bowed deeply to Aunt Pol. 'Lady Polgara,' he greeted her.

'Sadi,' she acknowledged with a brief nod.

'May I convey to you the heartfelt thanks of her Majesty's government?'

One of Aunt Pol's eyebrows rose inquiringly.

'The government, my Lady – not the queen herself. Your – ah – intervention, shall we say, has simplified things in the palace enormously. We no longer have to worry about Salmissra's whims and peculiar appetites. We rule by committee and we hardly ever find it necessary to poison each other any more. No one's tried to poison me for months. It's all very smooth and

237

civilized in Sthiss Tor now.' He glanced briefly at Garion. 'May I also offer my congratulations on your success with his Majesty? He seems to have matured considerably. He was really very callow when last we met.'

'Whatever happened to Issus?' Garion asked him, ignoring that particular observation.

Sadi shrugged. 'Issus? Oh, he's still about, scratching out a living as a paid assassin, probably. I imagine that one day we'll find him floating facedown in the river. It's the sort of end one expects for someone like that.'

There was a sudden blare of trumpets from just beyond the great doors at the back of the Hall. Garion started nervously, and his mouth quite suddenly went dry.

The heavy doors swung open, and a double file of Tolnedran legionnaires marched in, their breastplates burnished until they shone like mirrors, and the tall crimson plumes on their helmets waving as they marched. The inclusion of the legionnaires in the ceremony had infuriated Brand. The Rivan Warder had stalked about in icy silence for days after he had discovered that Garion had granted ambassador Valgon's request for a proper escort for Princess Ce'Nedra. Brand did not like Tolnedrans, and he had been looking forward to witnessing the pride of the empire humbled by Ce'Nedra's forlorn and solitary entrance into the Hall. The presence of the legionnaires spoiled that, of course, and Brand's disappointment and disapproval had been painfully obvious. As much as Garion wanted to stay on Brand's good side, however, he did not intend to start off the official relationship between his bride-to-be and himself by publicly humiliating her. Garion was quite ready to acknowledge his lack of education, but he was not prepared to admit to being *that* stupid.

When Ce'Nedra entered, her hand resting lightly on Valgon's arm, she was every inch an Imperial Princess. Garion could only gape at her. Although the Accords of Vo Mimbre required that she present herself in her wedding gown, Garion was totally unprepared for such Imperial magnificence. Her gown was of gold and white brocade covered with seed pearls, and its train swept the floor behind her. Her flaming hair was intricately curled and cascaded over her left shoulder like a deep crimson waterfall. Her circlet of tinted gold held in place a short veil that did not so much conceal her face as soften it into luminousness. She was tiny and perfect, exquisite beyond belief, but her eyes were like little green agates.

She and Valgon moved at stately pace down between the ranks of her tall, burnished legionnaires; when they reached the front of the hall, they stopped.

Brand, sober-faced and imposing, took his staff of office from Bralon, his eldest son, and rapped sharply on the stone floor with its butt three times. 'Her Imperial Highness Ce'Nedra of the Tolnedran Empire,' he announced in a deep, booming voice. 'Will your Majesty grant her audience?'

'I will receive the princess,' Garion declared, straightening a bit on his throne.

'The Princess Ce'Nedra may approach the throne,' Brand proclaimed. Though his words were ritual formality, they had obviously been chosen with great care to make it absolutely clear that Imperial Tolnedra came to the Hall of the Rivan King as a suppliant. Ce'Nedra's eyes flashed fire, and Garion groaned inwardly. The little princess, however, glided to the appointed spot before the dais and curtsied regally. There was no submission in that gesture.

'The Princess has permission to speak,' Brand

boomed. For a brief, irrational moment Garion wanted to strangle him.

Ce'Nedra drew herself up, her face as cold as a winter sea. 'Thus I, Ce'Nedra, daughter to Ran Borune XXIII and Princess of Imperial Tolnedra, present myself as required by treaty and law in the presence of His Majesty, Belgarion of Riva,' she declared. 'And thus has the Tolnedran Empire once more demonstrated her willingness to fulfill her obligations as set forth in the Accords of Vo Mimbre. Let other kingdoms witness Tolnedra's meticulous response and follow her example in meeting their obligations. I declare before these witnesses that I am an unmarried virgin of a suitable age. Will his Majesty consent to take me to wife?'

Garion's reply had been carefully thought out. The quiet inner voice had suggested a way to head off years of marital discord. He rose to his feet and said, 'I, Belgarion, King of Riva, hereby consent to take the Imperial Princess Ce'Nedra to be my wife and queen. I declare, moreover, that she will rule jointly by my side in Riva and wheresoever else the authority of our throne may extend.'

The gasp that rippled through the Hall was clearly audible, and Brand's face went absolutely white. The look Ce'Nedra gave Garion was quizzical, and her eyes softened slightly. 'Your majesty is too kind,' she responded with a graceful little curtsy. Some of the edge had gone out of her voice, and she threw a quick sidelong glance at the spluttering Brand. 'Have I your Majesty's permission to withdraw?' she asked sweetly.

'As your Highness wishes,' Garion replied, sinking back down onto his throne. He was perspiring heavily.

The princess curtsied again with a mischievous little twinkle in her eyes, then turned and left the Hall with her legionnaires drawn up in close order about her.

As the great doors boomed shut behind her, an angry buzz ran through the crowd. The word 'outrageous' seemed to be the most frequently repeated.

'This is unheard of, your Majesty,' Brand protested.

'Not entirely,' Garion replied defensively. 'The throne of Arendia is held jointly by King Korodullin and Queen Mayaserana.' He looked to Mandorallen, gleaming in his armor, with a mute appeal in his eyes.

'His Majesty speaks truly, my Lord Brand,' Mandorallen declared. 'I assure thee that our kingdom suffers not from the lack of singularity upon the throne.'

'That's Arendia,' Brand objected. 'This is Riva. The situations are entirely different. No Alorn kingdom has ever been ruled by a woman.'

'It might not hurt to examine the possible advantages of the situation,' King Rhodar suggested. 'My own queen, for example, plays a somewhat more significant role in Drasnian affairs than custom strictly allows.'

With great difficulty Brand regained at least some of his composure. 'May I withdraw, your Majesty?' he asked, his face still livid.

'If you wish,' Garion answered quietly. It wasn't going well. Brand's conservatism was the one stumbling block he hadn't considered.

'It's an interesting notion, dear,' Aunt Pol said quietly to him, 'but don't you think it might have been better to consult with someone before you made it a public declaration?'

'Won't it help to cement relations with the Tolnedrans?'

'Quite possibly,' she admitted. 'I'm not saying that it's a bad idea, Garion; I just think it might have been better to warn a few people first. What *are* you laughing at?' she demanded of Belgarath, who was leaning against the throne convulsed with mirth.

'The Bear-cult's going to have collective apoplexy,' he chortled.

Her eyes widened slightly. 'Oh, dear,' she said. 'I'd forgotten about them.'

'They aren't going to like it very much, are they?' Garion concluded. 'Particularly since Ce'Nedra's a Tolnedran.'

'I think you can count on them to go up in flames,' the old sorcerer replied, still laughing.

In the days that followed, the usually bleak halls of the Citadel were filled with color as official visitors and representatives teemed through them, chatting, gossiping, and conducting business in out-of-the-way corners. The rich and varied gifts they had brought to celebrate the occasion filled several tables lining one of the walls in the great throne room. Garion, however, was unable to visit or to examine the gifts. He spent his days in a room with his advisers and with the Tolnedran ambassador and his staff as the details of the official betrothal document were hammered out.

Valgon had seized on Garion's break with tradition and was trying to wring the last measure of advantage from it, while Brand was desperately trying to add clauses and stipulations to circumscribe Ce'Nedra's authority rigidly. As the two haggled back and forth, Garion found himself more and more frequently staring out the window. The sky over Riva was an intense blue, and puffy white clouds ran before the wind. The bleak crags of the island were touched with the first green blush of spring. Faintly, carried by the wind, the high, clear voice of a shepherdess singing to her flock wafted through the open window. There was a pure, un-schooled quality to her voice, and she sang with no hint of self-consciousness as if there were not a human ear within a hundred leagues. Garion sighed as the last notes of her song died away and then returned his attention to the tedious negotiations.

His attention, however, was divided in those early days of spring. Since he was unable to pursue the search for the man with the torn cloak himself, he was forced to rely on Lelldorin to press the investigation. Lelldorin was not always entirely reliable, and the search for the would-be assassin seemed to fire the enthusiastic young Asturian's imagination. He crept about the Citadel with dark, sidelong glances, and reported his lack of findings in conspiratorial whispers. Turning things over to Lelldorin might have been a mistake, but there had been no real choice in the matter. Any of Garion's other friends would have immediately raised a general outcry, and the entire affair would have been irrevocably out in the open. Garion did not want that. He was not prepared to make any decisions about the assassin until he found out who had thrown the knife and why. Too many other things could have been involved. Only Lelldorin could be relied upon for absolute secrecy, even though there was some danger in turning him loose in the Citadel with a license to track someone down. Lelldorin had a way of turning simple things into catastrophes, and Garion worried almost as much about that as he did about the possibility of another knife hurtling out of the shadows toward his unprotected back.

Among the visitors present for the betrothal ceremonies was Ce'Nedra's cousin Xera, who was present as the personal representative of Queen Xantha. Though shy at first, the Dryad soon lost her reserve – particularly when she found herself the center of the attention of a cluster of smitten young noblemen.

The gift of Queen Xantha to the royal couple was, Garion thought, somewhat peculiar. Wrapped in plain leaves, Xera presented them with two sprouted acorns. Ce'Nedra, however, seemed delighted. She insisted upon planting the two seeds immediately and rushed down to the small private garden adjoining the royal apartments.

'It's very nice, I suppose,' Garion commented dubiously as he stood watching his princess on her knees in the damp loam of the garden, busily preparing the earth to receive Queen Xantha's gift.

Ce'Nedra looked at him sharply. 'I don't believe your Majesty understands the significance of the gift,' she said in that hatefully formal tone she had assumed with him.

'Stop that,' Garion told her crossly. 'I still have a name, after all – and I'm almost positive you haven't forgotten it.'

'If your Majesty insists,' she replied loftily.

'My Majesty does. What's so significant about a couple of nuts?'

She looked at him almost pityingly. 'You wouldn't understand.'

'Not if you won't take the trouble to explain it to me.'

'Very well.' She sounded irritatingly superior. 'The one acorn is from my very own tree. The other is from Queen Xantha's.'

'So?'

'See how impossibly dense he is,' the princess said to her cousin.

'He's not a Dryad, Ce'Nedra,' Xera replied calmly.

'Obviously.'

Xera turned to Garion. 'The acorns are not really from my mother,' she explained. 'They're gifts from the trees themselves.'

'Why didn't you tell me that in the first place?' Garion demanded of Ce'Nedra.

She sniffed and returned to her digging.

'While they're still just young shoots, Ce'Nedra will bind them together,' Xera went on. 'The shoots will intertwine as they grow, embracing each other and forming a single tree. It's the Dryad symbol for marriage. The two will become one – just as you and Ce'Nedra will.'

'That remains to be seen,' Ce'Nedra sniffed, trowelling busily in the dirt.

Garion sighed. 'I hope the trees are patient.'

'Trees are very patient, Garion,' Xera replied. She made a little gesture that Ce'Nedra could not see, and Garion followed her to the other end of the garden.

'She does love you, you know,' Xera told him quietly. 'She won't admit it, of course, but she loves you. I know her well enough to see that.'

'Why's she acting the way she is, then?'

'She doesn't like being forced into things, that's all.'

'I'm not the one who's forcing her. Why take it out on me?'

'Whom else can she take it out on?'

Garion hadn't thought of that. He left the garden quietly. Xera's words gave him some hope that one of his problems, at least, might eventually be resolved. Ce'Nedra would pout and storm for a while, and then – after she had made him suffer enough – she would relent. Perhaps it might speed things along if he suffered a bit more obviously.

The other problems had not changed significantly. He was still going to have to lead an army against Kal Torak; Belgarath had still given no sign that his power was intact; and someone in the Citadel was still, so far as Garion knew, sharpening another knife for him. He sighed and went back to his own rooms where he could worry in private.

Somewhat later he received word that Aunt Pol

wanted to see him in her private apartment. He went immediately and found her seated by the fire, sewing as usual. Belgarath, dressed in his shabby old clothes, sat in one of the deep, comfortable chairs on the other side of the fire with his feet up and a tankard in his hand.

'You wanted to see me, Aunt Pol?' Garion inquired as he entered.

'Yes, dear,' she replied. 'Sit down.' She looked at him somewhat critically. 'He still doesn't look much like a king, does he, father?'

'Give him time, Pol,' the old man told her. 'He hasn't been at it for very long.'

'You both knew all along, didn't you?' Garion accused them. 'Who I was, I mean.'

'Naturally,' Aunt Pol answered in that maddening way of hers.

'Well, if you'd wanted me to behave like a king, you should have told me about it. That way I'd have had some time to get used to the idea.'

'It seems to me we discussed this once before,' Belgarath mentioned, 'a long time ago. If you'll stop and think a bit, I'm sure you'll be able to see why we had to keep it a secret.'

'Maybe.' Garion said it a bit doubtfully. 'All this has happened too fast, though. I hadn't even got used to being a sorcerer yet, and now I have to be a king, too. It's all got me off balance.'

'You're adaptable, Garion,' Aunt Pol told him, her needle flickering.

'You'd better give him the amulet, Pol,' Belgarath mentioned. 'The princess should be here soon.'

'I was just about to, father,' she replied, laying aside her sewing.

'What's this?' Garion asked.

'The princess has a gift for you,' Aunt Pol said. 'A ring. It's a bit ostentatious, but act suitably pleased.'

'Shouldn't I have something to give her in return?'

'I've already taken care of that, dear.' She took a small velvet box from the table beside her chair. 'You'll give her this.' She handed the box to Garion.

Inside the box lay a silver amulet, a bit smaller than Garion's own. Represented on its face in minute and exquisite detail was the likeness of that huge tree which stood in solitary splendor in the center of the Vale of Aldur. There was a crown woven into the branches. Garion held the amulet in his right hand, trying to determine if it had some of the same kind of force about it that he knew was in the one he wore. There was something there, but it didn't feel at all the same.

'It doesn't seem to be like ours,' he concluded.

'It isn't,' Belgarath replied. 'Not exactly, anyway. Ce'Nedra's not a sorceress, so she wouldn't be able to use one like yours.'

'You said "not exactly." It does have some kind of power then?'

'It will give her certain insights,' the old man answered, 'if she's patient enough to learn how to use it.'

'Exactly what are we talking about when we use the word "insight"?'

'An ability to see and hear things she wouldn't otherwise be able to see or hear,' Belgarath specified.

'Is there anything else I should know about it before she gets here?'

'Just tell her that it's a family heirloom,' Aunt Pol suggested. 'It belonged to my sister, Beldaran.'

'You should keep it, Aunt Pol,' Garion objected. 'I can get something else for the princess.'

'No, dear. Beldaran wants her to have it.'

Garion found Aunt Pol's habit of speaking of people long dead in the present tense a trifle disconcerting, so he didn't pursue the matter.

There was a light tap on the door.

'Come in, Ce'Nedra,' Aunt Pol answered.

The little princess was wearing a rather plain green gown open at the throat, and her expression was somewhat subdued. 'Come over by the fire,' Aunt Pol told her. 'The evenings are still a bit chilly this time of year.'

'Is it always this cold and damp in Riva?' Ce'Nedra asked, coming to the fire.

'We're a long ways north of Tol Honeth,' Garion pointed out.

'I'm aware of that,' she said with that little edge in her voice.

'I always thought it was customary to wait until *after* the wedding to start bickering,' Belgarath observed slyly. 'Have the rules changed?'

'Just practicing, Belgarath,' Ce'Nedra replied impishly. 'Just practicing for later on.'

The old man laughed. 'You can be a charming little girl when you put your mind to it,' he said.

Ce'Nedra bowed mockingly. Then she turned to Garion. 'It's customary for a Tolnedran girl to give her betrothed a gift of a certain value,' she informed him. She held up a heavy, ornate ring set with several glowing stones. 'This ring belonged to Ran Horb II, the greatest of all Tolnedran Emperors. Wearing it *might* help you to be a better king.'

Garion sighed. It was going to be one of those meetings. 'I'll be honored to wear the ring,' he replied as inoffensively as possible, 'and I'd like for you to wear this.' He handed her the velvet box. 'It belonged to the wife of Riva Iron-grip, Aunt Pol's sister.'

Ce'Nedra took the box and opened it. 'Why, Garion,' she exclaimed, 'it's lovely.' She held the amulet in her hand turning it to catch the firelight. 'The tree looks so real that you can almost smell the leaves.'

'Thank you,' Belgarath replied modestly.

'*You* made it?' The princess sounded startled.

The old man nodded. 'When Polgara and Beldaran were children, we lived in the Vale. There weren't very many silversmiths there, so I had to make their amulets myself. Aldur helped me with some of the finer details.'

'This is a priceless gift, Garion.' The tiny girl actually glowed, and Garion began to have some hope for the future. 'Help me with it,' she commanded, handing him the two ends of the chain and turning with one hand holding aside the mass of her deep red hair.

'Do you accept the gift, Ce'Nedra?' Aunt Pol asked her, giving the question a peculiar emphasis.

'Of course I do,' the princess replied.

'Without reservation and of your own free will?' Aunt Pol pressed, her eyes intent.

'I accept the gift, Lady Polgara,' Ce'Nedra replied. 'Fasten it for me, Garion. Be sure it's secure. I wouldn't want it to come undone.'

'I don't think you'll need to worry too much about that,' Belgarath told her.

Garion's fingers trembled slightly as he fastened the curious clasp. His fingertips tingled peculiarly as the two ends locked together with a faintly audible click.

'Hold the amulet in your hand, Garion,' Aunt Pol instructed him. Ce'Nedra lifted her chin and Garion took the medallion in his right hand. Then Aunt Pol and Belgarath closed their hands over his. Something peculiar seemed to pass through their hands and into the talisman at Ce'Nedra's throat.

'Now you are sealed to us, Ce'Nedra,' Aunt Pol told

the princess quietly, 'with a tie that can never be broken.'

Ce'Nedra looked at her with a puzzled expression, and then her eyes slowly widened and a dreadful suspicion began to grow in them. 'Take it off,' she told Garion sharply.

'He can't do that,' Belgarath informed her, sitting back down and picking up his tankard again.

Ce'Nedra was tugging at the chain, pulling with both hands.

'You'll just scratch your neck, dear,' Aunt Pol warned gently. 'The chain won't break; it can't be cut; and it won't come off over your head. You'll never have to worry about losing it.'

'*You* did this,' the princess stormed at Garion.

'Did what?'

'Put this slave chain on me. It wasn't enough that I had to bow to you; now you've put me in chains as well.'

'I didn't know,' he protested.

'Liar!' she screamed at him. Then she turned and fled the room, sobbing bitterly.

Chapter Fifteen

Garion was in a sour mood. The prospect of another day of ceremony and tedious conferences was totally unbearable, and he had risen early to escape from the royal bedchamber before the insufferably polite appointment secretary with his endless lists could arrive to nail down the entire day. Garion privately detested the inoffensive fellow, even though he knew the man was only doing his job. A king's time had to be organized and scheduled, and it was the appointment secretary's task to take care of that. And so, each morning after breakfast, there came that respectful tapping at the door, and the appointment secretary would enter, bow, and then proceed to arrange the young king's day, minute by minute. Garion was morbidly convinced that somewhere, probably hidden away and closely guarded, was the ultimate master list that laid out the schedule for the rest of his life – including his royal funeral.

But this day dawned too gloriously for thoughts of stuffy formality and heavy conference. The sun had come boiling up out of the Sea of the Winds, touching the snowfields atop the craggy peaks with a blushing pink, and the morning shadows in the deep valleys above the city were a misty blue. The smell of spring pushed urgently in from the little garden outside his window, and Garion knew he must escape, if only for an hour or so. He dressed quickly in tunic, hose, and soft Rivan boots, rather carefully selecting clothes as unroyal as his wardrobe offered. Pausing only long enough to belt on his sword, he crept out of the royal apartment. He even considered not taking along his guards, but prudently decided against that.

They were at a standstill in the search for the man who had tried to kill him in that dim hallway, but both Lelldorin and Garion had discovered that the outer garments of any number of Rivans needed repair. The grey cloak was not a ceremonial garment, but rather was something thrown on for warmth. It was a sturdy, utilitarian covering, and quite a number of such robes had been allowed to fall into a condition of shocking disrepair. Moreover, now that spring was here, men would soon stop wearing them, and the only clue to the attacker's identity would be locked away in a closet somewhere.

Garion brooded about that as he wandered moodily through the silent corridors of the Citadel with two mailed guards following at a respectful distance. The attempt, he reasoned, had not come from a Grolim. Aunt Pol's peculiar ability to recognize the mind of a Grolim would have alerted her instantly. In all probability the attacker had not been a foreigner of any kind. There were too few foreigners on the island to make that very likely. It had to be a Rivan, but why would a Rivan want to kill the king who had just returned after thirteen hundred years?

He sighed with perplexity over the problem and let his mind drift off to other matters. He wished that he were only Garion again; he wished that more than anything. He wished that it might be possible for him to awaken in some out-of-the-way inn somewhere and start out in the silver light of daybreak to ride alone to the top of the next hill to see what lay beyond. He sighed again. He was a public person now, and such freedom was denied him. He was coldly certain that he was never going to have a moment to himself again.

As he passed an open doorway, he suddenly heard a familiar voice. 'Sin creeps into our minds the moment we let our thoughts stray,' Relg was saying. Garion stopped, motioning his guards to silence.

'Must everything be a sin?' Taiba asked. Inevitably they were together. They had been together almost continually from the moment Relg had rescued Taiba from her living entombment in the cave beneath Rak Cthol. Garion was almost certain that neither of them was actually conscious of that fact. Moreover, he had seen evidence of discomfort, not only on Taiba's face, but on Relg's as well, whenever they were apart. Something beyond the control of either of them drew them together.

'The world is filled with sin,' Relg declared. 'We must guard against it constantly. We must stand jealous guard over our purity against all forms of temptation.'

'That would be very tiresome.' Taiba sounded faintly amused.

'I thought you wanted instruction,' Relg accused her. 'If you just came here to mock me, I'll leave right now.'

'Oh, sit down, Relg,' she told him. 'We'll never get anywhere with this if you take offense at everything I say.'

'Have you no idea at all about the meaning of religion?' he asked after a moment. He actually sounded curious about it.

'In the slave pens, the word religion meant death. It meant having your heart cut out.'

'That was a Grolim perversion. Didn't you have a religion of your own?'

'The slaves came from all over the world, and they prayed to many Gods – usually for death.'

253

'What about your own people? Who is your God?'

'I was told that his name is Mara. We don't pray to him though – not since he abandoned us.'

'It's not man's place to accuse the Gods,' Relg told her sternly. 'Man's duty is to glorify his God and pray to him – even if the prayers aren't answered.'

'And what about the God's duty to man?' she asked pointedly. 'Can a God not be negligent as well as a man? Wouldn't you consider a God negligent if he allowed his children to be enslaved and butchered – or if he allowed his daughters to be given as a reward to other slaves when they pleased their masters – as I was?'

Relg struggled with that painful question.

'I think you've led a very sheltered life, Relg,' she told the zealot. 'I think you have a very limited idea of human suffering – of the kinds of things men can do to other men – and women – apparently with the full permission of the Gods.'

'You should have killed yourself,' he said stubbornly.

'Whatever for?'

'To avoid corruption, naturally.'

'You *are* an innocent, aren't you? I didn't kill myself because I wasn't ready to die. Even in the slave pens, life can be sweet, Relg, and death is bitter. What you call corruption is only a small thing – and not even always unpleasant.'

'Sinful woman!' he gasped.

'You worry too much about that, Relg,' she advised him. 'Cruelty is a sin; lack of compassion is a sin. But that other little thing? I hardly think so. I begin to wonder about you. Could it be that this UL of yours is not quite so stern and unforgiving as you seem to believe? Does he really want all these prayers and rituals and grovelings? Or are they your way to hide from your God? Do you think that praying in a loud voice and

254

pounding your head on the ground will keep him from seeing into your heart?'

Relg was making strangled noises.

'If our Gods really loved us, they'd want our lives filled with joy,' she continued relentlessly. 'But you hate joy for some reason – probably because you're afraid of it. Joy is not sin, Relg; joy is a kind of love, and I think the Gods approve of it – even if you don't.'

'You're hopelessly depraved.'

'Perhaps so,' she admitted casually, 'but at least I look life right in the face. I'm not afraid of it, and I don't try to hide from it.'

'Why are you doing this?' he demanded of her in an almost tragic voice. 'Why must you forever follow me and mock me with your eyes?'

'I don't really know,' she replied, sounding almost puzzled. 'You're not really that attractive. Since we left Rak Cthol, I've seen dozens of men who interested me much more. At first it was because I knew that I made you nervous and because you were afraid of me. I rather enjoyed that, but lately there's more to it than that. It doesn't make any sense, of course. You're what you are, and I'm what I am, but for some reason I want to be with you.' She paused. 'Tell me, Relg – and don't try to lie about it – would you *really* want me to go away and never see you again?'

There was a long and painful silence. 'May UL forgive me!' Relg groaned finally.

'I'm sure he will, Relg,' she assured him gently.

Garion moved quietly on down the corridor away from the open door. Something he had not understood before had begun to become quite clear. *'You're doing this, aren't you?'* he asked silently.

'Naturally,' the dry voice in his mind replied.

'But why those two?'

'Because it's necessary, Belgarion. I don't do things out of whim. We're all compelled by necessity – even I. Actually, what's going on between Relg and Taiba doesn't remotely concern you.'

Garion was a little stung by that. 'I thought – well—'

'You assumed that you were my only care – that you were the absolute center of the universe? You're not, of course. There are other things almost equally important, and Relg and Taiba are centrally involved in one of those things. Your participation in that particular matter is peripheral at the most.'

'They're going to be desperately unhappy if you force them together,' Garion accused.

'That doesn't matter in the slightest. Their being together is necessary. You're wrong, though. It will take them a while to get used to it, but once they do, they're both going to be very happy. Obedience to necessity does have its rewards, after all.'

Garion struggled with that idea for a while, then finally gave up. His own problems intruded once more on his thoughts. Inevitably, as he always did when he was troubled, he went looking for Aunt Pol. He found her sitting before the cozy fire in her apartment, sipping a cup of fragrant tea and watching through the window as the rosy morning sunlight set the snowfields above the city ablaze. 'You're up early,' she observed as he entered.

'I wanted to talk to you,' he told her, 'and the only way I ever get the chance to do what I want is to leave my room before the man with my schedule for the day shows up.' He flung himself into a chair. 'They never give me a minute to myself.'

'You're an important person now, dear.'

'That wasn't *my* idea.' He stared moodily out the window. 'Grandfather's all right now, isn't he?' he asked suddenly.

'What gave you that idea?'

'Well – the other day, when we gave Ce'Nedra the amulet – didn't he – sort of—?'

'Most of that came from you, dear,' she replied.

'I felt something else.'

'That could have been just me. It was a pretty subtle thing, and even I couldn't be sure if he had any part in it.'

'There has to be some way we can find out.'

'There's only one way, Garion, and that's for him to do something.'

'All right, let's go off with him someplace and have him try – something sort of small, maybe.'

'And how would we explain that to him?'

'You mean he doesn't know?' Garion sat up quickly.

'He might, but I rather doubt it.'

'You didn't tell him?'

'Of course not. If he has any doubts whatsoever about his ability, he'll fail, and if he fails once, that will be the end of it.'

'I don't understand.'

'A very important part of it is *knowing* that it's going to work. If you aren't absolutely sure, then it won't. That's why we can't tell him.'

Garion thought about it. 'I suppose that makes sense, but isn't it sort of dangerous? I mean, what if something really urgent comes up, and he tries to do something about it, and we all of a sudden find out that he can't?'

'You and I would have to deal with it then, dear.'

'You seem awfully calm about it.'

'Getting excited doesn't really help very much, Garion.'

The door burst open, and Queen Layla, her hair awry and her crown slipping precariously over one ear, stormed in. 'I won't have it, Polgara,' she declared angrily. 'I absolutely won't have it. You've got to talk to

257

him. Oh, excuse me, your Majesty,' the plump little queen added, noticing Garion. 'I didn't see you.' She curtsied gracefully.

'Your Highness,' Garion replied, getting up hurriedly and bowing in return.

'With whom did you wish me to speak, Layla?' Aunt Pol asked.

'Anheg. He insists that my poor husband sit up and drink with him every night. Fulrach's so sick this morning that he can barely lift his head off the pillow. That great bully of a Cherek is ruining my husband's health.'

'Anheg likes your husband, Layla. It's his way of showing his friendship.'

'Can't they be friends without drinking so much?'

'I'll talk to him, dear,' Aunt Pol promised.

Mollified somewhat, Queen Layla departed, curtsying again to Garion.

Garion was about to return to the subject of Belgarath's infirmity when Aunt Pol's maid came in to announce Lady Merel.

Barak's wife entered the room with a somber expression. 'Your Majesty,' she greeted Garion perfunctorily.

Garion rose again to bow and politely respond. He was getting rather tired of it.

'I need to talk with you, Polgara,' Merel declared.

'Of course,' Aunt Pol replied. 'Would you excuse us, Garion?'

'I'll wait in the next room,' he offered. He crossed to the door, but did not close it all the way. Once again his curiosity overcame his good manners.

'They all keep throwing it in my face,' Merel blurted almost before he was out of the room.

'What's that?'

'Well—' Merel hesitated, then spoke quite firmly. 'My

lord and I were not always on the best of terms,' she admitted.

'That's widely known, Merel,' Aunt Pol told her diplomatically.

'That's the whole problem,' Merel complained. 'They all keep laughing behind their hands and waiting for me to go back to being the way I was before.' A note of steel crept into her voice. 'Well, it's not going to happen,' she declared, 'so they can laugh all they want to.'

'I'm glad to hear that, Merel,' Aunt Pol replied.

'Oh, Polgara,' Merel said with a helpless little laugh, 'he looks so much like a great shaggy bear, but he's so gentle inside. Why couldn't I have seen that before? All those years wasted.'

'You had to grow up, Merel,' Aunt Pol told her. 'It takes some people longer, that's all.'

After Lady Merel had left, Garion came back in and looked quizzically at Aunt Pol. 'Has it always been like that?' he asked her. 'What I mean is – do people always come to you when they've got problems?'

'It happens now and then,' she replied. 'People seem to think that I'm very wise. Usually they already know what they have to do, so I listen to them and agree with them and give them a bit of harmless support. It makes them happy. I set aside a certain amount of time each morning for these visits. They know that I'm here if they feel the need for someone to talk to. Would you care for some tea?'

He shook his head. 'Isn't it an awful burden – all these other people's problems, I mean?'

'It's not really that heavy, Garion,' she answered. 'Their problems are usually rather small and domestic. It's rather pleasant to deal with things that aren't quite so earthshaking. Besides, I don't mind visitors – whatever their reason for coming.'

The next visitor, however, was Queen Islena, and her problem was more serious. Garion withdrew again when the maid announced that the Queen of Cherek wished to speak privately with the Lady Polgara; but, as before, his curiosity compelled him to listen at the door of the adjoining chamber.

'I've tried everything I can think of, Polgara,' Islena declared, 'but Grodeg won't let me go.'

'The High Priest of Belar?'

'He knows everything, naturally,' Islena confirmed. 'All his underlings reported my every indiscretion to him. He threatens to tell Anheg if I try to sever my connection with the Bear-cult. How could I have been so stupid? He's got his hand around my throat.'

'Just how indiscreet have you been, Islena?' Aunt Pol asked the queen pointedly.

'I went to some of their rituals,' Islena confessed. 'I put a few cult members in positions in the palace. I passed some information along to Grodeg.'

'Which rituals, Islena?'

'Not *those*, Polgara,' Islena replied in a shocked voice. 'I'd never stoop to that.'

'So all you really did was attend a few harmless gatherings where people dress up in bearskins and let a few cultists into the palace – where there were probably a dozen or more already anyway – and pass on a bit of harmless palace gossip? – It *was* harmless, wasn't it?'

'I didn't pass on any state secrets, Polgara, if that's what you mean,' the queen said stiffly.

'Then Grodeg doesn't really have any hold over you, Islena.'

'What should I do, Polgara?' the queen asked in an anguished voice.

'Go to Anheg. Tell him everything.'

'I can't.'

'You must. Otherwise Grodeg will force you into something worse. Actually, the situation could be turned to Anheg's advantage. Tell me exactly how much you know about what the cult is doing?'

'They've begun creating chapters among the peasants, for one thing.'

'They've never done that before,' Aunt Pol mused. 'The cult's always been restricted to the nobility and the priesthood.'

'I can't be sure,' Islena told her, 'but I think they're preparing for something major – some kind of confrontation.'

'I'll mention it to my father,' Aunt Pol replied. 'I think he'll want to take steps. As long as the cult was the plaything of the priesthood and the minor nobility, it wasn't really all that important, but rousing the peasantry is quite another thing.'

'I've heard a few other things as well,' Islena continued. 'I think they're trying to penetrate Rhodar's intelligence service. If they can get a few people in the right places in Boktor, they'll have access to most of the state secrets in the West.'

'I see.' Aunt Pol's voice was as cold as ice.

'I heard Grodeg talking once,' Islena said in a tone of distaste. 'It was before he found out that I didn't want anything more to do with him. He'd been reading the auguries and the signs in the heavens, and he was talking about the return of the Rivan King. The cult takes the term "Overlord of the West" quite seriously. I honestly believe that their ultimate goal is to elevate Belgarion to the status of Emperor of all the West – Aloria, Sendaria, Arendia, Tolnedra – even Nyissa.'

'That's not how the term was meant to be interpreted,' Aunt Pol objected.

'I know,' Islena replied, 'but Grodeg wants to twist it

until it comes out that way. He's a total fanatic, and he wants to convert all the people of the West to Belar – by the sword, if necessary.'

'That idiot!' Aunt Pol raged. 'He'd start a general war in the West if he tried that – and even set the Gods to wrangling. What is there about Alorns that makes them continually want to expand to the south? Those boundaries were established by the Gods themselves. I think it's time for someone to put his foot down on Grodeg's neck – firmly. Go to Anheg immediately. Tell him everything and then tell him that I want to see him. I imagine that my father's going to want to discuss the matter with him as well.'

'Anheg's going to be furious with me, Polgara,' Islena faltered.

'I don't think so,' Aunt Pol assured her. 'As soon as he realizes that you've exposed Grodeg's plan, he'll probably be rather grateful. Let him think that you went along with Grodeg simply to get more information. That's a perfectly respectable motive – and it's the sort of thing a good wife would do.'

'I hadn't thought of that,' Islena said, already sounding more sure of herself. 'It would have been a brave thing to do, wouldn't it?'

'Absolutely heroic, Islena,' Aunt Pol replied. 'Now go to Anheg.'

'I will, Polgara.' There was the sound of quick, determined steps, and then a door closed.

'Garion, come back in here.' Aunt Pol's voice was firm.

He opened the door.

'You were listening?' It wasn't really a question.

'Well—'

'We're going to have to have a talk about that,' she told him. 'But it doesn't really matter this time. Go find your grandfather and tell him that I want to see him immediately. I don't care what he's doing. Bring him to me now.'

'But how do we know he can do anything?' Garion demanded. 'I mean, if he's lost his power—'

'There are many kinds of power, Garion. Sorcery is only one of them. Now go fetch him at once.'

'Yes, Aunt Pol,' Garion replied, already moving toward the door.

Chapter Sixteen

The High Priest of Belar was an imposing-looking man nearly seven feet tall. He had a long grey beard and burning eyes sunk deep in their sockets beneath bristling black eyebrows. He arrived from Val Alorn the following week after the seemingly endless negotiations had finally produced the official betrothal document. Accompanying him as a kind of retinue were two dozen hard-faced warriors dressed in bearskins.

'Bear-cultists,' Barak observed sourly to Garion and Silk as the three of them stood atop the wall of the Citadel, watching the High Priest and his men mounting the steps from the harbor in the bright spring sunshine.

'I didn't say anything about bringing soldiers with him,' Garion objected indignantly.

'I imagine he took it upon himself,' Silk replied. 'Grodeg's very good at taking things upon himself.'

'I wonder how he'd like it if I threw him into a dungeon,' Garion said hotly. 'Do I have a dungeon?'

'We could improvise one, I suppose.' Barak grinned at him. 'Some nice damp cellar someplace. You might have to import some rats, though. The island's reputed to be free of them.'

'You're making fun of me,' Garion accused his friend, flushing slightly.

'Now you know I wouldn't do that, Garion,' Barak replied, pulling at his beard.

'I'd talk with Belgarath before I had Grodeg clapped

in irons, though,' Silk suggested. 'The political implications might go a bit further than you intend. Whatever you do, don't let Grodeg talk you into letting him leave any of his men behind. He's been trying to get a foothold on the Isle of the Winds for twenty years now. Not even Brand has had the nerve to let him go that far.'

'Brand?'

'Isn't it obvious? I wouldn't want to say that Brand's a cult member, but his sympathies certainly lie in that direction.'

Garion was shocked at that, and a little sick. 'What do you think I ought to do?' he asked.

'Don't try to play politics with these people,' Barak replied. 'Grodeg's here to conduct the official betrothal ceremony. Just let it go at that.'

'He'll try to talk to me, though,' Garion fretted. 'He's going to try to make me lead an invasion of the southern kingdoms so that he can convert the Arends and Tolnedrans and Nyissans to the worship of Belar.'

'Where did you hear that?' Silk asked curiously.

'I'd rather not say,' Garion evaded.

'Does Belgarath know?'

Garion nodded. 'Aunt Pol told him.'

Silk chewed thoughtfully on a fingernail. 'Just be stupid,' he said finally.

'What?'

'Pretend to be a simple country bumpkin with no idea of what's going on. Grodeg's going to do everything he can to get you alone so he can wring concessions out of you. Just keep smiling and nodding foolishly, and every time he makes a proposal, send for Belgarath. Let him think that you can't make a single decision on your own.'

'Won't that make me seem – well—?'

'Do you really care what he thinks?'

'Well, not really, I guess, but—'

'It will drive him crazy,' Barak pointed out with a wicked grin. 'He'll think that you're a complete idiot – a ripe plum ready for picking. But he'll realize that if he wants you, he'll have to fight Belgarath to get you. He'll be tearing out his beard in frustration before he leaves.' He turned and looked admiringly at Silk. 'That's really a terrible thing to do to a man like Grodeg, you know.'

Silk smirked. 'Isn't it though?'

The three of them stood grinning at each other and finally burst into laughter.

The official betrothal ceremony was conducted the following day. There had been a great deal of haggling about who should enter the Hall of the Rivan King first, but that difficulty had been overcome by Belgarath's suggestion that Garion and Ce'Nedra could enter arm in arm. 'This is all in preparation for a wedding, after all,' he had pointed out. 'We might as well start off with a semblance at least of friendship.'

Garion was very nervous as the hour approached. His princess had been smoldering since the incident with the amulet, and he was almost certain that there was going to be trouble. But to his surprise, Ce'Nedra was radiant as the two of them waited alone together in a small antechamber while the official guests gathered in the Hall. Garion fidgeted a great deal and walked up and down, nervously adjusting his clothing, but Ce'Nedra sat rather demurely, patiently awaiting the trumpet fanfare which was to announce their entrance.

'Garion,' she said after a while.

'Yes?'

'Do you remember that time we bathed together in the Wood of the Dryads?'

'We did *not* bathe together,' Garion replied quickly, blushing to the roots of his hair.

'Well, very nearly.' She brushed his distinction aside.

'Do you realize that Lady Polgara kept throwing us together like that all the time we were travelling? She knew that all this was going to happen, didn't she?'

'Yes,' Garion admitted.

'So she kept shoving us at each other, hoping something might happen between us.'

Garion thought about that. 'You're probably right,' he concluded. 'She likes to arrange people's lives for them.'

Ce'Nedra sighed. 'Look at all the opportunities we missed,' she said somewhat regretfully.

'*Ce'Nedra!*' Garion gasped, shocked at her suggestion.

She giggled a bit wickedly. Then she sighed again. 'Now it's all going to be dreadfully official – and probably not nearly as much fun.'

Garion's face was flaming by now.

'Anyway,' she continued, 'that time we bathed together – do you remember that I asked you if you'd like to kiss me?'

Garion nodded, not trusting himself to speak.

'I never got that kiss, you know,' she said archly, standing up and crossing the small room to him, 'and I think I'd like it now.' She took hold of the front of his doublet firmly with both little hands. 'You owe me a kiss, Belgarion of Riva, and a Tolnedran always collects what people owe her.' The look she directed up through her lashes at him smoldered dangerously.

Just outside, the trumpets blared out an extended fanfare.

'We're supposed to go in now,' Garion sputtered a bit desperately.

'Let them wait,' she murmured, her arms sliding up around his neck.

Garion tried for a quick, perfunctory kiss, but his

267

princess had other ideas. Her little arms were surprisingly strong, and her fingers locked in his hair. The kiss was lingering, and Garion's knees began to tremble.

'There,' Ce'Nedra breathed when she finally released him.

'We'd better go in,' Garion suggested as the trumpets blared again.

'In a moment. Did you muss me?' She turned around so that he could inspect her.

'No,' he replied. 'Everything still seems to be in order.'

She shook her head rather disapprovingly. 'Try to do a little better next time,' she told him. 'Otherwise I might start to think that you're not taking me seriously.'

'I'm never going to understand you, Ce'Nedra.'

'I know,' she said with a mysterious little smile. Then she patted his cheek gently. 'And I'm going to do everything I can to keep it that way. Shall we go in? We really shouldn't keep our guests waiting, you know.'

'That's what I said in the first place.'

'We were busy then,' she declared with a certain grand indifference. 'Just a moment.' She carefully smoothed his hair. 'There. That's better. Now give me your arm.'

Garion extended his arm, and his princess laid her hand on it. Then he opened the door to the third chorus from the trumpets. They entered the Hall, and an excited buzz ran through the crowd assembled there. Taking his cue from Ce'Nedra, Garion moved at a stately pace, his face sober and regal-looking.

'Not quite so grim,' she whispered. 'Smile just a little – and nod occasionally. It's the thing to do.'

'If you say so,' he replied. 'I really don't know too much about this sort of thing.'

'You'll be just fine,' she assured him.

Smiling and nodding to the spectators, the royal

couple passed through the Hall to the chair that had been placed near the front for the princess. Garion held the chair for her, then bowed and mounted the dais to his throne. As always happened the Orb of Aldur began to glow as soon as he sat down. This time, however, it seemed to have a faint pink cast to it.

The official betrothal ceremony began with a rolling invocation delivered in a thunderous voice by the High Priest of Belar. Grodeg took full advantage of the dramatics of the situation.

'Tiresome old windbag, isn't he?' Belgarath murmured from his accustomed place at the right of the throne.

'What were you and Ce'Nedra doing in there?' Aunt Pol asked Garion.

'Nothing,' Garion replied, blushing furiously.

'Really? And it took you all that time? How extraordinary.'

Grodeg had begun reading the first clauses of the betrothal agreement. To Garion they sounded like pure gibberish. At various points Grodeg stopped his reading to look sternly at Garion. 'Does His Majesty, Belgarion of Riva, agree to this?' he demanded each time.

'I do,' Garion replied.

'Does Her Highness Ce'Nedra of the Tolnedran Empire agree to this?' Grodeg asked the princess.

Ce'Nedra responded in a clear voice, 'I do.'

'How are you two getting along?' Belgarath asked, ignoring the droning voice of the clergyman.

'Who knows?' Garion answered helplessly. 'I can't tell from one minute to the next what she's going to do.'

'That's the way it's supposed to be,' Aunt Pol told him.

'I don't suppose you'd consider explaining that.'

'No, dear,' she replied with a smile as mysterious as Ce'Nedra's had been.

'I didn't really think so,' he grumbled.

Garion thought about Ce'Nedra's rather open invitation to muss her during the interminable reading of the document which was firmly nailing down the remainder of his life, and the more he thought about it, the more he found the notion of a bit of polite mussing attractive. He rather hoped that the princess would linger after the ceremony and that they might go someplace private to discuss it. Following Grodeg's pompous benediction, however, Ce'Nedra was immediately surrounded by all the younger girls in the court and swept away for some private celebration of their own. From all the giggling and wicked little glances cast in his direction, he concluded that the conversation at their little get-together was going to be very frank, probably naughty, and that the less he knew about it the better.

As Silk and Barak had predicted, the High Priest of Belar tried several times to speak to Garion privately. Each time, however, Garion put on a great show of ingenuousness and sent immediately for Belgarath. Grodeg left the island with his entire retinue the following day. To add a final insult to the whole matter, Garion insisted that he and Belgarath accompany the fuming ecclesiast to his ship to see him off – and to be certain that no Bear-cultist might inadvertently be left behind.

'Whose idea was all of this?' Belgarath inquired as he and Garion climbed the steps back to the Citadel.

'Silk and I worked it out,' Garion replied smugly.

'I might have known.'

'I thought things went quite well,' Garion congratulated himself.

'You've made yourself a dangerous enemy, you know.'

'We can handle him.'

'You're getting to be very free with that "we," Garion,' Belgarath said disapprovingly.

'We're all in this together, aren't we, Grandfather?'

Belgarath looked at him helplessly for a moment and then began to laugh.

In the days that followed Grodeg's departure, however, there was little occasion for laughter. Once the official ceremonies were over, the Alorn Kings, King Fulrach, and various advisers and generals got down to business. Their subject was war.

'The most recent reports I have from Cthol Murgos indicate that Taur Urgas is preparing to move the southern Murgos up from Rak Hagga as soon as the weather breaks on the eastern coast,' King Rhodar advised them.

'And the Nadraks?' King Anheg asked.

'They appear to be mobilizing, but there's always a question about the Nadraks. They play their own game, so it takes a lot of Grolims to whip them into line. The Thulls just obey orders.'

'The Thulls don't really concern anyone,' Brand observed. 'The key to the whole situation is how many Malloreans are going to be able to take the field against us.'

'There's a staging area for them being set up at Thull Zelik,' Rhodar reported, 'but they're also waiting for the weather to break in the Sea of the East.'

King Anheg frowned thoughtfully. 'Malloreans are bad sailors,' he mused. 'They won't move until summer, and they'll hug the north coast all the way to Thull Zelik. We need to get a fleet into the Sea of the East as soon as possible. If we can sink enough of their ships and drown enough of their soldiers, we might be able to keep them out of the war entirely. I think we should strike in force into Gar og Nadrak. Once we get into the forests, my

271

men can build ships. We'll sail down the River Cordu and out into the Sea of the East.'

'Thy plan hath merit, your Majesty,' Mandorallen approved, studying the large map hanging on the wall. 'The Nadraks are fewest in number and farthest removed from the hordes of southern Cthol Murgos.'

King Rhodar shook his head stubbornly. 'I know you want to get to the sea as quickly as possible, Anheg,' he objected, 'but you're committing me to a campaign in the Nadrak forest. I need open country to maneuver in. If we strike at the Thulls, we can cut directly across to the upper reaches of the River Mardu, and you can sail on down to the sea that way.'

'There aren't that many trees in Mishrak ac Thull,' Anheg protested.

'Why build ships out of green lumber if you don't have to?' Rhodar asked. 'Why not sail up the Aldur and then portage across?'

'You want my men to portage ships up the eastern escarpment? Rhodar, be serious.'

'We have engineers, Anheg. They can devise ways to lift your ships to the top of the escarpment.'

Garion did not want to intrude his inexperience on the conference, but the question came out before he had time to think about it. 'Have we decided where the final battle's going to be?' he asked.

'Which final battle was that, Garion?' Rhodar asked politely.

'When we meet them head-on – like Vo Mimbre.'

'There won't be a Vo Mimbre in this war,' Anheg told him. 'Not if we can help it.'

'Vo Mimbre was a mistake, Garion,' Belgarath said quietly. 'We all knew it, but there wasn't anything we could do about it.'

'We won, didn't we?'

'That was pure luck, and you can't plan a campaign on the hope that you might get lucky. Nobody wanted the battle at Vo Mimbre – we didn't, and Kal Torak didn't, but nobody had any choice in the matter. We had to commit to battle before the second Angarak column arrived in the West. Kal Torak had been holding the southern Murgos and eastern Malloreans in reserve near Rak Hagga, and they started to march when he turned west from the siege of the Stronghold. If they'd been able to join forces with Kal Torak, there wouldn't have been enough men in all the West to meet them, so we had to fight. Vo Mimbre was the least objectionable battlefield.'

'Why didn't Kal Torak just wait until they arrived?' Garion asked.

'You can't stop an army in unfriendly territory, King Belgarion,' Colonel Brendig explained. 'You have to keep moving, or the local populace destroys all the food and starts coming out at night to cut up your people. You can lose half your army that way.'

'Kal Torak didn't want the meeting at Vo Mimbre any more than we did,' Belgarath went on. 'The column from Rak Hagga got caught in a spring blizzard in the mountains and bogged down for weeks. They finally had to turn back, and Torak was forced to fight at Vo Mimbre without any advantage of numbers, and nobody in his right mind goes into battle that way.'

'Thy force should be larger by a quarter than thine adversary's,' Mandorallen agreed, 'else the outcome must be in doubt.'

'By a third,' Barak corrected in a rumbling voice. 'By half if you can arrange it.'

'Then all we're going to do is spread out all over the eastern half of the continent and fight a whole series of little battles?' Garion demanded incredulously.

'That could take years – decades. It could go on for a century.'

'If it has to,' Belgarath told him bluntly. 'What did you expect, Garion? A short little ride in the sunshine, a nice easy fight, and then home before winter? I'm afraid it won't be like that. You'd better get used to wearing armor and a sword because you'll probably be dressed that way for most of the rest of your life. This is likely to be a very long war.'

Garion's illusions were crumbling rapidly.

The door to the council room opened, then, and Olban, Brand's youngest son, entered and spoke with his father. The weather had turned blustery, and a spring storm was raking the island. Olban's grey Rivan cloak was dripping as he entered.

Dismayed by the prospect of year after year of campaigning in the East, Garion distractedly stared at the puddle forming around Olban's feet as the young man talked quietly with Brand. Then, out of habit, he lifted his eyes slightly to look at the hem of Olban's cloak. There was a small tear on the left corner of the cloak, and a scrap of cloth seemed to be missing.

Garion stared at the telltale rip for a moment without realizing exactly what it was he saw. Then he went suddenly cold. With a slight start, he jerked his eyes up to look at Olban's face. Brand's youngest son was perhaps Garion's own age, a bit shorter, but more muscular. His hair was pale blond, and his young face was serious, reflecting already the customary Rivan gravity. He seemed to be trying to avoid Garion's eyes, but showed no other sign of nervousness. Once, however, he looked inadvertently at the young king and seemed to flinch slightly as guilt rose clearly into his eyes. Garion had found the man who had tried to kill him.

The conference continued after that, but Garion did not hear any more of it. What was he to do? Had Olban acted alone, or were others involved? Had Brand himself been a part of it? It was so difficult to know what a Rivan was thinking. He trusted Brand, but the big Warder's connection with the Bear-cult gave a certain ambiguity to his loyalties. Could Grodeg be behind all this? Or perhaps a Grolim? Garion remembered the Earl of Jarvik, whose soul had been purchased by Asharak and who had mounted rebellion in Val Alorn. Had Olban fallen perhaps under the spell of the bloodred gold of Angarak as Jarvik had? But Riva was an island, the one place in the world where no Grolim could ever come. Garion discounted the possibility of bribery. In the first place, it was not in the Rivan character. In the second, Olban had not likely ever been in a situation to come into contact with a Grolim. Rather grimly, Garion decided on a course of action.

Lelldorin, of course, had to be kept out of it. The hot-headed young Asturian was incapable of the kind of delicate discretion that seemed to be called for. Lelldorin would reach for his sword, and the whole business would disintegrate rather rapidly after that.

When the conference broke up for the day late that afternoon, Garion went looking for Olban. He did not take a guard with him, but he did wear his sword.

As chance had it, it was in a dim corridor not unlike the one where the assassination attempt had taken place that the young king finally ran Brand's youngest son down. Olban was coming along the passageway in one direction, and Garion was going the other. Olban's face paled slightly when he saw his king, and he bowed deeply to hide his expression. Garion nodded as if intending to pass without speaking, but turned after the two of them had gone by each other. 'Olban,' he said quietly.

Brand's son turned, a look of dread on his face.

'I noticed that the corner of your cloak is torn,' Garion said in an almost neutral tone. 'When you take it to have it mended, this might help.' He took the scrap of cloth out from under his doublet and offered it to the pale-faced young Rivan.

Olban stared wide-eyed at him, not moving.

'And as long as we're at it,' Garion continued, 'you might as well take this, too. I think you dropped it somewhere.' He reached inside his doublet again and took out the dagger with its bent point.

Olban started to tremble violently, then he suddenly dropped to his knees. 'Please, your Majesty,' he begged, 'let me kill myself. If my father finds out what I've done, it will break his heart.'

'Why did you try to kill me, Olban?' Garion asked.

'For love of my father,' Brand's son confessed, tears welling up in his eyes. 'He was ruler here in Riva until you came. Your arrival degraded him. I couldn't bear that. Please, your Majesty, don't have me dragged to the scaffold like a common criminal. Give me the dagger and I'll bury it in my heart right here. Spare my father this last humiliation.'

'Don't talk nonsense,' Garion told him, 'and get up. You look silly down there on your knees.'

'Your Majesty—' Olban began to protest.

'Oh, be still,' Garion told him irritably. 'Let me think for a moment.' Dimly he began to see the glimmer of an idea. 'All right,' he said finally, 'this is what we're going to do. You're going to take this knife and this wool scrap down to the harbor and throw them into the sea, and then you're going to go on about your life as if this had never happened.'

'Your Majesty—'

'I'm not finished. Neither you nor I will ever speak of

this again. I don't want any hysterical public confessions, and I absolutely forbid you to kill yourself. Do you understand me, Olban?'

Dumbly the young man nodded.

'I need your father's help too much to have this come out or for him to be distracted by personal tragedy. This did not happen, and that's an end of it. Take these and get out of my sight.' He shoved the knife and the wool scrap into Olban's hands. He was suddenly infuriated. The weeks of looking nervously over his shoulder had all been so unnecessary – so useless. 'Oh, one other thing, Olban,' he added as the stricken young Rivan turned to leave. 'Don't throw any more knives at me. If you want to fight, let me know, and we'll go someplace private and cut each other to ribbons, if that's what you want.'

Olban fled sobbing.

'*Very well done, Belgarion,*' the dry voice complimented him.

'Oh, shut up,' Garion said.

He slept very little that night. He had a few doubts about the wisdom of the course he had taken with Olban; but on the whole, he was satisfied that what he had done had been right. Olban's act had been no more than an impulsive attempt to erase what he believed to be his father's degradation. There had been no plot involved in it. Olban might resent Garion's magnanimous gesture, but he would not throw any more daggers at his king's back. What disturbed Garion's sleep the most during that restless night was Belgarath's bleak appraisal of the war upon which they were about to embark. He slept briefly on toward dawn and awoke from a dreadful nightmare with icy sweat standing out on his forehead. He had just seen himself, old and weary, leading a pitifully small army of ragged, gray-haired men into a battle they could not possibly win.

'*There's an alternative, of course – if you've recovered enough from your bout of peevishness to listen*,' the voice in his mind advised him as he sat bolt upright and trembling in his bed.

'What?' Garion answered aloud. 'Oh, that – I'm sorry I spoke that way. I was irritated, that's all.'

'*In many ways you're like Belgarath – remarkably so. This irritability seems to be hereditary.*'

'It's only natural, I suppose,' Garion conceded. 'You said there was an alternative. An alternative to what?'

'*To this war that's giving you nightmares. Get dressed. I want to show you something.*'

Garion climbed out of his bed and hastily jerked on his clothing. 'Where are we going?' he asked, still speaking aloud.

'*It isn't far.*'

The room to which the other awareness directed him was musty and showed little evidence of use. The books and scrolls lining the shelves along its walls were dust-covered, and cobwebs draped the corners. Garion's lone candle cast looming shadows that seemed to dance along the walls.

'*On the top shelf*,' the voice told him. '*The scroll wrapped in yellow linen. Take it down.*'

Garion climbed up on a chair and took down the scroll. 'What is this?' he asked.

'*The Mrin Codex. Take off the cover and start unrolling it. I'll tell you when to stop.*'

It took Garion a moment or two to get the knack of unrolling the bottom of the scroll with one hand and rolling up the top with the other.

'*There*,' the voice said. '*That's the passage. Read it.*'

Garion struggled over the words. The script was spidery, and he still did not read very well. 'It doesn't make any sense,' he complained.

278

'*The man who wrote it down was insane,*' the voice apologized, '*and he was an imbecile besides, but he was all I had to work with. Try it again – out loud.*'

Garion read: 'Behold, it shall come to pass that in a certain moment, that which must be and that which must not be shall meet, and in that meeting shall be decided all that has gone before and all that will come after. Then will the Child of Light and the Child of Dark face each other in the broken tomb, and the stars will shudder and grow dim.' Garion's voice trailed off. 'It still doesn't make any sense,' he objected.

'*It's a bit obscure,*' the voice admitted. '*As I said, the man who wrote it was insane. I put the ideas there, but he used his own words to express them.*'

'Who is the Child of Light?' Garion asked.

'*You are – for the moment at least. It changes.*'

'Me?'

'*Of course.*'

'Then who's this Child of Dark I'm supposed to meet?'

'*Torak.*'

'Torak!'

'*I should have thought that would be obvious by now. I told you once about the two possible destinies coming together finally. You and Torak – the Child of Light and the Child of Dark – embody those destinies.*'

'But Torak's asleep.'

'*Not any more. When you first put your hand on the Orb, the touch signalled his awakening. Even now he stirs on the edge of awareness, and his hand fumbles for the hilt of Cthrek-Goru, his black sword.*'

Garion went very cold. 'Are you trying to say that I'm supposed to fight Torak? *Alone?*'

'*It's going to happen, Belgarion. The universe itself rushes toward it. You can gather an army if you want, but* your army – or Torak's – won't mean anything. As the Codex says, everything will be decided when you fnally meet him. In the end, you'll face each other alone. That's what I meant by an alternative.'

'What you're trying to say is that I'm just supposed to go off alone and find him and fight him?' Garion demanded incredulously.

'*Approximately, yes.*'

'I won't do it.'

'*That's up to you.*'

Garion struggled with it. 'If I take an army, I'll just get a lot of people killed, and it won't make any difference in the end anyway?'

'*Not the least bit. In the end it will just be you, Torak, Cthrek-Goru, and the sword of the Rivan King.*'

'Don't I have any choice at all?'

'*None whatsoever.*'

'Do I have to go alone?' Garion asked plaintively.

'*It doesn't say that.*'

'Could I take one or two people with me?'

'*That's your decision, Belgarion. Just don't forget to take your sword.*'

He thought about it for the rest of the day. In the end his choice was obvious. As evening settled over the grey city of Riva, he sent for Belgarath and Silk. There were some problems involved, he knew, but there was no one else he could rely on. Even if his power were diminished, Belgarath's wisdom made Garion not even want to consider the undertaking without him. And Silk, of course, was just as essential. Garion reasoned that his own increasing talent for sorcery could see them through any difficulties if Belgarath should falter, and Silk could probably find ways to avoid most of the serious confrontations. Garion was confident that the three of them would be able to cope with whatever arose – until they found Torak. He didn't want to think about what might happen then.

When the two of them arrived, the young king was staring out the window with haunted eyes.

'You sent for us?' Silk asked.

'I have to make a journey,' Garion replied in a scarcely audible voice.

'What's bothering you?' Belgarath said. 'You look a bit sick.'

'I just found out what it is that I'm supposed to do, Grandfather.'

'Who told you?'

'*He* did.'

Belgarath pursed his lips. 'A bit premature, perhaps,' he suggested. 'I was going to wait a while longer, but I have to assume he knows what he's doing.'

'Who is this we're talking about?' Silk asked.

'Garion has a periodic visitor,' the old man answered. 'A rather special visitor.'

'That's a singularly unenlightening response, old friend.'

'Are you sure you really want to know?'

'Yes,' Silk replied, 'I think I do. I get the feeling that I'm going to be involved in it.'

'You're aware of the Prophecy?'

'Naturally.'

'It appears that the Prophecy is a bit more than a statement about the future. It seems to be able to take a hand in things from time to time. It speaks to Garion on occasion.'

Silk's eyes narrowed as he thought about that. 'All right,' he said finally.

'You don't seem surprised.'

The rat-faced little man laughed. 'Belgarath, nothing about this whole thing surprises me any more.'

Belgarath turned back to Garion. 'Exactly what did he tell you?'

'He showed me the Mrin Codex. Have you ever read it?'

'From end to end and backward and forward – even from side to side a couple of times. Which part did he show you?'

'The part about the meeting of the Child of Light and the Child of Dark.'

'Oh,' Belgarath said. 'I was afraid it might have been that part. Did he explain it?'

Dumbly, Garion nodded.

'Well,' the old man said with a penetrating look, 'now you know the worst. What are you going to do about it?'

'He gave me a couple of alternatives,' Garion said. 'I can wait until we get an army together, and we can go off and fight back and forth with the Angaraks for generations. That's one way, isn't it?'

Belgarath nodded.

'Of course that will get millions of people killed for nothing, won't it?'

The old man nodded again.

Garion drew in a deep breath. 'Or,' he continued, 'I can go off by myself and find Torak – wherever he is – and try to kill him.'

Silk whistled, his eyes widening.

'He said that I didn't have to go alone,' Garion added hopefully. 'I asked him about that.'

'Thanks,' Belgarath said dryly.

Silk sprawled in a nearby chair, rubbing thoughtfully at his pointed nose. He looked at Belgarath. 'You know that Polgara would skin the both of us inch by inch if we let him go off alone, don't you?'

Belgarath grunted.

'Where did you say Torak is?'

'Cthol Mishrak – in Mallorea.'

'I've never been there.'

'I have – a few times. It's not a very attractive place.'

'Maybe time has improved it.'

'That's not very likely.'

Silk shrugged. 'Maybe we ought to go with him – show him the way, that sort of thing. It's time I left Riva anyway. Some ugly rumors are starting to go around about me.'

'It is rather a good time of year for travelling,' Belgarath admitted, giving Garion a sly, sidelong glance.

Garion felt better already. He knew from their bantering tone that they had already made up their minds. He would not have to go in search of Torak alone. For now that was enough: there'd be time for worrying later. 'All right,' he said. 'What do we do?'

'We creep out of Riva very quietly,' Belgarath replied. 'There's nothing to be gained by getting into any long discussions with your Aunt Pol about this.'

'The wisdom of ages,' Silk agreed fervently. 'When do we start?' His ferret eyes were very bright.

'The sooner the better.' Belgarath shrugged. 'Did you have any plans for tonight?'

'Nothing I can't postpone.'

'All right then. We'll wait until everyone goes to bed, and then we'll pick up Garion's sword and get started.'

'Which way do we go?' Garion asked him.

'Sendaria first,' Belgarath replied, 'and then across Drasnia to Gar og Nadrak. Then north to the archipelago that leads to Mallorea. It's a long way to Cthol Mishrak and the tomb of the one-eyed God.'

'And then?'

'Then, Garion, we settle this once and for all.'

Part Three

DRASNIA

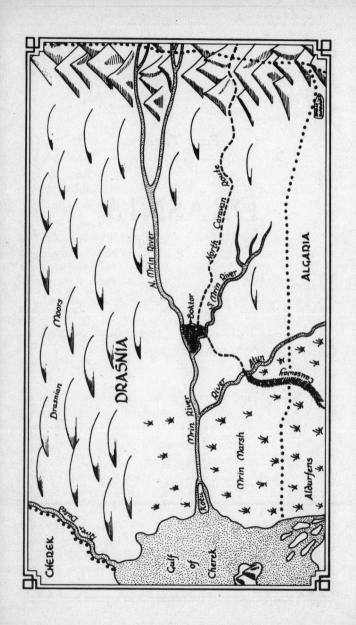

Chapter Seventeen

'Dear Aunt Pol,' Garion's note began, 'I know this is going to make you angry, but there's no other way. I've seen the Mrin Codex, and now I know what I have to do. The—' He broke off, frowning. 'How do you spell "Prophecy"?' he asked.

Belgarath spelled it out for him. 'Don't drag it out too much, Garion,' the old man advised. 'Nothing you say is going to make her happy about this, so stick to the point.'

'Don't you think I ought to explain why we're doing this?' Garion fretted.

'She's read the Codex, Garion,' Belgarath replied. 'She'll know why without your explanation.'

'I really ought to leave a note for Ce'Nedra, too,' Garion considered.

'Polgara can tell her what she needs to know,' Belgarath said. 'We have things to do and we can't afford to spend the whole night on correspondence.'

'I've never written a letter before,' Garion remarked. 'It's not nearly as easy as it looks.'

'Just say what you have to say and then stop,' the old man advised. 'Don't labor at it so much.'

The door opened and Silk came back in. He was dressed in the nondescript clothing he had worn on the road, and he carried two bundles. 'I think these should fit you,' he said, handing one of the bundles to Belgarath and the other to Garion.

'Did you get the money?' the old man asked him.

'I borrowed some from Barak.'

'That's surprising,' Belgarath replied. 'He isn't notorious for generosity.'

'I didn't tell him I was borrowing it,' the little man returned with a broad wink. 'I thought it would save time if I didn't have to go into long explanations.'

One of Belgarath's eyebrows shot up.

'We *are* in a hurry, aren't we?' Silk asked with an innocent expression. 'And Barak can be tedious when it comes to money.'

'Spare me the excuses,' Belgarath told him. He turned back to Garion. 'Have you finished with that yet?'

'What do you think?' Garion asked, handing him the note.

The old man glanced at it. 'Good enough,' he said. 'Now sign it and we'll put it where somebody'll find it sometime tomorrow.'

'Late tomorrow,' Silk suggested. 'I'd like to be well out of Polgara's range when she finds out that we've left.'

Garion signed the note, folded it and wrote, 'For Lady Polgara,' across the outside.

'We'll leave it on the throne,' Belgarath said. 'Let's change clothes and go get the sword.'

'Isn't the sword going to be a bit bulky?' Silk asked after Garion and Belgarath had changed.

'There's a scabbard for it in one of the antechambers,' Belgarath answered, opening the door carefully and peering out into the silent hall. 'He'll have to wear it slung across his back.'

'That glow is going to be a bit ostentatious,' Silk said.

'We'll cover the Orb,' Belgarath replied. 'Let's go.'

The three of them slipped out into the dimly lighted corridor and crept through the midnight stillness toward the throne room. Once, a sleepy servant going toward the kitchen almost surprised them, but an empty chamber provided them with a temporary hiding place until he had passed. Then they moved on.

'Is it locked?' Silk whispered when they reached the door to the Hall of the Rivan King.

Garion took hold of the large handle and twisted, wincing as the latch clacked loudly in the midnight stillness. He pushed and the door creaked as it swung open.

'You ought to have somebody take care of that,' Silk muttered.

The Orb of Aldur began to glow faintly as soon as the three of them entered the Hall.

'It seems to recognize you,' Silk observed to Garion.

When Garion took down the sword, the Orb flared, filling the Hall of the Rivan King with its deep blue radiance. Garion looked around nervously, fearful that someone passing might see the light and come in to investigate. 'Stop that,' he irrationally admonished the stone. With a startled flicker, the glow of the Orb subsided back into a faint, pulsating light, and the triumphant song of the Orb stilled to a murmur.

Belgarath looked quizzically at his grandson, but said nothing. He led them to an antechamber and removed a long, plain scabbard from a case standing against the wall. The belt attached to the scabbard had seen a certain amount of use. The old man buckled it in place for Garion, passing it over the young man's right shoulder and down across his chest so that the scabbard, attached to the belt in two places, rode diagonally down his back. There was also a knitted tube in the case, almost like a narrow sock. 'Slide this over the hilt,' Belgarath instructed.

Garion covered the hilt of his great sword with the tube and then took hold of the blade itself and carefully inserted the tip into the top of the scabbard. It was awkward, and neither Silk nor Belgarath offered to help him. All three of them knew why. The sword slid home and, since it seemed to have no weight, it was not too uncomfortable. The crosspiece of the hilt, however, stood out just at the top of his head and tended to poke him if he moved too quickly.

'It wasn't really meant to be worn,' Belgarath told him. 'We had to improvise.'

Once again, the three of them passed through the dimly lighted corridors of the sleeping palace and emerged through a side door. Silk slipped on ahead, moving as soundlessly as a cat and keeping to the shadows. Belgarath and Garion waited. An open window perhaps twenty feet overhead faced out into the courtyard. As they stood together beneath it, a faint light appeared, and the voice that spoke down to them was very soft. 'Errand?' it said.

'Yes,' Garion replied without thinking. 'Everything's all right. Go back to bed.'

'Belgarion,' the child said with a strange kind of satisfaction. Then he added, 'Good-bye,' in a somewhat more wistful tone, and he was gone.

'Let's hope he doesn't run straight to Polgara,' Belgarath muttered.

'I think we can trust him, Grandfather. He knew we were leaving and he just wanted to say good-bye.'

'Would you like to explain how you know that?'

'I don't know.' Garion shrugged. 'I just do.'

Silk whistled from the courtyard gate, and Belgarath and Garion followed him down into the quiet streets of the city.

It was still early spring, and the night was cool but not chilly. There was a fragrance in the air, washing down over the city from the high meadows in the mountains behind Riva and mingling with peat smoke and the salty tang of the sea. The stars overhead were bright, and the newly risen moon, looking swollen as it rode low over the horizon, cast a glittering golden path across the breast of the Sea of the Winds. Garion felt that excitement he always experienced when starting out at night. He had been cooped up too long, and each step that took him farther and farther from the dull round of appointments and ceremonies filled him with an almost intoxicating anticipation.

'It's good to be on the road again,' Belgarath murmured, as if reading his thoughts.

'Is it always like this?' Garion whispered back. 'I mean, even after all the years that you've been doing it?'

'Always,' Belgarath replied. 'Why do you think I prefer the life of a vagabond?'

They moved on down through the dark streets to the city gate and out through a small sallyport to the wharves jutting into the moon-dappled waters of the harbor.

Captain Greldik was a bit drunk when they reached his ship. The vagrant seaman had ridden out the winter in the safety of the harbor at Riva. His ship had been hauled out on the strand, her bottom scraped and her seams recaulked. Her mainmast, which had creaked rather alarmingly on the voyage from Sendaria, had been reinforced and fitted with new sails. Then Greldik and his crew had spent much of their time carousing. The effects of three months of steady dissipation showed on his face when they woke him. His eyes were bleary, and there were dark-stained pouches under them. His bearded face looked puffy and unwell.

'Maybe tomorrow,' he grunted when Belgarath told him of their urgent need to leave the island. 'Or the next day. The next day would be better, I think.'

Belgarath spoke more firmly.

'My sailors couldn't possibly man the oars,' Greldik objected. 'They'll be throwing up all over the deck, and it takes a week to clean up a mess like that.'

Belgarath delivered a blistering ultimatum, and Greldik sullenly climbed out of his rumpled bunk. He lurched toward the crew's quarters, pausing only long enough to be noisily sick over the rail, and then he descended into the forward hold, where with kicks and curses he roused his men.

The moon was high and dawn only a few hours off when Greldik's ship slid quietly out of the harbor and met the long, rolling swells of the Sea of the Winds. When the sun came up they were far out at sea.

The weather held fair, even though the winds were not favorable, and in two days' time Greldik dropped Garion, Silk and Belgarath off on a deserted beach just north of the mouth of the Seline River on the northwest coast of Sendaria.

'I don't know that I'd be in all that big a hurry to go back to Riva,' Belgarath told Greldik as he stepped out of the small boat onto the sand of the beach. He handed the bearded Cherek a small pouch of jingling coins. 'I'm sure you and your crew can find a bit of diversion somewhere.'

'It's always nice in Camaar this time of year,' Greldik mused, bouncing the pouch thoughtfully in his hand, 'and I know a young widow there who's always been very friendly.'

'You ought to pay her a visit,' Belgarath suggested. 'You've been away for quite some time, and she's sure to have been terribly lonely for you.'

'I think maybe I will,' Greldik said, his eyes suddenly bright. 'Have a good trip.' He motioned to his men, and they began rowing the small boat back toward the lean ship standing a few hundred yards offshore.

'What was that all about?' Garion asked.

'I'd like to get a bit of distance between us and Polgara before she gets her hands on Greldik,' the old man replied. 'I don't particularly want her chasing us.' He looked around. 'Let's see if we can find somebody with a boat to row us upriver to Seline. We should be able to buy horses and supplies there. '

A fisherman, who immediately saw that turning ferryboatman would provide a more certain profit than trusting his luck on the banks off the northwest coast, agreed to take them upriver; by the time the sun was setting, they had arrived in the city of Seline. They spent the night in a comfortable inn and went the following morning to the central market. Silk negotiated the purchase of horses, haggling down to the last penny, bargaining more out of habit, Garion thought, than out of any real necessity. Then they bought supplies for the trip. By midmorning, they were pounding along the road that led toward Darine, some forty leagues distant.

The fields of northern Sendaria had begun to sprout that first green blush that lay on damp earth like a faint jade mist and more than anything announced spring. A few fleecy clouds scampered across the blue of the sky, and, though the wind was gusty, the sun warmed the air. The road opened before them, stretching across the verdant fields; and though their mission was deadly serious, Garion almost wanted to shout out of pure exuberance.

In two more days they reached Darine. 'Do you want to take ship here?' Silk asked Belgarath as they crested the hill up which they had come so many months before with their three wagonloads of turnips. 'We could be in Kotu inside a week.'

Belgarath scratched at his beard, looking out at the expanse of the Gulf of Cherek, glittering in the afternoon sun. 'I don't think so,' he decided. He pointed at several lean Cherek warboats patrolling just outside Sendarian territorial waters.

'The Chereks are always moving around out there,' Silk replied. 'It might have nothing whatsoever to do with us.'

'Polgara's very persistent,' Belgarath said. 'She can't leave Riva herself as long as so many things are afoot there, but she can send people out to look for us. Let's avoid any possible trouble if we can. We'll go along the north coast and then on up through the fens to Boktor.'

Silk gave him a look of profound distaste. 'It will take a lot longer,' he objected.

'We aren't in all that great a hurry,' Belgarath remarked blandly. 'The Alorns are beginning to mass their armies, but they still need more time, and it's going to take a while to get the Arends all moving in the same direction.'

'What's that got to do with it?' Silk asked him.

'I have plans for those armies, and I'd like to start them moving before we cross into Gar og Nadrak if possible and certainly before we get to Mallorea. We can afford the time it will take to avoid any unpleasantness with the people Polgara's sent out to find us.'

And so they detoured around Darine and took the narrow, rocky road that led along the cliffs where the waves crashed and boomed and foamed, beating themselves to fragments against the great rocks of the north coast.

The mountains of eastern Sendaria ran down into the Gulf of Cherek along that forbidding shore, and the road, which twisted and climbed and dropped steeply again, was not good. Silk grumbled every mile of the way.

Garion, however, had other worries. The decision he

294

had made after reading the Mrin Codex had seemed quite logical at the time, but logic was scant comfort now. He was deliberately riding toward Mallorea to face Torak in a duel. The more he thought about it, the more insane it seemed. How could he possibly hope to defeat a God? He brooded about that as they rode eastward along the rocky coast, and his mood became as unpleasant as Silk's.

After about a week, the cliffs became lower, and the land more gently rolling. From the top of the last of the eastern foothills, they looked out and saw what appeared to be a vast, flat plain, dark-green and very damp-looking. 'Well, there they are,' Silk sourly informed Belgarath.

'What's got you so bad-tempered?' the old man asked him.

'One of the main reasons I left Drasnia in the first place was to avoid the possibility of ever being obliged to go anywhere near the fens,' Silk replied crisply. 'Now you propose to drag me lengthwise through the whole soggy, stinking expanse of them. I'm bitterly disappointed in you, old friend, and it's altogether possible that I'll never forgive you for this.'

Garion was frowning at the marshland spread out below. 'That wouldn't be Drasnia, would it?' he asked. 'I thought that Drasnia was farther north.'

'It's Algaria, actually,' Belgarath told him. 'The beginning of Aldurfens. Up beyond the mouths of the Aldur River is the Drasnian border. They call it Mrin marsh up there, but it's all the same swamp. It goes on for another thirty leagues or so beyond Kotu at the mouth of the Mrin River.'

'Most people just call it the fens and let it go at that,' Silk observed. 'Most people have sense enough to stay out of it,' he added pointedly.

'Quit complaining so much,' Belgarath told him bluntly. 'There are fishermen along this coast. We'll buy a boat.'

Silk's eyes brightened. 'We can go up along the coast then,' he suggested.

'That wouldn't be very prudent,' Belgarath disagreed, 'Not with Anheg's fleet scouring the Gulf of Cherek, looking for us.'

'You don't know that they're looking for us,' Silk said quickly.

'I know Polgara,' Belgarath answered.

'I feel that this trip is definitely growing sour on us,' Silk grumbled.

The fishermen along the marshy coast were a peculiar mixture of Algars and Drasnians, close-mouthed and wary of strangers. Their villages were built on pilings driven deep into the marshy earth, and there lingered about them that peculiar odor of long-dead fish that hovers over fishing villages wherever one finds them. It took some time to find a man with a boat he was willing to sell and even longer to persuade him that three horses and a few silver coins beside was a fair price for it.

'It leaks,' Silk declared, pointing at the inch or so of water that had collected in the bottom of the boat as they poled away from the reeking village.

'All boats leak, Silk,' Belgarath replied calmly. 'It's the nature of boats to leak. Bail it out.'

'It will just fill up again.'

'Then you can bail it out again. Try not to let it get too far ahead of you.'

The fens stretched on interminably, a wilderness of cattails and rushes and dark, slowly moving water. There were channels and streams and quite frequently small lakes where the going was much easier. The air was humid and, in the evenings, thick with gnats and mosquitoes. Frogs sang of love all night, greeting spring with intoxicated fervor – little chirping frogs and great, booming, bull-voiced frogs as big as dinner plates. Fish leaped in the ponds and lakes, and beaver and muskrats nested on soggy islands.

They poled their way through the confused maze of channels marking the mouths of the Aldur and continued northeasterly in the slowly warming northern spring. After a week or more, they crossed the indeterminate border and left Algaria behind.

A false channel put them aground once, and they were obliged to climb out to heave and push their boat off a mudbank by main strength. When they were afloat again, Silk sat disconsolately on the gunwale regarding his ruined boots that were dripping thick mud into the water. When he spoke, his voice was filled with profound disgust. 'Delightful,' he said. 'How wonderful to be home again in dear old mucky Drasnia.'

Chapter Eighteen

Although it was all one vast swampland, it seemed to Garion that the fens here in Drasnia were subtly different from those farther south. The channels were narrower, for one thing, and they twisted and turned more frequently. After a couple of days poling, he developed a growing conviction that they were lost. 'Are you sure you know where we're going?' he demanded of Silk.

'I haven't the vaguest idea,' Silk replied candidly.

'You keep saying that you know the way everywhere,' Garion accused him.

'There isn't any certain way here in the fens, Garion,' Silk told him. 'All you can do is keep going against the current and hope for the best.'

'There's got to be a route,' Garion objected. 'Why don't they put up markers or something?'

'It wouldn't do any good. Look.' The little man put his pole against a solid-looking hummock rising out of the water beside the boat and pushed. The hummock moved sluggishly away. Garion stared at it in amazement.

'It's floating vegetation,' Belgarath explained, stopping his poling to wipe the sweat from his face. 'Seeds fall on it, and it grows grass just like solid earth – except that it isn't solid. It floats wherever the wind and current push it. That's why there aren't any permanent channels and there's no definite route.'

'It's not always just wind and current,' Silk added

darkly. He glanced out at the lowering sun. 'We'd better find something solid to tie up to for the night,' he suggested.

'How about that one?' Belgarath replied, pointing at a brushy hummock that was somewhat higher than those surrounding it.

They poled their way to the clump of ground rising out of the surrounding water, and Silk kicked at it experimentally a few times. 'It seems to be stationary,' he confirmed. He stepped out of the boat and climbed to the top, frequently stamping his feet. The ground responded with a satisfactorily solid sound. 'There's a dry spot up here,' he reported, 'and a pile of driftwood on the other side. We can sleep on solid ground for a change, and maybe even have a hot meal.'

They pulled the boat far up onto the sloping side, and Silk took some rather exotic-seeming precautions to make certain that it was securely tied.

'Isn't that sort of unnecessary?' Garion asked him.

'It isn't much of a boat,' Silk replied, 'but it's the only one we've got. Let's not take chances with it.'

They got a fire going and erected their single tent as the sun slowly settled in a cloudbank to the west, painting the marsh in a ruddy glow. Silk dug out a few pans and began to work on supper.

'It's too hot,' Garion advised critically as the rat-faced little man prepared to lay strips of bacon in a smoking iron pan.

'Do you want to do this?'

'I was just warning you, that's all.'

'I don't have your advantages, Garion,' Silk replied tartly. 'I didn't grow up in Polgara's kitchen the way you did. I just make do the best I can.'

'You don't have to get grumpy about it,' Garion said. 'I just thought you'd like to know that the pan's too hot.'

'I think I can manage without any more advice.'

'Suit yourself – but you're going to burn the bacon.'

Silk gave him an irritated look and started slapping bacon slices into the pan. The slices sizzled and smoked, and their edges turned black almost immediately.

'I told you so,' Garion murmured.

'Belgarath,' Silk complained, 'make him leave me alone.'

'Come away, Garion,' the old man said. 'He can burn supper without any help.'

'Thanks,' Silk responded sarcastically.

Supper was not an absolute disaster. After they had eaten, they sat watching as the fire burned down and purple evening crept across the fens. The frogs took up their vast chorus among the reeds, and birds perched on the bending stalks of cattails, clucking and murmuring sleepily. There were faint splashes and rippling sounds in the brown water about them and occasional eruptions of bubbles as swamp gas gurgled to the surface. Silk sighed bitterly. 'I hate this place,' he said. 'I absolutely hate it.'

That night Garion had a nightmare. It was not the first he had suffered since they had left Riva; and as he sat up, sweat drenched and trembling, he was positive it would not be the last. It was not a new nightmare, but rather was one which had periodically haunted his sleep since boyhood. Unlike an ordinary bad dream, this one did not involve being chased or threatened, but consisted rather of a single image – the image of a hideously maimed face. Although he had never actually seen the owner of the face, he knew exactly whose face it was, and now he knew why it inhabited his darkest dreams.

The next day dawned cloudy with a threat of approaching rain. As Belgarath stirred up the fire and Silk rummaged through his pack for something suitable for breakfast, Garion stood looking out at the swamp around him. A flight of geese swept by overhead in a ragged V, their wings whistling and their muted cries drifting, lonely and remote. A fish jumped not far from the edge of the hummock, and Garion watched the ripples widening out toward the far shore. He looked for quite some time at that shore before he realized exactly what it was he was seeing. Concerned, then a bit alarmed, he began to peer first this way and then that.

'Grandfather!' he cried. 'Look!'

'At what?'

'It's all changed. There aren't any channels any more. We're in the middle of a big pond, and there isn't any way out of it.' He spun around, desperately trying to see some exit, but the edges of the pond in which they sat were totally unbroken. There were no channels leading out of it, and the brown water was absolutely still, showing no evidence of current.

Then in the center of the pond, without making so much as a ripple, a round, furred head emerged from the water. The animal's eyes were very large and bright; it had no external ears, and its little nose was as black as a button. It made a peculiar chirping noise, and another head emerged out of the water a few feet away.

'Fenlings!' Silk gasped, drawing his short sword with a steely rustle.

'Oh, put that away,' Belgarath told him disgustedly. 'They aren't going to hurt you.'

'They've trapped us, haven't they?'

'What do they want?' Garion asked.

'Breakfast, obviously,' Silk answered, still holding his sword.

'Don't be stupid, Silk,' Belgarath told him. 'Why would they want to eat a raw Drasnian when there's a whole swampful of fish available? Put the sword away.'

The first fenling which had poked its head up out of the water lifted one of its webbed forefeet and made a peremptory gesture. The webbed foot was strangely handlike.

'They seem to want us to follow them,' Belgarath said calmly.

'And you're going to do it?' Silk was aghast. 'Are you mad?'

'Do we have any choice?'

Without further discussion, Belgarath began taking down the tent.

'Are they monsters, Grandfather?' Garion asked worriedly as he helped. 'Like Algroths or Trolls?'

'No, they're just animals – like seals or beaver. They're curious and intelligent and very playful.'

'But they play very nasty games,' Silk added.

After they had stowed all their packs into the boat, they pushed it down the bank into the water. The fenlings watched them curiously with no particular threat or malice in their gaze, but rather a kind of firm determination on their furry little faces. The solid-looking edge of the pond opened then to reveal the channel that had been concealed during the night. The strangely rounded head of the fenling who had gestured to them moved on ahead, leading the way and glancing back often to be certain they were following. Several others trailed after the boat, their large eyes alert.

It began to rain, a few drops at first, and then a steady drizzle that veiled the endless expanse of reed and cattail stretching out on all sides of them.

'Where do you think they're taking us?' Silk asked, stopping his poling to wipe the rain out of his face. One of the fenlings behind the boat chattered angrily at him until he dug his pole into the muddy bottom of the channel again.

'We'll just have to wait and see,' Belgarath replied.

The channel continued to open before them, and they poled steadily along, following the round-headed fenling who had first appeared.

'Are those trees up ahead?' Silk asked, peering into the misty drizzle.

'It appears so,' Belgarath answered. 'I suspect that's where we're going.'

The large cluster of trees slowly emerged from the mist. As they drew closer, Garion could see a gentle rise of ground swelling up out of the reeds and water. The grove which crowned the island appeared to be mostly willows with long, trailing branches.

The fenling who had been leading them swam on ahead. When it reached the island, it emerged half out of the water and gave a strange, whistling cry. A moment or so later, a hooded figure stepped out of the trees and moved slowly down to the bank. Garion did not know what to expect, but he was more than a little startled when the brown-cloaked figure on the shore pushed back the hood to reveal a woman's face that, though very old, still bore the luminous traces of what had once been an extraordinary beauty.

'Hail, Belgarath,' she greeted the old sorcerer in an oddly neutral voice.

'Hello, Vordai,' he replied conversationally. 'It's been quite a while, hasn't it?'

The little creatures that had guided them to the island waded out of the water to gather around the brown-cloaked woman. They chirped and chattered to her, and she looked at them fondly, touching their wet fur with gentle fingers. They were medium-sized animals with short hind legs and little rounded bellies and they walked upright with a peculiar quick shuffle, their forepaws held delicately in front of their furry chests.

'Come inside out of the rain, Belgarath,' the woman said. 'Bring your friends.' She turned and walked up a path leading into the willow grove with her fenlings scampering along beside her.

'What do we do?' Garion whispered.

'We go inside,' Belgarath replied, stepping out of the boat onto the island.

Garion was not sure what to expect as he and Silk followed the old man up the path toward the dripping willows, but he was totally unprepared for the neat, thatch-roofed cottage with its small adjoining garden. The house was built of weathered logs, tightly chinked with moss, and a wispy tendril of smoke drifted from its chimney.

At the doorway, the woman in brown carefully wiped her feet on a rush mat and shook the rain out of her cloak. Then she opened the door and went inside without looking back.

Silk's expression was dubious as he stopped outside the cottage. 'Are you sure this is a good idea, Belgarath?' he asked quietly. 'I've heard stories about Vordai.'

'It's the only way to find out what she wants,' Belgarath told him, 'and I'm fairly sure we aren't going any farther until we talk with her. Let's go in. Be sure to wipe your feet.'

The interior of Vordai's cottage was scrupulously neat. The ceilings were low and heavily beamed. The wooden floor was scrubbed to whiteness, and a table and chairs sat before an arched fireplace where a pot hung in the flames from an iron arm. There were wildflowers in a vase on the table and curtains at the window overlooking the garden.

'Why don't you introduce your friends to me, Belgarath?' the woman suggested, hanging her cloak on a peg. She smoothed the front of her plain brown dress.

'As you wish, Vordai,' the old man replied politely. 'This is Prince Kheldar, your countryman. And this is King Belgarion of Riva.'

'Noble guests,' the woman observed in that strangely neutral voice. 'Welcome to the house of Vordai.'

'Forgive me, madame,' Silk said in his most courtly manner, 'but your reputation seems to be grossly inaccurate.'

'Vordai, the witch of the fens?' she asked, looking amused. 'Do they still call me that?'

He smiled in return. 'Their descriptions are misleading, to say the least.'

'The hag of the swamps.' She mimicked the speech of a credulous peasant. 'Drowner of travellers and queen of the fenlings.' There was a bitter twist to her lips.

'That's more or less what they say,' he told her. 'I always believed you were a myth conjured up to frighten unruly children.'

'Vordai will get you and gobble you up!' She laughed, but there was no humor in her laughter. 'I've been hearing that for generations. Take off your cloaks, gentlemen. Sit down and make yourselves comfortable. You'll be staying for a while.'

One of the fenlings – the one who had led them to the island, Garion thought – chattered at her in a piping little voice, glancing nervously at the pot hanging in the fire.

'Yes,' she answered quite calmly, 'I know that it's boiling, Tupik. It has to boil or it won't cook.' She turned back to her guests. 'Breakfast will be ready in a bit,' she told them. 'Tupik tells me you haven't eaten yet.'

'You can communicate with them?' Silk sounded surprised.

'Isn't that obvious, Prince Kheldar? Here, let me hang

your cloaks by the fire to dry.' She stopped and regarded Garion gravely. 'So great a sword for one so young,' she noted, looking at the great hilt rising above his shoulder. 'Stand it in the corner, King Belgarion. There's no one to fight here.'

Garion inclined his head politely, unbuckled the sword belt and handed her his cloak.

Another, somewhat smaller fenling darted out of a corner with a piece of cloth and began busily wiping up the water that had dripped from their cloaks, chattering disapprovingly all the while.

'You'll have to forgive Poppi.' Vordai smiled. 'She's obsessed with tidiness. I sometimes think that, if I left her alone, she'd sweep holes in the floor.'

'They're changing, Vordai,' Belgarath said gravely, seating himself at the table.

'I know,' she replied, going to the fireplace to stir the bubbling pot. 'I've watched them over the years. They're not the same as they were when I came here.'

'It was a mistake to tamper with them,' he told her.

'So you've said before – you and Polgara both. How is she, by the way?'

'Probably raging by now. We slipped out of the Citadel at Riva without telling her we were leaving, and that sort of thing irritates her.'

'Polgara was born irritable.'

'We agree on that point anyway.'

'Breakfast's ready.' She lifted the pot with a curved iron hook and set it on the table. Poppi scampered over to a cupboard standing against the far wall and brought back a stack of wooden bowls, then returned for spoons. Her large eyes were very bright, and she chittered seriously at the three visitors.

'She's telling you not to drop crumbs on her clean floor,' Vordai advised them, removing a steaming loaf of bread from an oven built into the side of the fireplace. 'Crumbs infuriate her.'

'We'll be careful,' Belgarath promised.

It was a peculiar sort of breakfast, Garion thought. The stew that came steaming from the pot was thick, with strange vegetables floating in it, and large chunks of fish. It was delicately seasoned, however, and he found it delicious. By the time he had finished eating, he rather reluctantly concluded that Vordai might even be as good a cook as Aunt Pol.

'Excellent, Vordai,' Belgarath complimented her, finally pushing his bowl away. 'Now suppose we get down to business. Why did you have us brought here?'

'To talk, Belgarath,' she replied. 'I don't get much company, and conversation's a good way to pass a rainy morning. Why have you come into the fens?'

'The Prophecy moves on, Vordai – even if sometimes we don't. The Rivan King has returned, and Torak stirs in his sleep.'

'Ah,' she said without much real interest.

'The Orb of Aldur stands on the pommel of Belgarion's sword. The day is not far off when the Child of Light and the Child of Dark must meet. We go toward that meeting, and all mankind awaits the outcome.'

'Except me, Belgarath.' She gave him a penetrating look. 'The fate of mankind is a matter of only the mildest curiosity to me. I was excluded from mankind three hundred years ago, you'll remember.'

'Those people are all long dead, Vordai.'

'Their descendants are no different. Could I walk into any village in this part of Drasnia and tell the good villagers who I am without being stoned or burned?'

'Villagers are the same the world over, madame,' Silk put in. 'Provincial, stupid, and superstitious. Not all men are like that.'

'All men are the same, Prince Kheldar,' she disagreed. 'When I was young, I tried to involve myself in the affairs of my village. I only wanted to help, but very soon not a cow died or a baby took colic without my being blamed for it. They stoned me finally and tried to drag me back to the village to burn me at the stake. They had quite a celebration planned. I managed to escape, though, and I took refuge here in the fens. After that I had very little interest in the affairs of men.'

'You probably shouldn't have displayed your talents quite so openly,' Belgarath told her. 'People prefer not to believe in that sort of thing. There's a whole catalogue of nasty little emotions curdling in the human spirit, and anything the least bit out of the ordinary raises the possibility of retribution.'

'My village learned that it was more than a possibility,' she replied with a certain grim satisfaction.

'What happened?' Garion asked curiously.

'It started raining,' Vordai told him with an odd smile.

'Is that all?'

'It was enough. It rained on that village for five years, King Belgarion – just on the village. A hundred yards beyond the last house everything was normal, but in the village there was rain. They tried to move twice, but the rain followed them. Finally they gave up and left the area. For all I know, some of their descendants are still wandering.'

'You're not serious,' Silk scoffed.

'Quite serious.' She gave him an amused look. 'Your credulity appears selective, Prince Kheldar. Here you are, going about the world in the company of Belgarath the Sorcerer. I'm sure you believe in his power; but you can't bring yourself to accept the idea of the power of the witch of the fens.'

Silk stared at her.

'I really am a witch, Prince Kheldar. I could demonstrate if you wish, but I don't think you'd like it very much. People seldom do.'

'That isn't really necessary, Vordai,' Belgarath said. 'What is it that you want exactly?'

'I was coming to that, Belgarath,' she replied. 'After I escaped into the fens, I discovered my little friends here.' She affectionately stroked the side of Poppi's furry little face, and Poppi nuzzled at her hand ecstatically. 'They were afraid of me at first, but they finally grew less shy. They began bringing me fish – and flowers – as tokens of friendship, and I needed friends very badly at that time. I altered them a bit out of gratitude.'

'You shouldn't have, you know,' the old man said rather sadly.

She shrugged. 'Should and shouldn't have very little meaning to me any more.'

'Not even the Gods would do what you did.'

'The Gods have other amusements.' She looked directly at him then. 'I've been waiting for you, Belgarath – for years now. I knew that sooner or later you'd come back into the fens. This meeting you spoke of is very important to you, isn't it?'

'It's the most important event in the history of the world.'

'That depends on your point of view, I suppose. You need my help, though.'

'I think we can manage, Vordai.'

'Perhaps, but how do you expect to get out of the fens?'

He looked at her sharply.

'I can open the way for you to the dry ground at the edge of the swamp, or I can see to it that you wander around in these marshes forever – in which case this meeting you're concerned about will never happen, will it? That puts me in a very interesting situation, wouldn't you say?'

Belgarath's eyes narrowed.

'I discovered that when men deal with each other, there's usually an exchange of some kind,' she added with a strange little smile. 'Something for something; nothing for nothing. It seems to be a sensible arrangement.'

'Exactly what did you have in mind?'

'The fenlings are my friends,' she replied. 'In a very special way, my children. But men look upon them as animals with pelts worth the taking. They trap them, Belgarath, and they kill them for their fur. The fine ladies in Boktor and Kotu dress themselves in the skins of my children and give no thought to the grief it causes me. They call my children animals and they come into the fens to hunt them.'

'They *are* animals, Vordai,' he told her gently.

'Not any more.' Almost without seeming to think, Vordai put her arm about Poppi's shoulders. 'It may be that you were right when you said that I shouldn't have tampered with them, but it's too late now to change it back.' She sighed. 'I'm a witch, Belgarath,' she continued, 'not a sorceress. My life has a beginning and an end, and it's approaching its end, I think. I won't live forever, as you and Polgara have done. I've lived several hundred years already and I'm growing very tired of life. As long as I'm alive, I can keep men from coming into the fens; but once I'm gone, my children will have no protection.'

'And you want me to take them into my care?'

'No, Belgarath. You're too busy; and sometimes you forget promises you don't care to remember. I want you to do the one thing that will make it forever impossible for men to think of the fenlings as animals.'

310

His eyes widened as what she was suggesting dawned on him.

'I want you to give my children the power of speech, Belgarath,' Vordai said. 'I can't do it. My witchcraft doesn't reach that far. Only a sorcerer can make it possible for them to talk.'

'Vordai!'

'That's my price, Belgarath,' she told him. 'That's what my help will cost you. Take it or leave it.'

Chapter Nineteen

They slept that night in Vordai's cottage, though Garion slept very little. The ultimatum of the witch of the fens troubled him profoundly. He knew that tampering with nature had far-reaching effects, and to go as far as Vordai wished might forever erase the dividing line between men and animals. The philosophical and theological implications of that step were staggering. There were, moreover, other worries. It was entirely possible that Belgarath could not do what Vordai demanded of him. Garion was almost positive that his grandfather had not attempted to use his will since his collapse months before, and now Vordai had set him an almost impossible task.

What would happen to Belgarath if he tried and failed? What would that do to him? Would the doubts then take over and rob him of any possibility of ever regaining his power? Desperately Garion tried to think of a way to warn his grandfather without arousing those fatal doubts.

But they absolutely had to get out of the fens. However reluctantly Garion had made the decision to meet Torak, he now knew that it was the only possible choice open to him. The meeting, however, could not be delayed indefinitely. If it were put off too long, events would move on, and the world would be plunged into the war they were all so desperately trying to head off. Vordai's threat to trap them all here in the fens unless

Belgarath paid her price threatened not only them, but the entire world. In a very real sense, she held the fate of all mankind in her uncaring hands. Try though he might, Garion could not think of any way to avoid the test of Belgarath's will. Though he would reluctantly have done what Vordai wished himself, he did not even know where to begin. If it could be done at all, his grandfather was the only one who could do it – if his illness had not destroyed his power.

When dawn crept through the misty fens, Belgarath arose and sat before the fire, brooding into the crackling flames with a somber face.

'Well?' Vordai asked him. 'Have you decided?'

'It's wrong, Vordai,' he told her. 'Nature cries out against it.'

'I'm much closer to nature than you are, Belgarath,' she replied. 'Witches live more intimately with her than sorcerers do. I can feel the turning of the seasons in my blood, and the earth is alive under my feet. I hear no outcry. Nature loves all her creatures, and she would grieve over the obliteration of my fenlings almost as much as I. But that's really beside the point, isn't it? Even though the very rocks shrieked out against it, I would not relent.'

Silk exchanged a quick look with Garion, and the little man's sharp face seemed as troubled as Belgarath's.

'Are the fenlings really beasts?' Vordai continued. She pointed to where Poppi still slept, her delicate forepaws open like little hands. Tupik, moving stealthily, crept back into the house, carrying a handful of dew-drenched swamp flowers. With precise care, he placed them about the slumbering Poppi and gently laid the last one in her open hand. Then, with an oddly patient expression, he sat on his haunches to watch her awakening.

Poppi stirred, stretched, and yawned. She brought the flower to her little black nose and sniffed at it, looking affectionately at the expectant Tupik. She made a happy little chirping sound, and then she and Tupik scampered off together for a morning swim in the cool water of the swamp.

'It's a courting ritual,' Vordai explained. 'Tupik wants Poppi to be his mate, and as long as she continues to accept his gifts, he knows that she's still fond of him. It will go on for quite some time, and then they'll swim off into the swamp together for a week or so. When they come back, they'll be mates for life. Is that really so different from the way young humans behave?'

Her question profoundly disturbed Garion for some reason he could not quite put his finger on.

'Look there,' Vordai told them, pointing through the window at a group of young fenlings, scarcely more than babies, at play. They had fashioned a ball out of moss and were rapidly passing it around in a circle, their large eyes intent on their game. 'Couldn't a human child join that group and not feel the slightest bit out of place?' Vordai pressed.

Not far beyond the game, a mature female fenling cradled her sleeping baby, rocking gently with her cheek against the little one's face. 'Isn't motherhood universal?' Vordai asked. 'In what way do my children differ from humans? – except that they're perhaps more decent, more honest and loving with each other?'

Belgarath sighed. 'All right, Vordai,' he said, 'you've made your point. I'll grant that the fenlings are probably nicer creatures than men. I don't know that speech will improve them, but if that's what you want—' He shrugged.

'You'll do it then?'

'I know it's wrong, but I'll try to do what you ask. I really don't have much choice, do I?'

'No,' she replied, 'you don't. Will you need anything? I have all the customary implements and compounds.'

He shook his head. 'Sorcery doesn't work that way. Witchcraft involves the summoning of spirits, but sorcery comes all from within. Someday, if we have the leisure, I'll explain the difference to you.' He stood up. 'I don't suppose you'd care to change your mind about this?'

Her face hardened. 'No, Belgarath,' she replied.

He sighed again. 'All right, Vordai. I'll be back in a bit.' He turned quietly and walked out into the mist-shrouded morning.

In the silence that followed his departure, Garion closely watched Vordai for some hint that her determination might not be as iron-hard as it seemed. It had occurred to him that if she were not blindly adamant, he might be able to explain the situation and persuade her to relent. The witch of the fens paced nervously about the room, picking things up absently and setting them down again. She seemed unable to concentrate her attention on any one thing for more than a moment.

'This may ruin him, you know,' Garion told her quietly. Bluntness perhaps might sway her where other attempts at persuasion had failed.

'What are you talking about?' she demanded sharply.

'He was very ill last winter,' Garion replied. 'He and Ctuchik fought each other for possession of the Orb. Ctuchik was destroyed, but Belgarath nearly died too. It's quite possible that his power was destroyed by his illness.'

Silk's gasp was clearly audible. 'Why didn't you tell us?' he exclaimed.

'Aunt Pol said that we didn't dare,' Garion said. 'We couldn't take any chance of word of it getting back to the Angaraks. Belgarath's power is the one thing that's held them in check all these years. If he's lost it and they find out, they'll feel free to invade the West.'

'Does *he* know?' Vordai asked quickly.

'I don't think so. Neither one of us said anything to him about it. We couldn't let him think for a moment that anything might be wrong. If he has one single doubt, it won't work for him. That's the main thing about sorcery. You have to believe that what you want to happen is going to. Otherwise, nothing happens at all – and each time you fail, it gets worse.'

'What did you mean when you said that this might ruin him?' Vordai's face looked stricken, and Garion began to have some hope.

'He may still have his power – or some of it,' he explained. 'But not enough to do what you've asked of him. It takes a tremendous effort to do even simple things, and what you've asked him to do is very difficult. It could be too much for him; but once he starts, he won't be able to stop. And the effort may drain his will and his life energy until he cannot ever recover – or until he dies.'

'Why didn't you tell me?' Vordai demanded, her face anguished.

'I couldn't – not without his hearing me, too.'

She turned quickly toward the door. 'Belgarath!' she cried. 'Wait!' She spun back to Garion. 'Go after him! Stop him!'

That was what Garion had been waiting for. He jumped to his feet and ran to the door. As he swung it open and was about to call out across the rainy yard, he felt a strange oppression as if something were almost happening – almost, but not quite. The shout froze on his lips.

'Go on, Garion,' Silk urged him.

'I can't,' Garion groaned. 'He's already begun to pull in his will. He wouldn't even hear me.'

'Can you help him?'

'I don't even know exactly what he's trying to do, Silk,' Garion replied helplessly. 'If I went blundering in there now, all I'd do is make things worse.'

They stared at him in consternation.

Garion felt a strange echoing surge. It was not at all what he expected, and so he was totally unprepared for it. His grandfather was not trying to move anything or change anything, but instead he was calling out – reaching across some vast distance with the voice of his mind. The words were not at all distinct, but the one word, 'Master,' did come through once quite distinctly. Belgarath was trying to reach Aldur.

Garion held his breath.

Then, from infinitely far away, Aldur's voice replied. They spoke together quietly for several moments, and all the while Garion could feel the force of Belgarath's will, infused and magnified by the will of Aldur, growing stronger and stronger.

'What's happening?' Silk's voice was almost frightened.

'He's talking with Aldur. I can't hear what they're saying.'

'Will Aldur help him?' Vordai asked.

'I don't know. I don't know if Aldur can use his will here any more. There's some kind of limitation – something that he and the other Gods agreed to.'

Then the strange conversation ended, and Garion felt Belgarath's will mounting, gathering itself. 'He's begun,' Garion said in a half-whisper.

'His power's still there?' Silk asked.

Garion nodded.

'As strong as ever?'

'I don't know. There's no way to measure it.'

The tension of it grew until it was almost intolerable.

What Belgarath was doing was at once very subtle and very profound. There was no rushing surge or hollow echo this time. Instead, Garion felt an odd, tingling whisper as the old man's will was unleashed with agonizing slowness. The whisper seemed to be saying something over and over – something Garion could almost understand, but which tantalizingly eluded him.

Outside, the young fenlings stopped their game. The ball dropped unnoticed as the players all stood, listening intently. Poppi and Tupik, returning hand in hand from their swim, froze in their tracks and stood with their heads cocked as Belgarath's whisper spoke gently to them, reaching down into their thoughts, murmuring, explaining, teaching. Then their eyes widened as if in sudden understanding.

Belgarath emerged finally from the misty willows, his step heavy, weary. He walked slowly toward the house, stopping just outside to look intently at the stunned faces of the fenlings gathered in the dooryard. He nodded then and came back inside. His shoulders were slumped with exhaustion, and his white-bearded face seemed drained.

'Are you all right?' Vordai asked him, her tone no longer neutral.

He nodded and sank into a chair by the table. 'It's done,' he said shortly.

Vordai looked at him, and her eyes narrowed suspiciously.

'No tricks, Vordai,' he said. 'And I'm too tired to try to lie to you. I've paid your price. If it's all right with you, we'll leave right after breakfast. We still have a long way to go.'

'I'll need more than just your word, Belgarath. I don't really trust you – or any human, for that matter. I want proof that you've paid.'

318

But there was a strange new voice from the doorway. Poppi, her furry little face contorted with the effort, was struggling with something. 'M-m-m-m-,' she stammered. Her mouth twisted, and she tried again. 'M-m-m-m-.' It seemed to be the hardest thing she had ever tried to do. She took a deep breath and tried once more. 'M-m-m-mo-therrr,' Poppi said.

With a low cry, Vordai rushed to the little creature, knelt, and embraced her.

'Mother,' Poppi said again. It was clearer this time.

From outside the cottage there came a growing babble of small, squeaky voices, all repeating, 'Mother, mother, mother.' The excited fenlings converged on the cottage, their voices swelling as more and more of them emerged from the swamps.

Vordai wept.

'You'll have to teach them, of course,' Belgarath said wearily. 'I gave them the ability, but they don't know very many words yet.'

Vordai looked at him with tears streaming down her face. 'Thank you, Belgarath,' she said in a faltering voice.

The old man shrugged. 'Something for something,' he replied. 'Wasn't that the bargain?'

It was Tupik who led them from the fens. The little creature's chirping to his fellows, however, now had words mixed in with it – faltering, often badly mispronounced, but words nonetheless.

Garion thought for a long time before he spoke, wrestling with an idea as he pushed on his pole. 'Grandfather,' he said finally.

'Yes, Garion,' the old man replied from where he rested in the stern of their boat.

'You knew all along, didn't you?'

'Knew what?'

'That it was possible that you couldn't make things happen any more?'

Belgarath stared at him. 'Where did you get that idea?' he asked.

'Aunt Pol said that after you got sick last winter, you might have lost all your power.'

'She said *what*?'

'She said that—'

'I heard you.' The old man was frowning, his face creased with thought. 'That possibility never even occurred to me,' he admitted. Suddenly he blinked and his eyes opened very wide. 'You know, she might have been right. The illness *could* have had that sort of effect. What an amazing thing.'

'You didn't feel any – well – weaker?'

'What? No, of course not.' Belgarath was still frowning, turning the idea over in his mind. 'What an amazing thing,' he repeated, and then he suddenly laughed.

'I don't see what's so funny.'

'Is that what's been bothering you and your Aunt for all these months? The two of you have been tiptoeing around me as if I were made out of thin glass.'

'We were afraid the Angaraks might find out, and we didn't dare say anything to you because—'

'Because you were afraid it might make me doubt my abilities?'

Garion nodded.

'Maybe in the long run it wasn't a bad idea at that. I certainly didn't need any doubts plaguing me this morning.'

'Was it terribly diffcult?'

'Moderately so, yes. I wouldn't want to have to try that sort of thing every day.'

'But you didn't really have to do it, did you?'

'Do what?'

'Show the fenlings how to talk. If you've still got your power, then between the two of us, you and I could have opened a channel straight through to the edge of the swamp – no matter what Vordai or the fenlings could have done to try to stop us.'

'I wondered how long it was going to be before that occurred to you,' the old man replied blandly.

Garion gave him an irritated look. 'All right,' he said, 'why did you do it then, since you didn't have to?'

'That question's rather impolite, Garion,' Belgarath chided. 'There are certain courtesies customarily observed. It's not considered good manners to ask another sorcerer why he did something.'

Garion gave his grandfather an even harder look. 'You're evading the question,' he said bluntly. 'Let's agree that I don't have very good manners, and then you can go ahead and answer anyway.'

Belgarath appeared slightly injured. 'It's not my fault that you and your Aunt were so worried. You don't really have any reason to be so cross with me.' He paused, then looked at Garion. 'You're absolutely going to insist?' he asked.

'Yes, I think I really am. Why did you do it?'

Belgarath sighed. 'Vordai's been alone for most of her life, you know,' he replied, 'and life's been very hard to her. Somehow I've always thought that she deserved better. Maybe this makes up for it – a little bit.'

'Did Aldur agree with you?' Garion pressed. 'I heard his voice when the two of you were talking.'

'Eavesdropping is really a bad habit, Garion.'

'I've got lots of bad habits, Grandfather.'

'I don't know why you're taking this tone with me, boy,' the old man complained. 'All right, since you're going to be this way about it, I did, as a matter of fact, have to talk rather fast to get my Master to agree.'

'You did all of this because you felt sorry for her?'

'That's not exactly the right term, Garion. Let's just say that I have certain feelings about justice.'

'If you knew you were going to do it anyway, why did you argue with her?'

Belgarath shrugged. 'I wanted to be sure that she really wanted it. Besides, it's not a good idea to let people get the idea that you'll do anything they ask just because you might feel that they have a certain claim on you.'

Silk was staring at the old man in amazement. 'Compassion, Belgarath?' he demanded incredulously. 'From *you*? If word of this ever gets out, your reputation's going to be ruined.'

Belgarath looked suddenly painfully embarrassed. 'I don't know that we need to spread it around all that much, Silk,' he said. 'People don't really have to know about this, do they?'

Garion felt as if a door had suddenly opened. Silk, he realized, was right. He had never precisely thought of it that way, but Belgarath *did* have a certain reputation for ruthlessness. Most men felt that there was a kind of implacableness about the Eternal Man – a willingness to sacrifice anything in his single-minded drive toward a goal so obscure that no one else could ever fully understand it. But with this single act of compassion, he had revealed another, softer side of his nature. Belgarath the Sorcerer was capable of human emotion and feeling, after all. The thought of how those feelings had been wounded by all the horrors and pain he had seen and endured in seven thousand years came crashing in on Garion, and he found himself staring at his grandfather with a profound new respect.

The edge of the fens was marked by a solid-looking

dike that stretched off into the misty distance in either direction.

'The causeway,' Silk told Garion, pointing at the dike. 'It's part of the Tolnedran highway system.'

'Bel-grath,' Tupik said, his head popping up out of the water beside the boat, 'thank-you.'

'Oh, I rather think you'd have learned to talk eventually anyway, Tupik,' the old man replied. 'You were very close to it, you know.'

'May-be, may-be-not,' Tupik disagreed. 'Want-to-talk and talk dif-ferent. Not-same.'

'Soon you'll learn to lie,' Silk told him sardonically, 'and then you'll be as good as any man alive.'

'Why learn to talk if only to lie?' Tupik asked, puzzled.

'It'll come to you in time.'

Tupik frowned slightly, and then his head slipped under the water. He came up one more time some distance away from the boat. 'Good-bye,' he called to them. 'Tupik thanks you – for Mother.' Then, without a ripple, he disappeared.

'What a strange little creature.' Belgarath smiled.

With a startled exclamation, Silk frantically dug into his pocket. Something a pale green color leaped from his hand to plop into the water.

'What's the matter?' Garion asked him.

Silk shuddered. 'The little monster put a frog in my pocket.'

'Perhaps it was meant as a gift,' Belgarath suggested.

'A frog?'

'Then again perhaps it wasn't.' Belgarath grinned. 'It's a little primitive perhaps, but it might just be the beginnings of a sense of humor.'

There was a Tolnedran hostel a few miles up the great causeway that ran north and south through the eastern edge of the fens. They reached it in the late afternoon and purchased horses at a price that made Silk wince. The following morning they moved out at a canter in the direction of Boktor.

The strange interlude in the fens had given Garion a great deal to think about. He began to perceive that compassion was a kind of love – broader and more encompassing than the somewhat narrow idea he had previously had of that emotion. The word love seemed, as he thought more deeply about it, to include a great number of things that at first glance did not seem to have anything whatsoever to do with it. As his understanding of this grew, a peculiar notion took hold of his imagination. His grandfather, the man they called Eternal, had probably in his seven thousand years developed a capacity for love beyond the ability of other men even remotely to guess at. In spite of that gruff, irritable exterior, Belgarath's entire life had been an expression of that transcendant love. As they rode, Garion glanced often at the strange old man, and the image of the remote, all-powerful sorcerer towering above the rest of humanity gradually faded; he began to see the real man behind that image – a complicated man to be sure, but a very human one.

Two days later in clearing weather, they reached Boktor.

Chapter Twenty

There was an open quality about Boktor that Garion noticed immediately as they rode through its broad streets. The houses were not for the most part over two stories high, and they were not jammed up against each other as they were in other cities he had seen. The avenues were wide and straight, and there was a minimum of litter in them.

He commented on that as they rode along a spacious, tree-lined boulevard.

'Boktor's a new city,' Silk explained. 'At least relatively.'

'I thought that it has been here since the time of Dras Bullneck.'

'Oh, it has,' Silk replied, 'but the old city was destroyed by the Angaraks when they invaded, five hundred years ago.'

'I'd forgotten that,' Garion admitted.

'After Vo Mimbre, when the time came to rebuild, it was decided to take advantage of the chance to start over,' Silk continued. He looked about rather distastefully. 'I don't really like Boktor,' he said. 'There aren't enough alleys and back streets. It's almost impossible to move around without being seen.' He turned to Belgarath. 'That reminds me of something, by the way. It probably wouldn't be a bad idea to avoid the central marketplace. I'm rather well-known here, and there's no point in letting the whole city know we've arrived.'

'Do you think we'll be able to slip through unnoticed?' Garion asked him.

'In Boktor?' Silk laughed. 'Of course not. We've already been identified a half dozen times. Spying is a major industry here. Porenn knew we were coming before we'd even entered the city.' He glanced up at a second floor window, and his fingers flickered a quick rebuke in the gestures of the Drasnian secret language. The curtain at the window gave a guilty little twitch. 'Just too clumsy,' he observed with profound disapproval. 'Must be a first-year student at the academy.'

'Probably nervous about seeing a celebrity,' Belgarath suggested. 'You are, after all, something of a legend, Silk.'

'There's still no excuse for sloppy work,' Silk said. 'If I had time, I'd stop by the academy and have a talk with the headmaster about it.' He sighed. 'The quality of student work has definitely gone downhill since they discontinued the use of the whipping post.'

'The what?' Garion exclaimed.

'In my day, a student who was seen by the person he was assigned to watch was flogged,' Silk told him. 'Flogging's a very effective teaching technique, Garion.'

Just ahead of them a door to a large house opened, and a dozen uniformed pikemen marched out into the street, halted and turned to face them. The officer in charge came forward and bowed politely. 'Prince Kheldar,' he greeted Silk, 'Her Highness wonders if you'd be so good as to stop by the palace.'

'You see,' Silk said to Garion. 'I told you she knew we were here.' He turned to the officer. 'Just out of curiosity, captain, what would you do if I told you that we didn't feel like being so good as to stop by the palace?'

'I'd probably have to insist,' the captain replied.

'I rather thought you might feel that way about it.'

'Are we under arrest?' Garion asked nervously.

'Not precisely, your Majesty,' the captain answered. 'Queen Porenn most definitely wishes to speak with you, however.' He bowed then to Belgarath. 'Ancient One,' he greeted the old man respectfully. 'I think that if we went around to the side entrance, we'd attract less attention.' And he turned and gave his men the order to march.

'He knows who we are,' Garion muttered to Silk.

'Naturally,' Silk said.

'How are we going to get out of this? Won't Queen Porenn just ship us all back to Riva?'

'We'll talk to her,' Belgarath said. 'Porenn's got good sense. I'm sure we can explain this to her.'

'Unless Polgara's been issuing ultimatums,' Silk added. 'She does that when she gets angry, I've noticed.'

'We'll see.'

Queen Porenn was even more radiantly lovely than ever. Her slimness made it obvious that the birth of her first child had already occurred. Motherhood had brought a glow to her face and a look of completion to her eyes. She greeted them fondly as they entered the palace and led them immediately to her private quarters. The little queen's rooms were somehow lacy and feminine with ruffles on the furniture and soft, pink curtains at the windows. 'Where have you been?' she asked them as soon as they were alone. 'Polgara's frantic.'

Belgarath shrugged. 'She'll recover. What's happening in Riva?'

'They're directing the search for you, naturally,' Porenn replied. 'How did you manage to get this far? Every road's been blocked.'

'We were ahead of everybody, Auntie dearest.' Silk

grinned impudently at her. 'By the time they started blocking roads, we'd already gone through.'

'I've asked you not to call me that, Kheldar,' she admonished him.

'Forgive me, your Highness,' he said with a bow, though still grinning mockingly.

'You're impossible,' she told him.

'Of course I am,' he answered. 'It's part of my charm.'

The queen sighed. 'What am I going to do with all of you now?'

'You're going to let us continue our journey,' Belgarath replied calmly. 'We'll argue about it, of course, but in the end that's the way it will turn out.'

She stared at him.

'You did ask, after all. I'm sure you feel better now that you know.'

'You're as bad or worse than Kheldar,' she accused.

'I've had more practice.'

'It's quite out of the question,' she told him firmly. 'I have strict orders from Polgara to send you all back to Riva.'

Belgarath shrugged.

'You'll go?' She seemed surprised.

'No,' he replied, 'we won't. You said that Polgara gave you strict orders to send us back. All right, then, *I* give you strict orders not to. Now where does that leave us?'

'That's cruel, Belgarath.'

'Times are hard.'

'Before we get down to serious squabbling, do you suppose we might have a look at the heir to the throne?' Silk asked. His question was artful. No new mother could resist the opportunity to show off her infant, and Queen Porenn had already turned toward the cradle standing in the corner of the room before she realized

328

that she was being cleverly manipulated. 'You're bad, Kheldar,' she said reprovingly, but she nonetheless pulled back the satin coverlet to reveal the baby that had become the absolute center of her life.

The Crown Prince of Drasnia was very seriously attempting to put one of his toes in his mouth. With a happy little cry, Porenn caught him up in her arms and hugged him. Then she turned him and held him out for them to see. 'Isn't he beautiful?' she demanded.

'Hail, cousin,' Silk greeted the baby gravely. 'Your timely arrival has insured that I will be spared the ultimate indignity.'

'What's that supposed to mean?' Porenn asked him suspiciously.

'Only that his little pink Highness has permanently removed any possibility of my ever ascending the throne,' Silk replied. 'I'd be a very bad king, Porenn. Drasnia would suffer almost as much as I would, if that disaster ever took place. Our Garion here is already a better king by accident than I could ever be.'

'Oh dear.' Porenn flushed slightly. 'That completely slipped my mind.' She curtsied somewhat awkwardly, her baby still in her arms. 'Your Majesty,' she greeted Garion formally.

'Your Highness,' Garion answered with the bow Aunt Pol had made him practice for hours.

Porenn laughed her silvery little laugh. 'That all seems so inappropriate.' She put one hand to the back of Garion's neck, drew his head down and kissed him warmly. The baby in her other arm cooed. 'Dear Garion,' she said. 'You've grown so tall.'

There wasn't much he could say to that.

The queen studied his face for a moment. 'Many things have happened to you,' she observed shrewdly. 'You're not the same boy I knew in Val Alorn.'

'He's making progress,' Belgarath agreed, settling himself into a chair. 'How many spies are listening to us at the moment, Porenn?'

'Two that I know of,' she replied, returning her baby to his cradle.

Silk laughed. 'And how many spies are spying on the spies?'

'Several, I'd imagine,' Porenn told him. 'If I tried to unravel all the spying that goes on here, I'd never get anything done. '

'I'll assume that they're all discreet,' Belgarath said with a meaningful glance around at the walls and draperies.

'Of course they are,' Porenn declared, sounding slightly offended. 'We do have standards, you know. Amateurs are never allowed to spy inside the palace.'

'All right, let's get down to business, then. Is it really going to be necessary for us to go through some long, involved argument about whether or not you're going to try to send us back to Riva?'

She sighed and then gave a helpless little laugh. 'I suppose not,' she surrendered. 'You are going to have to give me an excuse to give to Polgara, though.'

'Just tell her that we're acting on the instructions contained in the Mrin Codex.'

'Are there instructions in the Mrin Codex?' She sounded surprised.

'There might be,' he replied. 'Most of it's such unmitigated gibberish that no one can be absolutely sure one way or the other.'

'Are you asking me to try to deceive her?'

'No, I'm asking you to let her think that I deceived you – there's a difference.'

'A very subtle one, Belgarath.'

'It will be all right,' he assured her. 'She's always ready

330

to believe the worst about me. Anyway, the three of us are on our way to Gar og Nadrak. Get word to Polgara that we're going to need a diversion of sorts. Tell her that I said to stop wasting time looking for us and to mass an army somewhere in the south – make a lot of noise. I want the Angaraks all to be so busy watching her that they don't have time to look for us.'

'What on earth are you going to do in Gar og Nadrak?' Porenn asked curiously.

Belgarath looked suggestively at the walls behind which the official spies – as well as a few unofficial ones – lurked. 'Polgara will know what we're doing. What's the current situation along the Nadrak border?'

'Tense,' she replied. 'It's not hostile yet, but it's a long way from cordial. The Nadraks don't really want to go to war. If it weren't for the Grolims, I honestly think we could persuade them to stay neutral. They'd much rather kill Murgos than Drasnians.'

Belgarath nodded. 'Pass the word on to your husband that I'd like for him to keep a fairly tight rein on Anheg,' he continued. 'Anheg's brilliant, but he's a trifle erratic at times. Rhodar's steadier. Tell him that what I want in the south is a diversion, not a general war. Alorns sometimes get overenthusiastic.'

'I'll get word to him,' Porenn promised. 'When will you start?'

'Let's leave that a bit tentative.' The old man glanced once again at the walls of the queen's room.

'You'll stay the night, at least,' she insisted.

'How could we possibly refuse?' Silk asked mockingly.

Queen Porenn looked at him for a long moment. Then she sighed. 'I guess I should tell you, Kheldar,' she said very quietly. 'Your mother's here.'

Silk's face blanched. 'Here? In the palace?'

The queen nodded. 'She's in the west wing. I've given her that apartment near the garden she loves so much.'

Silk's hands had begun to tremble visibly, and his face was still ashen. 'How long has she been here?' he asked in a strained voice.

'Several weeks. She came before the baby was born.'

'How is she?'

'The same.' The little blond queen's voice was hushed with sadness. 'You'll have to see her, you know.'

Silk drew in a deep breath and squared his shoulders. His face, however, was still stricken. 'There's no avoiding it, I guess,' he said, almost to himself. 'I might as well get it over with. You'll excuse me?'

'Of course.'

He turned and left the room, his face somber.

'Doesn't he like his mother?' Garion asked.

'He loves her very much,' the queen replied. 'That's why it's so terribly difficult for him. She's blind – fortunately.'

'Fortunately?'

'There was a pestilence in western Drasnia about twenty years ago,' Porenn explained. 'It was a horrible disease, and it left dreadful scars on the faces of the survivors. Prince Kheldar's mother had been one of the most beautiful women in Drasnia. We've concealed the truth from her. She doesn't realize how disfigured her face is – at least we hope she doesn't. The meetings between Kheldar and his mother are heartbreaking. There's no hint in his voice of what he sees, but his eyes—' She broke off. 'Sometimes I think that's why he stays away from Drasnia,' she added. Then she straightened. 'I'll ring for supper,' she said, 'and something to drink. Kheldar usually needs that after he's visited with his mother.'

It was an hour or more before Silk returned, and he

332

immediately started drinking. He drank grimly like a man bent on reducing himself to unconsciousness as quickly as possible.

It was an uncomfortable evening for Garion. Queen Porenn cared for her infant son even while keeping a watchful eye on Silk. Belgarath sat silently in a chair, and Silk kept drinking. Finally, pretending a weariness he did not feel, Garion went to bed.

He had not realized how much he had depended on Silk in the year and a half he had known him. The ratfaced little Drasnian's sardonic humor and towering self-reliance had always been something to cling to. To be sure, Silk had his quirks and peculiarities. He was a highstrung, complex little man, but his unfailing sense of humor and his mental agility had seen them all through some very unpleasant situations. Now, however, all traces of humor and wit were gone, and the little man seemed on the verge of total collapse.

The dreadful confrontation toward which they rode seemed all the more perilous now for some reason. Although Silk might not have been able to help him when he finally faced Torak, Garion had counted on his friend to assist him through the terrible days leading up to the meeting. Now even that slight comfort seemed to have been taken away. Unable to sleep, he tossed and turned for hours; finally, well past midnight, he rose, pulled his cloak about him and padded on stockinged feet to see if his friend had made it to bed.

Silk had not. He still sat in the same chair. His tankard, unnoticed, had spilled, and he sat with his elbows in a puddle of ale and his face in his hands. Not far away, her face unreadable, sat the weary little blond queen of Drasnia. As Garion watched from the doorway, a muffled sound came from between Silk's hands. With a gentle, almost tender expression Queen Porenn rose, came around the table and put her arms about his head, drawing him to her. With a despairing cry Silk clung to her, weeping openly like a hurt child.

Queen Porenn looked across the little man's shaking head at Garion. Her face quite clearly revealed that she was aware of Silk's feelings for her. Her look was one of helpless compassion for this man of whom she was fond – but not in the way he wished – and combined with that was a deep sympathy for the suffering his visit with his mother had caused him.

Silently Garion and the Queen of Drasnia stood looking at each other. Speech was unnecessary; they both understood. When at last Porenn did speak, her tone was curiously matter-of-fact. 'I think you can put him to bed now,' she said. 'Once he's able to cry, the worst is usually over.'

The next morning they left the palace and joined an eastbound caravan. The Drasnian moors beyond Boktor were desolate. The North Caravan Route wound through low, rolling hills covered with sparse vegetation and scanty grass. Although it was the middle of spring, there seemed to be a sere quality to the moors, as if the seasons only lightly touched them; the wind, sweeping down from the polar ice, still had the smell of winter in it.

Silk rode in silence, his eyes on the ground, though whether from grief or from the aftereffects of the ale he had drunk, Garion could not guess. Belgarath was also quiet, and the three of them rode with only the sound of the harness bells of a Drasnian merchant's mules for companionship.

About noon, Silk shook himself and looked around, his eyes finally alert, though still a bit bloodshot. 'Did anybody think to bring something to drink?' he asked.

'Didn't you get enough last night?' Belgarath replied.

'That was for entertainment. What I need now is something therapeutic.'

'Water?' Garion suggested.

'I'm thirsty, Garion, not dirty.'

'Here.' Belgarath handed the suffering man a wineskin. 'But don't overdo it.'

'Trust me,' Silk said, taking a long drink. He shuddered and made a face. 'Where did you buy this?' he inquired. 'It tastes like somebody's been boiling old shoes in it.'

'You don't have to drink it.'

'I'm afraid I do.' Silk took another drink, then restoppered the wineskin and handed it back. He looked sourly around at the moors. 'Hasn't changed much,' he observed. 'Drasnia has very little to recommend it, I'm afraid. It's either too wet or too dry.' He shivered in the chilly wind. 'Are either of you aware of the fact that there's nothing between us and the pole to break the wind but an occasional stray reindeer?'

Garion began to relax. Silk's sallies and comments grew broader and more outrageous as they rode through the afternoon. By the time the caravan stopped for the night, he seemed to be almost his old self again.

Chapter Twenty-One

The caravan wound its slow way through the dreary moors of eastern Drasnia with the sound of mule bells trailing mournfully behind it. Sparse patches of heath, which had but lately begun to bloom with tiny, pink flowers, dotted the low, rolling hills. The sky had turned cloudy, and the wind, seemingly perpetual, blew steadily out of the north.

Garion found his mood growing as sad and bleak as the moors around him. There was one inescapable fact which he no longer could hide from himself. Each mile, each step, brought him closer to Mallorea and closer to his meeting with Torak. Even the whispered song of the Orb, murmuring continually in his ears from the pommel of the great sword strapped to his back, could not reassure him. Torak was a God – invincible, immortal; and Garion, not even yet full-grown, was quite deliberately trekking to Mallorea to seek him out and to fight him to the death. Death was a word Garion tried very hard not to think about. It had been a possibility once or twice during their long pursuit of Zedar and the Orb; but now it seemed a certainty. He would meet Torak alone. Mandorallen or Barak or Hettar could not come to his aid with their superior skill at swordsmanship; Belgarath or Aunt Pol could not intercede for him with sorcery; Silk would not be able to devise some clever ruse to allow him to escape. Titanic and enraged, the Dark God would rush upon him, eager for blood.

Garion began to fear sleep, for sleep brought nightmares which would not go away and which haunted his days, making each worse than the last.

He was afraid. The fear grew worse with each passing day until the sour taste of it was always in his mouth. More than anything, he wanted to run, but he knew that he could not. Indeed, he did not even know any place where he *could* run. There was no place in all the world for him to hide. The Gods themselves would seek him out if he tried and sternly drive him to that awful meeting which had been fated to take place since the beginning of time. And so it was that, sick with fear, Garion rode to meet his fate.

Belgarath, who was not always asleep when he seemed to doze in his saddle, watched, shrewdly waiting until Garion's fear had reached its peak before he spoke. Then, one cloudy morning when the lead-grey sky was as dreary as the moors around them, he pulled his horse in beside Garion's. 'Do you want to talk about it?' he asked calmly.

'What's the point, Grandfather?'

'It might help.'

'Nothing's going to help. He's going to kill me.'

'If I thought it was that inevitable, I wouldn't have let you start on this journey.'

'How can I possibly fight with a God?'

'Bravely,' was the unhelpful reply. 'You've been brave at some pretty inappropriate times in the past. I don't imagine you've changed all that much.'

'I'm so afraid, Grandfather,' Garion confessed, his voice anguished. 'I think I know how Mandorallen felt now. The fear's so awful that I can't live with it.'

'You're stronger than you think you are. You can live with it if you have to.'

Garion brooded about that. It didn't seem to help

much. 'What's he like?' he asked, suddenly filled with a morbid curiosity.

'Who?'

'Torak.'

'Arrogant. I never cared much for him.'

'Is he like Ctuchik was – or Asharak?'

'No. They tried to be like *him*. They didn't succeed, of course, but they tried. If it's any help to you, Torak's probably as much afraid of you as you are of him. He knows who you are. When you meet him, he isn't going to see a Sendarian scullery boy named Garion; he's going to see Belgarion, the Rivan King, and he's going to see Riva's sword thirsting for his blood. He's also going to see the Orb of Aldur. And *that* will probably frighten him more than anything.'

'When was the first time you met him?' Garion suddenly wanted the old man to talk – to tell stories as he had so long ago. Stories somehow always helped. He could lose himself in a story, and for a little while it might make things bearable.

Belgarath scratched at his short, white beard. 'Let's see,' he mused. 'I think the first time was in the Vale – it was a very long time ago. The others had gathered there – Belzedar, Beldin, all the rest – and each of us was involved in his own studies. Our Master had withdrawn into his tower with the Orb, and sometimes months would pass during which we didn't see him.

'Then one day a stranger came to us. He seemed to be about the same height as I, but he walked as if he were a thousand feet tall. His hair was black and his skin was very pale, and he had, as I remember, greenish-colored eyes. His face was beautiful to the point of being pretty, and his hair looked as if he spent a lot of time combing it. He appeared to be the kind of person who always has a mirror in his pocket.'

'Did he say anything?' Garion asked.

'Oh, yes,' Belgarath replied. 'He came up to us and said, "I would speak with my brother, thy Master," and I *definitely* didn't care for his tone. He spoke as if we were servants – it's a failing he's always had. Still, my Master had – after a great deal of trouble – taught me at least a few manners. "I shall tell my Master you have come," I told him as politely as I could manage.

' "That is not needful, Belgarath," he told me in that irritatingly superior tone of his. "My brother knows I am here." '

'How did he know your name, Grandfather?'

Belgarath shrugged. 'I never found that out. I assume that my Master had communicated with him – and the other Gods – from time to time and told them about us. At any rate, I led this over-pretty visitor to my Master's tower. I didn't bother to speak to him along the way. When we got there, he looked me straight in the face and said, "A bit of advice for thee, Belgarath, by way of thanks for thy service. Seek not to rise above thyself. It is not *thy* place to approve or disapprove of *me*. For thy sake I hope that when next we meet thou wilt remember this and behave in a manner more seemly."

' "Thank you for the advice," I told him – a bit tartly, I'll admit. "Will you require anything else?"

' "Thou art pert, Belgarath," he said to me. "Perhaps one day I shall give myself leisure to instruct thee in proper behavior." And then he went into the tower. As you can see, Torak and I got off on the wrong foot right at the very beginning. I didn't care for his attitude, and he didn't care for mine.'

'What happened then?' Garion's curiosity had begun to quiet the fear somewhat.

'You know the story,' Belgarath replied. 'Torak went up into the tower and spoke with Aldur. One thing led to another and finally Torak struck my Master and stole the Orb.' The old man's face was bleak. 'The next time I saw him, he wasn't nearly so pretty,' he continued with a certain grim satisfaction. 'That was after the Orb had burned him and he'd taken to wearing a steel mask to hide the ruins of his face.'

Silk had drawn closer and was riding with them, fascinated by the story. 'What did you all do then? After Torak stole the Orb, I mean?' he asked.

'Our Master sent us to warn the other Gods,' Belgarath replied. 'I was supposed to find Belar – he was in the north someplace, carousing with his Alorns. Belar was a young God at that time, and he enjoyed the diversions of the young. Alorn girls used to dream about being visited by him, and he tried to make as many dreams come true as he possibly could – or so I've been told.'

'I've never heard *that* about him,' Silk seemed startled.

'Perhaps it's only gossip,' Belgarath admitted.

'Did you find him?' Garion asked.

'It took me quite a while. The shape of the land was different then. What's now Algaria stretched all the way to the east – thousands of leagues of open grassland. At first I took the shape of an eagle, but that didn't work out too well.'

'It seems quite suitable,' Silk observed.

'Heights make me giddy,' the old man replied, 'and my eyes were continually getting distracted by things on the ground. I kept having this overpowering urge to swoop down and kill things. The character of the forms we assume begins to dominate our thinking after a while, and although the eagle is quite splendid-looking, he's really a very stupid bird. Finally I gave that idea up and chose the form of the wolf instead. It worked out much

340

better. About the only distraction I encountered was a young she-wolf who was feeling frolicsome.' There was a slight tightening about his eyes as he said it, and his voice had a peculiar catch in it.

'*Belgarath!*' Silk actually sounded shocked.

'Don't be so quick to jump to conclusions, Silk. I considered the morality of the situation. I realized that being a father is probably all well and good, but that a litter of puppies might prove embarrassing later on. I resisted her advances, even though she persisted in following me all the way to the north where the Bear-God dwelt with his Alorns.' He broke off and looked out at the gray-green moors, his face unreadable. Garion knew that there was something the old man wasn't saying – something important.

'Anyway,' Belgarath continued, 'Belar accompanied us back to the Vale where the other Gods had gathered, and they held a council and decided that they'd have to make war on Torak and his Angaraks. That was the start of it all. The world has never been the same since.'

'What happened to the wolf?' Garion asked, trying to pin down his grandfather's peculiar evasion.

'She stayed with me,' Belgarath replied calmly. 'She used to sit for days on end in my tower watching me. She had a curious turn of mind, and her comments were frequently a trifle disconcerting.'

'Comments?' Silk asked. 'She could talk?'

'In the manner of the wolf, you understand. I'd learned how they speak during our journey together. It's really a rather concise and often quite beautiful language. Wolves can be eloquent – even poetic – once you get used to having them speak to you without words.'

'How long did she stay with you?' Garion asked.

'Quite a long time,' Belgarath replied. 'I remember

that I asked her about that once. She answered with another question. It was an irritating habit of hers. She just said, "What is time to a wolf?" I made a few calculations and found out that she'd been with me for just over a thousand years. I was a bit amazed by that, but she seemed indifferent to the fact. "Wolves live as long as they choose to live," was all she said. Then one day I had to change my form for some reason or other – I forget exactly why. She saw me do it, and that was the end of any peace for me. She just said, "So *that's* how you do it," and promptly changed herself into a snowy owl. She seemed to take a great delight in startling me, and I never knew what shape I'd see when I turned around. She was fondest of the owl, though. A few years after that she left me. I was rather surprised to find that I missed her. We'd been together for a very long time.' He broke off and once again he looked away.

'Did you ever see her again?' Garion wanted to know.

Belgarath nodded. 'She saw to that – though I didn't know it at the time. I was running an errand for my Master somewhere to the north of the Vale and I came across a small, neatly thatched cottage in a grove of trees by a small river. A woman named Poledra lived in the cottage – a woman with tawny hair and curiously golden eyes. We grew to know each other, and eventually we were married. She was Polgara's mother – and Beldaran's.'

'You were saying that you met the wolf again,' Garion reminded him.

'You don't listen too well, Garion,' the old man said, looking directly at his grandson. There was a deep and ancient injury in his eyes – a hurt so great that Garion knew it would be there for as long as the old man lived.

'You don't mean—?'

'It took me a while to accept it myself, actually.

342

Poledra was very patient and very determined. When she found out that I couldn't accept her as a mate in the form of a wolf, she simply found a different shape. She got what she wanted in the end.' He sighed.

'Aunt Pol's mother was a *wolf*?' Garion was stunned.

'No, Garion,' Belgarath replied calmly, 'she was a woman – a very lovely woman. The change of shape is absolute.'

'But – but she started out as a wolf.'

'So?'

'But—' The whole notion was somehow shocking.

'Don't let your prejudices run away with you,' Belgarath told him.

Garion struggled with the idea. It seemed monstrous somehow. 'I'm sorry,' he said finally. 'It's unnatural, no matter what you say.'

'Garion,' the old man reminded him with a pained look, 'just about everything we do is unnatural. Moving rocks with your mind isn't the most natural thing in the world, if you stop and think about it.'

'But this is different,' Garion protested. 'Grandfather, you married a wolf – and the wolf had children. How could you do that?'

Belgarath sighed and shook his head. 'You're a very stubborn boy, Garion,' he observed. 'It seems that you're never going to understand until you've been through the experience. Let's go over behind that hill, and I'll show you how it's done. There's no point in upsetting the rest of the caravan.'

'Mind if I come along?' Silk asked, his nose twitching with curiosity.

'Might not be a bad idea,' Belgarath agreed. 'You can hold the horses. Horses tend to panic in the presence of wolves.'

They rode away from the caravan track under the

leaden sky and circled around behind a low, heath-covered hill. 'This should do,' Belgarath decided, reining in and dismounting in a shallow swale just behind the hill. The swale was covered with new grass, green with spring.

'The whole trick is to create the image of the animal in your mind,' Belgarath explained, 'down to the last detail. Then you direct your will inward – upon yourself – and then change, fitting yourself into the image.'

Garion frowned, not understanding.

'It's going to take too long if I have to explain it in words,' Belgarath said. 'Here – watch – and watch with your mind as well as your eyes.'

Unbidden, the shape of the great grey wolf he had seen on occasion before came into Garion's mind. He could clearly see the gray-shot muzzle and the silver ruff. Then he felt the surge and heard the hollow roaring sound in his mind. For an instant, the image of the wolf curiously mingled with an image of Belgarath himself – as if the two were trying to both occupy the same space. Then Belgarath was gone and only the wolf remained.

Silk whistled, then took a firmer grip on the reins of their startled horses.

Belgarath changed back again to an ordinary-looking old man in a rust-brown tunic and gray, hooded cloak. 'Do you understand?' he asked Garion.

'I think so,' Garion replied, a bit dubiously.

'Try it. I'll lead you through it one step at a time.'

Garion started to put a wolf together in his mind.

'Don't forget the toenails,' Belgarath told him. 'They may not look like much, but they're very important.'

Garion put the toenails in.

'Tail's too short.'

Garion fixed that.

'That's about right. Now fit yourself into it.'

Garion put his will to it. 'Change,' he said.

It seemed almost as if his body had grown somehow fluid, shifting, altering, flowing into the image of the wolf that he had in his mind. When the surge was gone, he sat on his haunches panting. He felt very strange.

'Stand up and let's have a look at you,' Belgarath told him.

Garion rose and stood on all four paws. His tail felt extremely peculiar.

'You made the hind legs a bit too long,' Belgarath noted critically.

Garion started to object that it was the first time he'd ever done it, but his voice came out in a peculiar series of whines and yelps.

'Stop that,' Belgarath growled. 'You sound like a puppy. Change back.'

Garion did that.

'Where do your clothes go?' Silk asked curiously.

'They're with us,' Belgarath replied, 'but at the same time they're not. It's kind of hard to explain, actually. Beldin tried to work out exactly where the clothes were once. He seems to think he's got the answer, but I never understood the whole theory. Beldin's quite a bit more intelligent than I am, and his explanations are sometimes a bit exotic. At any rate, when we return to our original shape, our clothing is always just as it was.'

'Even Garion's sword?' Silk asked. 'And the Orb?'

The old man nodded.

'Isn't it sort of dangerous having it floating around out there – unattached, so to speak?'

'It isn't really unattached. It's still there – but at the same time it's not.'

'I'll take your word for it,' Silk conceded dubiously.

'Try it again, Garion,' Belgarath suggested.

Garion switched back and forth several times until his wolfshape satisfied his grandfather.

'Stay with the horses,' the old man told Silk. 'We'll be back in a little bit.' He flickered and shimmered into the great grey wolf. 'Let's run for a bit,' he said to Garion. The meaning of what he said was conveyed directly from his mind to Garion's, aided only slightly by expressions and positions of his head and ears and a few brief barking sounds. Garion suddenly understood why the bond of the pack was so strong in wolves. Quite literally, they inhabited each others' minds. What one saw, they all saw; and what one felt, they all felt.

'Where do we run to?' Garion asked, not really surprised at how easily the speech of wolves came to him.

'No place in particular. I just need to stretch out a few kinks.' And the grey wolf bounded away with astonishing speed.

The tail was a definite problem at first. Garion kept forgetting that it was there, and its swishing back and forth kept jerking him off balance. By the time he got the hang of it, the old wolf was far out ahead of him on the gray-green moors. After a while, however, Garion found himself literally flying across the ground. His paws scarcely seemed to touch the earth as he bunched and stretched his body in great bounds. He marvelled at the economy of the running gait of the wolf. He ran not with his legs alone, but with his entire body. He became quite certain that, if need be, he could run for days without tiring.

The rolling moors were different somehow. What had seemed as desolate and empty as the dead sky overhead was suddenly teeming with life. There were mice and burrowing squirrels; in scrubby brown thickets, rabbits, petrified with fright, watched him as he loped by with his toenails digging into the springy turf. Silently he exulted in the strength and freedom of his new body. He was the lord of the plain, and all creatures gave way to him.

And then he was not alone. Another wolf ran beside him – a strangely insubstantial-looking wolf that seemed to have a bluish, flickering light playing about her. 'And how far will you run?' she asked him in the manner of wolves.

'We can stop if you'd like,' Garion replied politely, dropping back into a lope and then a trot.

'It's easier to talk if one isn't running,' she agreed. She stopped and dropped to her haunches.

Garion also stopped. 'You're Poledra, aren't you?' He asked it very directly, not yet accustomed to the subtleties of the language of wolves.

'Wolves have no need of names,' she sniffed. '*He* used to worry about that, too.' It was not exactly like the voice that had been in his mind since his childhood. He didn't actually hear her, but instead he seemed to know exactly what she wanted to say to him.

'Grandfather, you mean?'

'Who else? Men seem to have a need to classify things and put names on them. I think they overlook some very important things that way.'

'How is it that you're here? Aren't you – well—?'

'Dead, you mean? Don't be afraid of the word. It's only a word, after all. I suppose I am, though. It doesn't really feel all that much different.'

'Doesn't somebody have to do something to bring you back?' he asked. 'Like what Aunt Pol did that time when we were fighting with Grul in the mountains of Ulgo?'

'It's not entirely necessary. I can be summoned that way, but I can manage it myself if I have to.' She looked at him quizzically. 'You're really confused by all this, aren't you?'

'All of what?'

'Everything. Who you are; who we are; what you have to do.'

'A little,' he admitted.

'Let me see if I can explain it. Take him for instance. I never really saw him as a man, you know. There's something decidedly wolfish about him. I always rather thought that his being born in man-shape had been a mistake of some kind. Maybe it was because of what he had to do. The shape doesn't really matter, though.'

'It doesn't?'

'Did you really think it did?' She almost seemed to laugh. 'Here. Let me show you. Let's change.' She shimmered into air and was standing before him then in the form of a tawny-haired woman with golden eyes. Her gown was very plain and brown.

Garion shrugged himself back into his natural form.

'Am I really any different, Belgarion?' she asked him. 'Am I not who I am, whether as wolf or owl or woman?'

And then he understood. 'May I call you Grandmother?' he asked her, a bit embarrassed.

'If it makes you happy,' she replied. 'It's a bit inaccurate, though.'

'I know,' he said, 'but I feel a little more comfortable with it.'

'Have you finally accepted who you are?'

'I don't have much choice, do I?'

'But you're afraid of it and what you have to do, is that it?'

He nodded mutely.

'You're not going to be alone, you know.'

He looked at her sharply. 'I thought the Codex said—'

'The Codex doesn't really say everything that's involved,' she told him. 'Your meeting with Torak will be the coming together of two enormous, opposing forces. The two of you are really just the representatives of those forces. There'll be so much power involved in your meeting that you and Torak will be almost incidental to what's really happening.'

'Why couldn't somebody else do it then?' he asked quickly. 'Somebody better suited to it?'

'I said *almost* incidental,' she said firmly. 'It has to be you, and it's always been Torak. You are the channels through which the forces will collide. When it happens, I think you'll be surprised at how easy it all is.'

'Am I going to win?'

'I don't know. The universe itself doesn't know. That's why you have to meet him. If we knew how it would turn out, the meeting wouldn't be necessary.' She looked around. 'Belgarath's coming back. I'll have to leave you now.'

'Why?'

'My presence pains him – more than you could ever know.'

'Because—?' He broke off, not knowing how to say it.

'We were closer than others and we were together for a very long time. Sometimes I wish that he could understand that we haven't really been separated, but perhaps it's too early.'

'It's been three thousand years, Grandmother.'

'What is time to a wolf?' she asked cryptically. 'The mating of wolves is permanent, and the grief caused by separation is also permanent. Perhaps someday—' Her voice trailed off wistfully, and then she sighed. 'As soon as I leave, change back again. Belgarath will want you to hunt with him. It's sort of a formality. You'll understand when you're back in the shape of a wolf.'

Garion nodded and began to form the image of the wolf in his mind.

'One other thing, Belgarion.'

'Yes, Grandmother?'

'I do love you, you know.'

'I love you too, Grandmother.'

And then she was gone. Garion sighed and changed himself back into a wolf. And then he went out from that place to join Belgarath in the hunt.

Part Four

THE RIVAN QUEEN

Chapter Twenty-Two

The Princess Ce'Nedra was in a thoughtful, even pensive mood. Much as she had enjoyed the turmoil her periodic outbursts of temper had caused, she rather regretfully concluded that it was probably time to put them aside and make peace with Garion. They were going to be married, after all, and there was no real point in upsetting him any more than absolutely necessary. Her tantrums had established the fact that, although he might outrank her, she would not enter the marriage as his inferior, and that was really all she had wanted anyway. On the whole, the prospect of being married to Garion was not nearly as unpleasant as she pretended. She did love him after all, and now that he understood exactly how things were going to stand between them, everything was likely to be quite satisfactory. She decided to find him that very day and make peace with him.

The largest part of her attention that spring morning had been taken up by a book on protocol and a chart she was carefully drawing up. As Imperial Princess of Tolnedra *and* Queen of Riva, she would, of course, absolutely outrank every grand duchess of every house in the Empire. She was also fairly sure that she outranked Queen Islena of Cherek and Queen Silar of Algaria. Mayaserana's status as co-ruler of Arendia raised some problems, however. It was entirely possible that she and Mayaserana were equals. Ce'Nedra made a note on a scrap of parchment reminding herself to have Ambassador Valgon direct an inquiry to the chief of protocol in Tol Honeth concerning the matter. She felt a nice little glow as she surveyed the chart. With the exception of Lady Polgara and the motherly little Queen Layla of Sendaria, to whom everyone deferred because she was such a dear, Ce'Nedra concluded that she would in fact outrank or at least equal every noble lady in the West.

Suddenly there was a shattering thunderclap so violent that it shook the very walls of the Citadel. Startled, Ce'Nedra glanced at the window. It was a bright, sunny morning. How could there be thunder? Another rending crash ripped the silence, and there was a frightened babble in the halls. Impatiently, the princess picked up a small silver bell and rang for her maid.

'Go see what's happening,' she instructed the girl and returned to her study of the chart she had drawn. But there was another thunderous crash and even more shouting and confusion in the corridor outside. It was impossible! How could she concentrate with all that noise going on? Irritably she rose and went to the door.

People were running – actually fleeing. Just down the hall Queen Layla of Sendaria bolted from the door of Lady Polgara's private apartment, her eyes wide with terror and her crown very nearly falling off.

'What *is* the matter, your majesty?' Ce'Nedra demanded of the little queen.

'It's Polgara!' Queen Layla gasped, stumbling in her haste to escape. 'She's destroying everything in sight!'

'Lady Polgara?'

Another deafening crash sent the little queen reeling, and she clung to Ce'Nedra in terror. 'Please, Ce'Nedra. Find out what's wrong. Make her stop before she shakes down the entire fortress.'

'*Me?*'

'She'll listen to you. She loves you. Make her stop.'

Without pausing to consider the possible danger, Ce'Nedra went quickly to Lady Polgara's door and glanced inside. The apartment was a total shambles. Furniture was overturned; wall hangings had been ripped down; the windows were shattered and the air was full of smoke. Ce'Nedra had thrown enough tantrums in her own life to appreciate artistry when she saw it, but the disaster inside Polgara's apartment was so absolute that it went beyond art into the realms of natural catastrophe. Lady Polgara herself stood, wild-eyed and dishevelled in the center of the room, cursing incoherently in a dozen languages at once. In one hand she held a crumpled sheet of parchment; her other hand was raised like a claw before her, half clenched about an incandescent mass of blazing energy that she seemed to have summoned out of air itself and which she now fed with her own fury. The princess stood in awe as Polgara began a fresh tirade. The dreadful cursing began in a low contralto and rose in an awful crescendo into the upper registers and beyond. As she reached the limits of her voice, she began slashing the air with the blazing mass in her hand, punctuating each curse with a crackling burst of raw energy that sizzled from between her fingers like a bolt of lightning to shatter whatever her eyes fell upon. With a series of vile oaths, she detonated six teacups in a row into shards, then quite methodically she went back down the line, exploding the saucers upon which they had sat. Almost as an afterthought, she blew the table into splinters.

Ce'Nedra heard a strangled gasp directly behind her. King Anheg, the blood drained from his face, looked once through the door, then turned and ran.

'Lady Polgara,' Ce'Nedra remonstrated to the

sorceress, trying not so much to reason with her as to minimize the destruction.

Polgara shattered four priceless vases standing on the mantelpiece with four precisely separate explosions. Outside the window, the bright spring morning vanished as if the sun had suddenly been extinguished, and there was a sullen rumble of thunder that Ce'Nedra prayed devoutly was natural.

'Whatever is the matter?' the princess asked, hoping to draw the enraged sorceress into explanation rather than more curses. It was the curses that had to be headed off. Polgara seemed to have a deep-seated need to emphasize her oaths with explosions.

Polgara, however, did not reply. Instead she merely threw the parchment at Ce'Nedra, turned, and blew a marble statue into fine white gravel. Wild-eyed, she wheeled about, looking for something else to break, but there was very little left in the smoking room that she had not already reduced to rubble.

'No!' Ce'Nedra cried out sharply as the raging woman's eyes fell on the exquisite crystal wren Garion had given her. The princess knew that Polgara valued the glass bird more than anything else she possessed, and she leaped forward to protect the delicate piece.

'Get it,' Polgara snarled at her from between clenched teeth. 'Take it out of my sight.' Her eyes burned with a terrible need to destroy something else. She spun and hurled the incandescent ball of fire she had wielded out through the shattered window. The explosion, when it burst in the suddenly murky air outside, was ghastly. With her fists clenched tightly at her sides, she raised her distorted face and began to curse again. From roiling black clouds that had suddenly appeared out of nowhere, shattering bolts of lightning began to rain down on the island. No longer satisfied with localized destruction, Polgara expanded her rage to rake the Isle and the Sea of the Winds with sizzling fire and ear-splitting thunder. Then, with a dreadful intensity, she raised one fist and suddenly opened it. The downpour of rain she called was beyond belief. Her glittering eyes narrowed, and she raised her other fist. The rain instantly turned to hail – great, jagged chunks of ice that crashed and splintered against the rocks to fill the air with flying fragments and thick steam.

Ce'Nedra caught up the wren, stooped to grab the rumpled piece of parchment from the floor, and then she fled.

King Anheg poked his frightened face from around a corner. 'Can't you stop her?' he demanded in a shaking voice.

'Nothing can stop her, your Majesty.'

'Anheg! Get in here!' Polgara's voice rang above the thunder and the crashing deluge of hail that shook the Citadel.

'Oh, Belar,' King Anheg muttered devoutly, casting his eyes skyward even as he hurried toward Polgara's door.

'Get word to Val Alom immediately!' she commanded him. 'My father, Silk, and Garion slipped out of the Citadel last night. Get your fleet out and bring them back! I don't care if you have to take the world apart stone by stone. Find them and bring them back!'

'Polgara, I—' The King of Cherek faltered.

'Don't stand there gaping like an idiot! *Move!*'

Carefully, almost with a studied calm, the Princess Ce'Nedra handed the glass wren to her frightened maid. 'Put this someplace safe,' she said. Then she turned and went back to the center of the storm. 'What was that you just said?' she asked Polgara in a level voice.

'My idiot father, Garion, and that disgusting thief

decided last night to go off on their own,' Polgara replied in an icy voice made even more terrible by the super-human control that held it in.

'They did what?' Ce'Nedra asked flatly.

'They left. They sneaked away during the night.'

'Then you must go after them.'

'I can't, Ce'Nedra.' Polgara spoke as if explaining something to a child. 'Someone has to stay here. There are too many things here that could go wrong. He knows that. He did it deliberately. He's trapped me here.'

'Garion?'

'No, you silly girl! My father!' And Polgara began cursing again, each oath punctuated with a crash of thunder.

Ce'Nedra, however, scarcely heard her. She looked around. There was really nothing left to break in here. 'You'll excuse me, I hope,' she said. Then she turned, went back to her own rooms, and began breaking everything she could lay her hands on, screeching all the while like a Camaar fishwife.

Their separate rages lasted for several hours, and they rather carefully avoided each other during this period. Some emotions needed to be shared, but insane fury was not one of those. Eventually, Ce'Nedra felt she had exhausted the possibilities of her extended outburst, and she settled into the icy calm of one who has been mortally insulted. No matter what face his illiterate note put on the matter, it would be at the very most a week before the entire world knew that Garion had jilted her. The flight of her reluctant bridegroom would become a universal joke. It was absolutely intolerable!

She would meet the world, however, with a lifted chin and an imperious gaze. However she might weep and storm and rage in private, the face she presented to the world would betray no hint of how deeply she had been injured. All that was left for her was her pride, and she would never abandon that.

The Lady Polgara, however, seemed to feel no need for such imperial reserve. Once her initial fury had subsided to the degree that she allowed her private thunderstorm to pass, a few hardy souls assumed that the worst of it was over. The Earl of Trellheim went to her in an attempt to mollify her. He left her apartment moments later at a run with her crackling vituperation sizzling in the air about his ears. Barak was pale and shaken when he reported back to the others. 'Don't go near her,' he advised in a frightened voice. 'Do whatever she says as quickly as you can, and stay absolutely out of her sight.'

'Isn't she calming down at all?' King Rhodar asked.

'She's finished breaking the furniture,' Barak replied. 'I think she's getting ready to start on people.'

Thereafter, each time Polgara emerged from her apartment, the warning spread instantly, and the halls of Iron-grip's Citadel emptied. Her commands, delivered usually by her maid, were all variations of the initial orders she had given King Anheg. They were to find the vagrant trio and bring them back to face her.

In the days that followed, Princess Ce'Nedra's first rage settled into a sort of peevishness that made people avoid her almost as much as they avoided Polgara – all but gentle Adara, who endured the tiny girl's outbursts with a calm patience. The two of them spent most of their time sitting in the garden adjoining the royal apartments where Ce'Nedra could give vent to her emotions without fear of being overheard.

It was five days after Garion and the others had left before Ce'Nedra discovered the full implications of their departure.

The day was warm – spring came eventually even to a

bleak place like Riva – and the small bit of lawn in the center of the garden was a lush green. Pink, blue, and flaming red flowers nodded in their beds as bright yellow bees industriously carried kisses from blossom to blossom. Ce'Nedra, however, did not want to think about kisses. Dressed in her favorite pale green Dryad tunic, she bit rather savagely at an unoffending lock of hair and spoke to the patient Adara at length about the inconstancy of men.

It was about midafternoon when Queen Layla of Sendaria found them there. 'Oh, there you are,' the plump little queen bubbled at them. As always, her crown was a little awry. 'We've been looking all over for you.'

'Why?' was Ce'Nedra's somewhat ungracious reply.

Queen Layla stopped and looked critically at the princess. 'My,' she said, 'aren't we cross today? Just what is your problem, Ce'Nedra? You've barely been civil for days now.'

Ce'Nedra caught Adara's warning look to the queen, and that irritated her all the more. Her response was chilly. 'I'm finding the experience of being jilted to be just a bit annoying, your Highness,' she said.

Queen Layla's sunny face hardened. 'Would you excuse us, Adara?' she asked.

'Of course, your Highness,' Adara replied, rising quickly. 'I'll be inside, Ce'Nedra,' she said and went gracefully out of the garden.

Queen Layla waited until the girl was out of earshot, then sat down on a marble bench. 'Come here, Ce'Nedra,' she said firmly.

The princess looked at the motherly little woman, a bit startled by the iron in her voice. Obediently she went to the bench and sat.

'You really should stop interpreting everything that

happens in the world as a personal insult, you know,' Layla told her. 'That's a very unbecoming habit. What Garion, Belgarath, and Kheldar did has absolutely nothing to do with you.' She looked sternly at Ce'Nedra. 'Do you know anything at all about the Prophecy?'

'I've heard about it,' Ce'Nedra sulked. 'Tolnedrans don't really believe in that sort of thing.'

'Perhaps that's the problem,' Layla said. 'I want you to listen very carefully, Ce'Nedra. You may not believe, but you *will* understand.' The queen thought for a moment. 'The Prophecy clearly states that when the Rivan King returns, Torak will awaken.'

'Torak? That's nonsense. Torak's dead.'

'Don't interrupt, dear,' Layla told her. 'You travelled with them for all that time and you still don't understand? For a little girl who seems so bright, you're remarkably dense.'

Ce'Nedra flushed at that.

'Torak is a God, Ce'Nedra,' Layla continued. 'He's asleep, not dead. He did not die at Vo Mimbre, much as some people might like to think he did. The instant that Garion touched the Orb, Torak began to stir. Haven't you ever wondered why Polgara insisted that Errand carry the Orb back from Rak Cthol? Garion could have carried it just as easily, you know.'

Ce'Nedra hadn't thought of that.

'But if Garion had touched it – still on Angarak soil and without his sword – Torak might very well have jumped up and gone after him immediately, and Garion would have been killed.'

'Killed?' Ce'Nedra gasped.

'Of course, dear. That's what this is all about. The Prophecy says that Torak and the Rivan King will eventually meet, and that in their meeting shall be decided the fate of mankind.'

'*Garion?*' Ce'Nedra exclaimed, stunned and disbelieving. 'Surely you're not serious?'

'I've never been more serious in my life, child. Garion has to fight Torak – to the death – to decide the fate of the world. Now do you understand? That's why Belgarath and Kheldar and Garion left Riva so suddenly. They're on their way to Mallorea so that Garion can fight Torak. He could have taken an army with him, but he knew that would only cause needless deaths. That's why the three of them went alone. Now don't you think it's time that you grew up just a little bit?'

Ce'Nedra was greatly subdued after her conversation with Queen Layla. For perhaps the first time in her life, she began to think more about someone else than she did about herself. She worried constantly about Garion, and at night she had dreadful nightmares about the hideous things that could happen to him.

To make matters worse, there seemed to be a persistent buzzing in her ears that was at times quite maddening. It was rather like the sound of voices coming from a long way off – voices that verged just on the edge of being understandable, but never quite were. The buzzing sound, coupled with her anxiety about Garion, made her moody and frequently short-tempered. Even Adara began to avoid her.

The irritating sound in her ears continued for several days before she discovered, quite by accident, the significance of it. The weather on the Isle of the Winds was never really very good, and spring was a particularly unpredictable time of year. A series of storms, following one after another in dreary progression, lashed at the rocky coast, and nasty little rain squalls swept the city and the island. One somber, rainy morning the princess sat in her chambers looking glumly out the window at the soggy garden. The fire which crackled on her hearth did little to warm her mood. After a while she sighed and, for want of anything better to do, she sat at her dressing table and began to brush her hair.

The silver flicker at her throat distracted her eye momentarily as she looked at herself in the mirror. It was the medallion Garion had given her just after her birthday. She had by now grown accustomed to its being there, though the fact that she could not take it off still caused her periodic fits of anger. Without actually thinking about it, she stopped brushing and touched the amulet with her fingertips.

'– but we can't do a thing until the Arends and the Tolnedrans are fully mobilized.' It was the voice of King Rhodar of Drasnia. Ce'Nedra started and turned quickly, wondering why the portly monarch had entered her room. As soon as she removed her fingers from the silver amulet, the voice stopped. Ce'Nedra looked around, puzzled. She frowned and touched the amulet again. 'No, no,' another voice said, 'you don't add the spices until after it starts to boil.' Ce'Nedra again removed her fingertips from the talisman at her throat, and that voice too stopped abruptly. Fascinated, she touched it for the third time. 'You make up the bed, and I'll straighten up. We'll have to hurry. The Queen of Cherek might come back at any minute.'

Wonderingly, the princess touched the amulet again and again, and her ears ranged randomly through the Citadel.

'The fire's too hot. This iron will scorch anything it touches.'

Then she heard a snatch of whispered conversation. 'What if somebody comes?' It was a girl's voice.

'Nobody's going to come.' The young man's voice which replied had a peculiar wheedling quality. 'We're all safe and cozy here, and I really do love you.'

Ce'Nedra quickly jerked her fingers from the amulet, blushing furiously.

At first there was no direction to it; but as the princess experimented, she gradually learned to focus this peculiar phenomenon. After a couple of hours of intense concentration, she found that she could skim rapidly through all the talking that was going on in a given quarter of the Citadel until she found a conversation that interested her. In the process she learned many secrets, some very interesting, and some not very nice. She knew that she should feel guilty about her surreptitious eavesdropping, but for some reason she did not.

'Thy reasoning is sound, your Majesty.' It was Mandorallen's voice. 'King Korodullin is committed to the cause, though it will take some weeks for his call to arms to gather the forces of Arendia. Our major concern must be the position the Emperor will take in the affair. Without the legions, our situation is perilous.'

'Ran Borune has no choice in the matter,' King Anheg declared. 'He's bound by the provisions of the Accords of Vo Mimbre.'

Brand, the Rivan Warder, cleared his throat. 'I don't think it's that simple, your Majesty,' he said quietly in his deep voice. 'The Accords state that the Kingdoms of the West must respond to a call from the Rivan King, and Belgarion is not here to issue that call.'

'We're acting in his behalf,' King Cho-Hag asserted.

'The problem lies in convincing Ran Borune of that,' Rhodar pointed out. 'I know the Tolnedrans. They'll have whole battalions of legal experts working on the Accords. Unless Belgarion himself meets Ran Borune face to face and issues his command in person, the Emperor will take the position that he's not legally bound to join us. The Rivan King is the only one who can issue a call to war.'

Ce'Nedra let her fingertips drop from the amulet at her throat. An idea was beginning to take shape in her mind. It was an exciting idea, but she was not at all certain that she could bring it off. Alorns, she knew, were stubborn and reluctant to accept any new ideas. She quickly laid aside her hairbrush and went to a small chest standing against the wall near the window. She opened the chest and began rummaging through it. After a moment she found the tightly rolled parchment she had been seeking. She unrolled it and read through it quickly until she found the passage she wanted. She read it carefully several times. It seemed to say what she wanted it to say.

She considered the idea throughout the rest of the day. The possibility that anyone might succeed in catching up with Garion and stopping him was remote, to say the very least. Belgarath and Prince Kheldar were too skilled at evasion to allow themselves to be easily caught. Chasing them was simply a waste of time. Since Polgara was not yet rational enough to see things in this light, it fell to Ce'Nedra to take immediate steps to minimize Garion's danger once he had entered the lands of the Angaraks. All she had to do now was convince the Alorn Kings that she was the logical one to take those steps.

It was still raining the next morning, and she rose early to make her preparations. She must, of course, look positively regal. Her choice of an emerald velvet gown and matching cape was artful. She knew that she was stunning in green, and her circlet of gold oak leaves was enough like a crown to convey the right suggestion. She was glad she had waited until morning. Men were easier to deal with in the morning, she had discovered. They would fight her at first, and she wanted the idea implanted in their minds before they were fully awake.

As she gave herself a last-minute check in the tall mirror in her dressing room, she gathered her determination and marshalled all her arguments. The slightest objection must be met instantly. Carefully she put herself in an imperial frame of mind and, taking the rolled parchment, she moved toward the door.

The council chamber in which the Alorn Kings usually gathered was a large room high up in one of the massive towers of the Citadel. There were heavy beams on the ceiling, a deep maroon carpet on the floor, and a fireplace at the far end big enough to stand in. Maroon drapes flanked the windows where tatters of rain slashed across the solid stones of the tower. The walls of the chamber were covered with maps, and the large table was littered with parchments and ale cups. King Anheg, in his blue robe and dented crown, sprawled in the nearest chair, as shaggy and brutish-looking as always. King Rhodar was vast in his crimson mantle, but the other kings and generals wore rather plain clothing.

Ce'Nedra entered the chamber without knocking and stared regally at the somewhat confused men who struggled to their feet in acknowledgment of her presence.

'Your Highness,' King Rhodar began with a portly bow. 'You honor us. Was there—'

'Your Majesty,' she responded with a little curtsy, 'and gentlemen, I find that I need your advice in a matter of state.'

'We are all at your immediate disposal, your Highness,' King Rhodar replied with a sly little twinkle in his eyes.

'In the absence of King Belgarion, it appears that I must act in his stead,' Ce'Nedra announced, 'and I need your advice on how to proceed. I wish the transfer of power into my hands to go as smoothly as possible.'

They all stared at her disbelievingly.

King Rhodar recovered his wits first. 'An interesting proposal, your Highness,' he murmured politely. 'We have, however, made other arrangements. There's a long-standing precedent in the matter. We thank your Highness for her gracious offer nonetheless.'

'It was not precisely an offer, your Majesty,' Ce'Nedra told him, 'and any previous precedents have been superseded.'

King Anheg was spluttering, but Rhodar was already moving along smoothly. Ce'Nedra realized that the rotund Drasnian king was likely to be her most serious adversary – or her most effective ally. 'We'd all be fascinated to examine the instrument vesting your Highness with royal authority,' he said. 'I presume that the parchment you carry is relevant?'

'It is indeed, your Majesty,' Ce'Nedra declared. 'The document quite clearly lists my responsibilities.'

'May I?' Rhodar asked, extending his hand.

Ce'Nedra handed him the parchment and he carefully unrolled it. 'Uh – your Highness. This is your betrothal agreement. Perhaps you meant to bring a different document.'

'The pertinent material is contained in the fourth paragraph, your Majesty.'

Rhodar quickly read the paragraph, frowning slightly.

'What does it say, Rhodar?' King Anheg asked impatiently.

'Interesting,' Rhodar murmured, scratching his ear.

'Rhodar,' Anheg complained, 'what does it *say*?'

King Rhodar cleared his throat and began to read aloud. ' "It is agreed that King Belgarion and his Queen shall rule jointly, and that in his absence shall she assume fully the duties and authority of the Rivan Throne." '

'Let me see that,' Anheg demanded, snatching the parchment from Rhodar.

'It doesn't mean anything,' Brand declared. 'She isn't his queen yet. She won't be until after the wedding.'

'That's only a formality, my Lord Warder,' Ce'Nedra told him.

'A rather important one, I'd say,' he retorted.

'The precedent is well-established,' she said coolly. 'When a king dies, the next in line assumes the duties of the crown doesn't he, even though there hasn't been a formal coronation?'

'That's different,' Brand growled.

'I fail to see the difference, my Lord. I have been designated Belgarion's co-ruler. In his absence or an emergency I am obliged to take command. It is my right and my responsibility. The formalities may have to wait, but I *am* the Rivan Queen. This is King Belgarion's will and intent. Will you defy your king?'

'There's something to what she says, my Lord Warder,' the Earl of Seline mused. 'The document is quite clear.'

'But look at this,' Anheg said triumphantly. 'In paragraph two it says that should the wedding not take place, all gifts are to be returned. The wedding has not taken place.'

'I'm not sure that power is a gift, Anheg,' King Fulrach suggested. 'You can't give it and then take it back.'

'There's no way she could rule,' Anheg declared stubbornly. 'She doesn't know the first thing about Alorns.'

'Neither did Garion,' King Cho-Hag murmured in his quiet voice. 'She can learn the same way he did.'

Ce'Nedra had been rather carefully assessing their mood. Most of them seemed willing at least to consider her idea. Only the two conservatives, Brand and Anheg, were actually resisting. It seemed the time now for a dignified withdrawal coupled with a disarming offer. 'I will leave you gentlemen to discuss the matter,' she declared somewhat loftily. 'I would like you to know, however, that I realize the gravity of the situation confronting the West.' She deliberately put on a winsome, little-girl face. 'I'm only a young girl,' she confessed, 'unused to the intricacies of strategy and tactics. I could never make any decisions in that area without the fullest advice from you gentlemen.'

She curtsied then to King Rhodar, choosing him deliberately. 'Your Majesty,' she said, 'I shall await your decision.'

He bowed in response, a bit floridly. 'Your Majesty,' he replied with a sly wink.

Ce'Nedra retired and literally flew down the corridors to her own quarters. Breathlessly she closed the door behind her and touched the talisman at her throat with trembling fingertips. She sorted quickly through random conversation until she found the one she wanted.

'– refuse to be a party to an absurdity,' Anheg was saying.

'Anheg, my friend,' King Fulrach of Sendaria said with surprising firmness, 'you are my dear brother king, but you do have a few blind spots. Wouldn't it be more statesmanlike to consider the advantages and disadvantages of the situation dispassionately?'

'The Alorns will never follow her,' Anheg declared. 'That's a major disadvantage right there.'

'The Alorns will follow us, though,' King Cho-Hag said quietly. 'She's only going to be a figurehead, after all – a symbol of unity.'

'I suspect that Cho-Hag's hit the exact point we should examine most closely,' King Rhodar urged. 'My apologies, Baron Mandorallen, but the Arends are totally disunited. Asturia and Mimbre are hovering on the verge of reopening hostilities, and a call from King Korodullin could very possibly be ignored in northern Arendia – in which case the Mimbrate knights would almost be compelled to stay home to defend against possible Asturian uprisings. We have to have someone who can make them forget their squabbles and join with us. We need the Asturian bowmen and the Mimbrate knights.'

'I must sadly concur, your Majesty,' Mandorallen agreed. 'My poor Arendia must needs be united in one cause from the outside. We are not wise enough to unify ourselves.'

'Ce'Nedra can serve us there as well as Garion could have done,' Barak reasoned. 'I don't think anybody expected him to be a general. All we were going to do was put a crown on him and let him ride at the head of the army – and Arends get all gushy and romantic about pretty girls. That betrothal document makes her claim at least semi-legitimate. All we'd have to do is act as if we accepted her and talk very fast. Add the prospect of a nice little war someplace, and the Arends will unite behind us, I think.'

'The main point to consider, though,' King Rhodar emphasized, 'is the impact she's going to have in Tolnedra. Ran Borune dotes on her, and he might agree to lend her his legions – at least some of them – which he'd never do, if we were the ones asking it of him. He'll see the political advantage of having her in command almost immediately. We need those legions. I personally don't like Tolnedrans, but the legions are the finest fighting force in the world. I'll bend my knee to Ce'Nedra if I have to in order to get them. Let her play queen if she wants to.'

Ce'Nedra smiled. Things were going even better than she had expected. All in all, she was quite pleased with herself as she sat down at her dressing table and began to brush her hair, humming softly all the while.

Chapter Twenty-Three

Delban the armorer was a gruff, bald man with broad shoulders, huge callused hands and a grizzled beard. He was a craftsman, an artist, and he had absolutely no respect for anyone. Ce'Nedra found him to be impossible.

'I don't make armor for women,' was his initial response to her inquiry when she, accompanied by Durnik the smith, entered his workshop. He had then turned his back on her and begun pounding noisily on a sheet of glowing steel. It took the better part of an hour to convince him even to consider the idea. The heat shimmered out from his glowing forge, and the red brick walls seemed to reflect the heat and intensify it. Ce'Nedra found herself perspiring heavily. She had made some sketches of what she thought might be a suitable design for her armor. All in all, she thought it would look rather nice, but Delban laughed raucously when he saw them.

'What's so amusing?' she demanded.

'You'd be like a turtle in something like that,' he replied. 'You wouldn't be able to move.'

'The drawings are only intended to give you a general idea,' she told him, trying to keep a grip on her temper.

'Why don't you be a good girl and take these to a dressmaker?' he suggested. 'I work in steel, not brocade or satin. Armor like this would be useless, and so uncomfortable that you wouldn't be able to wear it.'

'Then modify it,' she grated from between clenched teeth.

He glanced at her design again, then deliberately crumpled her drawings in his fist and threw them into the corner. 'Foolishness,' he grunted.

Ce'Nedra resisted the urge to scream. She retrieved the drawings. 'What's the matter with them?' she persisted.

'Too much here.' He stabbed a thick finger at the shoulder represented on the drawing. 'You wouldn't be able to lift your arm. And here.' He pointed at the armhole on the breastplate she had drawn. 'If I make it that tight, your arms would stick straight out. You wouldn't even be able to scratch your nose. As long as we're at it, where did you get the whole notion in the first place? Do you want a mail shirt or a breastplate? You can't have both.'

'Why not?'

'The weight. You wouldn't be able to carry it.'

'Make it lighter then. Can't you do that?'

'I can make it like cobwebs if you want, but what good would it be if I did? You could cut through it with a paring knife.'

Ce'Nedra drew in a deep breath. 'Master armorer,' she said to him in a level voice, 'look at me. In all the world do you think there's a single warrior small enough for me to fight?'

He considered her tiny form, scratching his bald head and looking down at her with pursed lips. 'You *are* a bit undergrown,' he admitted. 'If you aren't going to fight, why do you need armor?'

'It's not actually going to be armor,' she explained to him rather impatiently, 'but I need to look like I'm wearing armor. It's sort of in the nature of a costume.' She saw instantly that her choice of words had been a mistake. Delban's face darkened, and he threw her drawings away again. It took another ten minutes to mollify him. Eventually, after much wheedling and outrageous flattery, she persuaded him to consider the whole notion as something in the nature of an artistic challenge.

'All right,' he surrendered finally with a sour look, 'take off your clothes.'

'*What?*'

'Take your dress off,' he repeated. 'I need exact measurements.'

'Do you realize what you're suggesting?'

'Little girl,' he said testily, 'I'm a married man. I've got daughters older than you are. You are wearing underclothes, aren't you?'

'Yes, but—'

'That will satisfy the demands of modesty. Take off the dress.'

With a flaming face, Ce'Nedra removed her dress. Durnik the smith, who had watched the entire exchange from the doorway with an open grin on his face, politely turned his back.

'You ought to eat more,' Delban told her. 'You're as scrawny as a chicken.'

'I can do without the comments,' she replied tartly. 'Get on with this. I'm not going to stand around in my chemise all day.'

Delban picked up a piece of stout cord with knots tied in it at regular intervals. He took a great many measurements with the cord, meticulously recording them on a piece of flat board. 'All right,' he said finally. 'That ought to do it. Go ahead and get dressed again.'

Ce'Nedra scrambled back into her dress. 'How long will it take?' she asked.

'Two or three weeks.'

'Impossible. I need it next week.'

'Two weeks,' he repeated stubbornly.

'Ten days,' she countered.

For the first time since she had entered his workshop, the blunt man smiled. 'She's used to getting her own way, isn't she?' he observed to Durnik.

'She's a princess,' Durnik informed him. 'She usually gets what she wants in the end.'

'All right, my scrawny little princess.' Delban laughed. 'Ten days.'

Ce'Nedra beamed at him. 'I knew you'd see it my way.'

Precisely ten days later, the princess, with Durnik once again in tow, returned to Delban's workshop. The mail shirt the craftsman had fashioned was so light that it could almost have been described as delicate. The helmet, hammered from thin steel, was surmounted with a white plume and was encircled with a gold crown. The greaves, which were to protect the fronts of Ce'Nedra's legs, fit to perfection. There was even an embossed shield rimmed with brass and a light sword with an ornate hilt and scabbard.

Ce'Nedra, however, was staring disapprovingly at the breastplate Delban had made for her. It would quite obviously fit – too well. 'Didn't you forget something?' she asked him.

He picked the breastplate up in his big hands and examined it. 'It's all there,' he told her. 'Front, back, all the straps to hook them together. What else did you want?'

'Isn't it a trifle – understated?' Ce'Nedra suggested delicately.

'It's made to fit,' he replied. 'The understatement isn't my fault.'

'I want it a little more—' She made a sort of curving gesture with her hands.

375

'What for?'

'Never mind what for. Just do it.'

'What do you plan to put in it?'

'That's my business. Just do it the way I told you to.'

He tossed a heavy hammer down on his anvil. 'Do it yourself,' he told her bluntly.

'Durnik,' Ce'Nedra appealed to the smith.

'Oh, no, princess,' Durnik refused. 'I don't touch another man's tools. That just isn't done.'

'Please, Delban,' she wheedled.

'It's foolishness,' he told her, his face set.

'It's important,' she coaxed. 'If I wear it like that, I'll look like a little boy. When people see me, they have to know that I'm a woman. It's terribly, terribly important. Couldn't you – well – just a little bit?' She cupped her hands slightly.

Delban gave Durnik a disgusted look. 'You had to bring her to my workshop, didn't you?'

'Everybody said you were the best,' Durnik replied mildly.

'Just a little bit, Delban?' Ce'Nedra urged.

Delban gave up. 'Oh, all right,' he growled, picking up his hammer. 'Anything to get you out of my shop – but not clear out to here.' He made an exaggerated gesture.

'I'll depend on your good taste, Delban.' She smiled, patting his cheek with a fond little laugh. 'Shall we say tomorrow morning?'

The armor, Ce'Nedra decided the following morning as she inspected herself in the mirror, was perfect. 'Well, what do you think, Adara?' she asked her friend.

'It looks very nice, Ce'Nedra,' the tall girl replied, although a bit dubiously.

'It's just exactly right,' Ce'Nedra said happily, turning so that the blue cape fastened to the shoulder pieces of the breastplate flared and swirled dramatically. The gleaming mail shirt she wore under the breastplate reached to her knees and wrists. The greaves covering her calves and the armguards reaching to her elbows were inlaid with brass; Delban had steadfastly refused the notion of gold. The armor did chafe a bit through the thick linen undershirt she wore, Ce'Nedra privately admitted, but she was prepared to accept that. She brandished her sword, studying the effect in her mirror.

'You're holding it wrong, Ce'Nedra,' Adara suggested politely.

'Show me,' Ce'Nedra said, handing over her sword.

Adara took the weapon and gripped it firmly, its point low. She looked extremely competent.

'Where did you ever learn to do that?' Ce'Nedra asked her.

'We're given instruction,' Adara replied, handing back the sword. 'It's traditional.'

'Help me on with my shield.'

Between them, they managed to gird the princess in all her warlike equipment.

'However do you keep it from getting tangled up in your legs?' Ce'Nedra demanded, fumbling with the long scabbard at her waist.

'Hold on to the hilt,' Adara told her. 'Do you want me to go along?'

Ce'Nedra thought about that as she smoothed her hair and settled her plumed helmet more firmly in place. 'I guess not,' she decided rather reluctantly. 'I think I'll have to face them alone. Do I really look all right?'

'You'll be fine,' Adara assured her.

A sudden thought struck the princess. 'What if they laugh?' she demanded in a frightened voice.

'You could draw your sword on them, I suppose,' Adara replied gravely.

'Are you making fun of me, Adara?'

'Of course not, Princess,' Adara answered with an absolutely straight face.

When Ce'Nedra reached the door to the council chamber, she drew in a deep breath and entered, once again without knocking. Knocking would have been inappropriate, suggesting somehow that she had doubts about her right to be there.

'Well, gentlemen?' she said to the assembled kings and generals as she stepped to the center of the room where they could all see her.

King Rhodar rose politely. 'Your Majesty,' he greeted her, bowing. 'We were curious about your absence. The reason is now abundantly clear.'

'Do you approve?' she could not help asking. She turned so they could all see her armor.

King Rhodar looked at her, his eyes speculative. 'It *is* impressive, don't you think?' he said to the others. 'Just the right touches in the right places. The Arends will flock to her, and the Tolnedrans – well, we'll have to see about the Tolnedrans.'

King Anheg looked like a man having a serious struggle with himself. 'Why do I feel that I'm being pushed into something?' he complained. 'The very notion of this makes my blood cold, but I can't think of any rational arguments against it.' He critically scrutinized Ce'Nedra. 'She doesn't really look all that bad, does she?' he conceded grudgingly. 'It's absolutely unnatural, of course, but the armor does add something. This might even work.'

'I'm so glad I meet with your Majesty's approval,' Ce'Nedra almost gushed at him. She tried to curtsy, but her armor made that impossible. She gave a helpless little laugh and fluttered her eyelashes at the brutish-looking King of Cherek.

'Don't do that, Ce'Nedra,' he told her irritably. 'I'm having enough trouble with this as it is.' He almost glared at her. 'All right,' he said finally, 'as long as we all understand that she's not going to make any decisions, I'll go along with the idea. I don't like it much, but that's beside the point, I suppose.' He stood up and bowed to her. 'Your Majesty,' he said, looking as if the words nearly choked him.

Ce'Nedra beamed at him and instinctively tried to respond to his bow.

'Don't bow, Ce'Nedra,' he advised her with a pained look. 'The Overlord of the West doesn't bow to anyone.' He turned in exasperation to the King of Drasnia. 'That isn't going to work, Rhodar. What are we going to call her? The Overlady of the West? We'll be the laughing-stock of the twelve kingdoms if we do.'

'We call her the Rivan Queen, my dear Anheg,' King Rhodar replied urbanely. 'And we break the head of any man who refuses to bow to her.'

'You can count on that.' Anheg scowled. 'If I bow to her, everybody's going to bow to her.'

'I'm glad that's all been settled,' a familiar voice came from a dim corner of the council chamber.

'Lady Polgara,' Ce'Nedra gasped with a certain confusion. 'I didn't realize you were here.'

'That's fairly obvious,' Polgara replied. 'You *have* been busy, haven't you dear?'

'I—' Ce'Nedra faltered.

Polgara carefully set down her teacup and moved into the light. Her face was serious, but there was a faintly amused twinkle in her eyes as she examined the armor-clad princess. 'Very interesting,' was all she said.

Ce'Nedra was crushed.

'Gentlemen,' Polgara said to the council, 'I'm sure you still have much to discuss. In the meantime, her

Majesty and I need to have a little discussion of our own. I'm sure you'll excuse us.' She moved toward the door. 'Come along, Ce'Nedra,' she said without so much as a backward glance.

Trembling, the princess followed her from the room.

Polgara said nothing until the door to her own chambers had closed behind them. Then she turned and looked gravely at the princess in her armor. 'I've heard about what you've been up to, Ce'Nedra. Would you care to explain?'

'They were all arguing so much,' Ce'Nedra began lamely. 'They needed somebody to unite them.'

'And you decided to take that upon yourself?'

'Well—'

'How did you know they were arguing?'

Ce'Nedra flushed guiltily.

'I see,' Polgara murmured. 'You've discovered how to use my sister's amulet. How clever of you.'

'Let me do it, Lady Polgara!' Ce'Nedra pleaded suddenly. 'Let me lead them; I know I can do it. Let me prove that I'm fit to be Garion's queen.'

Polgara gazed at her thoughtfully. 'You're growing up very rapidly, Ce'Nedra,' she said finally.

'You'll let me do it?'

'We'll talk about it. Take off your helmet and shield, dear, and stand your sword over in the corner. I'll make us a nice cup of tea, and you can tell me exactly what you've got in mind. I'd rather not have any surprises, once we get started in this.'

'You're going with us?' For some reason that startled Ce'Nedra.

'Of course I am,' Polgara told her. She smiled then. 'Possibly I can keep at least you out of trouble. I seem not to have had much success with Garion.' She stopped and looked rather pointedly at Ce'Nedra's breastplate. 'Isn't that a trifle overdone, dear?'

Ce'Nedra blushed. 'I thought it would be more – well—' She floundered with it defensively.

'Ce'Nedra,' Polgara told her, 'you don't have to be so selfconscious. You're still a young girl, after all. Give it some time. Things will improve.'

'I'm so flat,' the princess wailed, almost in despair about it. A thought occurred to her. 'Do you suppose you could – well—' She made a sort of a gesture.

'No, dear,' Polgara said firmly. 'That wouldn't be a good idea. It would do some very strange things to certain necessary balances within you, and those are not the sort of things to be tampered with. Just be patient. If nothing else, a few children will fill you out.'

'Oh, Lady Polgara,' Ce'Nedra said with a helpless little laugh, 'you seem to know everything. You're like the mother I never had.' Impulsively she threw her arms about Polgara's neck.

Polgara wrinkled her nose. 'Ce'Nedra,' she suggested, 'why don't you take off your armor? You smell like an iron pot.'

Ce'Nedra began to laugh.

In the days that followed, a number of people left Riva on important missions. Barak sailed north to Val Alorn to attend the outfitting of the Cherek fleet. Mandorallen left for Vo Mimbre to report to King Korodullin. The fiery young Lelldorin, who had received a pardon at Garion's request, took ship to return to Asturia to make certain preparations there. Hettar, Relg, and Colonel Brendig departed for Camaar, where they would separate and each would return home to oversee the final stages of the mobilization. Events, which always moved at their own pace, began to stir and quicken as the West moved inexorably toward war.

Chapter Twenty-Four

Princess Ce'Nedra soon discovered that Alorns were a surprisingly emotional people. She was forced from the outset to abandon the stereotyped Tolnedran view of this northern race as brutish savages, ravening on the extreme edges of civilization. She found them instead to be an extraordinarily complex people often capable of an extreme range of highly subtle emotions.

There was nothing subtle, however, about the apoplectic fury of King Anheg of Cherek when he came bursting into the council chamber a few days later with his eyes bulging and his face aflame. 'Do you have any idea what you've done?' he bellowed at Ce'Nedra.

'Done to what, your Majesty?' she replied calmly.

'To Cherek!' he shouted, his dented crown sliding down over one ear. 'This little game you've been playing gave my wife the brilliant idea that she's going to run my country while I'm gone.'

'She's your wife, King Anheg,' Ce'Nedra pointed out coolly. 'It's only proper that she should mind the kingdom in your absence.'

'*Mind?*' he almost screamed. 'Islena doesn't have a mind. There's nothing between her ears but empty air.'

'Why did you marry her then?'

'It certainly wasn't for her mind.'

'She might surprise you, Anheg,' King Rhodar suggested with an amused look on his face.

'The only thing that would surprise me would be to

find anything left when I get back,' Anheg retorted, collapsing in a chair. 'And there's nothing I can do to stop her. No matter what I say, she'll assume the throne as soon as I leave. It's going to be a disaster. Women have no business in politics. They're too weak-brained for it.'

'I'm afraid that suggestion won't endear you very much in this particular company, Anheg.' King Rhodar chuckled, glancing at Polgara. One of her eyebrows had shot up at Anheg's last remark.

'Oh – sorry, Polgara,' Anheg muttered, embarrassed. 'I didn't mean you, of course. I don't really think of you as a woman.'

'I wouldn't pursue it any further, Anheg,' King Rhodar advised him. 'You've blundered quite enough for one day already.'

'That's all right, Rhodar,' Polgara said in a frigid tone. 'I find the observations of the King of Cherek most interesting.'

Anheg winced.

'I really can't understand you, my friend,' King Rhodar said to Anheg. 'You've given yourself the finest education in the north. You've studied art and poetry and history and philosophy, but on this one subject you're as blind as an illiterate peasant. What disturbs you so much about the idea of a woman with authority?'

'It's – it's unnatural,' Anheg blurted. 'Women were not meant to rule. The whole idea violates the order of things.'

'I'm not certain that we're getting anywhere with this,' Polgara observed. 'If you gentlemen will excuse us, her Majesty and I still have preparations to make.' She rose and led Ce'Nedra from the council chamber.

'He's very excitable, isn't he?' Ce'Nedra said as the two of them passed through the corridors of Iron-grip's Citadel toward Lady Polgara's apartments.

'He tends to be overdramatic at times,' Polgara replied. 'These outbursts of his aren't always genuine. Sometimes he behaves the way he does because he thinks people expect it of him.' She frowned slightly. 'He's right about one thing, though. Isléna's not qualified to rule. I think we'll have to have a talk with her – and with the other ladies as well.' She opened the door to her apartment, and the two of them went inside.

Most of the damage that had resulted from Polgara's vast rage had been repaired, and there remained only a few scorchmarks on the stone walls to testify to the violence of her fury. She seated herself at a table and turned again to the letter which had arrived that morning from Queen Porenn in Drasnia. 'I think it's rather obvious that we're not going to be able to catch up with my father and the others now,' she observed somewhat regretfully, 'but at least there's one thing we won't have to worry about any more.'

'Which one is that?' Ce'Nedra asked, seating herself across the table from Polgara.

'There'd been some question about my father's recovery from that collapse he suffered last winter, but from what Porenn says, he's completely back to normal – although that's not an unmixed blessing.' She laid Porenn's letter aside. 'I think the time's come for us to have a little talk, Ce'Nedra. You've done a great deal of maneuvering and manipulating in the past few weeks. Now I want to know exactly what's behind it all. Precisely why have you seen fit to ram your new status down everybody's throat?'

Ce'Nedra flushed. 'I *am* the Rivan Queen after all, Lady Polgara,' she replied stiffly.

'Don't be absurd. You're wearing a fictional crown because Rhodar decided to let you wear it, and because he's convinced Anheg and Brand and Cho-Hag that

384

you're not going to do any damage. Now what's behind all this?' Polgara's look was very direct, and Ce'Nedra squirmed uncomfortably.

'We have to bring in the Arends and my father's legions,' she said as if that explained it.

'That's fairly obvious.'

'But the Alorn Kings wouldn't be able to do it.'

'Why not?'

'Because a committee can't win people's hearts.' It was out in the open now, and Ce'Nedra rushed on. 'Garion could have done it. The entire West would have risen at the call of the Rivan King, but Garion isn't here, so somebody else has to do it. I've studied history, Lady Polgara. No army led by a committee has ever succeeded. The success of an army depends on the spirit of the soldiers, and the soldiers have to have *one* leader –someone who fires their imagination.'

'And you've elected yourself?'

'It doesn't have to be anybody brilliant or anything – not really. It's just got to be somebody visible – and unusual.'

'And you think that a woman's going to be unusual enough and visible enough to raise an army – and incidentally to pose enough of a threat to attract the undivided attention of Taur Urgas and 'Zakath, the Mallorean Emperor?'

'Well, it's never been done before.' Ce'Nedra felt a little defensive about it.

'A lot of things have never been done before, Ce'Nedra. That's not necessarily the best recommendation – and what convinced you that I wasn't qualified?'

Ce'Nedra swallowed hard. 'You were so angry,' she faltered, 'and I wasn't sure how long you were going to stay angry. Somebody had to take charge immediately. Besides—' she hesitated.

'Go on.'

'My father doesn't like you,' Ce'Nedra blurted. 'He'd never order his legions to follow you. I'm the only one who has a chance to convince him that he ought to join us. I'm sorry, Lady Polgara. I don't mean to offend you.'

Polgara, however, waved that aside. Her face was thoughtful as she considered Ce'Nedra's arguments. 'It would seem that you have given the matter some thought,' she concluded. 'All right, Ce'Nedra, we'll try it your way – for now. Just don't do anything exotic. Now I think we'd better have a talk with the ladies.'

The conference that took place in Polgara's apartments that afternoon concerned matters of state. She waited quietly until the little group had all gathered, and then she spoke to them rather gravely. 'Ladies,' she began, 'in a very short time the Alorns and others will be taking the field on an expedition of some importance.'

'You mean war, Pol?' Queen Layla asked in a sinking voice.

'We're going to try to avoid that if it's at all possible,' Polgara replied. 'At any rate, the departure of your husband and the Alorn Kings will leave affairs at home in your hands – and the same holds true for each of you. I wanted to go over a few things with all of you before we left.' She turned to Queen Islena, who was splendidly gowned in red velvet. 'Your husband is somewhat less than enthusiastic about any arrangements that will leave you in charge of Cherek, Islena.'

Islena sniffed. 'Anheg can be tiresome at times.'

'Try not to agitate him. Drop a hint or two that you'll allow yourself to be guided by advisers he trusts. It will set his mind at rest a bit.' Polgara looked around at them. 'The campaign is not likely to take us so far away that you won't be able to stay in touch with us – not at first, anyway. If anything serious comes up, communicate with your husbands immediately. Deal with the day-to-day matters yourselves. I also think you should all stay in close contact with each other, once your husbands have left – and also with Porenn in Boktor and Mayaserana in Vo Mimbre. You all have your strengths and your weaknesses, but if you're not afraid to seek advice from each other, everything will be all right.'

'Possibly we should arrange for some kind of network for communications,' Queen Layla mused thoughtfully. 'Relays of horses, messengers, fast ships – that sort of thing. The Tolnedrans have done that for centuries.'

'I'm sure you'll be able to arrange it, Layla.' Polgara smiled at her. 'The one thing you all must remember is to pay close attention to anything Porenn tells you. I know she's very young and a bit shy about putting herself forward, but Drasnian intelligence will report directly to her, and she'll be aware of things long before any of the rest of you are. And I want you all to keep a particularly close watch on the Tolnedrans. They like to take advantage of periods of turmoil. Absolutely do not sign anything offered to you by a Tolnedran – no matter how attractive it looks. I trust Ran Borune about as much as I'd trust a fox in a henhouse – no offense intended, Ce'Nedra.'

'I know my father too, Lady Polgara,' Princess Ce'Nedra replied with a smile.

'Please, ladies,' Polgara told them finally, 'no adventures while I'm gone. Just try to keep things running smoothly, and don't be afraid to consult with one another. You'll also want to keep in touch with Xantha. The Dryads have access to a great deal of information about what's going on in the south. If any real emergency arises, get word to me immediately.'

'Will you want me to keep the little boy?' Merel asked. 'I'll be at Val Alorn with Islena, so he'll be safe with me. My girls are very fond of him, and he seems happy with us.'

Polgara thought about it for a moment. 'No,' she decided finally. 'Errand's going to have to go with me. Aside from Garion, he's the only person in the world who can touch the Orb. The Angaraks may realize that and try to take him.'

'I'll care for him,' Taiba offered in her rich voice. 'He knows me, and we're comfortable with each other. It will give me something to do.'

'Surely you're not planning to go along on the campaign, Taiba,' Queen Layla objected.

Taiba shrugged. 'Why not?' she replied. 'I don't have a house to keep or a kingdom to oversee. There are other reasons, too.'

They all understood. What existed between Taiba and Relg was so profound that it seemed somehow outside the sphere of normal human attachment, and the Ulgo's absence had caused the strange woman something rather close to physical pain. It was now obvious that she intended to follow him – even into battle if necessary.

Ariana, the blond Mimbrate girl who had accompanied Lelldorin of Wildantor to Riva, cleared her throat in preparation to raising a matter of some delicacy. 'The lives of women are circumscribed by proprieties,' she noted. 'Though battle doth rage about her and rude war turneth all to confusion, a lady must not be unattended in the midst of an army lest her reputation suffer. Lady Adara and I have of late held some conversation concerning this and have concluded that we must accompany Princess Ce'Nedra as her companions. We would do this out of duty even were we not impelled by love.'

'Very nicely put, Ariana,' Adara murmured without any hint of a smile.

'Oh dear.' Queen Layla sighed. 'Now I have two more to worry about.'

'I think that covers everything, then,' Polgara said. 'Running a kingdom isn't all that much different from running a house, and you've all had experience at that. Don't change any major policies, and don't sign any treaties. Aside from that, just let yourselves be guided by common sense. I think we can join the gentlemen now. It's getting on toward suppertime, and men tend to grow restless if they aren't fed regularly.'

A few days later, Barak returned to Riva, accompanied by a lean-faced Drasnian nobleman. The two of them immediately went to the council chamber to report to the kings. Princess Ce'Nedra considered following them into the conference, but decided against it. Her presence might inhibit the discussion, and she had another way to find out what was going on. She retired quickly to her rooms and touched her fingertips to the amulet at her throat.

'– going fairly well,' she heard Barak's voice say after she had finally located the conversation she wished to hear. 'The fleet's ready to move out of Val Alorn, and Queen Porenn's got the Drasnian pikemen gathering just south of Boktor. The mobilization's very nearly complete. I think we've got some problems, though. Count Kharel here has just returned from Thull Mardu. All the reports out of northern Cthol Murgos have been channeled to him, so he can give us a fairly clear assessment of the situation there.'

King Rhodar cleared his throat. 'Kharel's a very senior member of the intelligence service,' he said by way of introduction. 'I've always found his reports to be extremely accurate.'

'Your Majesty is too kind,' an unfamiliar voice responded.

'Have the southern Murgos begun their march north?' King Anheg asked.

'It goes a bit farther than that, your Majesty,' Kharel replied. 'All reports I have indicate that the march is nearly completed. There are somewhat in excess of four million of them encamped in the vicinity of Rak Goska.'

'What?' Anheg exclaimed.

'It appears that Taur Urgas began the march sometime last fall,' the Drasnian told him.

'In the winter?'

'It seems so, your Majesty.'

'I imagine that cost him a few of his men,' King Cho-Hag said.

'A hundred thousand or so, your Majesty,' Kharel answered, 'but human life doesn't mean that much to Taur Urgas.'

'This changes everything, Rhodar,' Anheg said tersely. 'Our advantage has always been the time that march was going to take. We've lost it now.'

'Unfortunately there's more, your Majesty,' Kharel continued. 'The western Malloreans have begun to arrive at Thull Zelik. Their numbers aren't really that significant yet, but they're ferrying in several thousand a day.'

'We've got to cut that off as quickly as we can,' Anheg growled. 'Rhodar, can you get your engineers to the eastern escarpment within a month? I'm going to have to portage a fleet across to the headwaters of the River Mardu. We've got to get ships into the Sea of the East as soon as possible. If we don't head off 'Zakath, his Malloreans will swarm us under.'

'I'll send word to Porenn immediately,' Rhodar agreed.

'One wonders if the noble count has any good news,' the Earl of Seline suggested dryly.

'There is some possibility of division in the enemy ranks, my Lord,' Kharel replied. 'Taur Urgas is behaving as if he considers himself the only possible choice as overgeneral of the Angarak armies; at the moment, he's got the advantage of numbers on his side. That may change if the Malloreans manage to land a big enough army. There are rumors that 'Zakath would like to dispute the leadership of Taur Urgas, but he's reluctant to try it in the face of four million Murgos.'

'Let's try to keep it that way,' Rhodar said. 'Taur Urgas is insane, and crazy men make mistakes. I've heard about 'Zakath, and I'd rather not face him in the field.'

King Cho-Hag spoke wryly. 'Even as it stands without the Malloreans, we're going to be taking the field at about a two to one disadvantage – and that's assuming that we can persuade the Arends and Tolnedrans to join us.'

'It's a rotten way to start a war, Rhodar,' Anheg complained.

'We'll just have to adjust our tactics,' Rhodar replied. 'We've got to avoid a pitched battle as long as possible to save as many men as we can.'

'I thought we weren't even considering a battle,' Barak objected, 'and Belgarath said that all he wants is a diversion.'

'The situation's changed, Barak,' King Rhodar declared. 'We hadn't counted on the southern Murgos or the Malloreans being in place this soon. We're going to have to do something a bit more significant than stage a few hit-and-run attacks. The Angaraks have enough men now to be able to ignore minor raids and skirmishes. If we don't make a major thrust – and very soon – they'll spread out all over the eastern half of the continent.'

'Belgarath doesn't like it when you change plans on him,' Anheg reminded Rhodar.

'Belgarath isn't here, and he doesn't know what's going on. If we don't act rather decisively, he and Belgarion and Kheldar haven't a hope of getting through.'

'You're talking about a war we can't win, Rhodar,' Anheg said bluntly.

'I know,' King Rhodar admitted.

There was a long silence. 'So that's the way it is, then,' Brand said finally.

'I'm afraid so,' Rhodar told them somberly. 'There has to be a diversion, or Belgarion and his sword will never get to the meeting with Torak. That's the only thing that really matters, and we'll all have to lay down our lives if necessary to make it happen.'

'You're going to get us all killed, Rhodar,' Anheg said bluntly, 'and all our armies with us.'

'If that's what it takes, Anheg,' Rhodar answered grimly.

'If Belgarion doesn't get to Torak, our lives don't mean anything, anyway. Even if we all have to die to get him there, it's still worth it.'

Ce'Nedra's fingertips slid numbly from her amulet as she fell back in her chair. Suddenly she began to weep. 'I won't do it,' she sobbed. 'I can't.' She saw before her a multitude – an army of widows and orphans all staring accusingly at her, and she shrank from their eyes. If she perpetrated this horror, the rest of her life would be spent in an agony of self-loathing. Still weeping, she stumbled to her feet, fully intending to rush to the council chamber and declare that she would have nothing further to do with this futile war. But then she stopped as the image of Garion's face rose in her mind – that serious face with the unruly hair she always wanted to straighten. He depended on her. If she shrank from this, the Angaraks would be free to hunt him down. His very life – and with it the future of the world – was in her hands. She had no choice but to continue. If only she did not know that the campaign was doomed! It was the knowledge of the disaster that awaited them that made it all so terrible.

Knowing that it was useless, she began to tug at the chain that held the amulet about her neck. Had it not been for the amulet, she would have remained blissfully ignorant of what lay ahead. Still sobbing, she yanked frantically at the chain, ignoring the sting as it cut into the soft skin of her neck. 'I hate you!' she blurted irrationally at the silver amulet with its crowned tree.

But it was useless. The medallion would remain chained about her neck for the rest of her life. Ashen-faced, Ce'Nedra let her hands drop. Even if she were able to remove the amulet, what good would it do? She already knew and she must conceal the knowledge in her heart. If the faintest hint of what she knew showed in her face or her voice, she would fail – and Garion would suffer for her failure. She must steel herself and face the world as if certain of victory.

And so it was that the Rivan Queen drew herself erect and bravely lifted her chin – even though her heart lay like lead in her breast.

Chapter Twenty-Five

Barak's new ship was larger by half than most of the other Cherek warboats in the fleet, but she moved before the spring breeze like a gull skimming low over the water. Fleecy white clouds ran across the blue sky, and the surface of the Sea of the Winds sparkled in the sunlight as the great ship heeled over and cut cleanly through the waves. Low on the horizon before them rose the green shoreline of the hook of Arendia. They were two days out from Riva, and the Cherek fleet spread out behind them in a vast crowd of sails, carrying the gray-cloaked Rivans to join the armies of King Fulrach of Sendaria.

Ce'Nedra nervously paced the deck near the prow, her blue cloak tossing in the wind and her armor gleaming. Despite the dreadful knowledge concealed in her heart, there was an excitement to all of this. The gathering of men, swords, and ships, the running before the wind, the sense of a unified purpose, all combined to make her blood race and to fill her with an exhilaration she had never felt before.

The coast ahead loomed larger – a white sand beach backed by the dark green of the Arendish forest. As they neared the shoreline, an armored knight on a huge roan stallion emerged from the trees and rode down the beach to the edge of the water where foamy breakers crashed on the damp sand. The princess shaded her eyes with one hand and peered intently at the gleaming knight.

Then, as he turned with a broad sweep of his arm which told them to continue up the coast, she saw the crest on his shield. Her heart suddenly soared. 'Mandorallen!' she cried out in a vibrant trumpet note as she clung to the ropes in the very prow of Barak's ship, with the wind whipping at her hair.

The great knight waved a salute and, spurring his charger, galloped through the seething foam at the edge of the beach, the silver and blue pennon at the tip of his lance snapping and streaming over his head. Their ship heeled over as Barak swung the tiller, and, separated by a hundred yards or so of foaming surf, the ship and the rider on the beach kept abreast of each other.

It was a moment Ce'Nedra would remember for all her life – a single image so perfect that it seemed forever frozen in her memory. The great ship flew before the wind, cutting the sparkling blue water, with her white sails booming; the mighty warhorse on the beach plunged through the gleaming foam at the edge of the sand with spray flying out from beneath his great hooves. Locked together in that endless moment, ship and rider raced along in the warm spring sunshine toward a wooded promontory a mile ahead, with Ce'Nedra exulting in the ship's prow and her flaming hair streaming like a banner.

Beyond the promontory lay a sheltered cove, and drawn up on the beach stood the camp of the Sendarian army, row upon orderly row of dun-colored tents. Barak swung his tiller over, and his sails flapped as the ship coasted into the cove with the Cherek fleet close behind.

'Ho, Mandorallen!' Barak bellowed as the anchor ropes sang and great iron anchors plunged down through crystal water toward the sandy bottom.

'My Lord Barak,' Mandorallen shouted his reply, 'welcome to Arendia. Lord Brendig hath devised a means to speed thy disembarking.' He pointed to where a hundred or so Sendarian soldiers were busily poling a series of large rafts into position, lashing them together to form a long floating wharf extending out into the waters of the cove.

Barak laughed. 'Trust a Sendar to come up with something practical.'

'Can we go ashore now?' King Rhodar asked plaintively as he emerged from the cabin. The king was not a good sailor, and his broad, round face had a pale greenish cast to it. He looked oddly comical in his mail shirt and helmet, and the ravages of seasickness on his face added little to his dignity. Despite his unwarlike exterior, however, the other kings had already begun to defer to his wisdom. Beneath his vast rotundity, Rhodar concealed a genius for tactics and a grasp of overall strategy that made the others turn to him almost automatically and accept his unspoken leadership.

A small fishing boat that had been pressed into service as a ferry drew alongside Barak's ship, almost before the anchors had settled, and the kings and their generals and advisers were transferred to the beach in less than half an hour.

'I think I'm hungry,' Rhodar announced the moment he stepped onto solid ground.

Anheg laughed. 'I think you were born hungry.' The king wore a mail shirt and had a broad swordbelt about his waist. His coarse features seemed less out of place somehow, now that he was armed.

'I haven't been able to eat for two days, Anheg.' Rhodar groaned. 'My poor stomach's beginning to think I've abandoned it.'

'Food hath been prepared, your Majesty,' Mandorallen assured him. 'Our Asturian brothers have provided goodly numbers of the king's deer – doubtless obtained lawfully – though I chose not to investigate that too closely.'

Someone standing in the group behind Mandorallen laughed, and Ce'Nedra looked at the handsome young man with reddish-gold hair and the longbow slung over the shoulder of his green doublet. Ce'Nedra had not had much opportunity to become acquainted with Lelldorin of Wildantor while they had been at Riva. She knew him to be Garion's closest friend, however, and she realized the importance of gaining his confidence. It should not be too hard, she decided as she looked at his open, almost innocent face. The gaze he returned was very direct, and one glance into those eyes told the princess that there was a vast sincerity and very little intelligence behind them.

'We've heard from Belgarath,' Barak advised Mandorallen and the young Asturian.

'Where are they?' Lelldorin demanded eagerly.

'They were in Boktor,' King Rhodar replied, his face still a trifle green from his bout of seasickness. 'For reasons of her own, my wife let them pass through. I imagine they're somewhere in Gar og Nadrak by now.'

Lelldorin's eyes flashed. 'Maybe if I hurry, I can catch up with them,' he said eagerly, already starting to look around for his horse.

'It's fifteen hundred leagues, Lelldorin,' Barak pointed out politely.

'Oh—' Lelldorin seemed a bit crestfallen. 'I suppose you're right. It would be a little difficult to catch them now, wouldn't it?'

Barak nodded gravely.

And then the blond Mimbrate girl, Ariana, stepped forward, her heart in her eyes. 'My Lord,' she said to Lelldorin, and Ce'Nedra remembered with a start that the two were married – technically at least. 'Thine absence hath given me great pain.'

397

Lelldorin's eyes were immediately stricken. 'My Ariana.' He almost choked. 'I swear that I'll never leave you again.' He took both her hands in his and gazed adoringly into her eyes. The gaze she returned was just as full of love and just as empty of thought. Ce'Nedra shuddered inwardly at the potential for disaster implicit in the look the two exchanged.

'Does anyone care that I'm starving to death right here on the spot?' Rhodar asked.

The banquet was laid on a long table set up beneath a gaily striped pavilion on the beach not far from the edge of the forest. The table quite literally groaned under its weight of roasted game, and there was enough to eat to satisfy even the enormous appetite of King Rhodar. When they had finished eating, they lingered at the table in conversation.

'Thy son, Lord Hettar, hath advised us that the Algar clans are gathering at the Stronghold, your Majesty,' Mandorallen reported to King Cho-Hag.

Cho-Hag nodded.

'And we've had word from the Ulgo – Relg,' Colonel Brendig added. 'He's gathered a small army of warriors from the caves. They'll wait for us on the Algarian side of the mountains. He said you'd know the place.'

Barak grunted. 'The Ulgos can be troublesome,' he said. 'They're afraid of open places, and daylight hurts their eyes, but they can see in the dark like cats. That could be very useful at some point.'

'Did Relg send any – personal messages?' Taiba asked Brendig with a little catch in her voice.

Gravely, the Sendar took a folded parchment from inside his tunic and handed it to her. She took it with a rather helpless expression and opened it, turning it this way and that.

'What's the matter, Taiba?' Adara asked quietly.

398

'He knows I can't read,' Taiba protested, holding the note tightly pressed against her.

'I'll read it to you,' Adara offered.

'But maybe it's – well – personal,' Taiba objected.

'I promise I won't listen,' Adara told her without the trace of a smile.

Ce'Nedra covered her own smile with her hand. Adara's penetrating and absolutely straight-faced wit was one of the qualities that most endeared her to the princess. Even as she smiled, however, Ce'Nedra could feel eyes on her, and she knew that she was being examined with great curiosity by the Arends – both Asturian and Mimbrate – who had joined them. Lelldorin in particular seemed unable to take his eyes from her. The handsome young man sat close beside the blond Mimbrate girl, Ariana, and stared openly at Ce'Nedra even while, unconsciously perhaps, he held Ariana's hand. Ce'Nedra endured his scrutiny with a certain nervousness. To her surprise, she found that she wanted this rather foolish young man's approval.

'Tell me,' she said directly to him, 'what are the sentiments here in Asturia – concerning our campaign, I mean?'

Lelldorin's eyes clouded. 'Unenthusiastic for the most part, your Majesty,' he replied. 'I'm afraid there's suspicion that this might all be some Mimbrate plot.'

'That's absurd,' Ce'Nedra declared.

Lelldorin shrugged. 'It's the way my countrymen think. And those who don't think it's a plot are looking at the idea that all the Mimbrate knights might join a crusade against the East. That raises certain hopes in some quarters.'

Mandorallen sighed. 'The same sentiments exist in some parts of Mimbre,' he said. 'We are a woefully divided kingdom, and old hatreds and suspicions die hard.'

Ce'Nedra felt a sudden wave of consternation. She had not counted on this. King Rhodar had made it plain that he absolutely had to have the Arends, and now the idiotic hatred and suspicion between Mimbre and Asturia seemed about to bring the entire plan crashing down around her ears. Helplessly she turned to Polgara.

The sorceress, however, seemed undisturbed by the news that the Arends were reluctant to join the campaign. 'Tell me, Lelldorin,' she said calmly, 'could you gather some of your less suspicious friends in one place – some secure place where they won't be afraid we might want to ambush them?'

'What have you got in mind, Polgara?' King Rhodar asked, his eyes puzzled.

'Someone's going to have to talk to them,' Polgara replied. 'Someone rather special, I think.' She turned back to Lelldorin. 'I don't think we'll want a large crowd – not at first, anyway. Forty or fifty ought to be enough – and no one too violently opposed to our cause.'

'I'll gather them at once, Lady Polgara,' Lelldorin declared, impulsively leaping to his feet.

'It's rather late, Lelldorin,' she pointed out, glancing at the sun hovering low over the horizon.

'The sooner I start, the sooner I can gather them,' Lelldorin said fervently. 'If friendship and the ties of blood have any sway at all, I will not fail.' He bowed deeply to Ce'Nedra. 'Your Majesty,' he said by way of farewell and ran to where his horse was tethered.

Ariana sighed as she looked after the departing young enthusiast.

'Is he always like that?' Ce'Nedra asked her curiously.

The Mimbrate girl nodded. 'Always,' she admitted. 'Thought and deed are simultaneous with him. He hath no understanding of the meaning of the word reflection,

I fear. It doth add to his charm, but it is sometimes disconcerting, I must admit.'

'I can imagine,' Ce'Nedra agreed.

Later, when the princess and Polgara were alone in their tent, Ce'Nedra turned a puzzled look upon Garion's Aunt. 'What are we going to do?' she asked.

'Not we, Ce'Nedra – you. You're going to have to talk to them.'

'I'm not very good at speaking in public, Lady Polgara,' Ce'Nedra confessed, her mouth going dry. 'Crowds frighten me, and I get all tongue-tied.'

'You'll get over it, dear,' Polgara assured her. She looked at the princess with a slightly amused expression. 'You're the one who wanted to lead an army, remember? Did you really think that all you were going to have to do was put on your armor, jump into the saddle and shout "follow me" and then the whole world would fall in behind you?'

'Well—'

'You spent all that time studying history and missed the one thing all great leaders have had in common? You must have been very inattentive, Ce'Nedra.'

Ce'Nedra stared at her with slowly dawning horror.

'It doesn't take that much to raise an army, dear. You don't have to be brilliant; you don't have to be a warrior; your cause doesn't even have to be great and noble. All you have to do is be eloquent.'

'I can't do that, Lady Polgara.'

'You should have thought of that before, Ce'Nedra. It's too late to go back now. Rhodar will command the army and see to it that all the details are taken care of, but *you're* the one who'll have to make them want to follow you.'

'I wouldn't have the faintest idea what to say to them,' Ce'Nedra protested.

'It'll come to you, dear. You do believe in what we're doing, don't you?'

'Of course, but—'

'You decided to do this, Ce'Nedra. You decided it all by yourself. And as long as you've come this far, you might as well go all the way.'

'Please, Lady Polgara,' Ce'Nedra begged. 'Speaking in public makes me sick at my stomach. I'll throw up.'

'That happens now and then,' Polgara observed calmly. 'Just try not to do it in front of everybody.'

Three days later, the princess, Polgara, and the Alorn Kings journeyed to the ruined city of Vo Astur deep in the silences of the Arendish forest. Ce'Nedra rode through the sunny woods in a state hovering on the verge of panic. In spite of all her arguments, Polgara had remained adamant. Tears had not budged her; even hysterics had failed. The princess was morbidly convinced that, even if she were to die, Polgara would prop her up in front of the waiting throng and make her go through the agony of addressing them. Feeling absolutely helpless, she rode to meet her fate.

Like Vo Wacune, Vo Astur had been laid waste during the dark centuries of the Arendish civil war. Its tumbled stones were green with moss and they lay in the shade of vast trees that seemed to mourn the honor, pride, and sorrow of Asturia. Lelldorin was waiting, and with him were perhaps fifty richly dressed young noblemen, their eyes filled with curiosity faintly tinged with suspicion.

'It's as many as I could bring together in a short time, Lady Polgara,' Lelldorin apologized after they had dismounted. 'There are others in the region, but they're convinced that our campaign is some kind of Mimbrate treachery.'

'These will do nicely, Lelldorin,' Polgara replied.

'They'll spread the word about what happens here.' She looked around at the mossy, sun-dappled ruins. 'I think that spot over there will be fine.' She pointed at a broken bit of one of the walls. 'Come with me, Ce'Nedra.'

The princess, dressed in her armor, hung her helmet and shield on the saddle of the white horse King Cho-Hag had brought for her from Algaria and led the patient animal as she tremblingly followed the sorceress.

'We want them to be able to see you as well as hear you,' Polgara instructed, 'so climb up on that piece of wall and speak from there. The spot where you'll be standing is in the shade now, but the sun's moving around so that it will be fully on you as you finish your speech. I think that will be a nice touch.'

Ce'Nedra quailed as she saw how far the sun had to go. 'I think I'm going to be sick,' she said in a quivering little voice.

'Maybe later, Ce'Nedra. You don't have time just now.' Polgara turned to Lelldorin. 'I think you can introduce her Majesty now,' she told him.

Lelldorin stepped up onto the wall and held up his hand for silence. 'Countrymen,' he announced in a loud voice, 'last Erastide an event took place which shook our world to its foundations. For a thousand years and more we have awaited that moment. My countrymen, the Rivan King has returned!'

The throng stirred at his announcement, and an excited buzz rippled through it.

Lelldorin, always extravagant, warmed to his subject. He told them of the flaming sword that had announced Garion's true identity and of the oaths of fealty sworn to Belgarion of Riva by the Alorn Kings. Ce'Nedra, almost fainting with nervousness, scarcely heard him. She tried to run over her speech in her mind, but it all kept getting jumbled. Then, in near panic, she heard him say,

'Countrymen, I present to you her Imperial Highness, Princess Ce'Nedra – the Rivan Queen.' And all eyes turned expectantly to her.

Trembling in every limb, she mounted the broken wall and looked at the faces before her. All her preparations, all the rehearsed phrases, evaporated from her mind, and she stood, white-faced and shaking, without the faintest idea of how to begin. The silence was dreadful.

As chance had it, one of the young Asturians in the very front had tasted perhaps more wine that morning than was good for him. 'I think her Majesty has forgotten her speech,' he snickered loudly to one of his companions.

Ce'Nedra's reaction was instantaneous. 'And I think the gentleman has forgotten his manners,' she flared, not even stopping to think. Incivility infuriated her.

'I don't think I'm going to listen to this,' the tipsy young man declared in a tone filled with exaggerated boredom. 'It's just a waste of time. I'm not a Rivan and neither are any of the rest of you. What could a foreign queen possibly say that would be of any interest to Asturian patriots?' And he started to turn away.

'Is the patriotic Asturian gentleman so wine-soaked that he's forgotten that there's more to the world than this forest?' Ce'Nedra retorted hotly. 'Or perhaps he's so unschooled that he doesn't know what's happening out there.' She leveled a threatening finger at him. 'Hear me, patriot,' she said in a ringing voice. 'You may think that I'm just here to make some pretty little speech, but what I've come to say to you is the most important thing you'll ever hear. You can listen, or you can turn your back and walk away – and a year from now when there is no Asturia and when your homes are smoking in ruins and the Grolims are herding your families to the altar of Torak with its fire and its bloody knives, you can look back on this day and curse yourself for not listening.'

And then as if her anger with this one rude young man had suddenly burst a dam within her, Ce'Nedra began to speak. She spoke to them directly, not with the studied phrases she had rehearsed, but with words that came from her heart. The longer she spoke, the more impassioned she became. She pleaded; she cajoled – and finally she commanded. She would never remember exactly what she said, but she would never forget how she felt as she said it. All the passion and fire that had filled the stormy outbursts and tantrums of her girlhood came into full play. She spoke fervently with no thought of herself, but rather with an all-consuming belief in what she said. In the end she won them over.

As the sun fell full upon her, her armor gleamed and her hair seemed to leap into flame. 'Belgarion, King of Riva and Overlord of the West, calls you to war!' she declared to them. 'I am Ce'Nedra, his queen, and I stand before you as a living banner. Who among you will answer Belgarion's call and follow me?'

It was the young man who had laughed at her whose sword leaped first into his hand. Raising it in salute, he shouted, 'I will follow!' As if his declaration were a signal, half a hundred swords flashed in the sunlight as they were raised in salute and pledge, and half a hundred voices echoed his shout. 'I will follow!'

With a broad sweep of her arm, Ce'Nedra drew her own sword and lifted it. 'Follow, then!' she sang to them. 'We ride to meet the fell hordes of Angarak. Let the world tremble at our coming!' With three quick steps, she reached her horse and literally threw herself into the saddle. She wheeled her prancing mount and galloped from the ruins, her sword aloft and her flaming hair streaming. The Asturians as one man rushed to their horses to follow.

As she plunged into the forest, the princess glanced back once at the brave, foolish young men galloping behind her, their faces exalted. She had won, but how many of these unthinking Asturians would she lead back when the war was done? How many would die in the wastes of the East? Her eyes suddenly filled with tears; but, dashing those tears away with one hand, the Rivan Queen galloped on, leading the Asturians back to join her army.

Chapter Twenty-Six

The Alorn Kings praised Ce'Nedra extravagantly, and hard-bitten warriors looked at her with open admiration. She lapped up their adulation and purred like a happy kitten. The only thing that kept her triumph from being complete was Polgara's strange silence. Ce'Nedra was a little hurt by that. The speech had not been perfect, perhaps, but it had won Lelldorin's friends completely, and surely success made up for any minor flaws.

Then, when Polgara sent for her that evening, Ce'Nedra thought she understood. The sorceress wished to congratulate her in private. Humming happily to herself, the princess went along the beach to Polgara's tent with the sound of waves on the white sand in her ears.

Polgara sat at her dressing table, alone except for the sleepy child, Errand. The candlelight played softly over her deep blue robe and the perfection of her features as she brushed her long dark hair. 'Come in, Ce'Nedra,' she said. 'Sit down. We have a great deal to discuss.'

'Were you surprised, Lady Polgara?' The princess could no longer contain herself. 'You were, weren't you? I even surprised myself.'

Polgara looked at her gravely. 'You mustn't allow yourself to become so excited, Ce'Nedra. You have to learn to conserve your strength and not squander it by dashing about in hysterical self-congratulation.'

Ce'Nedra stared at her. 'Don't you think I did well today?' she asked, hurt to the quick.

'It was a very nice speech, Ce'Nedra,' Polgara told her in a way that took all the fun out of it.

A strange thought occurred to the princess then. 'You knew, didn't you?' she blurted..'You knew all along.'

A faint flicker of amusement touched Polgara's lips. 'You always seem to forget that I have certain advantages, dear,' she replied, 'and one of those is that I have a general idea of how things are going to turn out.'

'How could you possibly—'

'Certain events don't just happen, Ce'Nedra. Some things have been implicit in this world since the moment it was made. What happened today was one of those things.' She reached over and picked up an age-darkened scroll from the table. 'Would you like to hear what the Prophecy says about you?'

Ce'Nedra felt a sudden chill.

Polgara ran her eyes down the crackling parchment. 'Here it is,' she said, lifting the scroll into the candlelight. ' "And the voice of the Bride of Light shall be heard in the kingdoms of the world," ' she read, ' "and her words shall be as a fire in dry grass, that the multitudes shall rise up to go forth under the blaze of her banner." '

'That doesn't mean anything at all, Lady Polgara,' Ce'Nedra objected. 'It's absolute gibberish.'

'Does it become any clearer when you find out that Garion is the Child of Light?'

'What is that?' Ce'Nedra demanded, staring at the parchment. 'Where did you get it?'

'It's the Mrin Codex, dear. My father copied it for me from the original. It's a bit obscure because the Mrin prophet was so hopelessly insane that he couldn't speak coherently. King Dras Bull-neck finally had to keep him chained to a post like a dog.'

408

'King Dras? Lady Polgara, that was over three thousand years ago!'

'About that long, yes,' Polgara agreed.

Ce'Nedra began to tremble. 'That's impossible!' she blurted.

Polgara smiled. 'Sometimes, Ce'Nedra, you sound exactly like Garion. I wonder why young people are so fond of that word.'

'But, Lady Polgara, if it hadn't been for that young man who was so insulting, I might not have said anything at all.' The princess bit her lip. She had not meant to confess that.

'That's probably why he was so insulting, then. It's quite possible that insulting you at that particular moment was the only reason he was born in the first place. The Prophecy leaves nothing to chance. Do you think you might need him to help you get started next time? I can arrange to have him get drunk again if you do.'

'Next time?'

'Of course. Did you think that one speech to a very small audience was going to be the end of it? Really, Ce'Nedra, you have to learn to pay more attention to what's going on. You're going to have to speak in public at least once a day for the next several months.'

The princess stared at her in horror. 'I *can't*!' she wailed.

'Yes, you can, Ce'Nedra. Your voice will be heard in the land, and your words shall be as a fire in dry grass, and the multitudes of the West shall rise up to follow your banner. Down through all the centuries, I've never known the Mrin Codex to be wrong – not once. The important thing at the moment is for you to get plenty of rest and to eat regularly. I'll prepare your meals myself.' She looked rather critically at the tiny girl. 'It would help if you were a bit more robust, but I guess we'll have to make do with what we have. Go get your things, Ce'Nedra. From now on, you'll be staying with me. I think I'm going to want to keep an eye on you.'

In the weeks that followed, they moved down through the moist, green Arendish forest, and word of their coming spread throughout Asturia. Ce'Nedra was dimly aware that Polgara was carefully controlling the size and composition of the audiences to be addressed. Poor Lelldorin was seldom out of his saddle as he and a carefully selected group of his friends ranged ahead of the advancing army to prepare each gathering.

Ce'Nedra, once she had finally accepted her duty, had assumed that speaking in public would grow easier with practice. Unfortunately, she was wrong. Panic still gripped her before each speech, and quite frequently she was physically sick. Although Polgara assured her that her speeches were getting better, Ce'Nedra complained that they were not getting easier. The drain on her physical and emotional reserves became more and more evident. Like most girls her age, Ce'Nedra could and often did talk endlessly, but her orations were not random talk. They required an enormous control and a tremendous expenditure of emotional energy, and no one could help her.

As the crowds grew larger, however, Polgara did provide some aid in a purely technical matter. 'Just speak in a normal tone of voice, Ce'Nedra,' she instructed. 'Don't exhaust yourself by trying to shout. I'll see to it that everybody can hear you.' Aside from that, however, the princess was on her own, and the strain became more and more visible. She rode listlessly at the head of her growing army, seeming sometimes almost to be in a trance.

Her friends watched her and worried.

'I'm not sure how much longer she can keep up this pace,' King Fulrach confided to King Rhodar as they rode directly behind the drooping little queen toward the ruins of Vo Wacune, where she was to address yet another gathering. 'I think we tend sometimes to forget how small and delicate she is.'

'Maybe we'd better consult with Polgara,' King Rhodar agreed. 'I think the child needs a week's rest.'

Ce'Nedra, however, knew that she could not stop. There was a momentum to this, a kind of accelerating rhythm that could not be broken. At first, word of her coming had spread slowly, but now it ran ahead of them, and she knew they must run faster and faster to keep up with it. There was a crucial point at which the curiosity about her must be satisfied or the whole thing would collapse and she'd have to begin all over again.

The crowd at Vo Wacune was the largest she had yet addressed. Half-convinced already, they needed only a single spark to ignite them. Once again sick with unreasoning panic, the Rivan Queen gathered her strength and rose to address them and to set them aflame with her call to war.

When it was over and the young nobles had been gathered into the growing ranks of the army, Ce'Nedra sought a few moments of solitude on the outskirts of the camp to compose herself. This had become a kind of necessary ritual for her. Sometimes she was sick after a speech and sometimes she wept. Sometimes she merely wandered listlessly, not even seeing the trees about her. At Polgara's instruction, Durnik always accompanied her, and Ce'Nedra found the company of this solid, practical man strangely comforting.

They had walked some distance from the ruins. The afternoon was bright and sunny, and birds sang among the trees. Pensively, Ce'Nedra walked, letting the peace of the forest quiet the agitated turmoil within her.

'It's all very well for noblemen, Detton,' she heard someone say somewhere on the other side of a thicket, 'but what does it have to do with us?'

'You're probably right, Lammer,' a second voice agreed with a regretful sigh. 'It was very stirring, though, wasn't it?'

'The only thing that ought to stir a serf is the sight of something to eat,' the first man declared bitterly. 'The little girl can talk all she wants about duty, but my only duty is to my stomach.' He stopped abruptly. 'Are the leaves of that plant over there fit to eat?' he asked.

'I think they're poisonous, Lammer,' Detton replied.

'But you're not sure? I'd hate to pass up something I could eat if there was any chance that it wouldn't kill me.'

Ce'Nedra listened to the two serfs with growing horror. Could anybody be reduced to that level? Impulsively, she stepped around the thicket to confront them. Durnik, as always, stayed close by her side.

The two serfs were dressed in mud-spattered rags. They were both men of middle years, and there was no evidence on their faces that either of them had ever known a happy day. The leaner of the two was closely examining a thick-leafed weed, but the other saw Ce'Nedra approaching and started with obvious fright. 'Lammer.' He gasped. 'It's her – the one who spoke today.'

Lammer straightened, his gaunt face going pale beneath the dirt that smudged it. 'Your Ladyship,' he said, grotesquely trying to bow. 'We were just on our way back to our villages. We didn't know this part of the forest was yours. We didn't take anything.' He held out his empty hands as if to prove his words.

'How long has it been since you've had anything to eat?' she demanded of him.

'I ate some grass this morning, your Ladyship,' Lammer replied, 'and I had a couple of turnips yesterday. They were a little wormy, but not too bad.'

Ce'Nedra's eyes suddenly filled with tears. 'Who's done this to you?' she asked him.

Lammer looked a little confused at her question. Finally he shrugged slightly. 'The world, I guess, your Ladyship. A certain part of what we raise goes to our lord, and a certain part to his lord. Then there's the part that has to go to the king and the part that has to go to the royal governor. And we're still paying for some wars my lord had a few years ago. After all of that's been paid, there isn't very much left for us.'

A horrible thought struck her. 'I'm gathering an army for a campaign in the East,' she told them.

'Yes, your Ladyship,' the other serf, Detton, replied. 'We heard your speech today.'

'What will that do to you?'

Detton shrugged. 'It will mean more taxes, your Ladyship – and some of our sons will be taken for soldiers if our lords decide to join you. Serfs don't really make very good soldiers, but they can always carry baggage. And when the time comes to storm a castle, the nobility seem to want to have a lot of serfs around to help with the dying.'

'Then you never feel any patriotism when you go to war?'

'What could patriotism have to do with serfs, my Lady?' Lammer asked her. 'Until a month or so ago I didn't even know the name of my country. None of it belongs to me. Why should I have any feelings about it?'

Ce'Nedra could not answer that question. Their lives were so bleak, so hopelessly empty, and her call to war meant only greater hardship and more suffering for them. 'What about your families?' she asked. 'If Torak

413

wins, the Grolims will come and slaughter your families on his altars.'

'I have no family, my Lady,' Lammer replied in a dead voice. 'My son died several years ago. My lord was fighting a war somewhere, and when they attacked a castle, the people inside poured boiling pitch down on the serfs who were trying to raise a ladder. My wife starved herself to death after she heard about it. The Grolims can't hurt either one of them now, and if they want to kill me, they're welcome to.'

'Isn't there anything at all you'd be willing to fight for?'

'Food, I suppose,' Lammer said after a moment's thought. 'I'm very tired of being hungry.'

Ce'Nedra turned to the other serf. 'What about you?' she asked him.

'I'd walk into fire for somebody who fed me,' Detton replied fervently.

'Come with me,' Ce'Nedra commanded them, and she turned and led the way back to the camp and the large, bulky supply wagons that had transported the vast quantities of food from the storehouses of Sendaria. 'I want these two men fed,' she told a startled cook. 'As much as they can eat.' Durnik, however, his honest eyes brimming with compassion, had already reached into one of the wagons and taken out a large loaf of bread. He tore it in two and gave half to Lammer and half to Detton.

Lammer stared at the chunk of bread in his hands, trembling violently. 'I'll follow you, my Lady,' he declared in a quavering voice. 'I've eaten my shoes and lived on boiled grass and tree roots.' His fists closed about the chunk of bread as if he were afraid someone might take it away from him. 'I'll follow you to the end of the world and back for this.' And he began to eat, tearing at the bread with his teeth.

Ce'Nedra stared at him, and then she suddenly fled. By the time she reached her tent she was weeping hysterically. Adara and Taiba tried without success to comfort her, and finally they sent for Polgara.

When the sorceress arrived, she took one brief look and asked Taiba and Adara to leave her alone with the sobbing girl. 'All right, Ce'Nedra,' she said calmly, sitting on the bed and gathering the princess in her arms, 'what's this all about?'

'I can't do it any more, Lady Polgara,' Ce'Nedra cried. 'I just can't.'

'It was your idea in the first place,' Polgara reminded her.

'I was wrong.' Ce'Nedra sobbed. 'Wrong, wrong! I should have stayed in Riva.'

'No,' Polgara disagreed. 'You've done something that none of the rest of us could have. You've guaranteed us the Arends. I'm not even sure Garion could have done that.'

'But they're all going to die!' Ce'Nedra wailed.

'Where did you get that idea?'

'The Angaraks are going to outnumber us at least two to one. They'll butcher my army.'

'Who told you that?'

'I – I listened,' Ce'Nedra replied, fumbling with the amulet at her throat. 'I heard what Rhodar, Anheg, and the others said when they heard about the southern Murgos.'

'I see,' Polgara said gravely.

'We're going to throw away our lives. Nothing can save us. And just now I even found a way to bring the serfs into it. Their lives are so miserable that they'll follow me just for the chance to eat regularly. And I'll do it, Lady Polgara. If I think I might need them, I'll deliberately take them from their homes and lead them to their deaths. I can't help myself.'

Polgara took a glass from a nearby table and emptied a small glass vial into it. 'The war isn't over yet, Ce'Nedra. It hasn't even begun.' She swirled the dark amber liquid around in the bottom of the glass. 'I've seen hopeless wars won before. If you give in to despair before you begin, you'll have no chance at all. Rhodar's a very clever tactician, you know, and the men in your army are very brave. We won't commit to any battle until we absolutely have to, and if Garion can reach Torak in time – and if he wins – the Angaraks will fall apart, and we won't have to fight them at all. Here.' She held out the glass. 'Drink this.'

Numbly, Ce'Nedra took the glass and drank. The amber liquid was bitter, and it left a strange, fiery aftertaste in her mouth. 'It all depends on Garion, then,' she said.

'It always has depended on him, dear,' Polgara told her.

Ce'Nedra sighed. 'I wish—' she began, then faltered to a stop.

'Wish what, dear?'

'Oh, Lady Polgara, I never once told Garion that I love him. I'd give anything to be able to tell him that – just once.'

'He knows, Ce'Nedra.'

'But it's not the same.' Ce'Nedra sighed again. A strange lassitude had begun to creep over her, and she had stopped crying. It was difficult somehow even to remember why she had been weeping. She suddenly felt eyes on her and turned. Errand sat quietly in the corner watching her. His deep blue eyes were filled with sympathy and, oddly, with hope. And then Polgara took the princess in her arms and began rocking slowly back and forth and humming a soothing kind of melody. Without knowing when it happened, Ce'Nedra fell into a deep and dreamless sleep.

The attempt on her life came the following morning. Her army was marching south from Vo Wacune, passing through the sunlit forest along the Great West Road. The princess was riding at the head of the column, talking with Barak and Mandorallen, when an arrow, buzzing spitefully, came out of the trees. It was the buzz that gave Barak an instant of warning. 'Look out!' he shouted, suddenly covering Ce'Nedra with his great shield. The arrow shattered against it, and Barak, cursing horribly, drew his sword.

Brand's youngest son, Olban, however, was already plunging at a dead run into the forest. His face had gone deathly pale, and his sword seemed to leap into his hand as he spun his horse. The sound of his galloping mount faded back among the trees. After several moments, there was a dreadful scream.

Shouts of alarm came from the army behind them and a confused babble of voices. Polgara rode forward, her face white. 'I'm all right, Lady Polgara,' Ce'Nedra assured her quickly. 'Barak saved me.'

'What happened?' Polgara demanded.

'Someone shot an arrow at her,' Barak growled. 'If I hadn't heard it buzz, it might have been very bad.'

Lelldorin had picked up the shattered arrow shaft and was looking at it closely. 'The fletching is loose,' he said, rubbing his finger over the feathers. 'That's what made it buzz like that.'

Olban came riding back out of the forest, his bloody sword still in his hand. 'Is the queen safe?' he demanded; for some reason, his voice seemed on the verge of hysteria.

'She's fine,' Barak said, looking at him curiously. 'Who was it?'

'A Murgo, I think,' Olban replied. 'He had scars on his cheeks.'

'Did you kill him?'

Olban nodded. 'Are you sure you're all right, my Queen?' he asked Ce'Nedra. His pale, blond hair was tousled, and he seemed very young and very earnest.

'I'm just fine, Olban,' she replied. 'You were very brave, but you should have waited instead of riding off alone like that. There might have been more than one.'

'Then I'd have killed them all,' Olban declared fiercely. 'I'll destroy anyone who even raises a finger against you.' The young man was actually trembling with rage.

'Thy dedication becomes thee, young Olban,' Mandorallen told him.

'I think we'd better put out some scouts,' Barak suggested to King Rhodar. 'At least until we get out of these trees. Korodullin was going to chase all the Murgos out of Arendia, but it looks as if he missed a few.'

'Let me lead the scouting parties,' Olban begged.

'Your son has a great deal of enthusiasm,' Rhodar observed to Brand. 'I like that in a young man.' He turned back to Olban. 'All right,' he said. 'Take as many men as you need. I don't want any Murgos within five miles of the princess.'

'You have my word on it,' Olban declared, wheeling his horse and plunging back into the forest.

They rode a bit more cautiously after that, and archers were placed strategically to watch the crowd when Ce'Nedra spoke. Olban rather grimly reported that a few more Murgos had been flushed out of the trees ahead of them, but there were no further incidents.

It was very nearly the first day of summer when they rode out of the forest onto the central Arendish plain. Ce'Nedra by that time had gathered nearly every able-bodied Asturian into her army, and her hosts spread out behind her in a sea of humanity as she led the way out onto the plain. The sky above was very blue as they left the trees behind, and the grass was very green beneath the hooves of their horses.

'And where now, your Majesty?' Mandorallen inquired.

'To Vo Mimbre,' Ce'Nedra replied. 'I'll speak to the Mimbrate knights, and then we'll go on to Tolnedra.'

'I hope your father still loves you, Ce'Nedra,' King Rhodar said. 'It will take a lot of love to make Ran Borune forgive you for entering Tolnedra with this army at your back.'

'He adores me,' Ce'Nedra assured him confidently.

King Rhodar still looked dubious.

The army marched down through the plains of central Arendia toward the capital at Vo Mimbre where King Korodullin had assembled the Mimbrate knights and their retainers. The weather continued fair, and they marched in bright sunshine.

One sunny morning shortly after they had set out, Lady Polgara rode forward and joined Ce'Nedra at the head of the column. 'Have you decided how you're going to deal with your father yet?' she asked.

'I'm not sure,' the princess confessed. 'He's probably going to be extremely difficult.'

'The Borunes usually are.'

'*I'm* a Borune, Lady Polgara.'

'I know.' Polgara looked penetratingly at the princess. 'You've grown considerably in the past few months, dear,' she observed.

'I didn't really have much choice, Lady Polgara. This all came on rather suddenly.' Ce'Nedra giggled then as a thought suddenly struck her. 'Poor Garion.' She laughed.

'Why poor Garion?'

'I was horrid to him, wasn't I?'

'Moderately horrid, yes.'

'How were any of you able to stand me?'

'We clenched our teeth frequently.'

'Do you think he'd be proud of me – if he knew what I'm doing, I mean?'

'Yes,' Polgara told her, 'I think he would be.'

'I'm going to make it all up to him, you know,' Ce'Nedra promised. 'I'm going to be the best wife in the world.'

'That's nice, dear.'

'I won't scold or shout or anything.'

'Don't make promises you can't keep, Ce'Nedra,' Polgara said wisely.

'Well,' the little princess amended, 'almost never anyway.'

Polgara smiled. 'We'll see.'

The Mimbrate knights were encamped on the great plain before the city of Vo Mimbre. Together with their men-at-arms, they comprised a formidable army, glittering in the sunlight.

'Oh dear,' Ce'Nedra faltered as she stared down at the vast gathering from the hilltop where she and the Alorn Kings had ridden to catch the first glimpse of the city.

'What's the problem?' Rhodar asked her.

'There are so many of them.'

'That's the whole idea, isn't it?'

A tall Mimbrate knight with dark hair and beard, wearing a black velvet surcoat over his polished armor, galloped up the hill and reined in some yards before them. He looked from face to face, then inclined his head in a polite bow. He turned to Mandorallen. 'Greetings to the Bastard of Vo Mandor from Korodullin, King of Arendia.'

'You still haven't gotten that straightened out, have you?' Barak muttered to Mandorallen.

'I have not had leisure, my Lord,' Mandorallen replied. He turned to the knight. 'Hail and well-met, Sir Andorig. I pray thee, convey our greetings to his Majesty and advise him that we come in peace – which he doubtless doth know already.'

'I will, Sir Mandorallen,' Andorig responded.

'How's your apple tree doing, Andorig?' Barak asked, grinning openly.

'It doth flourish, my Lord of Trellheim,' Andorig answered proudly. 'My care for it hath been most tender, and I have hopes of a bounteous harvest. I am confident that I have not disappointed Holy Belgarath.' He turned and clattered back down the hill, sounding his horn every hundred yards or so.

'What was that all about?' King Anheg asked his red-bearded cousin with a puzzled frown.

'We've been here before,' Barak replied. 'Andorig didn't believe us when we told him who Belgarath was. Belgarath made an apple tree grow up out of the stones of the courtyard, and that sort of convinced him.'

'I pray thee,' Mandorallen said then, his eyes clouded with a sudden pain. 'I see the approach of dear friends. I shall return presently.' He moved his horse at a canter toward a knight and a lady who were riding out from the city.

'Good man there,' Rhodar mused, watching the great knight as he departed. 'But why do I get the feeling that when I'm talking to him my words are bouncing off solid bone?'

'Mandorallen is my knight,' Ce'Nedra quickly came to the defense of her champion. 'He doesn't need to think. I'll do his thinking for him.' She stopped suddenly. 'Oh dear,' she said. 'That sounds dreadful, doesn't it?'

King Rhodar laughed. 'You're a treasure,

Ce'Nedra,' he said fondly, 'but you do tend to blurt things out on occasion.'

'Who are those people?' Ce'Nedra asked, curiously watching as Mandorallen rode to meet the couple who had emerged from the gates of Vo Mimbre.

'That's the Baron of Vo Ebor,' Durnik replied quietly, 'and his wife, the Baroness Nerina. Mandorallen's in love with her.'

'*What?*'

'It's all very proper,' Durnik assured her quickly. 'I didn't understand it at first myself, but I guess it's the sort of thing that happens here in Arendia. It's a tragedy, of course. All three of them are suffering terribly.' The good man sighed.

'Oh dear,' Ce'Nedra said, biting her lip. 'I didn't know – and I've treated him so badly at times.'

'I'm sure he'll forgive you, princess,' Durnik told her. 'He has a very great heart.'

A short time later, King Korodullin rode out from the city, accompanied by Mandorallen and a score of armored knights. Ce'Nedra had met the young King of Arendia several years before, and she remembered him as a pale, thin young man with a beautiful voice. On this occasion he was dressed in full armor and a crimson surcoat. He raised his visor as he approached. 'Your Majesty,' he greeted her gravely, 'we have awaited thy coming with great anticipation.'

'Your Majesty is too kind,' Ce'Nedra replied.

'We have marvelled at the stories of thy mobilization of our Asturian cousins,' the king told her. 'Thine oratory must be wondrously persuasive to move them to lay aside their customary enmities.'

'The day wears on, your Majesty,' King Rhodar observed. 'Her Majesty would like to address your knights – with your permission, of course. Once you've heard her, I think you'll understand her value to our cause.'

'At once, your Majesty,' Korodullin agreed. He turned to one of his men. 'Assemble the knights and men-at-arms of Mimbre that the Rivan Queen may disclose her mind to them.' he commanded.

The army which had followed Ce'Nedra down through the plains of Arendia had begun to arrive and was flowing down onto the plain before the city in a vast multitude. Drawn up to meet that force stood the glittering Mimbrate knights. The air crackled with suspicion as the two groups eyed each other.

'I think we'd better move right along,' King Cho-Hag suggested. 'An accidental remark out there could precipitate some unpleasantness we'd all prefer to avoid.'

Ce'Nedra had already begun to feel sick to her stomach. The feeling by now, however, was so familiar that it no longer even worried her. A platform had been erected on a spot that stood midway between Ce'Nedra's army and the armored knights of King Korodullin. The princess, accompanied by all her friends and the Mimbrate honor guard, rode down to the platform, where she nervously dismounted.

'Feel free to speak at length, Ce'Nedra,' Lady Polgara quietly advised. 'Mimbrates dote on ceremony and they're as patient as stones if you give them something formal to watch. It's about two hours until sunset. Try to time the climax of your speech to coincide with that.'

Ce'Nedra gasped. 'Two *hours*?'

'If you need longer, we can build bonfires,' Durnik offered helpfully.

'Two hours ought to be about right,' Lady Polgara surmised.

Ce'Nedra quickly began mentally revising her speech.

'You'll make sure they can all hear me?' she asked Polgara.

'I'll take care of it, dear.'

Ce'Nedra drew in a deep breath. 'All right, then,' she said, 'here we go.' And she was helped up onto the platform.

It was not pleasant. It never was, but her weeks of practice in northern Arendia had given her the ability to assess the mood of a crowd and to adjust the pace of her delivery accordingly. As Polgara had suggested, the Mimbrates seemed quite willing to listen interminably. Moreover, standing here on the field at Vo Mimbre gave her words a certain dramatic impact. Torak himself had stood here, and the vast human sea of the Angarak hordes had hurled themselves from here against the unyielding walls of the city gleaming at the edge of the plain. Ce'Nedra spoke, the words rolling from her mouth as she delivered her impassioned address. Every eye was upon her, and every ear was bent to her words. Whatever sorcery Lady Polgara used to make the Rivan Queen's voice audible at the farthest edge of the crowd was clearly working. Ce'Nedra could see the impact of what she was saying rippling through the hosts before her like a breeze touching a field of bending wheat.

And then, as the sun hovered in golden clouds just above the western horizon, the little queen moved into the climactic crescendo of her oration. The words 'pride,' 'honor,' 'courage,' and 'duty' sang in the blood of her rapt listeners. Her final question, 'Who will follow me?' was delivered just as the setting sun bathed the field with flaming light and was answered with an ear-splitting roar as the Mimbrate knights drew their swords in salute.

Perspiring heavily in her sun-heated armor, Ce'Nedra, as was her custom, drew her own sword in reply, leaped to her horse and led her now enormous army from the field.

'Stupendous!' she heard King Korodullin marvel as he rode behind her.

'Now you see why we follow her,' King Anheg told him.

'She's magnificent!' King Korodullin declared. 'Truly, my Lords, such eloquence can only be a gift from the Gods. I had viewed our enterprise with some trepidation – I confess it – but gladly would I challenge all the hosts of Angarak now. Heaven itself is with this marvellous child, and we cannot fail.'

'I'll feel better after I see how the legions respond to her,' King Rhodar observed. 'They're a pretty hard-bitten lot, and I think it might take a bit more than a speech about patriotism to move them.'

Ce'Nedra, however, had already begun to work on that. She considered the problem from every angle as she sat alone in her tent that evening, brushing her hair. She needed something to stir her countrymen and she instinctively knew what it must be.

Quite suddenly the silver amulet at her throat gave a strange little quiver, something it had never done before. Ce'Nedra laid down her brush and touched her fingertips to the talisman.

'I know you can hear me, father,' she heard Polgara say. A sudden image rose in Ce'Nedra's mind of Polgara, wrapped in her blue cloak, standing atop a hill with the night breeze stirring her hair.

'Have you regained your temper yet?' Belgarath's voice sounded wary.

'We'll talk about that some other time. What are you up to?'

'At the moment, I'm up to my ears in drunk Nadraks. We're in a tavern in Yar Nadrak.'

'I might have guessed. Is Garion all right?'

'Of course he is. I'm not going to let anything happen to him, Pol. Where are you?'

'At Vo Mimbre, We've raised the Arends, and we're going on to Tolnedra in the morning.'

'Ran Borune won't like that much.'

'We have a certain advantage. Ce'Nedra's leading the army.'

'Ce'Nedra?' Belgarath sounded startled.

'It seems that was what the passage in the Codex meant. She's been preaching the Arends out of the trees as if she owned them.'

'What an amazing thing.'

'Did you know that the southern Murgos are already gathered at Rak Goska?'

'I've heard some rumors.'

'It changes things, you know.'

'Perhaps. Who's in charge of the army?'

'Rhodar.'

'Good. Tell him to avoid anything major as long as possible Pol, but keep the Angaraks off my back.'

'We'll do what we can.' She seemed to hesitate for a moment. 'Are you all right, father?' she asked carefully. The question seemed important for some reason.

'Do you mean am I still in full possession of my faculties?' He sounded amused. 'Garion told me that you were worried about that.'

'I told him not to say anything.'

'By the time he got around to it, the whole question was pretty much academic.'

'Are you—? I mean can you still—?'

'Everything seems to work the same as always, Pol,' he assured her.

'Give my love to Garion.'

'Of course. Don't make a habit of this, but keep in touch with me.'

'Very well, father.'

The amulet under Ce'Nedra's fingers quivered again. Then Polgara's voice spoke quite firmly. 'All right, Ce'Nedra,' the sorceress said, 'you can stop eavesdropping now.'

Guiltily, Ce'Nedra jerked her fingers from the amulet.

The next morning, even before the sun came up, she sent for Barak and Durnik.

'I'm going to need every scrap of Angarak gold in the entire army,' she announced to them. 'Every single coin. Buy it from the men if you have to, but get me all the red gold you can lay your hands on.'

'I don't suppose you'd care to tell us why,' Barak said sourly. The big man was surly about being pulled from his bed before daylight.

'I'm a Tolnedran,' she informed him, 'and I know my countrymen. I think I'm going to need some bait.'

Chapter Twenty-Seven

Ran Borune XXIII, Emperor of Tolnedra, was livid with rage. Ce'Nedra noticed with a certain pang that her father had aged considerably in the year that she had been absent and she wished that their meeting might be more cordial than this one promised to be.

The Emperor had drawn up his legions on the plains of northern Tolnedra, and they faced Ce'Nedra's army as it emerged from the forest of Vordue. The sun was warm, and the crimson standards of the legions, rising from what seemed a vast sea of brightly burnished steel, waved imposingly in the summer breeze. The massed legions had taken up positions along the crest of a line of low hills and they looked down at Ce'Nedra's sprawling army with the tactical advantage of terrain in their favor.

King Rhodar quietly pointed this out to the young queen as they dismounted to meet the Emperor. 'We definitely don't want to provoke anything here,' he advised her. 'Try your best to be polite at least.'

'I know what I'm doing, your Majesty,' she replied airily, removing her helmet and carefully smoothing her hair.

'Ce'Nedra,' Rhodar said bluntly, taking her arm in a firm grasp, 'you've been playing this on your veins since the first day we landed on the hook of Arendia. You don't know from one minute to the next what you're going to do. I most definitely do not propose to attack the Tolnedran legions uphill, so be civil to your father or

I'll take you over my knee and spank you. Do you understand me?'

'Rhodar!' Ce'Nedra gasped. 'What a terrible thing to say!'

'I mean every word,' he told her. 'You mind your manners, young lady.'

'Of course I will,' she promised. She gave him a shy, little-girl look through fluttering eyelashes. 'Do you still love me, Rhodar?' she asked in a tiny voice.

He gave her a helpless look, and then she patted his broad cheek. 'Everything will be just fine, then,' she assured him. 'Here comes my father.'

'Ce'Nedra,' Ran Borune demanded angrily, striding to meet them, 'just exactly what do you think you're doing?' The Emperor was dressed in gold-embossed armor, and Ce'Nedra thought he looked rather silly in it.

'Just passing through, father,' she replied as inoffensively as possible. 'You've been well, I trust?'

'I was until you violated my borders. Where did you get the army?'

'Here and there, father.' She shrugged. 'We really ought to talk, you know – someplace private.'

'I don't have anything to say to you,' the bald-headed little man declared. 'I refuse to talk to you until you get this army off Tolnedran soil.'

'Oh, father,' she reprimanded him, 'stop being so childish.'

'Childish?' The Emperor exploded. '*Childish!*'

'Her Majesty perhaps chose the wrong word,' King Rhodar interposed, giving Ce'Nedra a hard look. 'As we all know, she tends at times to be a trifle undiplomatic.'

'What are you doing here, Rhodar?' Ran Borune demanded. He looked around quickly at the other kings. 'Why have the Alorns invaded Tolnedra?'

'We haven't invaded you, Ran Borune,' Anheg told

him. 'If we had, the smoke from burning towns and villages would be rising behind us. You know how we make war.'

'What are you doing here, then?'

King Cho-Hag answered in a calm voice. 'As her Majesty advised you, we're only passing through on our way to the East.'

'And exactly what do you plan to do in the East?'

'That's our business,' Anheg told him bluntly.

'Try to be civil,' Lady Polgara said to the Cherek king. She turned to the Emperor. 'My father and I explained to you what was happening last summer, Ran Borune. Weren't you listening?'

'That was before you stole my daughter,' he retorted. 'What have you done to her? She was difficult before, but now she's absolutely impossible.'

'Children grow up, your Majesty,' Polgara replied philosophically. 'The queen's point was well-taken, however. We do need to talk – preferably in private.'

'What queen are we talking about?' the Emperor asked bitingly. 'I don't see any queen here.'

Ce'Nedra's eyes hardened. 'Father,' she snapped, 'you know what's been happening. Now stop playing games and talk sense. This is very important.'

'Your Highness knows me well enough to know that I don't play games,' he told her in an icy tone.

'Your *Majesty*,' she corrected him.

'Your *Highness*,' he insisted.

'Your *Majesty*,' she repeated, her voice going up an octave.

'Your *Highness*,' he snarled from between clenched teeth.

'Do we really need to squabble like bad-tempered children right in front of the armies?' Polgara asked calmly.

'She's right, you know,' Rhodar said to Ran Borune. 'We're all beginning to look a bit foolish out here. We ought to try to maintain the fiction of dignity at least.'

The Emperor glanced involuntarily over one shoulder at the glittering ranks of his legions drawn up on the hilltops not far away. 'Very well,' he conceded grudgingly, 'but I want it clearly understood that the only thing we're going to talk about is your withdrawal from Tolnedran soil. If you'll follow me, we'll go to my pavilion.'

'Which stands right in the middle of your legions,' King Anheg added. 'Forgive me, Ran Borune, but we're not that stupid. Why don't we go to my pavilion instead?'

'I'm no stupider than you are, Anheg,' the Emperor retorted.

'If I may,' King Fulrach said mildly. 'In the interests of expediency, might we not assume that this spot is more or less neutral?' He turned to Brendig. 'Colonel, would you be so good as to have a large tent erected here?'

'At once, your Majesty,' the sober-faced Brendig replied.

King Rhodar grinned. 'As you can see, the legendary practicality of the Sendars is not a myth.'

The Emperor looked a bit sour, but finally seemed to remember his manners. 'I haven't seen you in a long time, Fulrach,' he said. 'I hope Layla's well.'

'She sends her regards,' the King of Sendaria replied politely.

'You've got good sense, Fulrach,' the Emperor burst out. 'Why have you lent yourself to this insane adventure?'

'I think that might be one of the things we ought to discuss in private, don't you?' Polgara suggested smoothly.

431

'How's the squabble over the succession going?' Rhodar asked in the tone of a man making small talk.

'It's still up in the air,' Ran Borune responded, also in a neutral manner. 'The Honeths seem to be joining forces, though.'

'That's unfortunate,' Rhodar murmured. 'The Honeths have a bad reputation.'

Under Colonel Brendig's direction, a squad of Sendarian soldiers were quickly erecting a large, bright-colored pavilion on the green turf not far away.

'Did you deal with Duke Kador, father?' Ce'Nedra inquired.

'His Grace found his life burdensome,' Ran Borune replied with a short laugh. 'Someone rather carelessly left some poison lying about in his prison cell, and he sampled it extensively. We gave him a splendid funeral.'

Ce'Nedra smiled. 'I'm so sorry I missed it.'

'The pavilion is ready now,' King Fulrach told them. 'Shall we go inside?'

They all entered and sat at the table the soldiers had placed inside. Lord Morin, the Emperor's chamberlain, held Ce'Nedra's chair for her.

'How has he been?' Ce'Nedra whispered to the brown-mantled official.

'Not well, Princess,' Morin replied. 'Your absence grieved him more than he cared to admit.'

'Is he eating well – and getting his rest?'

'We try, Highness.' Morin shrugged. 'But your father's not the easiest person in the world to get along with.'

'Do you have his medicine?'

'Naturally, Highness. I never go anywhere without it.'

'Suppose we get down to business,' Rhodar was saying. 'Taur Urgas has sealed his western border, and the southern Murgos have moved into position around

432

Rak Goska. 'Zakath, the Mallorean Emperor, has set up a staging area on the plains outside Thull Zelik to receive his troops as he ferries them in. We're running out of time, Ran Borune.'

'I'm negotiating with Taur Urgas,' the Emperor replied, 'and I'll dispatch a plenipotentiary to 'Zakath immediately. I'm certain this can be settled without a war.'

'You can talk to Taur Urgas until your tongue falls out,' Anheg snorted, 'and 'Zakath probably doesn't even know or care who you are. As soon as they've gathered their forces, they'll march. The war can't be avoided, and I for one am just as happy about that. Let's exterminate the Angaraks once and for all.'

'Isn't that just a bit uncivilized, Anheg?' Ran Borune asked him.

'Your Imperial Majesty,' King Korodullin said formally 'the King of Cherek speaks hastily perhaps, but there is wisdom in his words. Must we live forever under the threat of invasion from the East? Might it not be best forever to quell them?'

'All of this is very interesting,' Ce'Nedra interrupted them coolly, 'but it's really beside the point. The actual point at issue here is that the Rivan King has returned, and Tolnedra is required by the provisions of the Accords of Vo Mimbre to submit to his leadership.'

'Perhaps,' her father replied. 'But young Belgarion seems to be absent. Have you misplaced him somewhere? Or is it perhaps that he still had pots to scrub in the scullery at Riva so that you had to leave him behind?'

'That's beneath you, father,' Ce'Nedra said scornfully. 'The Overlord of the West requires your service. Are you going to shame the Borunes and Tolnedra by abrogating the Accords?'

'Oh, no, daughter,' he said, holding up one hand.

'Tolnedra always meticulously observes every clause of every treaty she's ever signed. The Accords require me to submit to Belgarion, and I'll do precisely that – just as soon as he comes here and tells me what he wants.'

'I am acting in his stead,' Ce'Nedra announced.

'I don't seem to recall anything that states that the authority is transferable.'

'I am the Rivan Queen,' Ce'Nedra retorted hotly, 'and I've been invested with co-rulership by Belgarion himself.'

'The wedding must have been very private. I'm a little hurt that I wasn't invited.'

'The wedding will take place in due time, father. In the meantime, I speak for Belgarion and for Riva.'

'Speak all you want, girl.' He shrugged. 'I'm not obliged to listen, however. At the moment, you're only the betrothed of the Rivan King. You are not his wife and therefore not his queen. If we want to be strictly legal about it, until such time as you do marry, you're still under my authority. Perhaps if you apologize and get out of that stupid-looking armor and put on proper clothing, I'll forgive you. Otherwise, I'll be forced to punish you.'

'Punish? *Punish!*'

'Don't scream at me, Ce'Nedra,' the Emperor said hotly.

'Things seem to be deteriorating rapidly,' Barak observed dryly to Anheg.

'I noticed that,' Anheg agreed.

'I *am* the Rivan Queen!' Ce'Nedra shouted at her father.

'You're a silly girl!' he shot back.

'That does it, father,' she declared, leaping to her feet. 'You will deliver command of your legions to me at once, and then you'll return to Tol Honeth where your servants can wrap you in shawls and feed you gruel, since you're obviously too senile to be of any further use to me.'

'*Senile?*' the Emperor roared, also jumping up. 'Get out of my sight! Take your stinking Alorn army out of Tolnedra at once, or I'll order my legions to throw you out.'

Ce'Nedra, however, was already storming toward the door of the tent.

'You come back here!' he raged at her. 'I haven't finished talking to you yet.'

'Yes you have, father,' she shouted back. 'Now *I'm* going to talk. Barak, I need that sack you have tied to your saddle.' She rushed from the tent and climbed onto her horse, spluttering with apparent fury.

'Are you sure you know what you're doing?' Barak asked her as he tied the sack of Angarak coins to her saddle.

'Perfectly,' she replied in a calm voice.

Barak's eyes narrowed as he looked at her. 'You seem to have regained your temper in a remarkably short time.'

'I never lost it, Barak.'

'You were acting in there?'

'Obviously. Well, at least partially. It will take my father an hour or so to regain his composure, and by then it will be too late. Tell Rhodar and the others to prepare the army to march. The legions will be joining us.'

'What makes you think that?'

'I'm going to go fetch them right now.' She turned to Mandorallen, who had just emerged from the tent. 'Where have you been?' she asked. 'Come along. I need an escort.'

'Where are we going, pray?' the knight asked.

'You'll see,' she told him, and she turned her mount

435

and rode at a trot up the hillside toward the massed legions. Mandorallen exchanged a helpless look with Barak and then clanged into his saddle to follow.

Ce'Nedra, riding ahead, carefully put her fingertips to her amulet. 'Lady Polgara,' she whispered, 'can you hear me?' She wasn't certain that the amulet would work that way, but she had to try. 'Lady Polgara,' she whispered again, a bit more urgently.

'What are you doing, Ce'Nedra?' Polgara's voice sounded quite clearly in the little queen's ears.

'I'm going to talk to the legions,' Ce'Nedra answered. 'Can you fix it so they'll hear me?'

'Yes, but the legions won't be much interested in a speech about patriotism.'

'I've got a different one,' Ce'Nedra assured her.

'Your father's having a fit in here. He's actually foaming at the mouth.'

Ce'Nedra sighed regretfully. 'I know,' she said. 'It happens fairly often. Lord Morin has the medicine with him. Please try to keep him from biting his tongue.'

'You goaded him into this deliberately, didn't you, Ce'Nedra?'

'I needed time to talk to the legions,' the princess replied. 'The fit won't really hurt him very much. He's had fits all his life. He'll have a nosebleed and a terrible headache when it's over. Please take care of him, Lady Polgara. I do love him, you know.'

'I'll see what I can do, but you and I are going to have a long talk about this, young lady. There are some things you just don't do.'

'I didn't have any choice, Lady Polgara. This is for Garion. Please do what you have to do so that the legions can hear me. It's awfully important.'

'All right, Ce'Nedra, but don't do anything foolish.' Then the voice was gone.

Ce'Nedra quickly scanned the standards drawn up before her, selected the familiar emblem of the Eighty-Third Legion, and rode toward it. It was necessary that she place herself in front of men who would recognize her and confirm her identity to the rest of her father's army. The Eighty-Third was primarily a ceremonial unit, and by tradition its barracks were inside the Imperial compound at Tol Honeth. It was a select group, still limited to the traditional thousand men, and it served primarily as a palace guard. Ce'Nedra knew every man in the Eighty-Third by sight, and most of them by name. Confidently, she approached them.

'Colonel Albor,' she courteously greeted the commander of the Eighty-Third, a stout man with a florid face and a touch of grey at his temples.

'Your Highness,' the colonel replied with a respectful inclination of his head. 'We've missed you at the palace.'

Ce'Nedra knew that to be a lie. The duty of guarding her person had been one of the common stakes in barracks dice games, with the honor always going to the loser. 'I need a small favor, colonel,' she said to him as winsomely as she could.

'If it's in my power, Highness,' he answered, hedging a bit.

'I wish to address my father's legions,' she explained, 'and I want them to know who I am.' She smiled at him – warmly, insincerely. Albor was a Horbite, and Ce'Nedra privately detested him. 'Since the Eighty-Third practically raised me,' she continued, 'you of all people should recognize me and be able to identify me.'

'That's true, your Highness,' Albor admitted.

'Do you suppose you could send runners to the other legions to inform them just who I am?'

'At once, your Highness,' Albor agreed. He obviously

saw nothing dangerous in her request. For a moment Ce'Nedra almost felt sorry for him.

The runners – trotters actually, since members of the Eighty-Third were not very athletic – began to circulate through the massed legions. Ce'Nedra chatted the while with Colonel Albor and his officers, though she kept a watchful eye on the tent where her father was recuperating from his seizure and also on the gold-colored canopy beneath which the Tolnedran general staff was assembled. She definitely did not want some curious officer riding over to ask what she was doing.

Finally, when she judged that any further delay might be dangerous, she politely excused herself. She turned her horse and, with Mandorallen close behind her, she rode back out to a spot where she was certain she could be seen.

'Sound your horn, Mandorallen,' she told her knight.

'We are some distance from our own forces, your Majesty,' he reminded her. 'I pray thee, be moderate in thine address. Even I might experience some difficulty in facing the massed legions of all Tolnedra.'

She smiled at him. 'You know you can trust me, Mandorallen.'

'With my life, your Majesty,' he replied and lifted his horn to his lips.

As his last ringing notes faded, Ce'Nedra, her stomach churning with the now-familiar nausea, rose in her stirrups to speak. 'Legionnaires,' she called to them. 'I am Princess Ce'Nedra, the daughter of your Emperor.' It wasn't perhaps the best beginning in the world, but she had to start somewhere, and this was going to be something in the nature of a performance, rather than an oration, so a bit of awkwardness in places wouldn't hurt anything.

'I have come to set your minds at rest,' she continued.

438

'The army massed before you comes in peace. This fair, green field, this sacred Tolnedran soil, shall not be a battleground this day. For today at least, no legionnaire will shed his blood in defense of the Empire.'

A ripple of relief passed through the massed legions. No matter how professional soldiers might be, an avoided battle was always good news. Ce'Nedra drew in a deep, quivering breath. It needed just a little twist now, something to lead logically to what she really wanted to say. 'Today you will not be called upon to die for your brass half-crown.' The brass half-crown was the legionnaire's standard daily pay. 'I cannot, however, speak for tomorrow,' she went on. 'No one can say when the affairs of Empire will demand that you lay down your lives. It may be tomorrow that the interests of some powerful merchant may need legion blood for protection.' She lifted her hands in a rueful little gesture. 'But then, that's the way it's always been, hasn't it? The legions die for brass so that others might have gold.'

A cynical laugh of agreement greeted that remark. Ce'Nedra had heard enough of the idle talk of her father's soldiers to know that this complaint was at the core of every legionnaire's view of the world. 'Blood and gold – our blood and their gold,' was very nearly a legion motto. They were almost with her now. The quivering in her stomach subsided a bit, and her voice became stronger.

She told them a story then – a story she'd heard in a half dozen versions since her childhood. It was the story of a good legionnaire who did his duty and saved his money. His wife had suffered through the hardships and separations that went with being married to a legionnaire. When he was mustered out of his legion, they had gone home and bought a little shop, and all the years of sacrifice seemed worthwhile.

'And then one day, his wife became very ill,' Ce'Nedra continued her story, 'and the physician's fee was very high.' She had been carefully untying the sack fastened to her saddle while she spoke. 'The physician demanded this much,' she said, taking three blood-red Murgo coins from the sack and holding them up for all to see. 'And the legionnaire went to a powerful merchant and borrowed the money to pay the physician. But the physician, like most of them, was a fraud, and the legionnaire's money might as well have been thrown away.' Quite casually, Ce'Nedra tossed the gold coins into the high grass behind her. 'The soldier's good and faithful wife died. And when the legionnaire was bowed down with grief, the powerful merchant came to him and said, "Where's the money I lent to you?" ' She took out three more coins and held them up. ' "Where's that good red gold I gave you to pay the physician?" But the legionnaire had no gold. His hands were empty.' Ce'Nedra spread her fingers, letting the gold coins fall to the ground. 'And so the merchant took the legionnaire's shop to pay the debt. A rich man grew richer. And what happened to the legionnaire? Well, he still had his sword. He had been a good soldier, so he had kept it bright and sharp. And after his wife's funeral, he took his sword and went out into a field not far from the town and he fell upon it. And that's how the story ends.'

She had them now. She could see it in their faces. The story she had told them had been around for a long time, but the gold coins she had so casually tossed away gave it an entirely new emphasis. She took out several of the Angarak coins and looked at them curiously as if seeing them for the first time 'Why do you suppose that all the gold we see these days is red?' she asked them. 'I always thought gold was supposed to be yellow. Where does all this red gold come from?'

'From Cthol Murgos,' several of them answered her.

'Really?' She looked at the coins with an apparent distaste 'What's Murgo gold doing in Tolnedra?' And she threw the coins away.

The iron discipline of the legions wavered, and they all took an involuntary step forward.

'Of course, I don't suppose an ordinary soldier sees much red gold. Why should a Murgo try to bribe a common soldier when he can bribe the officers – or the powerful men who decide where and when the legions are to go to bleed and die?' She took out another coin and looked at it. 'Do you know, I think that every single one of these is from Cthol Murgos,' she said, negligently throwing the coin away. 'Do you suppose that the Murgos are trying to buy up Tolnedra?'

There was an angry mutter at that.

'There must be a great deal of this red gold lying about in the Angarak kingdoms if that's what they have in mind, wouldn't you say? I've heard stories about that, though. Don't they say that the mines of Cthol Murgos are bottomless and that there are rivers in Gar og Nadrak that look like streams of blood because the gravel over which they flow is pure gold? Why, gold must be as cheap as dirt in the lands of the East.' She took out another coin, glanced at it and then tossed it away.

The legions took another involuntary step forward. The officers barked the command to stand fast, but they also looked hungrily toward the tall grass where the princess had been so indifferently throwing the red gold coins.

'It may be that the army I'm leading will be able to find out just how much gold lies on the ground in the lands of the Angaraks,' Ce'Nedra confided to them. 'The Murgos and the Grolims have been practicing this same kind of deceit in Arendia and Sendaria and the Alorn kingdoms. We're on our way to chastise them for it.' She stopped as if an idea had just occurred to her. 'There's always room in any army for a few more good soldiers,' she mused thoughtfully. 'I know that most legionnaires serve out of loyalty to their legions and love for Tolnedra, but there may be a few among you who aren't satisfied with one brass half-crown a day. I'm sure such men would be welcome in my army.' She took another red coin out of her dwindling supply. 'Would you believe that there's *another* Murgo gold piece?' she demanded and let the coin drop from her fingers.

A sound went through the massed legions that was almost a groan.

The princess sighed then. 'I forgot something,' she said regretfully. 'My army's leaving at once, and it takes weeks for a legionnaire to arrange for leave, doesn't it?'

'Who needs leave?' someone shouted.

'You wouldn't actually desert your legions, would you?' she asked them incredulously.

'The princess offers gold!' another man roared. 'Let Ran Borune keep his brass!'

Ce'Nedra dipped one last time into the bag and took out the last few coins. 'Would you actually follow me?' she asked in her most little-girl voice, 'just for this?' And she let the coins trickle out of her hand.

The Emperor's general staff at that point made a fatal mistake. They dispatched a platoon of cavalry to take the princess into custody. Seeing mounted men riding toward the ground Ce'Nedra had so liberally strewn with gold and mistaking their intent, the legions broke. Officers were swarmed under and trampled as Ran Borune's army lunged forward to scramble in the grass for the coins.

'I pray thee, your Majesty,' Mandorallen urged, drawing his sword, 'let us withdraw to safety.'

'In a moment, Sir Mandorallen,' Ce'Nedra replied quite calmly. She stared directly at the desperately greedy legionnaires running toward her. 'My army marches immediately,' she announced. 'If the Imperial Legions wish to join us, I welcome them.' And with that, she wheeled her horse and galloped back toward her own forces with Mandorallen at her side.

Behind her she heard the heavy tread of thousands of feet. Someone among the massed legions began a chant that soon spread. 'Ce-Ne-dra! Ce-Ne-dra!' they shouted, and their heavy steps marked time to that chant.

The Princess Ce'Nedra, her sun-touched hair streaming in the wind behind her, galloped on, leading the mass mutiny of the legions. Even as she rode, Ce'Nedra knew that her every word had been a deception. There would be no more wealth for these legionnaires than there would be glory or easy victory for the Arends she had gathered from the forests of Asturia and the plains of Mimbre. She had raised an army to lead into a hopeless war.

It was for love of Garion, however, and perhaps for even more. If the Prophecy that so controlled their destinies demanded this of her, there was no way she could have refused. Despite all the anguish that lay ahead, she would have done this and more. For the first time Ce'Nedra accepted the fact that she no longer controlled her own destiny. Something infinitely more powerful than she commanded her, and she must obey.

Polgara and Belgarath, with lives spanning eons, could perhaps devote themselves to an idea, a concept; but Ce'Nedra was barely sixteen years old, and she needed something more human to arouse her devotion. At this very moment, somewhere in the forests of Gar og Nadrak, there was a sandy-haired young man with a serious face whose safety – whose very life – depended on every effort she could muster. The princess surrendered finally to love. She swore to herself that she would never fail her Garion. If this army were not enough, she would raise another – at whatever cost.

Ce'Nedra sighed, then squared her shoulders and led the Tolnedran legions across the sunny fields to swell the ranks of her army.

Here ends Book Four of *The Belgariad*.
Book Five, *Enchanters' End Game*,
brings this epic to a brilliant conclusion
as Belgarion confronts evil Torak
to decide the fate of men, Gods, and Prophecies.

BELGARIAD 5: ENCHANTERS' END GAME
by David Eddings

The quest was over. The Orb of Aldur was restored. And once again, with the crowning of Garion, there was a descendant of Riva Iron-grip to rule as Overlord of the West.

But the Prophecy was unfulfilled. In the east, the evil God Torak was about to awaken and seek dominion. Somehow, Garion had to face the God, to kill or be killed. On the outcome of that dread duel rested the destiny of the world. Now, accompanied by his grandfather, the ancient sorcerer Belgarath, Garion headed towards the City of Endless Night, where Torak awaited him.

To the south, his fiancée, the Princess Ce'Nedra, led the armies of the West in a desperate effort to divert the forces of Torak's followers from the man she loved.

The Prophecy drove Garion on. But it gave no answer to the question that haunted him: How does a man kill an immortal God?

Thus ends the epic story of *The Belgariad*.

0 552 14811 3

THE MALLOREON
by David Eddings

A magnificent epic of immense scope set against a history of seven thousand years of the struggles of Gods and Kings and men – of strange lands and events – of fate and a prophecy that must be fulfilled!

It had all begun with the theft of the Orb that had so long protected the West from the evil God Torak. Before that, Garion had been a simple farm boy. Afterwards, he discovered that his aunt was really the Sorceress Polgara and his grandfather was Belgarath, the Eternal Man. Then, on the long quest to recover the Orb, Garion found to his dismay that he, too, was a sorcerer. Now, warned by the prophecy that a new and greater danger threatens the lands of the west, Garion, Belgarath and Polgara must begin another quest to save the lands from great evil.

The Malloreon, which continues the story of Garion, Polgara, Belgarath and the others is the sequel to *The Belgariad* and is an outstanding piece of imaginative storytelling, destined to achieve the classic status and following of Tolkien's *The Hobbit* or Stephen Donaldson's *Chronicles of Thomas Covenant*.

Book 1: GUARDIANS OF THE WEST   0 552 14802 4
Book 2: KING OF THE MURGOS   0 552 14803 2
Book 3: DEMON LORD OF KARANDA   0 552 14804 0
Book 4: SORCERESS OF DARSHIVA   0 552 14805 9
Book 5: SEERESS OF KELL   0 552 14806 7

POWERS THAT BE
by Anne McCaffrey
   and Elizabeth Ann Scarborough

The first collaboration between two of science fiction's mightiest names.

It was a world of ice and snow – a planet that just supported life and that had been terraformed from frozen uninhabitable rock. The people of Petaybee were hardy, self-reliant, friendly – and also very secretive.

Major Yana Maddock, medically discharged from the service, was shipped to Petaybee in the hope that her burnt-out lungs might just recover in the icy air. And at the last moment, she was given a special commission. Unauthorized life-forms had been seen on the planet and, more seriously, geologic survey teams had vanished into nowhere, the odd survivor being discovered abandoned and insane. It was Yana's task to infiltrate Petaybee society and find out who – or what – was causing the eerie events on the planet.

She discovered a primitive ice-bound community of extraordinary people – people who possessed some mysterious quality of surviving – and people whom Yana discovered she both liked and revered as she found herself becoming one of them.

0 552 14098 8

A SELECTED LIST OF FANTASY TITLES AVAILABLE FROM CORGI AND BLACK SWAN

☐	14802 4	**MALLOREON 1: GUARDIANS OF THE WEST**	*David Eddings*	£5.99
☐	14803 2	**MALLOREON 2: KING OF THE MURGOS**	*David Eddings*	£5.99
☐	14804 0	**MALLOREON 3: DEMON LORD OF KARANDA**	*David Eddings*	£5.99
☐	14805 9	**MALLOREON 4: SORCERESS OF DARSHIVA**	*David Eddings*	£5.99
☐	14806 7	**MALLOREON 5: SEERESS OF KELL**	*David Eddings*	£5.99
☐	14807 5	**BELGARIAD 1: PAWN OF PROPHECY**	*David Eddings*	£5.99
☐	14808 3	**BELGARIAD 2: QUEEN OF SORCERY**	*David Eddings*	£5.99
☐	14809 1	**BELGARIAD 3: MAGICIAN'S GAMBIT**	*David Eddings*	£5.99
☐	14811 3	**BELGARIAD 5: ENCHANTER'S END GAME**	*David Eddings*	£5.99
☐	14252 2	**THE LEGEND OF DEATHWALKER**	*David Gemmell*	£5.99
☐	14253 0	**DARK MOON**	*David Gemmell*	£5.99
☐	14254 9	**WINTER WARRIORS**	*David Gemmell*	£5.99
☐	14256 5	**SWORD IN THE STORM**	*David Gemmell*	£5.99
☐	08453 0	**DRAGONFLIGHT**	*Anne McCaffrey*	£5.99
☐	14436 3	**THE GIRL WHO HEARD DRAGONS**	*Anne McCaffrey*	£5.99
☐	13728 6	**PEGASUS IN FLIGHT**	*Anne McCaffrey*	£5.99
☐	14098 8	**POWERS THAT BE** *Anne McCaffrey & Elizabeth Ann Scarborough*		£5.99
☐	12475 3	**THE COLOUR OF MAGIC**	*Terry Pratchett*	£5.99
☐	12848 1	**THE LIGHT FANTASTIC**	*Terry Pratchett*	£5.99
☐	13105 9	**EQUAL RITES**	*Terry Pratchett*	£5.99
☐	13703 0	**GOOD OMENS**	*Terry Pratchett & Neil Gaiman*	£5.99
☐	13841 X	**THE ANTIPOPE**	*Robert Rankin*	£5.99
☐	13922 X	**THE BOOK OF ULTIMATE TRUTHS**	*Robert Rankin*	£5.99
☐	13833 9	**RAIDERS OF THE LOST CAR PARK**	*Robert Rankin*	£5.99
☐	13924 6	**THE GREATEST SHOW OFF EARTH**	*Robert Rankin*	£5.99
☐	99777 3	**THE SPARROW**	*Mary Doria Russell*	£6.99
☐	99811 7	**CHILDREN OF GOD**	*Mary Doria Russell*	£6.99